D1098734

KILLING IN
YOUR NAME

By Gary Donnelly

DI Owen Sheen series

Blood Will Be Born
Killing in Your Name
Never Ask the Dead

KILLING IN
YOUR NAME

GARY DONNELLY

Allison & Busby Limited
11 Wardour Mews
London W1F 8AN
allisonandbusby.com

First published in Great Britain by Allison & Busby in 2020.
This paperback edition published by Allison & Busby in 2021.

A CIP catalogue record for this book is available from
the British Library.

10 9 8 7 6 5 4 3 2 1

ISBN 978-0-7490-2542-7

Typeset in 11/16 pt Sabon LT Pro by
Allison & Busby Ltd.

FSC
www.fsc.org
MIX
Paper from
responsible sources
FSC® C020471

The paper used for this Allison & Busby publication
has been produced from trees that have been legally sourced
from well-managed and credibly certified forests.

Printed and bound by
CPI Group (UK) Ltd, Croydon, CR0 4YY

For my sisters
Jennifer, Leann, Rosemary and Baby Agnes
My sword and my shield

BLACK MAGIC FEAR IN TWO BORDER TOWNS

Sunday World (Northern Ireland) headline,
28th October 1973

'In those days Israel had no king'

Judges 19:1

PROLOGUE

Belfast, Northern Ireland
February 1976

Some say we regret the things we don't do in this life.

If only.

It was her fault. She let him slip past her unnoticed. If she'd been a little quicker, a little stronger, she could have caught him, dragged him back out the door. But she was slow and slight, and her arms were full of coats hastily shed and shoved her way.

She caught his eye though and dumped the coats. He glared back at her in a silent fury that spoke the words she'd heard from his lips many times:

'Go away, you're not my ma!'

Not his mother, that was true. But he had become her child in this last year, as surely as if she had borne him from her womb. Since the IRA visited death on their family and then the Catholic Church ripped apart what remained; she was the only mother he would ever have. And she was fifteen, Peter just two years younger.

He walked into the party room to her left and joined a small group of other boys, already voluminous with drink. Peter took a can of Tennent's, a colour image of a half-dressed woman printed on its side. It looked improbably large in his paw. He fumbled at the ring pull, finally opened the beer which foamed up. The yellow liquid ran down the side before he raised it to his mouth and drank.

Was that his first sip of beer? Yes, almost certainly. There were precious few opportunities for the boys in his home to socialise, even fewer chances of earning or stealing enough pocket money to buy a carry-out.

His eyes found her watching. He turned away with one hand jammed into his jeans pocket. From inside the party room came the swell of imbibed laughter, deep and grown-up.

There were men in there.

She'd been here to meet and greet them, had laid out the drinks table and snacks in advance of their arrival. Not for the first time: there'd been other parties like this. Some of the men were regulars, like the preacher. She'd seen him on the telly, but here he didn't wear the white dog collar. And there was the guy with the pinstripe suit, tall and softly spoken. She'd heard the others call him 'Counsellor'. He was usually here at the beginning. And there was the fat man. He was older, cheeks florid and always dressed in a three-piece suit. He carried a cane with a gold handle and he spoke with an accent that she couldn't place. Something between southern Irish and an upper-crust English drawl. These men she knew, but there were many she did not; they came and went.

What they had in common was their youth, and the power and wealth they exuded. That and the fact they were not much interested in her. She was developed enough to understand the intentions of men, and the baseness of their needs. These fellas were different. They hadn't come to the posh house off the Lisburn Road to meet young women or for the free drinks.

They'd come for the little boys.

A cold, dead thing pressed against her bare lower arms. She flinched and yelped. A man towered over her.

'When yer ready, love,' he said, and shoved his black leather jacket into her receiving hands. She muttered an apology and took the coat she'd thought was a carcase. She could smell the rich cow hide, and over it, the sweet fruit gum the man was chewing. She glanced up. He was tall, so big she had to tilt her head back to see his face. Strong jaw, mean mouth, a head of flaxen blonde hair worn swept back. And grey eyes, cold as the north Atlantic coast. She'd seen photos of SS officers in books. He fit the type exactly. But not just his features, it was the cruelty in his face. Beneath the sleazy slyness of this man she could feel it, like a cold river running through him and into her. There was badness here. She recoiled, but with nowhere to go, her back met the wall and she stopped dead. He clasped her cheeks in his hand, raised her face.

'You're a shy one, arn ya?' They were eye to eye.

His voice was rich, but she felt the menace and knew the question needed no answer because it was really an accusation.

'Why are you so spooked? Do you know me?'

She didn't, but she knew that he was different from the others, rougher. His coat was leather, not tweed or camel hair. His accent had the twang and truncation of the Belfast streets.

She tried for a smile, not easy. He examined her like a new-found species, the grey of his eyes now almost fully black. Just like Jaws from the film she'd sneaked in to see at the ABC on Great Victoria Street. His eyes were exactly the same: black and empty. She glanced away and he followed her eyes.

Her baby brother, animated now, was talking to another boy maybe a year or so older, their faces visibly flushed with the drink. The older boy and Peter walked out of frame. Counsellor emerged and strode their way. His smile was full of affable welcome, but his eyes showed calculated concern as he took in her predicament.

'Sure, it's grand to see you,' he said, extended his arm. The move worked. The man with the black eyes released her face and they shook hands.

'A'reet,' he replied. Counsellor handed her two folded pound notes. Her wages, and her signal to go.

She took her payment, fingers trembling, mumbled a thanks. But Counsellor had already turned his back and was walking his guest towards the party room. Counsellor was big, but even at that, not quite as tall as the man with black, soulless eyes. She took a hanger from the rail in the cloakroom beneath the stairs and hung the black-eyed man's coat up. A hard weight, inside pocket, knocked her hand. She reached her fingers into the jacket, felt cold steel. Slowly, she pulled out a butterfly knife, long as her hand. She put it back, but instead of leaving she walked slowly to the party room, the noise and the stink of tobacco smoke becoming thicker as she approached.

She peeped round the doorway. Groups of men with boys and youths, all drinking, most smoking, voices animated. The fat, old man with the funny accent was in an armchair in the corner, near the roaring open fire. A boy was seated on one of his boiled-egg thighs and the man's plump hand was rested on one of the boy's knees. She searched from face to face, looking for Peter. She spotted him, all alone again.

'Peter! I'm taking you home,' she shouted and started towards him—

An iron grip on her upper arm, hard enough to make her shriek, but nobody heard it. She turned to see Counsellor's flushed face in her own, his eyes wide and angry. She tried to pull away, but it was impossible; he was so strong, and she was so weak.

'Out!' he snarled, small globs of his spittle hitting her mouth as he said the words. Then she was dragged off, helpless to resist. She stole a final look at the room. The big, black eyed shark was on the move, headed to where her little brother stood alone.

Counsellor opened the front door and shoved her out hard enough to send her sprawling down the front steps and to her knees. Her threadbare coat followed and snagged in a big shrub.

'You're sacked, you stupid little bitch. Don't come back,' he hissed, casting a furtive look both ways. The halogen-lit street was the model of silent suburbia and answered not. He closed the front door with a rattle of the knocker. She watched first the lantern light over the small porch extinguish and then the hallway light. She got up, warmth and pain from her knees, thought about chucking a rock through the front window. Instead, she pulled her wretched coat off the bush and shuffled to the front gate, tears coursing down her face.

Peter was in there, and there was nothing she could do about it. She was just a girl, a weak nobody. And worst of all, she'd let him in. That man, who in her heart she knew was ten times, a hundred times worse than all the rest; she'd opened the door and let that evil man in. She reached into her blouse pocket where she'd put the precious pound notes. She scrunched the currency into a ball, raised her hand to throw it away and then she stopped.

Because this wasn't the movies, and this year she'd almost saved enough for the fare to England, enough for both of them. She returned the money to her pocket. She could feel the rage and the shame and the hopelessness scorch her throat and settle deep down in her fledgling breast where it had already started to burn.

She shuffled off, the wind slicing at her tear-wet face. When she closed her eyes all she could see was the great white predator on a course for her baby brother. She raised her face to the cold heavens and screamed, and her cry was swallowed up by the black Belfast night.

PART ONE

SKELETONS OF SOCIETY

CHAPTER ONE

Belfast, Northern Ireland, present day
Monday 17th December

The dead are silent in their graves, but at night they speak to Owen Sheen.

His brother Kevin, telling him to run after the football as it skimmed and bounced down the gloaming Sailortown street in Belfast so many years before, seconds before a car bomb exploded and obliterated him. He asks when Sheen will come visit him; tend his grave in Milltown Cemetery. He tells him that it's a disgrace; overgrown and forgotten.

John Fryer, the escaped IRA lunatic he'd hunted down last summer, speaks. His words, as always, an answer to Sheen's question when he finally cornered him: *Did you kill my brother?*

Maybe I did. I did so much but don't remember now.

Sheen had squeezed the trigger anyway. His own ineptitude with firearms was all that had stopped him from murdering Fryer. But the bullet he never shot had put a hole in his personal code; he'd killed a part of himself when he tried to shoot that unarmed man. He drags deep on the hot stub of his roll-up and winces at the burn, crushes it. The smoking is new, but it caught hold fast. This was John Fryer's lifetime addiction, and unless he quit, it would become his. Another voice speaks up, this one faint and far-off, and this one is worst of all.

What's my name, Owen Sheen? What's my name?

That's the voice of the boy.

His team had searched the bogland of County Monaghan and found the remains of the youth, Jimmy McKenna was his name, murdered and Disappeared there long ago by John Fryer. But no sooner had McKenna been found than another shout echoed across the drained bog. Another shout, and against all odds it was another body. It was decapitated, mutilated and buried in a wooden cask. And this boy was younger. But the child with no name was a chance discovery and was officially no business of Owen Sheen. As they were over the border in the Irish Republic, the Gardaí took control, and Sheen had walked away. But the boy had found him, time and again.

'What you going to do about it, Sheen?' he asked the empty room.

If the past three months were anything to go on, damn all was the answer. The Northern Ireland Assembly had stalled, and with it, the administrative arm of the Northern Ireland Office that oversaw his work with the Police Service of Northern Ireland was effectively out of action. Since locating and returning the remains of

Jimmy McKenna, he and his team had been put out to pasture. Paid to wait in limbo for the politicians to learn how to play nice.

He checked the digital glow of his bedside clock. It was just shy of 6.30 a.m. and outside his Laganside loft apartment he could hear the stirrings of another working week beginning for some. Sheen got up; he'd sat around for long enough. He scraped his car keys and phone off the table by the door. He checked for recent messages or missed calls. But it was one name he hoped to see. He had not spoken to Aoife McCusker in person since the day he had visited her in hospital in August. Not spoken at all since their stilted phone call about three months ago. A new distance and a thus far failed promise from him to call again. And, of course, not a whisper from Aoife. He pocketed his phone, glided down the stairs. She blamed him, probably fairly, for what had befallen her since the summer. But this week would be different; by the end of it he'd have got in touch, for better or worse.

He navigated the side streets and the slip roads, and, once on the M1, he let the Vauxhall Insignia Turbo go, driving south-west. Sheen was headed for the western edge of County Monaghan, a part of the Irish Republic that extended north and was flanked by Northern Ireland on two sides. The bogland, where he'd spent most of August excavating, was just across Monaghan's western border. He let his hands and feet do the driving. God knows they knew the way. At Dungannon the motorway disappeared, like it had given up as impossible its

21

attempt to extend modernity into the wilds of County Armagh and south Tyrone. Sheen adjusted his speed, looked out for farmers in tractors, and chewed over the names of the approaching townships as he ate up the miles: Aughnacloy, ford of the stone; Clogher, meaning stony place; Fivemiletown, originally known as Baile na Lorgan, meaning townland of the long ridge.

The gradient steepened and the relief changed from arable land to upland bog. If he kept going he would reach the village of Welshtown, the last settlement on the Northern Ireland side of the border in County Tyrone, and the place where he and his team had been based in August. Beyond it, the land changed seamlessly into County Monaghan, and the Irish Republic. The lonely desolation of Coleman's bog was all that awaited the wanderer from here to where the land dropped once more, leading eventually into Monaghan town. Sheen drove on, hardly adjusting his speed, beams on full. There'd been a lot of talk about the threat of a hard border, but talk was all it would ever be in this wild land. The idea of a border was as meaningless here now as it had been when they first drew a line in the map. Sheen pulled in and stopped at a passing place.

He got out, breathed in the damp morning air and listened to the rustling sounds of the darkness which greeted him, as he changed his shoes for the stout hiking boots he kept on a plastic sheet in his boot, and pulled on the thermal-lined waterproof rolled up beside them. The blue beanie hat he kept in the pocket was still there and he pulled it down over his ears. He felt in the other pocket of the jacket and found the snug shaft of the powerful little Maglite. He turned it on and off, and in the light he saw the short-handle shovel he had carried with him every day while searching for the body of the young man, Jimmy McKenna. He had rarely used it on the dig, the main forensic work had been carried out by excavation experts or heavy-duty earth movers, but like the leather Brief of St Anthony he had round his neck, a gift from Aoife McCusker, it was a talisman. And it had worked. He unlatched the silver stainless steel gate by the road and closed it again behind him before starting up the dirt track.

Twenty minutes later he stopped. The thin path he'd been on had faded away and the land dissolved into an expanse of waterlogged swamp. Somewhere close by was where they had finally unearthed the body of McKenna. He veered due south, searching for the place where the second cry of 'Body found!' had been raised, searching for the marker he needed. Sheen squinted in the half-light at the excavation trenches his teams had made in the peat bog adjacent. The metal spikes they had used to tape off the area were still impaled waist height in the earth, though they should have been removed. He stopped at the dead-looking tree, its blackened arms stretched from west to east, and jumped down the ridge to reach its exposed roots. The cavity was still visible under its trunk where the cask containing the body had been discovered.

He could see rust deposits where the metal bands of the cask had been, and the vague impression of the wood in the sheltered core of the cave. He reached into the cavity, dug his hand into the cold, wet peat, felt it embed under his nails and cool his blood and bones instantly. He took out a handful and raised it to his face, breathed its rich, nearly disinfectant odour. He tossed the loose earth into the hole. Someone had dumped a child here, to cover unspeakable things. Sheen stood up and clapped his hands clean of earth. This was not his manor. Technically, not even his country. But he'd discovered the body and that made it his responsibility; he would never be able to let it go.

'I found you and now I am going to find out who did this to you,' said Sheen. A muffled pop then another in quick succession some distance away, coming from the east. The shotgun fired again, both barrels. Sheen scanned the horizon but couldn't see a soul. He moved off and then saw a rabbit, followed by another bouncing from one grassy knoll to another before both disappeared into the earth. The guns barked again as Sheen trudged back across the border. He wasn't the only person out hunting at dawn after all.

CHAPTER TWO

Sheen bit into the soft, flour-dusted soda farl, still warm from the oven. Melted butter escaped, a rich contrast to the naturally acerbic taste of the bread. Three or four big bites and it was gone. He dabbed his mouth with the paper bag. Maureen set his tea on the counter, plus two fat pancakes that he'd not ordered.

'Those are on the house. You've ailed,' she said. Maureen had not changed a bit since he was last here at the end of the summer; she still looked somewhere between eighty and National Trust protected status. Stick-thin with blue rinse hair under a netted hat; she had a puckered smoker's mouth and teeth too perfect and too white to be anything but part-time occupants in her head.

Sheen thanked her without comment. The haggard-looking man who'd stared back from the mirror over his bathroom sink this morning was dark-eyed and a bit too thin. The overall look wasn't helped by the thick rash of stubble approaching beard status. A bad time in life to first grow one, apparently; there was lots of grey and, alarmingly, more than a little ginger too. Sheen wasn't sure which was worse. He attacked the pancakes and moved out of the way for the next in line. Mostly they were thick-booted farmhands and municipal labourers wearing high-visibility coats, loading up on calories for the day ahead. Maureen's hands set to work making the next order, but she spoke to Sheen.

'Not seen your face for a while,' she said, and twirled a paper bag until it sealed closed with two pointed Doberman ears.

'Been busy. Back in Belfast,' he said.

Maureen fixed him with a stare. 'But you're back in Welshtown today all the same. Think you'll be busy in these parts again?' she asked. Maureen had made him welcome and never pried about his business while they were on the dig, which he'd appreciated. His team had given her good trade in return. But Sheen had read the hostility and resentment on the faces of the locals. The discovery of McKenna's body, albeit just across the border in County Monaghan, had brought Welshtown an unwanted notoriety. Like the little town of Lockerbie in Scotland, one bad event from the past had changed it permanently. He set the money he owed her on the counter.

'No, just woke up and knew that nothing but Maureen's would do,' he said.

'Smooth-talking bastard,' commented Maureen.

Sheen had polished off the pancakes, took a slurp of the tea, strong and hot, so good.

'Same again?' said Maureen.

'They call people like you feeders, Maureen. I'm done, thanks,' he said.

She cocked her chin to the wall behind Sheen. 'Our boys are having some season,' she said.

Sheen glanced up at a framed clipping from a sports page. It was the *Irish News,* the Belfast daily paper. MAGUIRE PLAYS IT SWEETLY FOR THE HARPS. Beneath the headline was a muscle-roped young man wearing a gold and green jersey captured mid sprint, hurley extended with a ball apparently glued to the end.

'Welshtown Harps?' asked Sheen. Local Gaelic athletic club.

'That was from the quarter final a couple of months back. This week's the semi against Monaghan.' Sheen could hear the disdain in her voice at the mention of the rivals.

'Good luck to them,' said Sheen.

Maureen folded her arms and nodded, looked grim but clearly happy with Sheen's reply. An old gent tapped his cane on the floor a few times and nodded his agreement. He had a net of broken veins over the tops of his cheeks and Sheen could hear the wheeze of his breathing as well as a faint smell of menthol coming off him. But there was also a packet of battered-looking filterless cigarettes protruding from his fleece pocket. For him a tap was easier than spoken agreement. Real men saved their last breath for a smoke. This would be him some day unless he, as his Belfast colleagues liked to put it, caught himself on and quit the stupidity of smoking while he still had time. Nonetheless, having drained his tea, the glimpse of tobacco had sent his hand in search of his own. He jammed it into his jacket pocket. Then something else caught his eye.

. . . SATANIC PANIC

It was half a headline from a story that was featured on the opposite page of the cutting, much of it missing. Sheen searched for the date, noted that it was from two months previous. He recalled that about that time there had been a scheduled release of Ministry of Defence records pertaining to Northern Ireland, a glut of material that had previously been withheld and dating back up to forty-five years. A number of newspapers had run stories on the declassified files, and he'd read a few with interest. This was almost certainly one of them, but Sheen had missed it.

He scanned the text, felt his heart quicken as he pieced together the broken sentences and extracted the meaning. An undercover British Army unit engaged in psych ops to falsely link paramilitary groups with black magic and devil worship. Black candles and inverted crucifixes in country lanes; fake news '70s style. But Sheen had found a child's body, probably from the same time, a child who had been ritualistically murdered, but for real. He noted the name of the journalist who'd penned it: Dermot Fahey.

'You read this?' he asked Maureen.

The old boy answered him. 'I remember it,' he said hoarsely.

'Seriously? Black magic and bogeymen?' asked Sheen.

'It went on, boy,' he replied, and beckoned Sheen outside where he sparked up a tab with yellow-tipped fingers. The blue smoke wafted Sheen's way. 'Thon bastards killed my brother's donkey in the fields. Cut the poor creature's head clean aff,' he said.

'Animals were sacrificed?' asked Sheen.

'Certainly. Animals destroyed, and worse, cut to ribbons, tortured,' he said, and then broke into a coughing fit. But what if decapitating and mutilating animals was not where this story ended? What if someone involved got a taste for the real thing, or found a way to practise even darker acts, under the cloak of such secrecy? Like torturing and killing a child, for instance?

'Do you know if that article mentioned any names, people who might have been involved?' asked Sheen.

The old man shrugged mid cough.

Maureen spoke up from the counter. The breakfast rush was over; the small shop was quiet and empty. 'The soldiers were based at Aughnacloy army base. It's gone now,' she said. Aughnacloy made sense. Close to the border, easy access to farms and towns, not too far from Belfast. But also close to Welshtown and Coleman's bog too, a place where bad men buried dark deeds. Sheen wanted to speak to the journalist, Fahey. But first he needed to have a proper look at the boy's body. It wouldn't be easy, but he had a plan. He thanked Maureen and said goodbye.

'Hope the farl was worth the drive,' she said.

He told her it was as good as ever. 'Hope the home team win,' added Sheen.

'Bit of luck and a lot of prayer,' she replied, and as Sheen drove out of Welshtown he reflected that that was probably what he needed.

CHAPTER THREE

After leaving Welshtown, Sheen pulled in, careful not to veer too far to the left and get bogged down. He scrolled through the contact list on his phone, found Pixie McQuillan's name and called her. Pixie was a sergeant with An Garda Síochána, the Republic of Ireland's National Police Service. She'd joined Sheen and his team as they excavated over the border, searching for the body of Jimmy McKenna. Pixie's presence had been a token of co-operation from the Gardaí, but also a set of ears and eyes for her superiors. Sheen and his team were under no obligation to report to Dublin.

'Owen Sheen,' said Pixie, sounding sleepy. Sheen checked the clock, just gone 8.30 a.m. If she'd been on a night shift, he had probably woken her. 'I've woke up with you in my bed after all,' she teased. Sheen winced. Three weeks into the dig and a few pints of stout later, Sheen had made a pass. Clumsy and badly timed; Pixie was just about to start showing him photos of her girlfriend and their two kids. Awkward, and, though she'd laughed it off, she'd made sure Sheen hadn't forgotten it. In retrospect her fine features and blonde hair gave Pixie a likeness to someone else, maybe the person Sheen had really wanted to be with after a few drinks on an August evening. He ignored her jibe, opted for the direct approach.

'Pixie, do you know where they took the body? The one in the cask, from the bog?' said Sheen. No immediate reply but the sound of splashing water. Pixie had overseen the body after one of Sheen's guys had made the discovery.

'Monaghan General,' she said. Sheen nodded, it made sense. Monaghan was the closest hospital of any size and probably had a mortuary and cold storage. The hospital was south of the border, where Sheen was a civilian.

'It's not even active, you know. Straight to a cold case file until some retiree with spare time gets pulled in to look into it,' she said, voice free from her slumber and, Sheen noted with some encouragement, a bit of an edge. Pixie had not forgotten the body.

'Autopsy?'

'Aye, but routine,' she said.

Sheen gritted his teeth, and slowly shook his head. In cases like this one, where a crime was clearly involved, a forensic autopsy rather than a routine one was standard. Primarily because the increased level of scrutiny often yielded evidence for the criminal investigation. But the investigation into this child's awful death had obviously ended before it had begun.

'You're kidding me,' said Sheen flatly.

'Budget,' she replied, which at least partly made sense. A forensic cost a lot more than a routine one. But Pixie's meaning was more far-reaching than the cost of the medical examination. 'Powers that be see it as a Northern case, Troubles' legacy. No one's pushing for results; the media's been kept at bay. We've got enough on our plate to keep the Gardaí stretched to the limit down here,' she explained.

All of which meant the case was as cold as the earth that had kept the body hidden for so long. Without the benefit of a forensic report to use, Sheen was at a disadvantage, but it didn't mean there was no value in seeing the body. And just because her superiors didn't care, it did not mean Pixie had given up.

'Can you help me get access to the body?'

'This official, Sheen?' she asked. Pixie might be sympathetic to an investigation, but he wanted to insulate her from any blowback. The direct approach had its limits.

'Far as anyone who comes asking later, I'm telling you it is. I'll take the rap. My word,' he offered.

She laughed. 'Jesus, Sheen, could you be any more melodramatic? I have stuff to do this morning, but I'll be done by one. Meet me at Monaghan General at one-thirty,' she said.

Sheen thanked her and ended the call.

Sheen's Internet connection was weak and his search was slow work, but eventually he found the service he needed, plus one or two other details he was interested in. Microfilm archives were located at the library in Clones, a town south-west of Monaghan, right on the border with County Fermanagh and Northern Ireland. He tapped the address into the car's GPS. Thirty minutes away, but this was Monday morning. He put the Sig in gear and hit shuffle on his music player. The Beach Boys 'Good Vibrations' twirled out from the speakers, and he welcomed it gratefully.

It was shortly after 9.30 a.m. when he pulled into a parking space outside Clones Library. Not what he'd expected. It was an impressive modernist structure; interlinked concrete blocks, tinted glass window walls, clean lines. It reminded Sheen of the millionaire mansions whose lines and corners peeked from behind security gates and high fences on the hills leading from Highgate down into Hampstead Heath in London. Sheen entered and the automatic doors sealed behind him, the hush of the library settled. Mostly vacant seats and tables, but a few teenagers had already bagged window stalls that ran along one wall. They were plugged into white headphones with fat textbooks, coloured study cards and segregated folders of notes spread before them. The reception desk was empty.

He picked up an information leaflet and saw that the microfilm readers and printers were available on Tuesday, Wednesday and Friday only. Not looking good.

'Can I assist you?' Sheen looked up. A woman, mid twenties, was now behind the counter. She had dark hair politely pinned off a full face which was pale apart from the rose of her cheeks. Her conservative cardigan and blouse combo jarred with the chrome eyebrow bar and the coloured petal of a tattooed flower that was part of a much larger piece concealed under her sleeve.

'Hope so,' replied Sheen. He reached into his jacket and flipped open his PSNI warrant card. She glanced at his card, and then met his eyes again.

'Are you from London?' she said.

'Spot on. DI Sheen. I'm with the PSNI, though I came from the Met Police,' he said, his ungainly backstory feeling like a right mouthful. But better to keep talking and make it personal. He had a favour to ask and if he offered a bit of background, she might be more inclined to help him out.

'I'm Lucy. Are you, like, on official business?' she replied.

'Thing is, Lucy,' said Sheen confidentially, 'I am, and I'm on the clock. I'm looking for something that might be stored on microfilm here,' he said.

'Access hours for the readers and printers is Tuesday, Wednesday and Friday only,' she said.

'Which I have just found out, after travelling all the way from Belfast this morning,' said Sheen, holding up the information leaflet between them.

'We need another member of staff present, someone to run and fetch. Plus, people need to be overseen when using the equipment,' she said.

'Can you make an exception?' asked Sheen.

'You asking me to break the rules, Mr Policeman Sheen?' she asked. A silver tongue stud flashed into view, the metal bead clasped fleetingly between her front teeth. Sheen actually felt himself redden. Ridiculous. He was tired. Too late to stop, as Van Morrison once sang. He leant his elbows on the counter.

'I think I am,' he said. She glanced over at the students whose backs were still arched over their work, and then beckoned Sheen with a twitch of her eyebrow. She walked straight into a room which was pitch-black. He stayed at the open door as the overhead LED spots came to life. Lucy was already standing halfway across a room where three plastic-covered stations waited against the far wall, a large printer adjacent.

'Movement activated lights. Come on in, I won't bite you,' she said.

Sheen entered the room, not entirely convinced.

'Now what exactly are you after?' she asked.

'Old newspaper editions, but I'm not sure which,' he said.

She nodded in response, her tongue bolt on display again but business mode now.

'Is there a local paper that serves both sides of the border, maybe covering Monaghan, south Armagh, Fermanagh?' He told her he was interested in the mid seventies onwards, but not what he was interested in finding. Not that he really held much hope of finding anything of great value. But the fact was that a newspaper article had given him an unexpected lead, so why not do a bit more digging while he was in the neighbourhood? Made more sense than driving all the way back to Belfast, and he had a few hours to kill before his planned meeting with Pixie at Monaghan General. Lucy took a few seconds to consider his needs.

'I'd start with the *Northern Standard*. It's well established so we have back copies from those dates, and well before that. Circulation covers the area you just listed, bit more besides,' she said.

'Is the *Northern Standard* daily or weekly?' he enquired.

'Weekly.' Good news. This meant fewer copies and more chance of picking out patterns across a period of time. Sheen gave her the range of years he wanted.

'Was there anything else?' she asked, a smile playing on her lips. Sheen wasn't sure if they were back on tease mode, but if so, he had little time to play the game just now.

Sheen shook his head, but then thought of the article on Maureen's wall in Welshtown. He wanted to read the piece in full to pick up any details he might have missed.

'Do you stock recent copies of the *Irish News*?' he asked. She nodded, told him there was a daily copy in the reading room on the rack.

'I need to see an article from about two months ago,' he said.

'We keep a six-month paper archive, then they get moved into microfilm,' she replied. Sheen gave her the date of the edition he needed. She'd made it to the door when he called after her.

'Don't suppose there's any danger of a coffee?' he asked.

The tongue bolt flashed and so did her smile. 'No hot drinks permitted in the microfilm room, bottles of water only,' she said.

Sheen gave her a small salute. 'The rules,' he said.

CHAPTER FOUR

Ten minutes later Sheen was scrolling through his first batch of weekly microfilm editions of the *Northern Standard*, a steaming mug of black coffee next to him and two remaining chocolate digestives left on his plate. The investigative report he had read on Maureen's wall in Welshtown had said the covert army unit were most active between 1974 and 1976. This made sense. While Sheen had checked online for library services and opening times, he had also found a macabre ready reckoner for the number of people killed in Northern Ireland's Troubles across all years, each total helpfully broken down according to types of victims: 'Police/Army', 'Paramilitary', and 'Civilian'.

Apart from 1972, by far the single darkest year of the conflict, the years between 1974–6 had the worst run of violence that was seen over the near thirty-year period of the Troubles. Like 1972, these years were infamous because proportionally more innocent civilians died in comparison with active combatants. Sheen could read the story behind the numbers. The country had been sliding headlong into all-out anarchy. If there was a time for disinformation and black propaganda to alienate the population from paramilitaries, this was it. Question was, did it begin and end with scare tactics and make-believe?

Sheen had started with 1973, just to be sure. He was just about getting the hang of the speed control by the time he completed the year, but saw nothing that made him pause and print. Still, even though he'd readied himself, the constant reports of violence from all sides were truly frightening. He mentally worked out what age his parents had been. Both were Belfast-based, not yet married at this time, and living on opposite sides of the divide. Too late to ask either of them what their lives had been like in those years. Sheen was aware that a short time after marrying they had looked into going to live in Australia. Sheen changed the reel and started on 1974 and pretty soon could see why newly-weds would think of emigrating.

There was death and destruction in every edition, a war played out in slow motion. Any single event transplanted to modern times would dominate headline news for weeks on end, but in this deep valley, one atrocity merged into the next: the IRA attacking off-duty police and soldiers, loyalists murdering innocent Catholics, tit following tat. But even in times of violence and chaos, some atrocities can still stand out. On 17th May of that year, no warning car bombs were detonated during rush hour in Dublin and Monaghan, killing thirty-four (including an unborn child) and injuring hundreds more. It was the single deadliest attack of the Troubles and it had gone unclaimed at the time.

Sheen pushed his chair back, took a mouth full of cold coffee, and swallowed it with a grimace. He checked his phone, just gone 11.30 a.m. If he skipped lunch then he'd make his appointment at the mortuary with Pixie in Monaghan, but he needed to pick up his pace. He set to work, and soon paused to study a story. Local farmers had complained about the British Army illegally crossing the border through their land, damaging outbuildings and fences during clandestine searches in the middle of the night. He scrolled on, his eyes started to glaze, his mind wandered to thoughts of a lunch break after all.

He stopped and removed his hand from the forward button like he'd just taken a mains voltage kick.

Sheen slowly reversed the direction, eyes alert and focused again, searching for what he thought he had seen. He stopped, took his finger off the cursor and read the headline.

LIVESTOCK DESTROYED IN DEAD OF NIGHT

'OK then,' he said softly. Pat Ney, Monaghan livestock farmer, had found two of his weaning calves missing from the barn and dead in the field, their throats cut. The carcases of the animals had been laid out with their heads touching. This was the second instance of what the article described as 'livestock destruction' in as many months. Sheen drummed the tabletop with his fingers, then pressed print, heard the chunky Laserjet whirl to life and efficiently deposit a copy of the story in the tray. His alertness sparked now, he moved meticulously and speedily through the weeks and months, drawing 1974 to a close. He quickly replaced it with 1975. Almost immediately, he got a direct hit.

EVIDENCE OF BLACK MASS FOUND

Beneath the headline was a black and white photograph of what looked like upended tin pots with dried grass protruding from one. In the background was the burnt out remains of what had been a thick, black candle. He printed and continued but not for long. He stopped again in March 1975.

BLACK MAGIC FEAR IN TWO BORDER TOWNS

This report had made the front page, contained more photographs and verbal testimonies from a number of frightened witnesses whose farm animals and pets had gone missing, some found horrifically mutilated. The report claimed that a British Army patrol had stumbled across a black magic ceremony being held in the foundations of an abandoned castle close to the border. The suspects managed to get away, Sheen was not surprised to learn.

Sheen studied a photograph taken in the bowels of the castle ruins. An inverted pentagram was enclosed inside a circle, both traced in what looked like salt. The gutted remains of thick black candles marked the apex points, and symbols had been shaped, again in salt, adjacent to each one. But right at the heart of the pentagram, and much larger and more prominent than the rest, was another symbol. Sheen at first thought it was an inverted cross, but after drawing nearer the image saw it was more like a sword, with a half-moon arching from its blade. Whatever it was, it meant something to those responsible for creating this superstitious panic, which meant it could well be important for Sheen's investigation. He had worked countless cases in which small details like this ended up turning cases, and more often than not they'd been staring detectives in the face from the murder file all along. Sheen pressed print and took out his phone. He searched the details of the symbol and felt a flutter of exhilaration and satisfaction when he read the first result.

'Saturn,' he said.

He scrolled quickly through the information. The second largest planet in the solar system was also a central symbol of the occult and astrology, associated with the harvest and the night. What he'd mistaken for a half-moon was in fact a scythe, the origins of the popular image of the grim reaper. Whoever had traced the symbol in salt had really done their homework. Or had really believed in what they were up to. Sheen clicked open the next image.

'Bloody hell,' he whispered. It was the 1636 painting *Saturn Devouring His Son* by the Flemish artist, Peter Paul Rubens. Sheen stared at it; Saturn in human form, old and grey, devouring one of his children. Sheen emailed himself the link, certain that this was significant, and returned his attention to the microfilm. He was dying for another brew and a smoke.

He forged on, got partway through 1976 when he checked the time on his phone and saw a missed call from Pixie. It had just gone 1 p.m. Sheen cursed silently, sent her a text to say he was on his way and went back to flying through weekly news stories, already aware he was growing numb, his alertness all but blunted. He stopped.

HORRIFIC DONKEY SACRIFICE TERRIFIES BORDER COMMUNITY

The image which accompanied the piece was the most graphic he'd seen yet. The carcase of a donkey, on its side in a field, its head hacked off and resting some feet away, its eyes gouged out. An inverted cross had been carved into the animal's back. He scanned the story, found much of the same outrage and dismay as in previous articles, but with one exception. He read a quote from an unnamed local woman:

'It's just a matter of time before these evil people go for a human sacrifice. It's what they really want.'

Sheen pressed print, continued to scan, but found nothing more as the hot summer of 1976 faded to early winter. By the last week of November, he was ready to call time when he saw it.

LOCAL LAD MISSING: FEARS MOUNT

'Jesus wept,' whispered Sheen. He'd expected some reports of animal destruction, but not this. He read the article, digested it quickly and sat back.

Declan O'Rawe, aged twelve, had been on his bike travelling home from a friend's farmhouse near Terrytole, but never made it home. Sheen closed his eyes and racked his mind to remember where he'd heard that name before. He saw it, as it flashed past him on a small sign at the side of the B road he had driven from Welshtown to get here. Close enough to where the body in the bog had been discovered. His heart picked up, excitement ballooning in his chest. If Declan O'Rawe was a missing child who had never turned up, a DNA check with any remaining family could quickly identify the boy's body. Sheen hit scroll, approached the end of 1976. No more mention of the boy until the first week of December when his bicycle was uncovered by a farmer from a hedgerow in Armagh, over the county line and over the Irish border. Sheen slowed as he approached the end of the year, more certain now he was onto a winner, and then stopped when he found Declan.

O'Rawe's body had been found burned, dismembered and bearing signs of torture near the River Lagan in Belfast. He had been wrapped in a blanket and dumped on waste ground.

O'Rawe was not his body after all, and the facts did not fit. This boy had been dumped and probably murdered in Belfast. His death had been just one more that made up the horrific civilian death toll in the mid 1970s, many of them picked off streets, taken away and tortured before being dumped. Then again, he'd come from Monaghan, fairly close to where they'd discovered the boy's body in the bog. But right now, Sheen couldn't see the woods, let alone the trees. One last time he pressed print.

'Sheen, you all right?' It was Lucy, standing by his side, a newspaper in hand. Sheen turned and stared at her mutely, suddenly aware that no, he probably wasn't. His detour into the 1970s had left him shaken and sickened. It was as though the ordinary rules of civilised society had been tossed out the window and murderers and sociopaths had enjoyed a free hand. He'd read somewhere that at the height of the Troubles, the psychiatric ward that treated aggressive psychopaths in Belfast had to close down because of a lack of patients. If the news reports that Sheen had just scanned through were anything to go on, it was because they were running wild on the streets.

'Fine,' he said, with a weak smile.

'And forgetful. You wanted this *Irish News* back issue. Plus you owe me for those printouts,' she said, handing Sheen the newspaper. Sheen took the paper, found the article and asked if he could get a photocopy. Lucy brought it back a few moments later.

'How much do I owe you?' he asked.

'Three euros per microfilm, plus fifty cents for the photocopy. Unless you're able to sign it off as official state business, in which case it's free,' she said. Sheen handed her his credit card which she charged at the reception desk. At least the coffee and biscuits were on the house.

As Sheen exited the sealed world of the library, the gusting wind knocked him from one side, and he just about managed to clasp his printed pages to his chest as he texted Pixie to say he'd been a bit delayed but was en route.

As he headed off the N54 for Monaghan he thought again about the small sign he'd passed for Terrytole, dead children and the words of warning from a farmer's wife too terrified to give her name in 1976.

So far Sheen had two bodies, ritual and sacrilege. In a world where murder and destruction had become a background noise, it seemed that evil men had been free to indulge their darkest fantasies and get away with it.

But now Sheen was on their case.

CHAPTER FIVE

Pixie was waiting for Sheen at the entrance to Monaghan General Hospital. They clapped hands, made a fist and then she took him by surprise and drew him in for a hug and a slap on the back of the shoulders. Sheen reciprocated, but for him the gesture felt alien, his embrace ill practised and stiff.

Pixie led the way to the wide lifts which, after an almost imperceptible descent opened to a low-lit basement corridor painted an institutional light green. The hospital smell was thicker here; Sheen could taste that heavy combination of antiseptic, like warm pitch tar, and stale, recycled air.

'This is it,' said Pixie.

Sheen noted that some of the healthy colour had seeped from her cheeks. He pushed open one of the hinged rubber doors and they entered a brightly lit tiled room, its whiteness glaring and brilliant in comparison to the murk of the corridor. A man wearing a white coat stopped what he was doing at an open metal tray where an array of steel instruments was spread. His hair was dark and rich, but on the retreat, his tailored moustache flecked with white. He greeted the strangers in his domain with a smile.

'Can I help you?' he asked.

Pixie introduced them both and showed her identification. She quickly explained what they had come to see, asked if the body was still in the mortuary. The attendant introduced himself as Michael Mulligan and they shook hands.

'Yes, we are still in possession of the remains. Pending identification, and investigation, I presume,' he said.

'Did the autopsy take place here, Michael?' asked Sheen. He could see the raised steel table across the room, the drainage channels feeding into the plughole in the floor.

'That's correct, sir, yes. The acting deputy state pathologist was sent up from Dublin,' he replied.

Sheen quickly tried to assimilate the jargon. In Sheen's experience, the bigger the case, the better established the pathologist. He didn't need inset training to know that an acting deputy being sent up from Dublin meant a case wasn't a top priority.

He turned to Pixie. 'Were you present?' he asked. She shook her head. *Fair enough*, thought Sheen, a senior investigating officer (SIO) sometimes was, in the way Sheen himself had been invited and attended the autopsy of Jimmy McKenna in Belfast. But more often, the officer present would be a senior officer. Sheen enquired whether one of Pixie's superiors attended as a representative of the Gardaí, and she told him she didn't believe so.

Sheen sighed. The picture that was emerging confirmed his gut feeling; the child's body had been given the bare minimum of institutional attention and was not even yet being actively investigated.

'Do you have a copy of the report here?' Sheen asked Michael.

'No, sir,' said Mulligan. Sheen had expected as much.

'What about a copy of the pink form?' he asked. Michael Mulligan looked confused. The pink post-mortem form was the original record made during the autopsy examination, sometimes in duplicate, and used to inform the final write-up. Sheen explained, and Michael Mulligan disappeared into a side room and emerged less than a minute later holding what Sheen had requested. This form was blue; clearly a duplicate of an original, but it was legible and would give Sheen a window into the post-mortem. Sheen asked to see the remains.

Michael led them into the cold storage facility, opened a wall tray and deftly slid the sheet-draped contents onto a waiting gurney. The cargo was small, less than half the length of an average-sized body. Michael wheeled it back into the well-lit autopsy suite and removed the cover. Sheen stepped forward; his eyes fixed on what had been revealed to the cutting glare of the overhead lights.

The headless torso was tanned a deep peat brown, fixed in a foetal position, and rested on its side. The arms were clasped close to the chest, and the legs hitched right up, knees over elbows. It had clearly shrunk. This, added to the discolouration and perfect preservation from the acid waters of the peat bog, made the remains other-worldly, alien. Sheen completed a tour round the remains, opening his senses for an important first impression.

'Remains' seemed fitting. What lay before him seemed to hardly qualify as human, but of course, that was what this had once been. Sheen swallowed, forcing himself to get anchored.

This was a child's body. And this was an unlawful death. Given the strong similarities between this body and that of Jimmy McKenna, Sheen judged it to date from around the same era.

The body was naked. And though his genitals were obscured from view, Sheen could tell it was male. He took another slow circuit round the boy's body, this time with his phone in hand taking snaps as he went. He spoke, detailing what he observed as much for himself as for Pixie and Michael, who had given him space.

'Head has been removed,' commented Sheen, now hunkering down, examining the ragged stump of the boy's neck. On closer inspection, Sheen observed the yellowed bone of the neck and spinal column. It looked like the killer had taken more than one cut to dismember the boy.

'Appears that decapitation,' he paused, searching for the best term, 'was the result of hacking,' he finished. Not exactly what he wanted, but he wasn't a medical professional.

Then Michael spoke up. 'I've seen similar wounds, though never on a body like this.'

Sheen glanced through the form; saw no mention of a possible weapon.

'Axe?' he opined.

'I'd say a shovel,' Michael replied. Which made sense. The boy's body had been found in a buried cask. Someone had been digging.

'So, perhaps, the head of this boy may be buried close to where the original body was discovered in the bog?' pondered Sheen. No response to this from Michael this time, or Pixie.

He doubted that the dig had missed something as obvious as the head of a little boy. Instinct told him that it was gone and would never be recovered, certainly not from the Monaghan bog that had yielded his torso. Perhaps the decapitation, like that of the donkey, was part of the masquerade to suggest a sick ritual, or maybe this was genuine, or perhaps just a means to conceal the identity of the child victim?

Sheen cleared his throat; the better to shake away this analysis, that could come later, and right now it was beginning to interfere with his absorption of the evidence. He brought his face close to the boy's auburn, leathery torso where the arms were still pressed against his thin chest. A faint whiff exuded from it: iodine and suede.

'Both hands have been removed, just above the wrist,' he said. The yellowed tusk of the boy's lower arm bones protruded where the flesh and skin had either receded over time or through tanning and dehydration.

'Cleaner cut,' interjected Michael. 'But probably with the same instrument.'

Sheen nodded a quick reply. The same instrument meant the flat blade of a shovel. Easier to nick and slice off a little boy's hands than his head. Sheen changed position to examine the boy's back. It had been carved, like a side of wood, the deep cuts now indented over time. Sheen felt sparks ignite in his ribcage: recognition and excitement, but anger too at what he was seeing.

Michael joined him. 'Is that an inverted cross?'

'Yes and no,' replied Sheen, coming closer to the body, again taking photographs. The 'T' of what indeed appeared to be a cross had been sliced deeply into the skin of the boy, ending, as though inverted, a little shy of the base of his spine. The shaft scored the length of his back. Sheen traced his gloved finger along the line of the cut.

'This part is, but it's not what I think we're looking at,' Sheen explained. He moved a fingertip along the curved arc of another cut. This one emerged from the shaft of the inverted cross just south of the 'T' and swept in a wide arc across the breadth of the child's back, ending in a tight kink like a cat's tail, or the blade of a sickle at the boy's shoulders. Sheen recognised it instantly. The same symbol had been traced in salt at the centre of an inverted pentagram in the old newspaper report he'd found at Clones Library earlier. The excitement of the find was in his voice when he spoke.

'Taken together this is the symbol of Saturn. The crescent below the cross, it means the victory of the earth over the soul, or something like that,' said Sheen. Michael made a faint sound, something between agreement and accolade.

Sheen moved to the boy's shrunken feet. His blackened heels were like basalt eggs. Sheen recorded more images. With the hands and head missing, identification would be very difficult. DNA testing could be done on a skin sample but would be helpful only if there was a record of the child's genetic code on file. Given that this crime likely dated from the 1970s, he had more chance of finding the kid's head if he went digging with his lucky shovel in Monaghan. Sheen's eyes lingered on the red horn of his large toenail. He clicked his fingers, reached into his pocket with his free hand.

'I'm gonna need to take a small nail sample,' Sheen said.

Michael's expression was blank, but not yet dismissive. He looked where Pixie stood waiting against the desk. She was Gardaí; their body, her call. She turned a questioning stare back at Sheen.

'I want to have it sent off for testing, a bone spectrum analysis,' he explained.

Pixie smiled, nodded. 'Clever. You're trying to determine whether this was a country or a city boy?' she asked.

'Exactly, a bone spectrum reading can tell us the environment this child lived in, using toxicology and pollution readings. In the absence of any other forensics it might just give us something to go on,' confirmed

Sheen. And it paid not to fall into the trap of making assumptions in the absence of evidence. From his library research he knew that another boy, Declan O'Rawe, had disappeared around the same time this crime likely took place. O'Rawe was a Monaghan child, and his body had been dumped far from home on a Belfast street.

The smile fell from Pixie's face. 'Who's authorising this?' she asked.

Sheen didn't miss a beat. Experience taught him that self-assurance often got the result you needed, in the short term anyway. 'I'll sign it off on behalf of DCI Conor Daly, PSNI Serious Crimes. Can't say much more, Pixie, but I'm working with the big man directly on this, cross-border issue,' he said.

Daly had recently taken the helm at Serious Crimes in Belfast, had transferred from the Dublin Gardaí, something that had previously been unheard of. He'd replaced the late Irwin Kirkcaldy and he was a well-known ball-breaker.

'Oh, aye, and that's why you had to drag my arse out of bed this morning?'

Sheen affected surprise, then hurt. 'I wanted to see you again,' he replied.

Pixie shook her head, but the mention of Daly's name had clearly done the trick. Only a fool would cross him. Sheen had never met him in his life and hoped that wouldn't change at any time soon.

'Go ahead, then,' she agreed.

Michael walked to a filing cabinet and fished out a

sealable plastic bag and handed it to Sheen.

'Cheers,' he replied. He was about to use the small nail cutters he'd taken from his pocket, but Michael held up a hand before he could try, and after a few seconds came back holding a more industrial-looking version of Sheen's personal manicure tool.

'This is what we need,' he said. Michael deftly removed a portion of the boy's large toenail and dropped it in the bag. Sheen explained what he wanted done, and Michael scribbled the details on the bag using a Sharpie.

'I'll complete the paperwork later. Just sign here,' he instructed. Sheen signed the bottom of an intricate-looking form, including the authorisation which he'd spuriously claimed to have.

'Michael, it says in the report here there was anal obstruction,' read Sheen. 'That mean evidence of sexual abuse?' he asked, trying to translate the jargon.

Michael's face lit up. 'Given the length of time that's passed it's virtually impossible to say for certain. No possibility of checking for internal bruising, abnormal secretions, that sort of thing. But there was something else,' he continued, once again walking off briskly before he'd had a chance to complete his explanation. He returned with a transparent plastic bag identical to the one Sheen had used for the toenail sample. He handed it over. Inside was the stem of a plant, presumably once green but now dyed peat brown as the body it had been extracted from. Along its length was the shrivelled remains of unopened buds, pod-like and pendulous.

'It was lodged in the anus, definitely not ingested, someone inserted it there,' Michael clarified.

Pixie spoke up. 'That's Solomon's seal,' she said, pointing at the bag. 'It's a cottage remedy, grows naturally in early summer. My old granny used to grind it up into a paste, good for aches and pains.'

Sheen took a photo, made a mental note. 'What about the cask the child was found in?' he asked.

Michael shook his head. 'I haven't seen it,' he replied. Which made sense; if it was anywhere it would be locked up in Gardaí secure evidence storage. But then again, that's exactly where the herbs should be.

'Hold on though,' he said. Another little excursion, same drawer as before, and he was back, another bag in hand. 'This was in the bag with the body. We presumed it must have been at the bottom of the cask and accidently sent to us. We alerted the Gardaí, but nobody's come to collect,' he said, glancing at Pixie.

Sheen took the bag. There was a semi-disintegrated brogue inside, the heel half missing. Sheen guessed probably an adult size six or seven. Sheen turned the shoe over, examined the sole. It was rubber, well worn down, but faintly the impression of what looked like an imprinted name ran along the right outside rim. He adjusted the angle and snapped the best photos he could manage, but it was still indistinct. Block capitals, perhaps a child's name, though he'd never known shoes to be printed as such.

ORAN

'Look, Sheen, I have to get going now.' It was Pixie. And this was her day off.

Sheen quickly wrote his email address down on a sheet of paper using Michael's Sharpie. 'When that lab report comes back, could you send it my way, mate?' Michael said no bother. 'And if you have a spare minute, can you scan the blues and send them my way too?' asked Sheen. He was pushing his luck, but not as far as Michael was concerned.

Pixie had turned to go. Michael was now busy covering the body. Sheen didn't think; he closed his hand over the shoe and pocketed it. It was the only thing here that seemed real from the child that had been, and he couldn't leave that remnant of the little boy in this sterile place. Anyway, the Gardaí had abandoned this piece of evidence as surely as they'd betrayed the memory of a murdered child. He headed back down the bleak corridor after Pixie.

In his mind's eye he could see Saturn's cross and scythe, carved cruelly into the back of that other-worldly body. And then something else, Saturn in human form, the ancient and insane god, devouring a screaming boy child held in one giant palm.

PART TWO

THE EVIL THAT MEN DO

CHAPTER SIX

Belfast, Northern Ireland
Tuesday 18th December

'Body of Christ,' said Aoife McCusker, holding up the Communion host to the face of the Mass-goer in one hand, not unlike the way she had at one time held her PSNI warrant card to the eyes of unbelievers when she was a detective. She was volunteering as a lay assistant, serving Communion at dawn Mass in the church that adjoined Clonard Monastery, off Falls Road in West Belfast. Though not strictly accurate, the church was known to most as 'Clonard' or 'the monastery'.

The man looked like he was in his late seventies, well-tanned and well presented. He made a layered plate of his palms in which Aoife set the host and he uttered a husky 'Amen', before he reverentially took the disc between one finger and thumb. He closed his eyes and put it into his mouth before blessing himself with the sign of the cross.

Aoife stared at his intently closed eyelids, willing to see something of his faith, before the man turned and walked slowly away. A woman stepped up to take his spot. Aoife repeated the ritual. The woman whispered her acceptance with closed eyes and offered her tongue, unwilling to sully the sanctity of the sacramental bread with her hand. Aoife slipped the wafer into her mouth with a practised ease, no longer anxious she might drop it.

Aoife raised another, but there was nobody left to serve or to save. The small congregation had accepted Christ and were now returning to their seats, most with the aid of walking sticks or on the arms of assisting relatives or carers. To her right Father Phil Rafferty bowled over to her from the other side. He'd come from the back of the church, serving those too infirm to walk up to the main altar. He was all business and energy despite the still night-time feel of the place and the fact he was well past eighty years old. As he approached, he started a hymn, his rich baritone pitch perfect; 'Hail glorious St Patrick, dear saint of our isle,' he announced, and his prompt was quickly picked up and spread. He stopped singing as abruptly as he had started, swished over to Aoife, and raised the big, silver-plated goblet that contained the few remaining hosts.

'The Body of Christ,' he intoned, though Father Phil Rafferty should know better. Still, he always tried, and Aoife was thankful. She lowered her head slowly, and with one hand covered her breast, a gesture of respectful decline. Father Phil made a sign of the cross on her forehead. Aoife appreciated the touch of his warm skin if nothing else. She glanced over at the front pew where she had left her handbag, coat and walking stick. Her thoughts turned to Ava and how once, not too long ago, her feet would just about scrape the floor if she were sitting there. The thought brought with it a pang that was deeper and more painful than the recurrent throb from the gunshot wounds she'd received several months before on her first and last case as a detective. Unlike the red scar tissue on her shoulder and stomach, the pain of having lost Ava to the social care system wasn't going to be soothed by the OxyContin tablets she'd been abusing on and off since leaving hospital in September.

Father Phil navigated an efficient path to the end of the Mass. His final blessing was returned as always with a full-hearted reply from the congregation, herself included, but the emptiness inside her felt bigger than the cold vacuum of the monastery's vaulted ceiling over their heads. Aoife had found unexpected solace in the social structure of organised religion, but it didn't mean she had any faith.

She waited for the small crowd to drift off, then headed to the Altar of St Gerard where she lit a candle and placed it in a red glass holder, its light joining the dozen or more that flickered in various stages of life and near-death. She turned to the white marble statue of the saint, a cross held to his breast, and made the same petition as always, but no more secure in the moment now than before.

'Return her to me,' she whispered. Gerard was the patron saint of expectant mothers. Not strictly true in her case, but if she stopped believing, *expecting* that Ava would come home again, then . . . She turned away from the statue, found a pound coin in her purse and deposited it in the box embedded in the wall next to the candles. God's always watching, so her mother used to tell her.

'Aoife, look who it is.' She turned at the sound of Father Phil's voice and saw Hayley White standing by his side.

'How's it going?' enquired Hayley, and gave her a small hug and a peck on the cheek.

As on the first day Aoife had met Hayley some two months before, she noted her strong-featured face, cheekbones and nose as angular as her hairstyle, but mostly her soft green eyes that smiled as she did. She also noted Hayley's Adam's apple that was only partly concealed by the neck scarf, and the strong, wide hands that now held her own. Hayley was also a lay volunteer but tended to work different Masses. The afternoons and early mornings they'd spent together cleaning the monastery or helping with the soup kitchen had been welcome highlights for Aoife. She counted her as a mate and had been able to open up to her about things. Hayley had suggested they hit the tiles and go for a drink the week before, but as usual Aoife had made an excuse and declined.

'All right, thanks,' replied Aoife.

Father Phil was looking even further north of pleased than usual, still in his purple and gold vestments, hands clasped before him.

'I asked Hayley to drop in. Thought you could do with a bit of a break,' he said.

Aoife had all but rebutted him, but then stopped the words before they escaped with one eye on the budding flame of the little candle she'd lit. Another of her mother's sayings, her voice clear and alive in her mind: *Prayers will always be answered, but you don't always get what you want.*

'Good of you,' she said, and then ran her eyes over Hayley's dark blue coat; pressed wool and tailored to die for. 'Where did you get that coat? It's gorgeous,' she said. Aoife mentioned a brand name she adored but knew there was no store here in Belfast.

'Yes, that's right. And aye, there's one in town, opened last week,' replied Hayley.

'I really wish you'd never told me that,' said Aoife. They both laughed.

Father Phil made a pantomime of staring at his shoes and turning on his heel to leave.

'Right, ladies, I'm going to leave you two to crack on. Go and have a cup of tea, sure you could even do a bit of shopping,' he said.

'Hey, that's stereotyping,' said Aoife to Father Phil's back as he strode off.

'Aye, well, God forgive me, sure it probably is too.' He paused and half turned. 'You need a break, Aoife, from all this.' He waved generally at the stunning baroque decor, the mosaic tiled floor. 'St Gerard won't forget you, and the poor, as the big man once said, will always be with us.

They'll be waiting when you come back,' he said, walking off again. He reached the door to the sacristy where he would change. 'I will too,' he shouted, his voice echoing across the monastery before disappearing under the booming slam of the wooden door shutting in his wake.

CHAPTER SEVEN

The monastery was predawn cool but the woman who was seated right at the very back burned in its shadows.

Her heart convulsed. It pounded against her chest which was scarred and pruned so as to never offer succour to man or child again. The disease was rampant in her now; she could feel it consuming her, eating her alive. But still, she coursed with power. And very soon more would be tapped. Pain, keen as a blade, stabbed her from within. She clenched her black robes and rode the agony. Her gaze remained fixed on the priest, Rafferty, as he strode away up the central aisle, so full of vigour. In his hand was the chalice he'd brought to her lips. On the roof of her mouth, the bland, cardboard strangeness of the wafer he had set on her tongue.

Priests and doctors – their visits only ever spelt bad news.

She'd given up on the doctors; they'd done nothing but show her how to die with no dignity. And priests? She'd lost faith in those shamans long, long ago.

She listened, tight-mouthed as the congregation took to song.

'Hail glorious St Patrick, dear saint of our isle.'

She spat the host the priest had served her on the stone floor and ground it under foot.

It was fitting that the priest would be her first.

Time passed in a slow pour. The ceremony ended and the congregation melted away, but she remained still and unnoticed. She listened; voices speaking from the front, followed by a laugh from the priest and a few moments later the slam of a door as he exited to his chambers. Soon enough all was quiet and empty.

She emerged from the shadows and slowly walked the length of the monastery walls, out of sight of the spying eye focused on the main altar. She stopped at the Altar of St Gerard, and one by one tipped the burning tealights onto the thin iron tray. Her gloved hand killed each in turn. The waxy smoke briefly filled the air and stung her eyes. She lowered her head and retraced her steps, followed the outer wall to the opposite side of the monastery. The big wooden door to the sacristy was unlocked and she slipped inside.

The click of its closing echoed in the empty chamber where Aoife McCusker's extinguished prayer turned cold and hard under the statue's stone eyes.

CHAPTER EIGHT

The coffee at Harlem Cafe in Belfast city centre was strong and smooth. Aoife's stomach growled as she absorbed the sights and smells of those enjoying their breakfasts at surrounding tables. She and Hayley managed to get stool seats on a raised bench that overlooked the rest of the diners. To her left, a woman had just been served eggs Benedict on soda bread and it looked good enough to kill for. That was Aoife's mind made up, and she closed the laminated menu and set it down. She glanced up to see Hayley approach from the other side of the bar where the toilets were located. Aoife had time to wonder whether Hayley had used the men's or ladies' room. She dropped her eyes abruptly at the intrusive thought, admiring for the second time that morning Hayley's beautiful navy coat draped on the back of the stool opposite.

'Well, I know what I'm having,' said Aoife.

Hayley nodded, and voiced Aoife's breakfast decision before she had time to speak it.

'It's a winner,' confirmed Hayley, her voice, as before in Clonard, was little over a whisper, but clearly audible despite its softness.

'Same for you, then?' asked Aoife, nodding to a waiter who weaved his way towards them.

'Not today. Salmon and cream cheese bagel for me,' she replied.

The waiter took their orders and whisked their menus away, returning in advance of the breakfasts with two iced waters. Aoife watched as Hayley took a sip, her eyes scanning Bedford Street at Aoife's back. Her free hand was balled into a soft fist, and like the wary expression she wore her gesture seemed vulnerable and somehow lonely. Aoife shifted on her stool, careful not to topple the walking stick she had balanced on the bench edge next to her. She took a sip of water. How much of what she had just sensed from Hayley had Father Phil seen in her over recent months? Their pairing was far from random.

'Father Phil's a good man,' said Hayley, her eyes moving to rest on Aoife. 'But he thinks we both are in need of company. Doesn't mean we have to become besties, you know. A coffee and a shop around, no pressure,' she continued.

Aoife noted she'd successfully followed her thinking for the second time. She'd have made a decent copper. 'I know. About his kindness, I mean. But I'm not exactly doing you a favour here. The opposite's true, actually. Keeps telling me I need to be out and about more,' said Aoife.

Father Phil's assessment was an understatement. She'd used a full deck of excuses not to get together with her good friend Marie. Fact was Aoife could not bear to be with her because so much of their time together had involved their girls playing or sharing sleepovers. To see Sinead, Marie's daughter, would be to see a ghost of Ava, and that was too much to cope with. She'd also stopped using social media, which she'd been so entranced with in what she loosely now referred to as her 'Previous Life'. Despite Hayley's words, she was the only real friend she had now – fact.

'Oh, he's all for people getting out and enjoying things: "Get out and spread yerself around a bit, girl!"' Hayley said, pushing her shoulders forward and jutting out her chin. Aoife choked on her mouthful of water, turned away and strained to swallow, barely managing it before exploding with laughter. The woman next to them put her cutlery down and stared over at them, but Aoife was past caring. She laughed, hard and true, and it felt glorious. Food came, she dabbed her eyes with her white cotton napkin and watched as Hayley started her bagel. The giggles were still bubbling; her unexpected catharsis had left her borderline hysterical.

'Ah God, he said that to you too? Some advice from a Catholic priest, that,' she said.

'Redemptorist Catholic priest,' corrected Hayley.

'He is a good man, you're right,' said Aoife, suddenly sombre again. 'How long have you known him?' she asked.

Hayley finished a mouthful of her breakfast and glanced to the right. A tell of someone speaking the truth, accessing her memory rather than her creative imagination, Aoife noted. Previous Life skills died hard it would seem.

'Just over a year,' she said, nodding. 'I've worked in England on and off for the last twenty years or so, teaching, in the north-east mainly, Newcastle upon Tyne. When I first moved away, I went to London, but I was only there for a year. But you reach an age. I decided it was time to return. I've done agency work since coming back. Don't get holiday or sick pay, but the rates are good. Suits me,' she said. Aoife processed this, registered the fact that Hayley had been out of Ireland for a fair portion of her adult life. The slight lilt in her accent was easier to place now she had the information.

'I haven't known him that long, really, only a few months,' said Aoife, dropping her eyes. 'Previous to that I was in the PSNI,' she said quietly, 'but I'm taking time out.' Aoife had already confided to Hayley that Ava had been taken into care, but not why. When she'd first told her, Hayley had listened, no suggestion of judgement.

'I know. About your job, I mean. I heard about what happened to you over the summer,' replied Hayley. Of course, in the public mind she was still a hero, injured in the line of duty averting a catastrophe. 'Seriously brave,' said Hayley. Aoife set her utensils down, appetite suddenly gone.

'I'm not what you think I am,' said Aoife quietly. Hayley smiled weakly, her expression polite but confused, and Aoife couldn't blame her. She could barely make sense of how screwed up things had got, and how quickly. Aoife took a breath and gave her a potted summary starting with the drugs found in her locker at Ladas Drive PSNI station, the internal investigation, her ongoing suspension and how it resulted in Ava being taken into care. She looked Hayley in the eye and assured her she had nothing to do with the drugs. On that count, at least, she had a grain of dignity left. When she had finished, Hayley was shaking her head once more, but now her expression had turned sour. She sniffed and cast a look over Aoife's shoulder at the world beyond. The passers-by who looked would see the flame in her eyes as Aoife now could.

'Don't be taking offence, but in general I've got little time for peelers,' she said, returning her gaze to Aoife. Her face had softened, but not much. 'Present company excluded, they're an old boys' network and they look after their own,' she said.

'None taken,' replied Aoife. She thought about how she had been hung out to dry by Paddy Laverty, now a DI in Serious Crimes. Not a phone call, not a visit, just a cold suspension letter. Internal Investigations was the only member of the police family who wanted to know her now.

Though, perhaps, not the only.

Sheen had visited her in hospital, and he'd kissed her

73

too, so tenderly. But it was also Sheen's double-speak that had talked her into disobeying orders. And that had nearly got her killed, left her with half a pancreas and put Ava in the line of fire. Golden Gun Sheen could wait in the cold, indefinitely, as far as she was concerned. And she was not at all concerned or interested in seeing him. Her mind returned to that kiss. Perhaps she had dreamt that?

'As a matter of fact, I happen to agree with you,' said Aoife.

'I want to tell you something. About me,' said Hayley. Aoife nodded for her to continue but said nothing. If Hayley was comfortable to talk about the fact that she was transgender, she would listen, but had promised herself never to pry.

'I did a bit of work for the police, in London, about twenty years ago,' she said. 'It didn't end well.' This was not what she had anticipated.

'So, you were on the force?' asked Aoife.

'Consultant,' she replied.

Aoife quickly played with the few facts in front of her. Hayley was a teacher, perhaps a linguist? 'Do you have an additional language, something they could find a use for?' she attempted.

Hayley gave her a whimsical look. 'No, I'm not a linguist, but I can see you must have been good at your job,' she said, then laughed, dryer and less hearty than earlier.

Aoife waited. Hayley exhaled.

'Do you know what an intuitive is?'

'No.'

'Psychic?'

'Like a spiritualist?' attempted Aoife.

'Like that, but minus the crystal ball and people joining hands round a card table in a candlelit room,' she said.

Aoife smiled. That was exactly what she had thought of, but she doubted it took a mind-reader to work it out.

'OK, but why does this link to police work?'

'It doesn't. Not directly. In fact, I'm of a mind that it has no place there whatsoever,' she said.

Now Aoife asked about the work she had done. Hayley didn't answer directly, instead took her further back.

'When I was six years old, my big sister took me out one Saturday shopping. She brought me up to Ardoyne. Not our side of town, to a house where they were selling knocked-off Ralph Lauren hoodies, all the rage and a fraction of the price.

In the front bedroom a guy was waiting, lots of stolen goods, including the Polo tops. And he had a knife. He kept asking us questions: where we were from, what schools we went to, you know? All the time he was cutting nicks into the side of one of the boxes with that huge knife. But it was not him who was frightening me,' she said. Her voice had dropped to a lower whisper than before.

Aoife put her elbows on the bench, leant closer to Hayley, who was still staring into a faraway place out the big window.

'What scared you?' she prompted gently.

'What scared me was the man who was sitting behind him, in the corner. I remember seeing him in black and white, like an old film. He wore older-fashioned clothes, a pair of flares and a shirt, but his armpits were stained in wide dark patches. And he was staring right at me. His eyes were black, I'll never forget that, big black discs.'

'Bloody hell,' said Aoife. She rubbed the gooseflesh that had spread up her arms. 'And then?'

'Then the man looked over my shoulder, to where the door was. I turned around too and when I did the guy with the big knife followed my gaze, nothing there, just the closed door. When I looked back the man was shaking his head, he shouted something, but it was like the film was on mute. I knew what he'd said; I screamed the words for him: "No!" I had not realised I'd wet myself until I looked down. My sister grabbed me by the arm and trailed me away,' she finished.

'That's spooky,' said Aoife.

Hayley had gone pale. She was telling her the truth, as she believed it anyway. Aoife had heard enough liars to spot the difference. And if Hayley had a gift, it made sense that police could make use of it.

'So, you used your gifts to help the police?' she asked.

'Didn't prove very helpful in the end,' she replied, her voice more serrated, cutting above a whisper.

Aoife watched her jaw tighten, and then relax. 'Would I know the case?' she prompted.

'Charlotte Claridge,' Hayley replied.

'Right,' said Aoife. Of course she recognised the name, everyone over a certain age would. Charlotte Claridge was a journalist and television presenter. She'd started on breakfast TV and at the time she was murdered she had been best known for a consumer rights show that prided itself with righting wrongs and exposing corruption. The next name Aoife spoke was almost as well-known as Claridge, and for a different reason was also remembered as a victim.

'Wilmott Kettering,' she said. The guy had a history of stalking and harassing women, and one conviction for sexual assault. He lived a few streets away from Claridge's south London home in Brixton. Kettering was sent down for murder, but was released on appeal the following year, only to overdose. Aoife remembered the media hype, and vaguely recalled some controversy about the investigation being led astray by bogus advice from a psychic.

'After Kettering got out, the press turned on the police, and they turned on me,' she said.

'They said you gave them Kettering?' asked Aoife.

'Yip, not in so many words, but the press joined the dots.'

'Not true?' asked Aoife.

'Blatant lie. I had nothing to do with Kettering, but they liked him for it,' she said.

'What did you tell them? Did you see something? I mean like when you were a child?'

'It doesn't always happen like that. That was very vivid, very specific. Most of the time it's snippets, fleeting sensations, like picking up a trace of perfume or cigarette smoke after someone's left a room,' replied Hayley. 'They took me to her home; let me stand in the doorway where she'd been shot. I thought I wasn't going to get anything, and then I dropped down and touched the doorstep. That was where, you know, her head had been. The tile was chipped, where the bullet had lodged,' said Hayley, looking away. She took another sip of water before continuing. 'I was able to tell them that their murderer was a white male, that he fired the gun using his left hand. I told them that his breath smelt of garlic and a tiger was important,' said Hayley.

'I remember something about a tiger now,' said Aoife.

'Wilmott Kettering had a tiger tattoo on his chest,' confirmed Hayley.

Aoife shook her head. 'But he was also black, right?'

'Yeah, they didn't mention that. The press picked up the tiger angle and ran with it. I was named, photographers on the doorstep, hate mail,' said Hayley.

'Christ, that's so unfair. That was when you left London?'

Hayley agreed with a nod. 'Thank God it was pre-Facebook and social media. The world wouldn't have been big enough for me to run. As it was, the north-east seemed distant enough, plus there was work,' said Hayley.

Aoife's brow creased. 'Didn't Claridge get involved in helping Albanian refugees before she was killed, and they were looking into a Serbian connection? What was his name?' asked Aoife.

'Arkan,' replied Hayley. She pulled out her phone and searched. She slid the phone over the bench to Aoife, who quickly scanned the image and text beneath it.

'The Tigers,' said Aoife.

'That was the name of Arkan's Serbian paramilitary group in the Yugoslav Wars,' said Hayley. Aoife glanced down at the phone again. She studied the image of the dead-eyed thug in military garb; in one hand he held an automatic rifle, in the other he clutched a tiger cub by the scruff. Around him, dressed in similar uniforms and also heavily armed were his men, their faces hidden behind black balaclavas. Whether Belgrade or Belfast, it seemed clear the men of violence were the same: their guns, their masks, and their bullshit machismo.

Aoife pushed Hayley's phone back across the table as the waiter set their bill down. They paid and she followed Hayley to the exit, thought about how she had guessed her breakfast order. She asked her about it, and in response Hayley laughed.

'Don't be daft. I saw you staring at that woman's plate,' replied Hayley. For the third time in just one morning Aoife laughed too, and mentally noted that she was going to thank Father Phil for setting her up on this date. The laughter was the best drug she'd had in the past four months.

'Come on, we'll take a dander round to that shop, see if something catches our eye,' said Hayley, turning into the wind and walking. 'And by the way I always use the ladies',' she said.

CHAPTER NINE

Dermot Fahey, the investigative reporter who'd written the piece Sheen had spotted on Maureen's wall in Welshtown, had agreed to meet at the John Hewitt in Belfast city centre. As soon as Sheen entered the pub a little after 11.30 a.m., he recognised his face from the headshot that had been printed beside the *Irish News* article. Music played, but low enough to ignore. The place was mostly empty, just three people: a man and woman seated on stools at the bar dressed for business, phones front and centre, soft drinks and matching sandwiches either side. The third looked to be a regular, already a half-empty pint of lager held in his hand, big gut sagging over his belt. He stared unblinking at the preamble to a horserace on the screen above the bar.

Fahey stood up as Sheen approached, extended his hand and gave a strong shake. He had the crumpled orderliness of a man with little interest in style but an attention to detail. And, Sheen noted, a moral compass.

Sheen recognised his trainers as a brand which had publicly denounced sweatshops. His checked shirt boasted no label. Apart from a wedding band, the thin MacBook that was open on the round table in front of him was his only luxury. In short, a thoroughbred investigative journalist: crusading, obsessive and all about the job.

Sheen went for his warrant card, but Fahey waved him to not bother as he sat back down.

'I recognise you,' he explained.

Sheen's media coverage had been brief but bright. And with Jimmy McKenna's funeral scheduled for tomorrow, he could be back in the spotlight once again.

'You too,' said Sheen.

'Bloody wonder,' replied Fahey with a grin; he ran his freckled hand through the remaining wisps of his springy red hair. There'd been much more of it in his mugshot.

'You have kids?' he asked. Sheen told him no. 'Stock up on the Grecian 2000 before you do, that's my advice.' His Dublin lilt barely touched on each word. The barman came to them; they ordered drinks: pot of tea for Sheen, an Americano for Fahey. He raised his eyebrows when the barman departed, Sheen's cue to begin.

'I need an inside angle on the Satanic panic stoked by the British Army along the Irish border,' he said.

'This official?' he asked.

In short, no, and half-truths told to bulldog journalists tended to come back to bite you, in his experience. More seriously, if Sheen's masters in the Northern Ireland Office and PSNI got wind of him pursuing a cowboy investigation under their badge, he'd be pulled over the coals. But if Fahey thought there was no mileage for him in terms of a story, then why would he talk? Time to bait the line.

'We found a body, last summer,' he said. Fahey blinked slowly. 'I don't mean the McKenna boy, another one,' continued Sheen.

'Heard about it,' said Fahey. The case had been given almost zero coverage, so it was unlikely he'd heard much. Their drinks arrived. A silence settled.

'What you didn't hear is that the body was decapitated, hands missing, had an occult symbol, Saturn, cut into the torso. And it was a boy's body, no more than thirteen, if I was pushed to guess,' said Sheen. His bait was cast, the best he had. He'd not told Fahey this was an Historical Offences case, but neither had he denied it. Fahey lifted his absurdly large bowl of black Americano and took a slurp, set it back into its groove in the saucer.

'So, you think the British Army were behind this?' he asked.

Sheen shrugged. He was nibbling.

'I don't know. The guys operating out of Aughnacloy barracks were reading a bit of Dennis Wheatley before bedtime. And according to your investigation, they did a good enough job of raising a black magic scare. People believed it. Maybe there was more,' said Sheen.

'Seems plausible, in a world gone buck mad of course, but that's what it was,' said Fahey. 'If you're interested go to the Public Record Office of Northern Ireland web page. You can access the Conflict Archive. I did. They're all there for the reading,' he said. Which of course was true, but not what he needed. Fahey's article had referred to 'Soldier A', 'Captain Y' and so on. Those still alive, and maybe even those dead had their identities redacted.

'If I get a name, you get the story, exclusive. I can't go on the record, but I'll open every door I can,' said Sheen.

Another question from Fahey in response, but less dismissive now than a moment before. 'You seriously think these boys took things to that level? What the fuck would the point be for them? They were highly trained, professional soldiers. What they did saved lives, you know. I didn't go down that route in the article, but that's also true. They did some nasty business, but it kept civilians away from target areas, helped separate players from the public, know what I mean?' he said.

Sheen said he did. 'It's a starting point, best I have. Surely it's worth investigating?' he said.

Fahey made a clicking sound with the side of his cheek. 'Plus, whoever murdered the kid you found is probably dead anyway,' he said.

A memory came to Sheen: his feet numb with cold after walking the night beat in London, still in uniform, not long finished his probation. A call to Tower Bridge and a dark shape in the mudbank below, the orange shorts glaring in the dim dawn light. A child's torso, limbs and head expertly cleaved, and his lifeblood drained, his essence stolen for Muti witchcraft.

'I found the body of that child who was dumped in the Thames, the one they started off calling Eli. Remember that?' asked Sheen.

'Yeah, I do,' said Fahey.

'I was just a green PC. First on the scene,' he said. 'You know when I looked over the edge, I refused to believe what I was seeing. Told myself it was a doll, a dummy. But those orange shorts, it was what made it real. They made you stare, you couldn't look away, you know?'

'The shorts were the calling card, the way the bastards announced the sacrifice, made it known. What are the odds of you finding another body?' said Fahey softly.

'Yeah,' said Sheen; he had to agree. 'Whoever did this thing is an evil person, just like the man who bled that kid Eli and made potions from his body. Muti. Devil worship. You see, Fahey, I really don't give a flying fuck what the sick bastards like to call it or how they choose to dress it up,' said Sheen. He'd leant his elbows on the table, moved into Fahey's space, getting angry, not caring. Fahey did not retreat, kept calm. 'But I know if I knock on enough doors or enough heads together then sooner or later I'm going to find out who did this, and I don't care if they're dead or alive. But I need a name, a place to start.'

Fahey turned his mouth down, nodded, sat back and folded his arms.

'Now don't think badly of me. But when you do, it's going to be one fucking good story too,' he said.

'Yip, I suppose that's true,' said Sheen. Bleeding journalists.

Fahey tapped the table with his index finger and then nodded a few times, as though making a decision. But his eyes were still wary, and he came back at Sheen with another question.

'You heard of a guy called Dylan Martin, one of us?' asked Fahey. By which Sheen assumed he meant press. He was about to reply in the negative, then paused, recalling a book he'd read as a teen on the Troubles, something about collusion between the old Royal Ulster Constabulary, army reservists and loyalist paramilitaries. Sheen clicked his fingers, his shadowy memory for once coming to his aid.

'*Dirty Deeds . . .*' he started, and Fahey completed what Sheen could not.

'*And Secret Signs*,' said Fahey. 'That's the one. You can still buy it, but it's out of print. Collusion, path-beating stuff, linked the Ulster Volunteer Force to rogue police and army, all of them sharing the same funny handshakes,' he said.

Sheen raised his eyebrows; he'd forgotten the ties the book had made to the Masons, long time since he'd read it. He waited for Fahey to get to the point, at last feeling this was going somewhere useful.

'Dylan was a mentor to me as a younger man; took me under his wing, served me stories. No need to, but that was him. Anyway, he was working on a follow-up, something that he wouldn't share, not even with me. Only thing I got from him was a name. Captain Trevor McHenry. Army Intelligence. Dylan told me he was a communications officer, but that wasn't the half of it,' said Fahey.

'Never heard of him,' said Sheen.

'Well, indeed. British Army officer, but an Ulster man, home-grown. Well-bred, public-schooled, but he made his own way. I don't even know if Dylan made contact, or if he was just sniffing. If you google him, you'll find him but not the full story.'

'What's the full story?' asked Sheen.

Fahey drained the last of his black coffee and winced, sucking the dregs through his front teeth.

'No idea. But Dylan got hammered one night, though he was never a drinker. Told me McHenry was once the head of army psychological warfare in the North. Said he had an elite troop, SAS, but just for him, guys who worked well below the radar. Also said he was onto something else big, wouldn't be budged on what. Looking back, I think he was frightened.'

'The Satanic panic. This McHenry was behind it?' asked Sheen.

'Looks that way, doesn't it?' answered Fahey.

Sheen felt the rustle and draw of his new addiction calling him now he'd drained the last of his tea. Not the time to nip out to the front doorway though.

'You said I'd see a story if I google him. What's the deal?'

'McHenry fell, catastrophically so,' replied Fahey.

'Go on,' said Sheen.

'Whatever his job had been in the early '80s, by the 1990s he was involved in running agents; IRA members who were willing to co-operate in exchange for a bit, often a lot, of money on the side.' Sheen rubbed the side of his face, frowned.

'That's a Special Branch role, or maybe MI5. Had McHenry taken a sidestep from his psych ops job in the army?'

Fahey shrugged. 'Or was he always standing with a foot in both camps? Wheels within wheels and fires within fires,' he said.

'So, he fell,' prompted Sheen.

'Hard and far. Landed in an eight by nine cell and did fourteen years,' said Fahey.

Sheen played the numbers against his knowledge of the criminal justice system. McHenry hadn't just been creaming off cash or disobeyed an order.

'Murder?' chanced Sheen.

'Manslaughter,' corrected Fahey.

'The well-known republican he had allegedly been handling as an informer, Paco Hillen was his name, was found dead in his Belfast home with head injuries. McHenry was found unconscious in his car on the shore of Lough Neagh, whiskey on his breath and the blood of the IRA man all over him,' said Fahey. He paused to let Sheen absorb the facts. Then he gave him one more, and the pieces slotted together seamlessly. 'When they searched McHenry's home, they found a lot of money under his mattress, bundles of it that couldn't be accounted for. The dead guy's prints were all over them,' he said.

'McHenry was on the take and being blackmailed,' said Sheen.

Fahey rocked his head, mouth turned down. 'It was never said in court, but whispers came my way that the handler had been turned by his own agent. McHenry had started selling information about fellow military and police personnel to the IRA. The Provo had started to blackmail him rather than paying him, so the stories went, and McHenry killed him before he could be compromised.'

Sheen sat back on his small stool as best he could, folded his arms, chin lowered.

'Don't buy it, eh?' asked Fahey.

Sheen shook his head.

'Guy is top brass, a pioneer in his field. And at that later stage in his career he gets turned by a Belfast Provo for *money*?'

Sheen again shook his head.

'Hear ya, though it was a lot of cash, to be fair. Judge sent McHenry down despite his denials,' said Fahey.

Not a jury, just a judge, Sheen noted. The so-called Diplock court system, set up in Northern Ireland for special cases to protect civilians from retribution who would otherwise be called to sit on juries and make terrorist convictions. It was also very useful when the decision or sentence was expedient for the state.

'Same time your mate Dylan Martin was talking to him,' said Sheen.

'See where it's taking you?' asked Fahey.

Sheen did. McHenry was shafted because someone discovered he'd been speaking to a journalist with a record of digging up filth. Speaking, most probably, about the nefarious activities of his troop over a decade before, in the badlands of south Armagh and Monaghan, the very place where Sheen had discovered the body of a child who had suffered a terrible death.

'Jesus. Did Martin not publish?' asked Sheen.

Fahey sighed deeply. 'Any attempt to print whispers about McHenry's fall was met with legal action. Powerful people were happy to spread the poison by mouth, but wanted their man out of the spotlight, like forgotten,' said Fahey.

'What happened to publish or be damned?' said Sheen.

'Yeah, well, Dylan's nerves were frayed, he took a holiday, went to Morocco, wanted his head showered, you know? Someone stuck a broken bottle in his neck in an alleyway the night before he was scheduled to return. Stole his traveller's cheques, but whoever did it left his watch and wedding ring.'

Sheen let the gravity of what Fahey was telling him sink in. One man locked up and shut up, another dispensed with brutally.

'Not a classic mugging,' said Sheen.

'No,' agreed Fahey.

'Dylan Martin's wife still alive?' asked Sheen.

'No idea. We never got on, and she wanted nothing to do with me after he died,' said Fahey.

'But if Martin was close to something there might be evidence?' suggested Sheen.

'Maybe,' agreed Fahey. 'I can try, but as I said, she despised me.'

'Persistence beats resistance,' said Sheen.

'Here, giz your phone,' Fahey said. Sheen unlocked it and handed it over. Fahey's fingers worked the screen and seconds later his own phone started to vibrate on the table next to his computer. He killed the call on Sheen's phone, handed it back. 'We've exchanged numbers, let's keep in touch,' he said, getting up and shrugging on his coat. It was army surplus. Sheen had him hooked.

'McHenry?'

'He's out, good few years now. Don't bother looking for him, he's gone,' he said.

Sheen's stomach sank. Just when he thought he'd taken a step closer.

Fahey laughed. 'Jesus, you have a face like a well-scalped arse,' he said. 'The name you need is Paul Craigavon. McHenry got himself a new identity when he was released. Don't ask me how I know that. I won't tell you,' warned Fahey.

Sheen asked him for an address.

'That I don't know, but I've heard reliably that Paul Craigavon's in Belfast. A search in one of those all-seeing police databases will probably turn it up.'

Sheen waited by the doorway as Fahey walked off, unlocked his mountain bike that was chained to a lamp post further along and cycled off. No helmet. He sparked up a rollie, first of the week, and allowed himself three good draws before crushing it against the steel mesh of the butt bin. His phone vibrated and he saw a text from Fahey; he must have sent it while cycling.

Good luck, thanks for the meet. Remember Dylan Martin.

A fair point; he was a man who'd gone searching and had ended up with his throat full of broken glass, dead on a foreign street. Sheen opened Safari, did a search for McHenry, and found only a little of what Fahey had just told him. He enlarged the black and white image, on the screen, and studied the uniformed officer staring resolutely back at him. Straight back, broad-shouldered and clipped moustache, his eyes were hard and intelligent. McHenry had been the very picture of all that was strong and upright. But a man who had also fallen from a great height and into the darkness, like Lucifer himself.

CHAPTER TEN

Sheen pulled up on the Glencairn estate in north Belfast close to where the satnav told him he could find McHenry, living now under a new identity: Paul Craigavon. The place looked like it was built in the 1960s, shoulder to shoulder pebble-dashed homes, municipal and unattractive. From where Sheen was parked, their ascending roofs resembled steps leading the way up to the foot of Divis Mountain, bulbous and green above them. Across the road was a building with a roof pitched like a teepee. Above the double doors a banner spelt out THE WORD IS THE TRUTH and in the middle of a patch of grass that separated this road from its neighbour, Sheen could make out the still-blackened outline where a massive bonfire had burned into the July night over the 12th weekend.

Here was a place where two things mattered more than any other: God and Ulster. Sheen got out of his car and headed for McHenry's house, still using his phone to navigate. The kerbstones were painted red, white and blue. Sheen wondered if any of McHenry's neighbours knew he'd been convicted of murdering a top IRA man, but only because he'd been selling him state secrets.

The rattle of a police helicopter overhead took his attention. It swooped into view before turning in a large circle, its tail to Sheen. He turned the corner into McHenry's street, saw police tape stretched across the far end, armour-plated Land Rovers blocked the road. Beyond, he caught a glimpse of a tactical aid unit on their hands and knees, going over the road inch by inch and wearing blue protective suits. The newsreader's announcement from the car radio as he drove here returned to him.

'. . . *in his thirties shot and killed, a former prisoner who had served time for Ulster Defence Association membership and racketeering offences.*'

The feud that had torn the UDA apart since Cecil Moore's untimely demise on the 12th of July simmered on. The latest victim had been shot in the groin while holding a three-month old baby. As Sheen reached number 13, McHenry's home, he spotted Paddy Laverty behind the tape. Laverty had shaved off his moustache, made him look younger. He was on a call, distracted and not looking Sheen's way. Still, Sheen kept his head low and headed into McHenry's front garden. Sheen and Laverty had history, and Paddy Laverty was a man who knew how to hold a grudge. Into the bargain, Laverty had been overlooked for the top job in Serious Crimes. Conor Daly, another blow-in, from south of the border no less, had been shoehorned in ahead of him.

Laverty was angry at Daly, jealous and angry at Sheen, and had taken it all out on the only person he had authority to punish: Aoife McCusker. Sheen knew she'd been suspended and cold-shouldered as the slow-moving sludge of an Internal Investigations enquiry approached. Laverty had thrown her to the wolves when he could have had her back. These things mattered, especially when it came to Internal Investigations; everyone reads between the lines. Laverty's message to them was clear: guilty. Sheen paused, racked his brain for the psychological term for Paddy's behaviour, but could not find it. He raised a fist and banged McHenry's scuffed front door.

At last the technical term he had been looking for came to him.

'Fucking arsehole,' he said quietly.

No answer. Sheen looked through an opening in the drawn curtains of the front room. An old television was on a table in the corner, screen dark and grey. Boulder-shaped, not flat-screened. A saggy-looking sofa was shipwrecked against the far wall, an off-white duvet with no cover, rolled up at one end. Empty beer cans were strewn over the warped laminate floor. No dog, at least that he could see. In Sheen's experience knocking doors across London, it was better to know. He banged the door again, felt it rattle, but got no response. He could feel the emptiness of the house beating back at him.

'All right?'

A woman was standing in the open doorway of the house to his left, arms crossed over her substantial bosom. She fixed him with two small eyes set deep at the root of her long branch of a nose. Sheen noted the knot halfway down; broken and mended, home job, perhaps on both counts. A dog barked from behind her.

'Said all right?' she repeated. Her greeting was pure Belfast; a hello, an enquiry into his well-being and a what the fuck do you want? Sheen took out his warrant card and flipped it open in front of her for half a second. She didn't need to study it; she just needed to know who was in charge.

'He about?' he said, cocking his head at McHenry's front door. She registered a momentary surprise at his accent.

'How would I know?' she said.

Sheen imagined there was not a lot this woman did not make her business, maybe that explained her bobbled nose. The look in her eye said that she was not going to offer any help, so he turned away with a shrug. He strolled off. His apathy play worked. It usually did with nosey parkers like her.

'Anyway, you lot have already had a word the day with Paul. Why do you need to bother the poor creature again?' she asked, a sly look playing on her face.

The murder on the estate; it made sense.

'Not to worry, just following up with something,' he said, turning and walking off again.

'Try the offy. That's where he's usually to be found if he's not rattling round that front room. Or drinking down the allotment,' she shouted after him.

Sheen heard her door slam shut. The muffled sound of the dog barking stopped. Sheen stopped too, thought of the beer cans that were strewn across the front room.

The off licence was not hard to find, the only closed shop at the end of a row that included a kebab joint, hair salon and a minimarket. Its sad-looking fruit and vegetables were on display beneath an awning that looked like it had caught more rain than sunshine over the years. In London, McHenry could have walked into any corner shop to purchase alcohol. But Northern Ireland was, in this regard as with so much else, different. Over the past few months, Sheen had been caught out more than once when he fancied a glass of red with his microwave meal. The alcohol licencing laws were tighter here: if you wanted booze you either went to a bar, the fenced-off section of most big supermarkets (and even then, only after midday), or one-stop shops like this one, again, subject to strict opening times. The Bible, just like the gun, was never far from day-to-day dealings in this place.

Sheen slowed as he approached the off licence, took note of the two men standing outside the shuttered front of Andy's Booze Hut. At first he thought he was out of luck and then recognised McHenry, but only just.

The man in the grainy black and white photo was all but gone. The straight-backed poise and high-raised chin had transformed into a slumped old man, his grubby Puffa coat not fully disguising his too-thin frame. It was his eyes that gave him away. He had taken the time to glance back in the direction of Sheen's approaching footsteps, something the young man standing by the door of the off licence in front of him had not. They had the same intelligent gleam of the younger man and the same unafraid toughness which spoke of experienced soldiery. Sheen glanced down as McHenry slowly turned his back to him and dug his hands in his coat pockets. Sheen noted his shoes as he did so. They were polished to an improbably high shine. Definitely his captain; even though his world had fallen down a toilet, McHenry still polished his shoes like an officer.

'Hello, Captain McHenry. Spare me five minutes?' said Sheen, joining the queue behind him.

McHenry remained still for a long moment. Then, without turning around, he spoke, just above a rough whisper.

'Nobody calls me that any more. That man's dead,' he said.

Sheen waited and McHenry turned to him, his face impassive. He flipped open his warrant card. McHenry ignored it.

'Fuck off and leave me be,' he said. He was ordering, not pleading, from a man who still knew how to issue commands.

Sheen raised his warrant card and held it prominently between them. McHenry's eyes momentarily dropped from Sheen's face, took it in and returned.

'I spoke to some Julie this morning, got me out of my bed,' he said.

'Murder's not why I'm here, Captain McHenry. Not that one anyway,' Sheen persisted, taking care to use McHenry's now-defunct official title. If he was riled, he might let something slip, especially a man who was yet to have his hair of the dog. 'Want to chat about the body of a child that I dug up just over the border. Whoever put him there cut his fucking head off and sliced symbols into him. About the same time you and your boys were sacrificing chickens and burning black candles in sheds across south Armagh,' said Sheen. His voice was almost convivial, at odds with the horror.

The shutters of the Booze Hut rattled open and McHenry stood aside abruptly, turning his face from Sheen. The man in the queue beside them was staring at them.

'Five minutes, walk,' said McHenry and he moved off, leaving the concrete pathway in front of the shops and headed across the patchy grass beyond. Sheen followed. McHenry stopped as they entered an outdoor gym and playground, the equipment sweating with recent rainfall. Sheen leant against the pillar of a pull-up bar, felt the cold line of steel digging into his shoulder blades.

'Call me that again and I will punch you in the jaw. I boxed in the army,' he said.

'No need for that,' said Sheen, glancing away.

In his day this man was probably formidable, but not now. The chopper rattled overhead, a woman pushed a rickety-looking buggy past them, an oversized child squeezed in its sagging seat, bottle of Coke in his hand. McHenry's blood-cracked eyes were still on Sheen when he returned his attention to him.

'The *Irish News* article,' said McHenry, not a question.

'I found a body, Trevor. A kid's body,' started Sheen, but McHenry cut him off fast as a whip.

'I know what you found, Owen Sheen,' he said.

Sheen's turn to stab a glance at McHenry. Despite his dishevelment he was still sharp, the sort of sharp that took a man to the head of Military Intelligence at twenty-four.

'What's that, then?' he asked. Instead of answering, McHenry broke his gaze and turned towards the mist-shrouded hump of Divis, fast disappearing as the cloud sank in. Though not yet gone 2.30 p.m., the deepening gloom spoke of dusk.

'Now you see it, now you don't,' he said, nodding at the mountain.

'Teach you that in MI? How to be evasive, say nothing?' said Sheen. 'Someone killed that boy; I have a photo,' said Sheen, reaching for his phone. 'Want to see what a body looks like after you dig it up from a peat bog? Remarkably intact, at least the bits your boys didn't remove first,' he continued.

'Put the phone away; I've no interest,' said McHenry, returning his eyes to Sheen's.

Sheen returned his phone to his jacket pocket.

'Smoke and mirrors, is that what you're telling me, Trevor? Pure coincidence that your troop was beheading livestock and putting Communion wafers in excrement at the same time and same place that some kid was carved up, beheaded and buried in a barrel?' he said.

'I had no hand in what you're describing,' he said.

'Which bit? The black magic hysteria or the killing of a little boy?' said Sheen.

'You read the news article. What was printed was the truth. And old news dressed as new. The archives are public, go and read them and leave me be,' he said, starting to move, headed back in the direction of Andy's Booze Hut.

'Sacrificing animals, desecrating graves, all in a day's work, huh, Trevor? Easy pay for a man like you?' spat Sheen. He could grab the old soldier by the arm, drag him back and pin him over the cold bars of the stationary bike, but he let him walk.

McHenry stopped, turned and came to Sheen instead.

'Easiest thing I ever did,' he hissed.

'Did it stop at that?' asked Sheen, holding steady.

Again, McHenry ducked and weaved, answering as he wished.

'It was the end of the world along the border back then, Sheen. All bets were off. In bandit country you did what you could because the farmers by day became bogeymen at night. We made the locals drunk and slow on their own superstitions. And we saved lives, we saved lives,' he said, his words thick through clenched, yellow teeth.

Sheen could smell the phantom whiff of sick, sweet drink exuding from his pores.

'But someone took a boy's life, made a depraved fucking art form out of it,' persisted Sheen.

'Not my men. It was black propaganda, not black masses, get real,' he said. McHenry shook his head, turned again, but this time with an air of finality.

Sheen grabbed him below his elbow, felt more bone than meat through the soft fabric of his coat.

'You're about to add to your life's tally of mistakes, boy,' he said quietly.

Sheen softened his grip, felt McHenry draw away. He opted for a different line.

'Trevor. The Dublin man, Fahey, who wrote the article about you and your men, said you did good work, sabotaged arms dumps, kept locals out of the line of fire,' said Sheen.

McHenry stopped and looked to the mucky grass at their feet, his eyes a world away.

'And he told me you were stitched up, mate. Someone hung you out to dry, Trevor. After everything you did for this country, they fucked you over. They only do that when a man gets too close to a truth that's been buried for bad reasons,' said Sheen.

McHenry's face was once again turned to the hills,

all but obscured now by an off-white bank of cloud.

'It's gone two and I need to drink,' he said, his momentary resurgence totally gone.

'What about your boys? Maybe one of them will talk to me? And do the right thing,' said Sheen pointedly.

McHenry did not turn, but he answered Sheen.

'Lost touch long ago. I know one is in Australia, lives in the outback, off the grid. Some are dead,' he said.

Sheen followed him. McHenry paused, he turned.

'One of them's in Belfast still,' he said.

Sheen nodded, his face asking for more.

'That'll do you. He's close enough; you'll find him,' said McHenry.

Not a lot but better than leaving empty-handed.

'Owen Sheen. The man who wants to own the past,' he said.

Sheen waited, remembering now that McHenry had clocked him, probably without the help of his warrant card. He'd been in the news, more than he cared for. Sheen continued to wait, McHenry watched him, and Sheen could not read the old soldier's cracked eyes. Like his black arts, they held both light and dark.

'John Fryer didn't murder your brother, you know. Don't know who put those words in his mouth, but I can tell you it wasn't him,' he said.

Sheen wanted more, but McHenry was done. He turned away, sharp on his heel, and entered the maw of Andy's Booze Hut. Sheen headed towards his car. The mist now threatened to swallow the whole estate. Sheen was unclear if he had been administered a poison or given the antidote.

As he pulled away, his phone bleated through the powerful speakers and the name he'd been waiting for flashed on his display.

Aoife McCusker.

CHAPTER ELEVEN

Perhaps it was the two crows, big and black, that were perched on the gate post of Clonard Monastery when she returned to her parked car. Or, maybe, it was the closed sacristy door. Father Phil kept it open as a rule, a form of welcome to anyone in need who wanted to enter the house of God. Either way, Aoife's high spirits from just moments before had suddenly dipped.

She glanced over at the closed door as she popped the boot of her rusted Micra and deposited the two bags of clothes she had bought while in town with Hayley White. For no reason at all that she could think of, her mind turned to a memory of her mum, sitting at her kitchen table that day when Aoife had popped by. She'd had her head in her hands and when she looked up, Aoife knew immediately that not only did she have bad tidings, but that her mum was dying.

She slammed the boot closed on the thought and the black birds flew off. She hesitated, considered getting in her car and driving home, and then headed to the sacristy. It was exactly this kind of negativity and swings in mood that she needed to get on top of. Father Phil had been right when he told her to get out and spread herself about a bit, but he hadn't told her not to drop in and thank him for pushing her in the right direction. She reached the door and paused, but not for deliberation this time. The wispy hairs on her arms stood erect under the cover of her PVC jacket, her stomach muscles and jaw had clenched. She stared at the old wooden door.

This was the back brain at work, instinct and animal.

Something was very wrong here.

She reached for her personal protection weapon under her left arm, a reflex response, but of course it was gone. Aoife dropped her walking cane, took her mobile out of her jacket pocket, and fast-tracked to the speed dial function for emergency services, finger poised. She stepped slowly forward, eyes never leaving the door and slowly turned the handle. She edged it open, just a few inches, stopping shy of where she knew the hinges would screech in complaint. Aoife waited, listening, but all was quiet from within. Either Father Phil wasn't there or . . .

Aoife frowned, sniffed the air. The odour was faint, but unmistakeable.

It was blood. Coppery, dull and sickly bland.

Words swirled in her mouth, she shouted Father Phil's name, followed by the naive query as to whether her friend was all right. At last, training took over. Her voice, strong and commanding now: 'Armed police. We have weapons trained. Come out with your hands up. Now!'

In her peripheral vision she clocked a woman with a buggy, who'd stopped and was staring at her from the wide entrance gates. Aoife raised her hand in a stop gesture without turning away from the door, and then waved the woman to get back. After a momentary pause she did, pulling the buggy backwards in the direction she had come from. Aoife took another step forward, same hand now tentatively placed against the door. She blinked into the darkened hallway within and counted two seconds, her pulse audibly beating in her ears.

Aoife took a breath and tasted the blood now, like sucking an old brown coin. No more hesitation. She threw her shoulder against the door, put all her weight and strength behind it. The squawk of the hinges was drowned out by a gigantic clap and boom as the oak slammed against the stone wall and Aoife moved on its wave, stormed inside. Shock and awe, just like she'd been trained in police college, but now it was the sound of the door, not a flash bang from her utility belt. And in her hand was only her mobile, not her Glock.

What greeted her arrived in still images, not a flow of events. And like stored images on a phone, they would always be waiting, but never to be deleted.

Father Phil's robe, broad-shouldered and flowing like a delta on a hanger and hooked to the door opposite that led into the church. On its ornate needlework were new spots of gleaming red, awful pomegranate garnish, making his emerald-coloured advent garb even more obscenely festive.

The small porcelain sink where she had many times washed the serving bowls and offering plates for pre-consecrated bread and wine, was glazed sticky red. The incessant drip had carved an ivory stream through the smeared blood.

The dark oak sideboard was in disarray and thick with black blood; silver chalices smeared. It had seeped to the edge and dripped viscously to the stone floor. Where the long sideboard met the wall, blood had been sucked up hungrily by the neatly folded white cotton napkins and touched the open pages of a Bible. Aoife looked to her right.

Father Phil Rafferty was sat in the high-backed wooden chair with the sagging cushion that needed reupholstering. His feet were positioned neatly on the little step, same as he liked to have them in his moments of repose before saying Mass. She gasped as she saw his black cotton trousers bunched at his ankles and Father Phil's blood-smeared bare legs. His genitals were exposed. Aoife averted her eyes, not wanting to see any more, but there was more, and it was much worse. His hands were limp at his sides, and his black shirt ripped open, his chest exposed. His white skin was rinsed rouge and a sign had been carved into his torso, the lines of the cut a deeper red, but lined with yellow fat. It was an inverted cross, a half-moon shape arcing from it like a tail. Her eyes inched up, found the source of the blood, so much blood. Father Phil's head had been removed. It was lodged on the apex of the high-backed chair. His eyes, as dead as an iced fish, stared up at the ceiling above her head.

Words now from Aoife, spoken in a voice thick with tears but not yet weeping: 'God, oh God,' she gasped. A voice spoke in return, from the other end of a wormhole that led back to an ordinary world, one where she had bought a new coat and two new jumpers, and where she'd enjoyed a breakfast and laughed hard enough to cry.

'Emergency services. What service do you require?'

Aoife's throat was dry. She murmured the same words as before, felt her feet turn Judas and begin to back away, suck and stick.

'Hello, I can hear you. Can you hear me? What's your emergency?'

Aoife raised the phone to her ear and spoke with the voice of the police officer she had been, calm and clear, relayed her location, asked for the police. Her heartbeat like a skin drum, a line of hot battery acid bile had risen in her throat. She swallowed it down and spoke again to the operator. Her eyes caught on the sodden red tongue that had once been Father Phil Rafferty's white dog collar.

'And what's the nature of your emergency?'

'There's been a murder,' replied Aoife, and gave her location. The operator explained that police were on their way; she should not leave the scene. She asked for Aoife's name. Aoife understood, but she replied:

'Father Phil. Father Phil Rafferty. He's my friend,' she said.

She killed the emergency call, breathing in hitching sobs, and Aoife hit speed dial on the number her fingers found, put the phone to her ear and heard Owen Sheen's voice after just one ring.

'Aoife,' he said, tentatively. He paused; spoke again, this time a thread of urgency laced his words. 'Aoife, are you OK, darling?' he asked.

Darling. That was what did it.

'Yes,' she replied, but as she said the word the tears came and they would not stop.

CHAPTER TWELVE

As Sheen pulled to a stop on Clonard Drive to lay claim to the last parking space, he could see the entrance to the monastery up on the right. He sat in the idling car, eyes on the commotion up ahead. He recognised it as the typical first stage of an urban murder scene: a small crowd of mostly teens, some on mountain bikes or huddled in small groups, smoking, shoving and having a laugh. A few adults too, one man in a dark leather jacket, self-appointed expert no doubt, now pointing over the fluttering police tape, where a big PSNI officer in uniform stood like a dark statue, nursing a submachine gun. Adjacent to him, blocking the road, was a PSNI Land Rover and beside it, a saloon car not unlike his own, windows darkened, blue bulb on its roof, though not flashing. First responders and assigned detectives, Sheen could only assume.

The other adults who had gathered round the man in the leather jacket listened with rapt attention, heads shaking. Crimes, catastrophes and bad weather came with a licence to share with the stranger. Sheen had no doubt his account, like all our stories and memories, had become more embellished and decorated with each telling. By lunchtime he would be ready to take his show on the road. And he'd do well too.

Sheen hit redial on Aoife's name. The tone filled the car. He was about to give up, and then she answered.

'Yeah?' Her voice was hoarse, clotted with emotion.

'I'm here. Where are you?' he asked.

'Finishing up giving a statement. I'm in the back of a Land Rover,' she clarified.

'I see it. I'll walk your way. Parked down the street,' he said.

'Don't bother. I'll come to you,' she said, and hung up.

Sheen got out and started to make his way up the hill anyway. He saw a young man in a suit talking to two uniforms. The suit was probably the detective, though surely not the lead; the guy looked like a sixth-form student on work experience. Sheen watched as he started to finger the screen of a tablet device as the uniforms waited. Finally, the suit gave them a command and they both nodded more or less in unison and set off down the hill. One of them raised his eyes to the sky, the other said something that lasted two words as they marched off. Sheen didn't need to be within earshot to know it wasn't 'Great guy'.

Hopefully he'd sent them off to knock on doors; Sheen would have. Sheen glanced back at him: he was back on that tablet, vigorously tapping and flicking. Maybe he had his detective's training manual on it. If this was who Paddy Laverty had for a cold-blooded murder in broad daylight (well, very dull light), then Serious Crimes was stretched tighter than a funeral drum. And in Sheen's experience a case like this could be an opportunity for the right man in the right place.

Movement drew his eye to the left side of the parked Land Rover. Aoife McCusker emerged, pale and drawn, hair pulled in an unforgiving but not altogether unflattering small bun at the back of her head, her profile caught in sharp relief for an instant before she turned. Sheen stopped. Her eyes, red and tear-worn, picked him out. Sheen smiled weakly and raised his right hand in a limp hello. He nodded, noting that she looked smaller than he had remembered her in the summer, too much of her hospital bed walking with her. And, Sheen also noted, his smile waning, she was not alone.

A tall woman had one hand on Aoife's shoulder, her expensive-looking coat draped rather unnecessarily over Aoife's back. They were talking, not observing him. Sheen used the few seconds he had. He noted the set jaw, not as lantern wide as the big uniform securing the tape, but unmistakeably different to Aoife, masculine. Sheen noted the shoulders, though not stacked with muscles, were coat-hanger wide, and hour-glassed down a slim torso to narrow hips. The hand that still rested, almost proprietorially, on

Aoife McCusker's shoulder was a big one. Under the silk neck scarf would be a man's neck with an Adam's apple bobbing like a cork in a vase.

'I'm Owen Sheen. Pleased to meet you,' he started, offering his hand.

'Hayley White,' responded the woman. Her voice was gentle, almost a whisper, not a trace of male about it. She took his hand as offered, returned his shake. White's hand was as big as his own and her nutcracker grip was at variance with the soft purr of her voice. 'I'm Aoife's friend,' she added. Which, to be fair, was probably more than he could claim in this moment.

Sheen nodded. He turned his attention to Aoife.

'Hello, Sheen. Thanks for coming. I shouldn't have called you. It was a shock—'

Sheen raised his palms in a gentle stop gesture.

'Aoife, I'm really glad. That you did. Not glad that this has happened, but I'm glad. How are you? You look tired,' he responded, finally shutting his muttering mouth before he could say anything else.

'Still the charmer, I see. You look like you've got lost in the woods. What's going on with that furniture on your face?' Hayley White watched him, the hint of a smile in her green eyes. He glanced away, one hand rasping over his cheek.

The sixth form detective was on his phone, still looking perplexed.

'Paddy Laverty back there?' Sheen asked, gesturing with his chin towards the monastery.

Aoife shook her head. 'Thankfully, no. Some kid barely out of police college is working this. Paramedics had to sit him down and give him the once-over after he saw the body,' she said. No hint of emotion in her voice, but Sheen could see she was struggling, red-rimmed eyes filling on cue. She added, 'Father Phil, I meant. Not "the body".'

If the flurry of horrific details which Aoife had relayed to him on her call earlier was anything to go on, he could almost sympathise with the young lad. Even probationary PCs saw their fair share of the dead, more often than not in their first days on the job. But old folk who had gone quietly and started to smell in the heat of summer, or homeless souls who had frozen solid under the bridge were different to what lay behind the gates of the big monastery on the hill.

'No way is this case being left to that teenager up there. Father Phil was a friend, to both of us, Sheen,' continued Aoife, nodding to Hayley, who mirrored the gesture. 'I'm going to find who did this. And you are going to help me,' she said.

This was news. Sheen glanced from Aoife's determined blue eyes to Hayley's green, and then turned his face to the gunmetal grey of the low clouds above, trying to keep his voice calm.

'Aoife, I'm in forced bloody retirement here. How?'

'You work on the how, Owen Sheen,' she fired back, brass in her voice. 'You're very damn persuasive when it suits you.'

Sheen took the blow, felt his face redden, shame not anger. The too-thin woman before him should be Paddy Laverty's first choice detective right now, not the sixth former. And she should be heading back to her daughter at the end of the day, but instead Ava was in care, and Sheen had so far done bugger all to help her. The fact that she'd kept her distance was neither here nor there. But now she was asking for his help, this was his chance.

'If, and it's a very big if, I was able to help, you don't even have a warrant card. One call to Ladas Drive and you'd be in a world of trouble,' he argued.

'I'm already in a world of trouble, Sheen,' she replied.

Which was true, but pursuing an active murder investigation when not an authorised police officer was one way to prove that however shit things are, they can always get worse. Sheen said nothing.

'Hayley is going to help too. She's an intuitive,' Aoife said.

Hayley's face dropped.

'A what?' said Sheen.

This time it was Hayley who spoke. 'I am a spiritual intuitive. I have done work for the Church through Clonard,' she said softly.

'What sort of work?' asked Sheen, but he'd already pieced it together. Hayley was a psychic, a poison in any murder investigation. Offender profilers came in a close second in terms of irrational destructiveness and misdirection for a case. The former he'd personally locked horns with; the latter he'd heard horror stories about from his DCI in London.

It's like putting the inmates in charge of the asylum, Sheen. Never, ever, ever again, mate . . .

'I use my abilities to sense things, in places where there is energy. Where the energy is negative, it tends to stay around, leave a trace. I can pick up the traces,' she said.

Aoife McCusker was staring right at him; he didn't need to be a detective to know that how he responded here was going to get a mark out of ten.

'I see. There's a fair bit of bad energy right here, but, ehm, Hayley, I sort of fail to see what your powers have got to do with police work. No offence,' he added, tried for a smile.

'I don't have powers,' she replied. 'And none taken. I happen to agree with you,' she added, looking at Aoife, eyes full of pleading.

Silence from all three. Sheen counted out fat seconds, listened to the rise and fall of excited voices from the ever-swelling crowd of teens gathering to pay their respects up the street.

'If Hayley can get close to the crime scene, she'll be able to help,' picked up Aoife, and rested a hand on Hayley's arm.

Sheen kept his face at what he hoped was engaged and on board. He nodded.

'I can try to help,' corrected Hayley, but with more warmth than her last reply to Sheen. 'But absolutely off the record,' she added.

'Oh, I hear you on that. Look, Aoife, I've heard tell of it working in the past,' said Sheen. 'Never on my watch, mind,' he offered. Aoife returned a small nod; for the first time her eyes were, if not warmer, then a little less cold. 'First time for everything, they say,' he added.

'So, what happens next?' asked Aoife.

'I know this is hard, but can you go back over the details of what you saw when you found Father Phil?' asked Sheen.

He'd got the gist; Aoife had mentioned decapitation and something carved into the priest's chest. He'd closed down his impulse to make the obvious parallels to the bog body, but as Aoife went on to relay the grisly details of what she'd come across on Father Phil Rafferty's remains, frame by bloody frame, there was no supressing the excitement, and alarm, in his gut.

'You said the sign was like a cross?' asked Sheen.

'Sort of, but there was a curve coming off one side,' she said, making a curving slash in the air between them with her forefinger.

Sheen could see this was hard for her, but it had to be done. He rummaged for his notebook from the inside pocket of his jacket, clicked his ballpoint to life which had been in there with it.

'Like this?' he asked, holding up the quick sketch he had just made on a blank page.

Aoife nodded but said nothing, her eyes set on the image. Saturn, the same symbol he'd found on the boy's torso, and had uncovered during his microfilm search at Clones Library. Seemed barely plausible, but it was impossible to argue away the evidence.

'Mean something?' asked Aoife.

'I really hope not,' he replied. Sheen glanced again at the befuddled-looking young detective, again searching for answers on his tablet. He could see a way this might just work.

'Listen, Aoife, I'm going to try to make this right. Not just what's happened today, I'm also going to find out who framed you. I should have been all over it already, and I'm sorry—'

'You just get me, us, access to this case, Sheen. I don't need you to fight my battles. I'll find the bastard that put drugs in my locker, and I'm going to clear my name and get my life back. You're not the only one that should have been doing more the last few months,' she said. Sheen wasn't so convinced of the mechanics involved in that, but he said he was there if she needed him. At last, the same resolute woman he'd paired up with in July had made an appearance, fire in her eyes, a flash of colour in her cheeks.

'Me too,' chimed in Hayley White. Her words, Sheen observed, elicited a touch from Aoife, who squeezed her arm and kept her hand there. They'd walked as far as Sheen's parked car; Sheen's eye was drawn to the smooth lines of his dark turbo saloon.

'Aoife, where's your walking stick?' asked Hayley.

Aoife stopped and examined each hand in turn.

'Dropped it, up there,' she said, and gestured at the crime scene.

Hayley said they'd wait, pick it up later. Sheen knew better; at best it would be hours, at worst she'd never get it back.

Aoife shook her head. 'I don't want it. And I don't need it any more,' she said.

'Can I give you a lift somewhere?' asked Sheen.

'New wheels? The previous owner a travelling salesman?' asked Aoife.

Airport car hire company, in fact, after he'd used it to drive all the way to London and back to avoid flying. Sheen laid a hand on the hood, explained that she was wrong as Hayley actually smiled at her joke.

'My car's parked up there too. I want to wait until Father Phil's remains are removed,' she said.

'May take all night,' countered Sheen.

'Then I'll wait,' she said.

'I'll stay with you,' said Hayley.

'Right. I'll be off. I'll keep in touch,' he said.

Aoife nodded, turned to go and then said, 'Thanks, Sheen. For coming and for saying you'll help.'

He nodded and smiled. Aoife and Hayley headed back up Clonard Drive.

Sheen inched out of his space and did a three-point turn, drove back down the hill. He needed to speak with Paddy Laverty, and at Jimmy McKenna's funeral tomorrow morning he'd have his chance. What he said to Laverty had best be convincing. He glanced in his rear-view, caught a final sight of the police tape that protected a ghastly crime scene. In Belfast a violent past was playing out in the present, and you didn't need to be a psychic to tell that this was just the beginning.

CHAPTER THIRTEEN

In the shadows of the evening, the black-robed woman watched from behind the wheel of her parked car. The girl waved goodbye to her father, but absently; all her young attention was fixed on the phone in her hands. The car, a big German saloon, sleek and seamless, pulled away from the double yellow it had briefly parked on outside the Methodist Church on the Lisburn Road in south Belfast. Seconds later it disappeared round the next corner with a double beep of its horn. The girl languidly raised a hand before it dropped back to her phone. She slowly moved closer to where the woman silently waited and watched in her parked vehicle.

A final goodbye between the father and the daughter; there would not be another.

The woman braced herself for the cold and opened the door of her car, flinched anyway when it cut through her layers of clothing. She'd had to wait. The strength and heat that had coursed through her an hour before had dimmed. The slicing wind met her face, her eyes filled with water. The girl had stopped, but her fingers were working, eyes discs of mute concentration. No hat, the scarf she'd been wearing when she jumped from the car now off and slung over one arm.

The woman made her way to the footpath and headed in the girl's direction as fast as she could, which was not very fast at all. If the girl turned and marched up the well-lit church steps, she would get away. There'd be no point pursuing her if she passed the threshold of that place. The woman edged closer, taking care to remain in the shadows as her gloved hand searched in her coat pocket, not finding the rosary beads she knew were there. She fixed a smile on her face, despite the searing pain that had returned to cut her from within. At last, her fingers pinched a hard pebble and her false smile lit up for real, but colder than the wind that blew. She removed the rosary and then pulled the sanctified beads between her clenched fists. The rosary tightened but held. She growled, clenched her teeth and pulled again, felt it give, and then the thin links of the chain tore apart and obsidian beads exploded across the pavement like buckshot. She uttered a cry of triumph and the girl looked at her for the first time. Surprise and concern washed over her features like two consecutive waves.

'Oh my God, are you OK?' asked the girl, stepping towards her, closer to the shadows. Her words were articulated in the clear, well-pronounced elocution of the Belfast upper crust. Before the woman could reply, the girl was down on her hands and knees, collecting the scattered beads as best she could. Well-spoken and well-mannered too. Well-protected, until right now, against the harder realities of existence. The woman's pulse ticked in her neck as she watched the child stretch and lunge after the aberrant beads.

'There, it's going to be lost,' she said, pointing at the gleaming silver crucifix that had landed on the kerb, beside the passenger door of her parked car. The girl nodded, rose and ran over. She bent down to retrieve the cross, her back turned, both of them now encased in the dark. The woman took a febrile look about; a couple further up had paused, were facing a shop window, perhaps reading a menu. The far side of the street was a desolate place and, for now, even the traffic had lulled. Only the voice of the biting wind sounded; and, fainter and sounding very far away indeed, the church organ burping stray chords.

The woman reached into her other pocket, more carefully than before, stepped closer to the girl, bent over on her haunches now, in one hand the dish, the other still pecking the ground for the scattered rosary.

'Please, open the car door, child, set the pieces on the front seat.' She told her she was for ever grateful.

The girl did as she was asked, taking care to empty her dish on the seat, her back to the woman, and head and shoulders in the vehicle.

'Thank you, child,' she said, unsheathing the syringe from its clear plastic cap, taking aim at the denim-clad behind that filled her passenger door. With an accustomed precision, she slipped the steel point of the needle into the girl's gluteus maximus, and pressed the cargo home, all the way. The girl gave a small yelp of surprise, jerked and knocked her head on the roof of the car. The woman had enough time to withdraw the needle and toss it into the footwell, before the girl deflated into the car. Panting now, nose wet and throat dry, she shoved her into the front seat, felt her soft skin touch her face.

She gagged on the girl's cheap floral scent and tugged the loose hanging seat belt, felt the smooth polyester slip from her gloved fingers. She tried again and this time grasped the hard tooth of the steel hasp. With one quivering arm pinning the girl's chest to the seat, she drew the restraint across the girl's body and locked it in place. The girl slumped forward but the belt caught her. The woman pulled the lever on the side of the seat and the back dropped, taking the now-unconscious child with it. She heaved first one leg, then the next into the footwell.

The woman raised a gloved hand and wiped the dampness from her top lip. The couple who were further along had gone; perhaps they were ordering their first drink? She stood her ground, watched and waited as cars passed in both directions, streams of moving light. She walked to the driver's door, head down, and got in. Seconds later she saw what she needed; a big articulated lorry approached from the oncoming lane. She turned the ignition, indicated right and when it was three, maybe four car lengths away she edged out, ignored an angry beep behind her, and edged across the road. The lorry hissed, slowed, and then pulled to a stop. With a deep double honk of its horn the driver flashed her twice, blinding bursts from its big full beams. She did not wait. She quickly swerved the car in a loop, drove on, and let the big boy tower over her from behind, kept her speed low enough to tease him closer as she emerged from shadow and into the lamplit road.

After a couple of hundred metres she took a left turn into the quiet grid of side streets off the main road, freeing up the tail of traffic that had built up behind her. She stopped only once, found the girl's mobile phone in her jeans pocket, turned it off and removed the SIM. She crept along the kerb, leant out of the car and posted both phone and SIM into the black cavity of a storm drain, before driving away. Coloured lights danced fleetingly through the dark interior of her car as she passed homes illuminated with Christmas decorations and gaudy trees. Neither these nor the blasting hot air in the car served to warm her. She was cold from within.

CHAPTER FOURTEEN

Gordon Sterrit checked his watch on his chest of drawers as he heard his wife flush the toilet in the en suite bathroom. It had just gone 9.15 p.m. and his daughter, Rhonda, was running late. He'd dropped her to her choir practice at their Methodist Church on the Lisburn Road just before 7 p.m. and she had promised to come straight home. He had agreed for her to take a bus with her friend Bethany, whose family lived close to them on the Malone Road. A good family: Gordon and Bethany's father, Willis, were brothers at their local Black Preceptory Lodge, a Protestant fraternal society with a very select membership.

Gordon quickly did the numbers as he fumbled around for his tartan bow. Their choir practice should have ended at 8 p.m. Gordon allowed the girls fifteen minutes to dilly-dally the fairly short distance between the more or less parallel Malone and Lisburn roads, plus same again to get themselves on a bus and home.

Gordon had suggested that they could have walked all the way, but his daughter and her friend would not hear of it. Rhonda then needed only to walk down Newforge Lane. She should have arrived through the door of his detached and gated home no later than 8.45 p.m. He'd lost track of the time, started reading the file for a dispute resolution between a waterfront entertainment complex and an independent car park management firm. The complex wanted free staff parking and the management firm wanted to charge an adjusted, but still sizeable, rate. If Rachel had not called him, he'd still be immersed in his work as one of Northern Ireland's leading barristers.

In truth he had not even thought about Rhonda until right now. He pulled his dinner jacket from its plastic body bag and shook it on. His mind was still strong as a trap when it came to the law, but at times like this, he often pondered whether becoming a father for the first time in his late fifties had been such a good idea after all.

During the darker days of the Troubles, Gordon would not have entertained the idea of his thirteen-year-old daughter taking a bus, let alone walking the curving solitude of Newforge Lane to their home. But these were changed times. Also, he'd told Rhonda to ring him, should she need to, and she had not. His eyes now searched the top of the chest of drawers for his mobile, but it was not there. He squinted, trying to recall if it was on his desk in his study, then remembered he had plugged it in to charge in the car.

That had been almost two hours ago.

A ripple of unease spread from his chest down his arms, making him feel suddenly chilled despite the cosy, heated air of their large bedroom.

Rachel emerged from the bathroom, large towel round her torso, smaller one wrapped around her head. Her expression crumpled from ease to concern as she read his expression in the mirror.

'What's the matter?' she asked.

'Can't find my tartan tie,' he lied.

She flipped her eyes to the ceiling and set about hand-drying her hair, her back to him. She dropped the towel on the floor, and started to use her hairdryer, with its industrial noise. She raised her voice over it.

'Wear another one. We're going to be late. Babysitter's due. And go and remind Rhonda to put the pizzas in the oven, will you?'

Gordon strode out of the room without replying, thankful for the sonic barrier the hairdryer had placed between them, thankful she had not enquired whether or not their daughter was home yet, trying to outpace the rising panic that threatened to drown him. He descended the wide, oak-floored staircase and drank in the silence of the ground-floor hallway and the spotlit, open-plan kitchen beyond. He called his daughter's name. More silence in response, and then the flat drone of the intercom at the front door burred in reply. Gordon flinched, and marched to it, anger in charge now. Late and no key; he'd kill her. The live feed next to the door offered a grainy black and white box on the world beyond the front gate. No one there, though someone must have pushed the button. On the periphery of the screen what looked like a black plastic bin bag propped against his gate. He pressed the intercom.

'Rhonda?' His voice sounded reedy, pleading. It was an old man's voice asking a senile question. His panic elbowed anger out of the way and took the controls once more. His heart stammered unpleasantly in his chest. He spoke his daughter's name again, eyes fixed on the shape that remained, unmoving against his gate. It was not a black bag of dumped rubbish. The intercom camera timed out, leaving him in shadow. In his mind he saw the shape once more. He knew what it was.

Gordon Sterrit lurched away from the screen, snatched his car keys from the table and threw open the front door, not caring as it banged thunderously against the wall in a way he had told Rhonda countless times not to do. His mobile phone, he needed to get to it; it was how this was going to turn out all right in the end. There would be a message from his daughter, pushing her luck, explaining that there was a problem with the buses, that they'd decided to stop for a milkshake or a bag of chips, that she was in Bethany's house and could she please, please stay the night, it was fine with her dad. He launched himself out, remotely unlocked the car which chirped in greeting. The security light triggered from above him as he opened the Mercedes. From within the house Rachel's voice, shrill:

'Rhonda! How many times have we told you?' He leant over the driver's seat, tasted the leather interior and faint whiff of peppermint gum in the air and opened the armrest to get his phone.

Four missed calls. Two were from the church, two from Willis. Gordon drew his palm over his mouth. He stared at the glowing screen as the interior light of the car started to dim, his finger hovering over Willis's name. He threw the phone down and turned to face the gate. That was where his answer lay. Rachel appeared at the open front door, clutching herself, looking confused. Gordon Sterrit pressed the fob attached to his key ring. The gate slowly started to slide open.

The thing that leant against the gate was wrapped in a dark grey blanket. As the gate rolled back, the bars bumped against it, rocked it first forwards and then over on its side. Gordon slowly approached, eyes not leaving the figure (that's what it was, a slumped figure). Gordon Sterrit stopped. An unruly mop of brownish-red hair fell loose and on the car ramp.

'What is it, Gordon?' Rachel called. Her tone was irate, but not yet hysterical. That would come, soon it would come.

'Stay there,' he ordered, and his younger wife obeyed.

He leant over the figure, hesitated, and then pulled the blanket aside. Rhonda's face, her cheek flush against the stone-paved entrance ramp. Her eyes were closed, expression composed, peaceful even, as though in sleep. But his little girl would never again open her eyes. Her lips were blue. He reached out and touched her forehead, withdrew his hand with a gasp as though scalded. She was icy cold to the touch. He tugged the filthy-smelling blanket from her, cried out.

Rhonda's right arm rested on her body, but her hand was missing. In its place was a raw stump, off-pink meat and a fork of clean bone. Gordon felt his gut convulse and he gagged on sour bile and hot water, stepped back, and then stopped.

Inserted into Rhonda's left hand was a rolled sheaf of paper, typed script visible in the half-light. Gordon could make out one word, but it was enough to cut through the unreality of this terrible moment. He looked left and right for watching eyes, saw none and snatched the document from his dead child's stiff grip, quickly scanned it and secreted it in his inner jacket pocket. Another sound emitted from him, a cross between a groan and a plea. He swallowed the sick in his throat and turned his eyes once again to Rhonda's face, and then to that awful stump. In his pocket he could feel the weight of the paper he'd found, as heavy as the stone tablets carried by Moses.

Rachel's voice, coming from what felt like far away: 'Is that Rhonda? Tell her to get in, she's late,' she said.

'Call the police,' Gordon shouted back, but instead his voice was thin and paper dry, barely audible to his own ears.

'Hurry up, Gordon. Both of you, get inside. The cold's getting in. And good news, I found your tartan bow tie,' she called.

CHAPTER FIFTEEN

Costa del Sol, Spain
Wednesday 19th December

McKeague ended the call without saying goodbye, slid the phone into the thin net lining of his swim shorts, and pulled the weight of the double-glazed balcony door open with a grunt. The sound of the sea magnified immediately, joined now by the cries of men on the beach below who were aligning plastic paddle boats into rows and securing a tarpaulin in place over them. It had just gone 5.30 a.m. and the pine-board walk that stretched west to the threshold of Marbella, and east for another few kilometres before abruptly ending well before Fuengirola and Torremolinos was, like the beach, all but empty. The wind that gusted up from the water wasn't cold, but carried a cool reminder that this was winter, even on the costa. He glanced up at the overcast sky. Not for the first time in the twenty years since McKeague had taken up residency in Calahonda did he conclude that there were few things more depressing than this summertime paradise in winter.

He came back inside, sparked up his laptop and quickly searched for flights from Málaga, booked a seat for later that morning, one that would land him in Belfast's International Airport by lunchtime. But it'd cost him. He hesitated momentarily, then made a one-click reservation for a budget hotel chain based in the city centre and a hire car. The street on which the hotel was located he knew, the hotel he did not. He'd been considering another trip to North Africa for a frolic and then none other than Gordon Sterrit had called him.

He'd not spoken to Sterrit in over two decades, but McKeague had made sure Gordon always had his number. Good thing too. There'd been a killing: his daughter. And not just murder: her body had been posed, hand chopped off. Another tingle of anticipation; Sterrit was right to call him in. The wannabe hunter was soon to discover that for this big cat, they were nothing more than fair game. But there was more. Sterrit had sounded scared and had held something back. McKeague could taste it down the phone line. The fridge in the small kitchen cracked loudly, like it was splitting apart, but McKeague did not flinch, or look towards the familiar sound of the icebox auto-defrosting. He closed his eyes. From way deep down, the faintest tinkle of a servant's bell in his mind, triggered by something Sterrit had said. Nothing came. Outside the window mist had settled on the far horizon, North Africa just beyond. His mind turned again to his recent frolic.

Probably best to avoid Morocco for a while, let the dust settle. McKeague smiled at his own humour and the face that looked back at him from the mirrored wall of his bedroom was strong-jawed and topped with the same dense wave of hair from his youth, though blonde from a bottle these days, no longer natural flax. But his cold eyes were the same, unthawed by time and jest alike.

He went to his built-in wardrobe, found his old leather jacket and jeans inside the dust cover. A few seconds later he found his boots. It had been a long time since he had wintered further north than the Pyrenees. But that was now about to change. Belfast had called him back, like a husky old whore who had croaked his name from her doorway and beckoned him in, just one more time. A thin rustle of anticipation started under his ball sack, rose through his gut and into his throat. His heart started to run. It would be good to see the old slag again. There was hunting to be had there too.

On this thought he turned, went down on his knees, strong and flexible yet, and found his safe, embedded in the floor beneath a carpet tile under his bed. He inputted the six-figure number into the digital touchscreen and heard the low drill of the mechanism unlock. The chunky grey door popped. He reached into his safe and carefully removed the boxy Polaroid camera, then the knife, its edge sheathed but still razor-sharp in the envelope of its smooth bone handle. He set his tools down and reverentially removed his book.

He eased it out and sat with his back to the side of his bed, book in hands. He ran his palm over its goatskin cover, savouring the oily sleekness followed by the rougher resistance against the run of the hair. Not the book's first cover, but his favourite by far. He'd seen the fear boil in the animal's eyes, black and glassy and full of the fire's flames. He'd swallowed its squeal, as it rose from panic to the purity of pain, its neck sliced open. Then the goat's eyes glazed over into dead stones. As it is for goats, it is for man. He opened the book. One last visit before he left; the book would stay.

The photographs had been placed meticulously, four to a page, each one neatly labelled in his near-perfect capitalised script, never more than a single location, and a single three-part date. At the back of the album were the most recent kills, most of the faces brown and almost all of them children. McKeague moved slowly from page to page, counting back the years, the images becoming more jaded and yellowed.

Some things, however, had not changed.

Each image was a death moment, lived in the throes of blinding agony, captured by the man who collected souls. McKeague's well-manicured fingers delicately caressed the arranged faces of his gallery of the dead, drinking in their life force again as he had done so long ago: a visual, visceral, dark communion. McKeague rested an index finger on one of his oldest souls, let the choking grimace of horror and agony hot-wire his brain and body. He closed his eyes, concentrated on the dream-like sound of the muffled sea, going back through all the streets he'd prowled, until the waves became the sound of a hundred captured souls, whispering for mercy that would never come.

CHAPTER SIXTEEN

Belfast, Northern Ireland
Wednesday 19th December

Sheen scanned the crowd as they snaked like a slow, black serpent behind Jimmy McKenna's coffin, following it into Milltown Cemetery.

The cortège stopped, and black-coated funeral directors started to organise the pallbearers. Sheen permitted himself a few seconds of fascinated spectating. The consequences of mismanaging the changeover were unthinkable, but the men in black were experts. Each bearer was disengaged and replaced by another with an assured ease, the lid of the coffin stayed as plumb as the deck of a ship on horse latitudes.

Behind the narrow bottleneck that ended at the coffin, was the widening fantail of mourners. Sheen moved his eyes in short, focused bursts, parsing the sea of faces into imaginary grids, working methodically first in horizontal lines, then up vertical ladders as he had once been trained and in turn had trained others.

Hundreds of faces, some old; flat-capped men with wet,

fat noses, yellowed handkerchiefs in hand to dab and blow, and pensioner-aged women with headscarves trussed tight over ears and hair, rosary beads in hand. Younger men and women too, and segregated gaggles of same-sex teens, most with phones in hands. No older, Sheen considered briefly, than Jimmy McKenna had been in the last days of his life. Tourists today, like Sheen himself, visiting a past that was as alien to them now as the Troubles had been to any young person in any other city of the United Kingdom when it had burned on and on.

Many faces, though the man he wanted, DI Paddy Laverty, was not to be seen. But he was in there somewhere. Laverty was a bit of a wanker, but he was old-school. In murder investigations the family came first. Sheen stood atop a squidgy tuft of grass to get an angle over the casket. The saturated soil gave way under his weight, his boot skidded off and he just managed to save himself the indignity of a fall. The other option was to stand on the marble border of an adjacent grave which he wouldn't do. Instead he gently probed into the assembled, close enough now to touch the cold wood of Jimmy McKenna's coffin.

A firm hand folded over the meat of his forearm, insistent but not pinching. The taller of the two funeral directors, a tight head of gelled curls, his clean face cocked close to Sheen's ear, as though to impart a kiss.

'You'll take a turn, sir,' not an order, but not a question. The guy's grip was as assured as any lifetime beat copper; the hand of God would have been easier to resist. Sheen was guided to the front space at the right of the coffin and slotted in. The director adjusted Sheen's posture and positioned Sheen's left arm under the unseen guy's ribs on the other side. The stranger's tight palm was doing the same to Sheen, as the hard angles of the casket rested on their shoulders. Salt and pepper hair right next to him; he recognised the voice.

'No, no, not me,' Paddy Laverty repeated. He turned around and saw Sheen as the glare of a television camera's light flooded the coffin, Sheen at the head. The press had taken the spot on the grave he'd avoided. Laverty shook his head, eyes full of dull reproach. As far as he was concerned, Sheen's status as an attention-seeking outsider was sealed. Sheen looked away and watched as Mrs McKenna drifted by, black hat on head, a big man who looked like a bouncer linked to her right arm.

They walked the coffin in slow, scuffing silence, shouldering that strange burden of foreshortened manhood in the shape of Jimmy McKenna. When at last he was relieved of his station, Sheen looked left and right for Laverty at the graveside, but he wasn't there. A thin priest spoke the service, a fluttering book of psalms in hand. He splashed holy water from a silver urn. It rattled on the coffin lid.

After the body was lowered into the ground Mrs McKenna dropped a trowel of clay on top, and then, with a blessing that was always going to be an anti-climax, it was over. Sheen stood his ground as mourners floated off like black ash on the breeze, the faint drone of the M1 in the near distance. He glanced over the rows of headstones. Unmarked amongst these graves was where his brother's scant remains and then his mother's thin corpse had been laid to rest. And now, if McHenry's taunt was to be believed, both brother and mother were still unavenged.

'You planning on moving in?'

Sheen snapped back to the moment, and the voice. It was Laverty.

'I didn't intend to get in front of the cameras,' replied Sheen.

Paddy Laverty shrugged, hands buried in his leather jacket, a gesture that said he didn't give a shit either way.

'Show's over. What is it you want?'

'Who said I want anything?' countered Sheen.

'The fact that you were searching for my mug from when I walked in here,' Laverty responded.

Sheen was about to deny it but decided there was no point.

'I want to propose something. How about a pint?' suggested Sheen.

Laverty made a hissing sound, lips barely parted.

'"Propose something",' he mimicked. 'No one's ever proposed anything to me, Sheen. Not even a pint,' he said.

A small flicker of anger sparked up in Sheen's gut. Laverty just wanted an argument, and he had half a mind to give him one.

Sheen swallowed, snuffing it out. He needed a yes from Laverty. Aoife needed it.

'The pint is just a pint. We need to talk. I think I can help you,' said Sheen.

Laverty responded with a blank gaze, but when he turned and walked it was in sour agreement, not dismissal. Sheen made to follow, watching his footing.

'DI Sheen,' said a voice, female, behind him. He turned, Laverty did too. Mrs McKenna was standing on the path just below him, the big boy who looked like a doorman was a few steps behind her. He had one eye that looked damaged, permanently half-closed. As Sheen made it to the path, the man smiled, brief warmth, though sad.

'Hello, Mrs McKenna.'

'I want to thank you, for agreeing to carry the coffin. It was right that you brought him to the grave,' she said. Her voice was clean, youthful even, but her face was haggard and drink-worn, and when she raised her hands and took one of Sheen's in both of hers, they were shaking lightly. But no smell of booze; she'd done this sober.

'I'm glad I could,' he replied, and though it came out on impulse, he meant it.

Mrs McKenna, who had become an expert in tears over her days, filled up, and Sheen felt them push to enter him. Grief, like panic, can jump between us. She drew him in and clasped him in an embrace. Sheen jauntily returned the hug, his arms folding her up entirely. At last, she released him; they stood apart.

'You may not believe this yourself, but you are a

good man, DI Sheen,' she said. And then she turned and on the arm of the big man, she walked off. Laverty was waiting, his face as blank as before, but his eyes no longer reproachful.

'Come on, hero. You can buy me a pint,' he said.

CHAPTER SEVENTEEN

McKeague stood at the very front of the oval viewing platform at the apex of Belfast's Victoria Square shopping centre. He clasped the cool metal rail and leant over the edge, only a clear Perspex dome now between him and the panorama of Belfast city in the late afternoon.

He took back what he'd thought about Calahonda on an overcast day like this. Belfast was far more fucking depressing by a long stretch. Behind him, the soft squeak of slowly approaching feet. Not the feet that he was waiting for either. These belonged to the so-called security guard who had bid him 'Good morning, sir' as McKeague had exited the lift and joined him on the platform. McKeague had clocked him for a former peeler, probably a reservist. The fat clown filled that pressed jacket like only a pretender can. His greeting had confirmed him as a chatty bastard too.

'Every man desires to live long, but no man wishes to be old,' he said, now occupying the space to McKeague's left, approximately five off twelve. Fucking God help us. McKeague turned his eyes to the two yellow shipyard cranes in Harland and Wolff in the near distance, their high brows touched briefly by the mist that cloaked the bowl of the city. He nodded, as much to himself as his uninvited companion.

'Aye,' he commented. The guard had a point at least.

'This wee city, it has produced an uncanny amount of talent. Those words are from the pen of none other than Jonathan Swift, whose most famous tale is of course *Gulliver's Travels*,' he continued.

McKeague knew this. School had given him little, but he was a reader, and had learnt that it paid to be so. So, he also knew what was coming next.

'Some are convinced the inspiration for the tale came when Swift ministered a parish north of Belfast in Ballynure and Kilroot,' he said, pointing now to their left and north where the low cloud had momentarily lifted off the granite nose of Cave Hill in the distance. McKeague followed the security man's extended finger, which now seemed to touch the dark monolith and the gothic sandstone edifice of Belfast Heights psychiatric hospital crouching at its base.

'He wrote it in Dublin,' countered McKeague.

The guard continued. 'Swift spotted the cliff face overlooking Belfast as he travelled into the city, so the story goes. Later he found himself in Lilliput Street and so it was that he called the little people the Lilliputians. This was 1720 and the book came out in 1726.'

McKeague feigned impressed surprise; hopefully enough to send him on his way. No such joy.

He started on about how if you turned your head to a certain angle, when the weather was right of course, Cave Hill could appear to be a man's face, resting in profile. McKeague zoned his voice out, took in the panorama of Belfast. His first view of it in two decades confirmed what he'd gathered already as he wandered the streets in a daze, waiting for the text message that had told him to come to this place.

Yeah, the iconic cranes were still there at least, but the world had changed. Gone were the dirty red-bricked old factories and derelict mills. Gone were many of the office blocks that had stood sentinel by bomb-damaged cavities. Gone were the high antenna towers of the police and army barracks. Gone were the RUC, flanked by the soldiers, the spikes of long rifles breaking their silhouettes. Gone were the checkpoints, the bag searches at the entrance of brand department stores. Gone was the ring of steel that had caged the city centre from bomb couriers. Gone were the single file barbed-wire-crowned entrance points. Gone all, and in their place a new world of unbroken paving, glass-fronted hotels, offices and shops left unshattered. He even had to trace his steps back to his hotel at one point to get an illustrated map of the city centre to find this place. This spot used to be a Littlewoods, or maybe a BT office, or maybe just a broken cobblestoned old street between the two. Belfast had *quarters* now, five of them for fuck's sake, and everywhere you went seven shades of humanity walked the city streets where once every face was white, and blood ran only green or orange.

This city had become new while McKeague had, gracefully albeit, apparently grown old. In response to this rather unpleasant epiphany, a shiver moved from his gut and set his breast a-trot. McKeague placed it as something close to concern, which was as close to fear as he could manage.

McKeague closed his eyes, pinched the bridge of his nose, felt the pressure on the bone, the hard marble under his boot heel, seeking the moment. The muffled sounds of pre-Christmas traffic leaked in from the streets far below. Closer, the security guard was still talking, saying something to do with George Best.

'Are you a visitor, sir, or are you from here?'

'Both,' replied McKeague. Behind them he heard the gentle ping of the lift, then the faint swish of the twin metal doors parting.

'I worked in Gallaher's. First here, but then took a job in England with them. I'm retired too,' he said.

The tobacco manufacturer was a keystone of the Northern Irish economy over the last hundred years, up there with the big cranes in the shipyard in the near distance. Saying he had been employed there had always proved a sound cover, strong under pressure and difficult to falsify in the cut and thrust of meaningless conversation like this. And, of course, a cover was required. McKeague's work defending Ulster hadn't exactly been a nine-to-five job. Especially the one he was best at, and still missed: extracting confessions from touts in the ranks. He'd been in demand, worked freelance for different loyalist groups. His thoughts skipped to his book; a good few early faces there had been official jobs. But pretty soon he'd got a taste for it and his frolics had become a passion, not a job.

He could hear the shuffle of approaching people from the lift. His man would be in that number. Always did keep time.

The guard asked him if he'd worked on the Silk Cut manufacturing line where, he was at pains to tell him, a brother-in-law was a deputy foreman. Deputy no less.

McKeague nodded. 'In my day I must have worked every line they had, and smoked every tab they made,' he said, breaking an arctic smile for what he understood was convivial effect, but the guard was gone, had squeaked round to about twenty past the hour where the new group waited.

Another set of footsteps, purpose in their stride.

'All right, Counsellor,' said McKeague without turning around.

Sterrit appeared on his right, closer to him than the guard had been at five past the hour, maybe three.

'Don't speak so loudly,' he said. The warm fumes of his breath tasted strong and brown like the peaty Scotch that had fathered them. Sterrit had his vices, but drink had never been one of them as far as McKeague recalled. But here he was, shit-faced and not yet four in the afternoon.

'Sorry about your loss, Sterrit.' He didn't really give a shit one way or the other about Sterrit's dead sprog. But they had history. He turned to face his old mucker. Grey hair, spongy but thinned so McKeague could see his pink scalp under the backcomb, face dropped to jowls, high red points on his once-proud cheekbones, and fuller at the waist than the shoulders, all draped in a midnight blue pinstripe suit and an expensive-looking overcoat. He'd aged with good living.

'We need to be discreet,' said Sterrit, ignoring McKeague's condolence. Unnecessary. McKeague had heard him the first time.

He stared at Sterrit who held his gaze, but then dropped his eyes.

'Thank you for coming. You look to be in hale shape,' Sterrit said. In comparison with Sterrit that was certainly true. But then McKeague swam most days, jogged too, neither drank nor smoked and never had. Not to say he was a man without vices. McKeague noted that, compliments aside, Sterrit had not said how good it was to see him.

'You too, Sterrit. Prosperous,' he judged after a short pause.

There was a moment's quiet between them. The guard was talking shit and taking stupid questions.

Sterrit spoke. 'The PSNI are involved, of course. Investigating my daughter's murder,' he started.

McKeague spoke up, stopping him. 'I'll be discreet, Gordon. I'll find the fucker who did your daughter and

I'll give them a death they deserve. No charge, for old time's sake. And I'll not cross paths with the peelers. They couldn't pour pish from a shoe back then. I doubt much has changed,' he said.

'Retribution is not why I summoned you here,' replied Sterrit, turning now to face McKeague.

Summoned by fucking God. McKeague bit back his reply, only just.

'Rhonda's murder is only one part of this,' he continued.

At the mention of the dead girl's first name Sterrit's voice started to crack, and he paused. McKeague exhaled, counting the slow seconds. Sterrit removed a little pewter flask from his inside jacket pocket, screwed off the lid and took a long swig with an unsteady hand. He tried to pass it to McKeague, who shook his head, eyes raised to the dreary sky above.

'Sauce won't help,' said McKeague.

'Won't make it any fucking worse than it is, will it? I've not drunk in over forty years, Leonard. But I'm bloody well drinking now. I'm drinking now,' he said, draining the contents of the flask as though to emphasise his point.

'Get on with it, Sterrit. If this isn't about helping you get the bastard who killed your kid, then why did you drag me up here? In December too,' added McKeague.

'This is about containment, Leonard. Find who's behind this before they have a chance to leak anything else.'

'What you on about?'

Sterrit pulled out his phone, big thing larger than his hand. He moved his fingers over the screen, passed it to McKeague, who took it and studied the picture for almost a full minute, keeping the phone low and to his chest. McKeague let out a breath, slowly returned the phone to Sterrit's waiting hand, screen facing the floor.

'Fuck did this come from?'

'It was left with Rhonda's body. Right outside my front garden gate,' said Sterrit.

'That's a photo. Where's the original?'

'I burnt it. This copy is not backed up, on the Cloud I mean,' said Sterrit.

McKeague involuntarily looked up to where Belfast was offering an abundance of them. He didn't pursue it; he'd look like a wanker. Presumably Sterrit meant it was secure.

'Get rid of it,' he replied.

Sterrit took the phone out again, played with the screen, returned it to his coat.

'It's only code names, no identities there,' started McKeague, but his heart was ticking again, and that same unpleasant chill was working its way through him. The document Sterrit had photographed and found on his dead daughter's body should not even exist. Until a few minutes ago, McKeague had no idea it had.

'Get real, Leonard!' hissed Sterrit, his drunken breath coated McKeague's face. His eyes were a scrawl of red lines on yellowed whites. 'I know the names, same as you. And whoever murdered my Rhonda, cut off her hand

151

and dumped her at my gate like a bag of trash obviously bloody well knows which one was my name too! Did you read what that document said, Leonard? Almost all of it's me. Code name or no code name, it's me.'

McKeague said he did, his mind was moving in another direction. Something Sterrit had just said, something about his daughter's hand. That barely audible bell in the basement of his brain chimed again. For no reason he could explain, his book of souls came to mind. If he could touch it now and walk through its hallowed pages, he would connect, see what he now could not. But his thoughts were slow-moving sludge in an old canal.

'And you're afraid what has been in darkness will be brought into the light. Even with your daughter dead, all you're worried about is saving your hide,' noted McKeague.

Sterrit glared at him. 'Not just my hide, it's yours too, Leonard. They'll hang us high if this gets out. It's not like old times. This is a changed land,' he said.

McKeague couldn't argue with that. 'You think there's more documents,' he concluded.

'Course there is,' said Sterrit, his words laced with impatience.

So this was the real reason he'd called. To contain the situation. In other words, find and kill the fucker.

'You think it might have come from the old man?' asked McKeague.

'Perhaps. Originally. But he's dead, long time,' replied Sterrit.

152

'His family? Someone who might have dug up something like this?'

Sterrit shook his head, again exuding impatience. He had clearly gone over this ground in his own mind. Before he'd decided to *summon* McKeague.

'Grown-up children abroad, youngest son is severely disabled, still lives on the estate, twenty-four-hour care. He can't wipe his own arse, let alone do this,' explained Sterrit.

'Must be one of us,' said McKeague. The pronoun slipped out unintentionally, its shape strange on his tongue after so many years. One man came to mind, someone who'd been put back in line once before. McKeague said his name.

'Could be,' replied Sterrit.

McKeague asked him where he was to be found.

'No idea. He changed his name after he was released. If he has any sense he'll be in Brazil.'

'Aye, but he never did have much sense, Sterrit,' offered McKeague. 'What about your mate Golding?'

Sterrit eyed him icily, sniffed at his mention. 'Oh, *he's* around. Can't see how he'd know how to find him,' he said. Sterrit explained Golding's set-up.

'Fucking brass neck,' said McKeague. Then he said nothing, tried to think, but his brain felt slow and felt old. Twenty years away was a long stretch.

'What are you thinking?' enquired Sterrit.

'That this is a fuck-up that needs to be unfucked. Beyond that, I don't know yet,' admitted McKeague.

'Eloquent,' said Sterrit. He started to button up his

overcoat. He told him to keep in touch, walked off, unsteady on his legs.

McKeague watched him leave. 'Aye, and you keep a lid on the jungle juice,' he said. The lift opened and Sterrit stepped in, a big man filling the space. McKeague turned back to the vista, tapped the steel handrail with the tip of his finger. To unfuck things he'd need to work fast and think faster. And now he was back in Belfast, there was only one thing that would get his motor running. Just like old times. He took the tourist map of the city from his inside pocket and walked over to the guard, greeting him with a small smile.

'I wonder would you show me where I should best avoid. After dark, I mean. So many changes since I've left, I feel like I'm a tourist in my own town. Don't want to find myself in the wrong area, you know?' he confided, handed the map to the guard. The helpful bastard couldn't wait to oblige. He produced an expensive-looking ballpoint from the breast pocket of his jacket and set about outlining and then shading small areas of the city that his neat key designated as 'Dangerous: No Go'. He held the map open for McKeague, who pointed to one such hatched area where Castle Street fed into Divis Street and the west of the city.

'Big druggie problem, especially now the guns have been put down,' explained the guard.

McKeague understood; since the end of the conflict, both sides had more or less abandoned punishment beatings and shootings as a sanction against antisocial behaviour. And with the cat away, the rats had clearly had the run of things. McKeague tutted, said he'd be careful. And he would too, careful he wasn't ripped off when he went there to score.

'Cheers, my friend,' he said, tugging his map from the hands of the watchman. He deftly folded it up and pocketed it.

'Welcome, sir,' the man replied quietly.

McKeague dropped him a wee wink and turned on his boot heel, clocked over to the lift. He glanced back at the view; Cave Hill was unveiled of cloud for now, and brooded over Belfast like, well, like a giant's head. But Samson was soon to be unleashed, and there'd be no sleep till Calahonda, no rest for the wicked at all. The lift pinged, and as it opened so did a long-sealed synapse in McKeague's memory. It was a quote, Swift, and McKeague spoke it out, as best he could recall.

'*The bulk of your natives are the most pernicious race of little odious vermin that nature ever suffered to crawl upon the surface of the earth.*'

Silence and staring faces were his only response. The doors sealed closed on McKeague, and the little people and Belfast beyond them disappeared from view.

CHAPTER EIGHTEEN

It took a while, but Sheen at last reached the bar in McEaney's, or the Gravedigger's Arms, across the road from the entrance to Milltown Cemetery. He returned with a larger top for Laverty and a pint of stout for himself. They headed for the stairs and the first-floor saloon after a cursory look around gave them no quarter; grieving was thirsty business in Belfast.

'You look like you could do with a few more of those,' said Laverty, nodding at Sheen's settling stout and echoing Maureen's observation from two days before.

'Been keeping busy,' retorted Sheen.

Laverty did one of his give-a-shit shrugs. He took half his pint in one big gulp, his eyes not leaving Sheen as he swallowed.

'That a fact? Thought your historical work was a shut shop, courtesy of your shenanigans over the 12th weekend?'

Laverty was toying with him, but he was correct: the frozen operations of the Serious Historical Offences Team, like the stalled Stormont Assembly and never-ending rounds of elections, could be traced back to Sheen's pursuit of John Fryer the previous July and the calamity that had ensued.

'You know it is. Man needs to keep himself occupied. Idle hands and all that,' said Sheen.

He took a first draw on his pint. Mac's did a good one, in a town where the standard was high. The black bitter was cool, but not ice cold, the liquid as smooth and rich as double cream and many times more drinkable. He could see how Brendan Behan, the Irish writer and would-be revolutionary, had more or less lived on the stuff.

'Going to tell me what you want to talk about. Or should I say "propose"?' asked Laverty.

Sheen cast a nonchalant glance out the window, his eyes immediately drawn to the green and granite of the cemetery across the main road. He'd done his homework. After hearing about the murder of the teenage girl in south Belfast last night, the first thing he did was call MacBride, his CSI mate who'd worked the first murder that started the ball rolling last summer. As luck would have it, he was also on the case in south Belfast. MacBride was a joker, but not about his job. Took some arm-bending and pleading for Sheen to get the few scant details he needed. But it had been enough to convince him that the murder and mutilation of the teenage girl was connected to that of Father Phil Rafferty, and in turn both were rooted in what he'd discovered in the Monaghan bog. What he didn't know yet was how and why.

'I could say that I am not busy enough. You, on the other hand . . .' Sheen let the observation hang in the air between them.

'I can cope,' said Laverty.

'Sure about that? You have the UDA feuding and spreading the fight to other groups from north Belfast right up the Antrim coast,' replied Sheen, starting to count his points on thumb and then fingers, leaning into the table. 'You have a backlog of cases that is growing deeper by the week. You are three active detectives down from July if you include Irwin, me and Aoife McCusker. And unless I'm very wrong, I'd say you have a serial offender on your patch who is just getting warmed up, two bodies in and more to come. I wouldn't call that busy, I call it overstretched. Believe me, mate, I know what it's like, pressure from above, the tide rising around you from below, your back to the wall. Sleeping all right, are you?' asked Sheen, slipping in the personal question like a blade at the end of his words.

Laverty's eyes widened, involuntarily registering a cut. 'So I'm busy. What do you want, Sheen?'

'To offer you some help,' replied Sheen, tone softer, leaning back in his chair.

'Make this a weekly thing, will we? Pints and good listening, new friendship forged?'

'Deputise me into Serious Crimes. Let me help,' said Sheen, at last lobbing his pitch.

'Impossible,' said Laverty.

'Not at all, technically SHOT is under SC while it's back on ice. Same as when I arrived in July,' said Sheen.

Laverty's eyes again flickered. He must have been aware of what Sheen had just told him, but knowing something and accessing it, as Sheen knew all too well, could be two different things.

Sheen pushed on, advancing his small gain. 'Let me take the reins on the serial case, the one involving the priest. It'll free you up. You're best placed to work the paramilitary feud, Paddy. It's your manor and you know them. But I have good form with serial murders. You know about the Railway Cutter. Me and my lads cracked that one, even after the original team had let it go cold,' said Sheen.

'Didn't that boy murder four prostitutes? Is that what you lads in London call a good result?' said Laverty, but Sheen could tell he'd not lost him, maybe not entirely.

'Yes, four *women* died, Paddy,' said Sheen, 'but not on my watch. And that bastard would still be killing them today if I hadn't nailed him.'

Laverty had drained his shandy, but he still held the foam-rinsed glass, which he was rolling slowly on its circular base.

'It was a smart move to map the murders to the train line and not the localities. Not many would have thought of that,' he conceded.

'And this will be your collar, not mine. You retain SIO status, all the spoils to you. As far as the history lesson will be told, I was just one of your team, and a visitor at that,' said Sheen. This was Sheen's best card.

'You got good form for that too, do you think?' asked Laverty, his face hardening visibly. He set the empty down with a small clack, started to push his chair back from the table.

'No cowboy behaviour. No repeat of last summer, my word, Paddy,' said Sheen. But Laverty was on his feet, and this time he looked like a man who was really going. Sheen stood up too. 'How can I convince you?'

'You can't.' He walked a few paces round Sheen, making his way through the deserted upstairs lounge of Mac's. Laverty was almost at the mouth of the steep stairs that led to the rowdy bar beneath.

Sheen stood up. 'I bet one of her hands was missing. Your dead girl from last night,' said Sheen.

Laverty stopped and did an about-face, started to retrace his steps back to Sheen, his face swimming between curiosity, outrage and shock. It settled on outrage.

'How the fuck can you know that? That crime scene's airtight,' he said. His eyes flicked side to side, scanning the thin carpet between their feet, seeing something else, probably the faces of the personnel who'd signed in at the tape. 'Did one of the uniform—'

'No one's talked to me about the girl,' interrupted Sheen. 'I told you I was busy, old cold case, body from the '70s. My own thing, not through the SHOT,' said Sheen.

'And what?' asked Laverty.

'There's a link. My body had its hands missing, head

too. There's a connection, but I'm not sure how, not yet,' said Sheen.

Details of Father Phil's death had been in the press. His knowledge of the decapitation and its significance wouldn't raise an alarm for Laverty. He'd dished Laverty up a mixed platter of truth and lies, the best we can hope for in this world.

'Like the way you made the link to the railway line, huh?'

'Exactly so,' replied Sheen, resisting the urge to exhale. Laverty had thrown him a rope, maybe because what Sheen was offering was too tempting to let swim away, maybe because the guy was almost burnt out and to bring Sheen aboard was effectively going to rescue him too. Sheen couldn't say and didn't care.

'Say I bring you in, and I'm not saying I *will*, but let's speak hypothetically,' responded Laverty.

'OK, say,' said Sheen.

'You will keep me updated, every day, and no exceptions.'

'Yes.'

'I get to say what is actioned off the back of these updates, there will be no negotiation and there will be no magician's tricks from you,' he continued, a finger now raised and pointing at Sheen's chest.

'None,' agreed Sheen, thinking about the false authorisation he'd already issued on behalf of Laverty's boss, Conor Daly. Laverty looked like a man about to plunge his hand into a wicker basket in search of his wedding ring, knowing that it probably also housed a snake.

'OK then,' said Laverty.

'Just one thing,' said Sheen. He kept his hands in his coat pockets, shoulders relaxed.

'Jesus Christ, I should have known not to listen. What?'

'I'll wrap this up for you, Paddy, and tie it with a bow. You'll smell of more roses than that flower stall across the road. But I want your word, same as you wanted mine. I'm going to find out who stitched up Aoife McCusker, which we both bloody well know is exactly what has happened. I'm going to build a case and you are going to rubber-stamp it and back her against Internal Investigations. If it holds, she re-joins Serious Crimes and you draw a line under last summer,' said Sheen.

'Good luck with that, Sheen. I'm not having you to do a home job to help your girlfriend,' said Laverty.

'I'm not asking you to. I've been hard at it, one of the things that's been keeping me up at night, see,' said Sheen. 'I just need the right man to take it to the right people,' he said.

Sheen put out his hand, waiting for Laverty to shake. Laverty glanced down at Sheen's open palm.

'It had better be a smoking gun, Sheen. Nothing else will do,' replied Laverty.

He raised his palm, spat a little on it and clasped it into Sheen's waiting hand with a clap. His grip was strong, and Sheen returned it, held him dead centre.

'I'm didicoi, you know,' he said, reading Sheen's confusion. 'My mother's side were travellers a long way back. They made their deals this way, pacts that had best never be broken,' he said.

'The job will be done, Paddy,' said Sheen.

Laverty let his hand fall. He turned again. 'Get to work, Sheen. I'll let it be known. First update in no more than twenty-four,' said Laverty.

'Sure. But just another . . . one more thing,' said Sheen.

Laverty stopped, lowered his head, and turned once more to face Sheen, the theatrics of a broken man.

'I'm gonna need another copper, someone to help with the paper, do a bit of running, door-knocking, you know what I mean,' said Sheen.

If he was going to make good on what he'd just set out he needed some support, someone with a bit of depth and he knew exactly who that was going to be.

'Whole point is I'm stretched like a circus tent, mate. I can spare you a DC, two days a week only,' said Laverty, after a pause for contemplation.

'No need. Let me bring in Geordie Brown. He's already getting a full wage like me, and like me he's wasted, sits at home watching daytime movies. Not good for a man,' said Sheen.

Brown had been successfully plucked from early retirement by Sheen for the SHOT. He was as old-school as they came; even in his early days on the Met Sheen hadn't encountered anything like the guy.

'Geordie Brown? Your business taking him on for the SHOT, but thon boy's unmanageable,' said Laverty.

'You won't have to. I'll manage him, you give me the orders,' said Sheen.

Laverty was shaking his head.

'He's free. He's available. A green DC is worse than useless to me and you know it,' argued Sheen.

Laverty made a groaning sound, pushed his fingers through his hair and turned away.

'Fuck's sake, yes. Do it. I'm going to regret it, but do it,' he said and strode away.

'Thanks, Paddy. And by the way, man, Aoife McCusker's not my girlfriend, for the record,' said Sheen.

Laverty gave him another who-gives-a-shit shrug.

'Well, word is that Internal Investigations are finally about to get to work on her. So best get moving on that collar if you want young McCusker, *not* your girlfriend, to be in a happy place again.'

CHAPTER NINETEEN

McKeague spotted his man.

He was half concealed in an alcove that was probably used as a loading bay on Fountain Lane, close to what had once been Belfast's Primark store. That building was now a fire-blackened skeleton and McKeague could taste its burnt remains in the air from a couple of streets away as he marched up the wide alleyway towards his man. He was parallel with Castle Street on the threshold of West Belfast. Not exactly a bullseye for the guard's map, but it was close enough, give him his credit. And this deserted stretch was an even better choice for the prospective dealer or a scumbag out to smash and grab; easy getaway points from both ends, but quiet and dark for the work at hand.

His man was barely that, eighteen, maybe younger. Big frame, but not yet filled. He was dead still, in the shadows, hands stuffed into the nylon front pockets of his expensive brand tracksuit top. But his eyes moved restlessly, searchlights scoping his surroundings. McKeague stopped about five metres from him, pulled out his map, made a show of studying it. He could feel the dealer's eyes on him, but only momentarily. McKeague stole a look his way, but he'd already dismissed him, had eyed two youths now approaching from the opposite direction on mountain bikes.

The tracksuit had seen an old man: prey, not a predator. But he was wrong about that.

The dealer gave the youths an almost imperceptible nod as they flew past him. Seconds later they swished either side of McKeague, almost close enough to send him flying. He ignored their play, headed straight for the young drug dealer standing in the doorway. The dealer focused on his approach, gave him his full attention now. In the air, the ammonia stink of a thousand drunken alleyway pisses and a muffled din coming from the pub hidden from view at the far end of the alley. And now the hiss of approaching tyres from behind him. No doubt it was the return of the two wankers on the mountain bikes. He stopped and smiled at the young entrepreneur. His man was tall, eye to eye with McKeague.

'Lost, old man?' He was chewing gum, a wireless phone port in one ear. His gold and black trainers matched his tracksuit.

'Not a bit of it. Been looking for you,' replied McKeague.

A shadow of uncertainty flared in the dealer's eyes at this but was quickly gone. On either side, McKeague was now flanked by the two mountain bikers, leaning their weight on the handlebars. A quick glance confirmed that both were of similar age, wore similar wannabe gangster garb and had the same hard look in their eyes.

'And now I've found you.'

'What you want?' the dealer said.

'Got speed?' enquired McKeague.

'Dead on, this fucker's a fed,' said the youth on his right, the one who was wearing a hooded top, already making moves to back his bike up.

The dealer fired him a small shake of his head, stony-eyed. The wheel on McKeague's right stopped moving. The dealer returned his eyes to McKeague, appraising. Here was the brain of the operation. A small nod, this time for McKeague, and the dealer pulled open his tracksuit bottoms, reached inside and took out a medium plastic ziplock, inside it several smaller brothers, each with different products, but in small quantities. He showed McKeague the speed, two or three wraps, kept it close to his chest. He named a price, sounded about right. He was in no form to haggle. McKeague moved to take the product.

'Money,' said the dealer.

McKeague slid out his wallet and opened it, not attempting to hide the wedge of sterling notes, still fresh from the exchange booth at Málaga. He picked out what he needed, held it up with two fingers; the dealer took it. McKeague pinched the small bag from his hand. The dealer secreted the money, eyes again on the alley. McKeague opened the bag, swallowed the wraps. Swears and laughter from either side. Not from the dealer.

'That was a starter. I need an ounce, more if you have it,' he said.

Same reaction from the two hyenas, same unfazed response from his man. McKeague was beginning to like this kid; had some nerve. He told the other two to shut up, sent them to fetch what McKeague had asked for. Definitely a brain; only the small amounts he would carry. The big stash was always somewhere else, probably in a safe drop. It was the same system the world over from Belfast to the streets of Philly. Moments later, the two mountain bikers returned, skidding to a halt. Cue handover from the one who was wearing a red and black tracksuit. McKeague sized it up. Looked to be the ticket, and if it was from the same batch he'd just parachuted, it would hit the spot nicely. He could already feel the tell-tale rustle of the amphetamine as it started to course in his bloodstream, strikes of internal lightning sparking from his brain down his arms and into his fingertips, and everything starting to speed up, gently at first, but in no time he'd be a rocket man.

'How much?' he said, reaching for his wallet.

'All of it,' the dealer replied.

McKeague slowly looked up from his deck of notes, saw the blade, glowing steel in the twilight, pointed and angled close to his face. He saw the dealer's eyes glint with a cocktail of fear and zeal from behind it, watched as his pupils blossomed into black holes, slowly, slowly. He felt the wallet and the pack of drugs slip from his hands, viscous as glue.

Then his world sped up like an igniting supernova.

McKeague exploded; his right hand shot up, past the knife, into the dealer's face, his index finger hard and piercing as the point of a spear. He felt his man's left eyeball instantly puncture; his finger disappeared almost to the second knuckle. It was hot and soft, as a grilled tomato on a plate. The dealer convulsed, tried to pull away, but too late; McKeague was faster. He bent his finger into a hook and ripped it out with a suck. McKeague stepped back, slapped the blade from his hand. As it clattered to the ground the eyeball hit the wall with a small splat, rolled and stopped.

His action over, the others, so slow, now moved. Shrieks and curses came from the two wankers on the bikes as they clambered and fell off their steeds, making distance. The dealer staggered forward, emitting a sound somewhere between a moan and a scream, one hand over the hole in his head, blood coursing past his fingers. McKeague deftly sidestepped, let him go, and he staggered towards his helpers, who cringed from him as though his agony was contagious. The one in the hoodie pushed him away and the dealer staggered towards McKeague, thought better of it, and started to lope off in the direction of the pub, taking it in zigzags.

'I'm fucking disappointed with you,' McKeague shouted. Then, added, 'You're very lucky I'm not carrying a blade.' He glanced down to where the dealer's weapon now lay. He shook his head. It was a kitchen knife.

McKeague hunkered down, picked up the drugs and

his wallet, approached the dazed-looking one in the red and black tracksuit. He froze, eyes wide, started to retreat.

'Do you want to get paid or not?'

He stopped, looked at his hoodie-wearing partner, who'd got back on his bike, and then back to McKeague. He nodded. McKeague stepped forward, wiped his index finger on the boy's tracksuit top and counted out the money. After a moment's hesitation, it was taken from his hand.

'The one-eyed man is only king in the land of the blind. Do you know what I'm saying?' he asked.

The kid nodded his head. He clearly hadn't a clue, pearls to swine. McKeague told him to fuck off and he quickly obliged, following his hooded pal into the dusk, headed west.

McKeague started moving too, the opposite direction, where the evening traffic flashed past and fused with the colours of festive street decorations. His accelerating thoughts matched the streaks. He was back, feeling just as good as he ever had in his home town and impossible to put down. But he did need a knife, and the right tool for the job. Then he'd find whoever had decided to play at being a killer, and who wanted to tell tales from McKeague's past. He'd cut this city wide open if he had to, but he'd find them, rip out their heart and eat their soul.

PART THREE

RUNNIN' WITH THE DEVIL

CHAPTER TWENTY

Belfast, Northern Ireland
Thursday 20th December

Sheen's loft apartment could feel cramped when it was just him. This morning four people occupied the small living area that led from his windowless kitchenette. In attendance were Sheen, Geordie Brown, Aoife McCusker and Hayley White. Sheen closed the front door behind him, then unzipped the large skylight Velux window of its blackout blind and opened it a little. Scant grey light and a waft of cool air entered. In its wake came a medley of sounds from the Lagan and Belfast city centre below; the cry of a gull repeating into the distance, a riverboat engine, and the fainter hum of traffic.

'Make yourselves at home,' offered Sheen, and stepped into the little kitchen area and filled the kettle. The three adults continued to stand their ground. The living space contained a single armchair in front of a small flatscreen portable television on the floor, a mess of wires, a wireless broadband box at its feet and a small printer. The armchair was piled up with Sheen's laundry, most of it smalls – all clean, at least. Aside from that there was an IKEA desk with a flimsy blue net-backed swivel chair which he saw Geordie eyeing like it had been deposited from the rear end of a passing dog. Along the flat wall, adjacent to Sheen's bed and partially obscuring the window, were three boards, one pin and two dry-wipe. Sheen had set them up on easels he'd purchased from the same arts and crafts shop in the city centre where he'd bought the boards.

He had spent the best part of yesterday evening printing off the images he wanted to keep in mind from the unidentified bog body now stored in Monaghan General, to which he had added the scanned copies of the blues, the original record made during the autopsy examination which Michael Mulligan had sent him. Sheen also had the microfilm printouts from Clones Library detailing the Satanic panic orchestrated by the covert British Army troop in the mid 1970s. On the breakfast bar were the case notes for Father Phil Rafferty's and Rhonda Sterrit's murders. He'd written both names and dates of death on a whiteboard, but as yet had not had time to stick key photographs and documents to the boards and begin drawing links. Just as well. His guests, not surprisingly, now stared at what he'd posted. Aoife's eyes rested on Father Phil's name. Sheen reached over and pulled out the single stool that was under the breakfast bar, offered it to Aoife. She turned to him but didn't accept his offer.

'You've had a shave,' she stated.

Sheen unnecessarily ran a hand over his smooth jaw. He'd also put on some aftershave. Aoife's jibe had been what he needed. As soon as his face was clean, he'd felt ready for work again; ritual and routine so much more important than inspiration.

Her brow creased and she sniffed the air. 'Have you started smoking?' she asked. He could hear the disdain.

'No,' he said, scoffed. He danced his eyes across the few surfaces of the apartment, looking for evidence, saw none. 'Previous tenant,' he said.

Aoife said it was disgusting, he should complain, and he agreed he would.

Geordie nodded at the spindle-legged stool he'd offered Aoife, made a noise that was something between a grunt and a sigh, and claimed the armchair without waiting for the women to choose their seats. He reversed into the pile of Sheen's underwear and T-shirts, shuffling his rear end to find the required purchase. Sheen winced. Geordie was wearing a suit that looked like it may have fitted him around about the time a British prime minister thought it was cool to shake hands with rock stars in Downing Street. His charcoal-grey woollen overcoat just about fitted over it, but it wasn't going to button up this year. Sheen could hear him wheezing lightly following their single-file trek up the three flights of stairs to get here.

'I hope that's the kettle on.' Sheen said it was.

Aoife and Hayley were still standing, Hayley slightly hunched but unnecessarily, despite the low ceiling of his apartment, much in the way those who are over-tall, or those who feel they are, often do. He'd offered the seats; he wasn't going to beg anyone to take one. Sheen found that he had four mugs, to his mild surprise. A quick check of his abandoned fridge confirmed what he already knew.

'Black tea or coffee OK?' he asked the group.

Geordie answered. 'Do I look like I'm a Turk or something? Who do you know that takes their tea black?' He told Sheen he'd take a coffee, one sugar. Aoife said she'd pass.

'I'd love a black tea, one sugar. Thank you,' added Hayley, softly, her voice barely more than a whisper.

Sheen nodded, returned her politeness with a small smile and quickly appraised, or perhaps more fairly, re-appraised Hayley White, whom he'd been so quick to dismiss the day before. Behind that modesty Sheen sensed strength of dignity, maybe some steel too. Despite her soft tone and effort to remain diminutive, her very presence had as much weight as Geordie, for all his heft and volume. He could see what attracted Aoife to her new friend, if 'attract' was the correct term. Perhaps that same sense of self had intimidated him a bit when he'd first met her, if truth be told. He hoped so; the alternative was raw prejudice, something he did not want to consider.

His eyes moved to Geordie. He was staring at Hayley, as though also properly noticing her for the first time, even though there had been cursory greetings downstairs. The expression on his blood-vessel-cracked face suggested that Geordie Brown was trying to make sense of more than Hayley White's preference for black tea.

The kettle boiled and Sheen poured. He served up and leant against the breakfast bar, the stool still vacant. Aoife had opted for the swivel chair and Hayley remained standing, but some of her earlier awkwardness had gone as she sipped the tea he had given her and leant the back of her wide shoulders against the gradient of the loft. Sheen took a sip of his brew. Hayley was right; the black tea was sweet and good.

'Right. Thanks for coming here. As you know, Paddy Laverty has agreed to assign me to Father Phil Rafferty's murder and, it now would seem, the connected case of Rhonda Sterrit, who was found dead outside her south Belfast home night before last,' he said.

Aoife cocked her head to the side, a small crease forming between her eyebrows. Sheen could practically hear the mental machinery whirring.

'Aoife, Paddy has no idea that you will be working with me. If he did there was no way he'd have agreed. And it's essential we keep your profile low,' he said. At that she opened her mouth, her face filling with argument. Sheen set his drink down. 'But you will be working this case, you have my word,' he said quickly.

She nodded; Aoife understood the need for it to be on the quiet, even if she clearly didn't like it.

'This will be our de facto operations room, but as far as Laverty is concerned the shadow version of this,' he said, gesturing to the display boards, 'down at

Ladas Drive is the real thing. I'm going to keep him up to speed, and Geordie and I will make an appearance there when we can,' explained Sheen.

He scanned their faces; no one asked a question. Sheen continued, his words now largely directed at Aoife, but speaking to the room.

'I took the liberty of briefing Geordie about what's happened to you, and he has agreed to take the lead on finding out who stitched you up, and why,' he said.

Geordie nodded gravely three or four times. No playacting; now that conversation had turned to Aoife's suspension and the threat she faced from Internal Investigations, he was all business.

Aoife looked primed and ready to launch, but Sheen waved her down with both palms, asked that she hear him out. Sheen quickly recounted what he had also explained to Geordie over a pint the night before, when he had also walked Geordie through what he knew about the two Belfast murders this week and how there could be a link to the body found in the bog.

Geordie had agreed to take sole management of working the case of Aoife McCusker's stitch-up. Sheen did not need to resort to flattery when he told him he was the best man for the job; experienced, connected, but also out of the game for long enough not to draw eyes and cries from the street corners. The fact that he'd been hounded into early retirement by an internal investigation meant he also had the sort of hunger that Sheen and Aoife needed. Plus, he'd be a valuable sounding board and another pair of feet for the main murder investigation too.

In contrast, if Aoife showed up asking questions without a warrant card it would not only prove futile but raise questions with Paddy Laverty that could not be easily answered. Added to this, her face was well-known, not least by those who'd set her up. She'd serve only to alert any guilty parties that she was on their tail. What Sheen didn't spell out was that he wanted her with him, investigating the murders. He could lead legitimately and with some care; she could enter the doors he could open. She was the edge he needed to solve the case, his first choice. And not simply because she was maybe the best rookie detective he'd ever worked with either. As he finished, Aoife still had disagreement written all over her face, but she nodded once, reluctant consent.

'It's for the best, the only way really,' added Geordie. He rummaged around the inside pocket of his overcoat, took out a small black notebook and unclicked a pen. 'For it to happen, I'm gonna need to have a few questions answered. In private if you prefer,' he said, glancing up at Sheen and Aoife, and then looking at Hayley. 'A list of people you think might have had it in for you, any personal reasons that might help explain why someone went to the effort and risk of dropping a bag of coke that size in your work locker. You'll need to be candid and you'll need to trust me,' he said.

Softly delivered words, well targeted; Geordie was good. Sheen had taken one further liberty over the pint the previous night and told Geordie that he suspected that the late Cecil Moore had had something that he was holding over Aoife McCusker.

'I'll tell you what I know. No need for a confessional, Geordie. Cecil Moore was blackmailing me. He'd managed to get his hands on a secret video recording,' she took a breath, continued, 'of me and that waster Charlie Donaldson, somewhere up in Derry, in a hotel,' she said.

Geordie's right hand was discreetly adding shorthand notes to his black book, but his eyes remained on Aoife. He nodded, asked her to go on.

'Sort of thing that might be classed as revenge porn,' she said quietly, but her chin was raised.

Sheen felt his neck redden and that pilot light of old anger in his chest, never really extinguished, flared up at her words. Nothing burned fiercer than the accelerant of jealousy.

'But the clincher was Charlie vacuuming up lines of coke before I entered stage right and the main act took place,' she said with a dry, mirthless laugh.

Hayley moved the few steps across the room and set a hand on Aoife's shoulder. Geordie was implacable, hand scribbling.

Sheen could hear his pulse in his ears. He wanted to flay this Donaldson alive, once for having Aoife and once again for exposing her to such risks. But that bastard Moore, if he could bring him back to life to beat him to death, he'd do it right now. And when they found out who had done this to Aoife at his bidding, they'd cry for their mothers, he would see to it himself. He pulled his eyes from Aoife's stony face, looked out the loft window at the grey rectangle of Belfast sky and tried to steady his breathing. In that space he could see the video he had never watched. That was what was on Cecil Moore's SIM card, the one he had taken from the crime scene where Moore had been killed, the one he'd destroyed at Aoife's request. This was what had been hanging over Aoife last summer and what she had fought so desperately to keep secret and neutralise.

'The drugs are what he had you on, but because of your daughter, right?' said Geordie, pausing momentarily and flicking the page of his notebook. He had noted some particulars from Sheen last night. 'Wee Ava?' he finished.

Aoife flinched visibly at the mention of her child's name, then nodded once more, sharp and short. Geordie waited; seconds passed. Aoife spoke, her voice unsteady.

'Yes. Ava. Moore threatened to expose me, and he knew the social services would take her away. If drugs were involved, I mean,' she said.

Hayley's hand moved from her shoulder to her back. Aoife did not pull away.

'So he wanted what? Information, the inside leg on Serious Crimes in exchange for keeping quiet about the video?'

'Yes,' said Aoife.

'I know of this Donaldson fella. Had a name as a drinker, which takes some going in this game, I can tell you. Ladies' man too,' he said more quietly, no jibe in his voice, just the fact.

'Charlie was an idiot. But he was good to me. In fact, he tried to warn me that Moore had something on me. He wasn't behind this. He's just weak,' she said.

The black flame in Sheen's chest blazed.

'Sheen tells me that you're straight, you didn't give Moore anything,' said Geordie. Not a question, but the way in which he'd floated it required some response.

Smart Geordie; thorough, thought Sheen. He'd been through enough in his time to know that if you wanted the answer to a question, best to do the asking yourself. Sheen got it; he'd be the same. Geordie trusted Sheen's opinion, but he wanted to look Aoife in the eyes and know he could trust her too.

'I spoke to the press, up at Belfast Heights, when we were hunting the killer of Cecil Moore's mother last summer,' she said.

Aoife raised her chin and looked directly at Sheen, her face was open, the look in her pale blue eyes somewhere between pleading and proud. Sheen almost moved to her, barely resisted the urge to walk over and take her hands in his, get down on one knee like this was bloody *La La Land* or something.

'Moore ordered me to do that and I obeyed him,' she said contemptuously. 'I'm sorry. I was scared,' she said.

Sheen remembered the moment, and his confusion at the time. His cheeks flushed once more, not with rage this time. He had assured Geordie that he'd had all the facts, but clearly not.

'Aye, I remember watching that. You blamed it on

Dissident republicans, right? I was in a boozer,' said Geordie, rather more sheepishly.

'Sheen took the rap for that. Irwin was furious. That spook Oswald was waiting, warned us off the political angle, remember?' she asked Sheen.

He nodded, pleased that she mentioned his gallantry, but eclipsed as his mind turned to Oswald for the first time since meeting him briefly in July. The spook that had conveniently appeared and laid down what they could and could not investigate and then, just disappeared, as spooks will. Or, perhaps, he had just disappeared from view.

'Thanks for being honest. If it's any consolation, Aoife, I can understand. And if there's a peeler in this town who hasn't got a dirty secret or two, then they've been doing a different job than I did,' he said. Geordie let silence settle. 'Was there anything else? Did you—'

'No,' she replied, voice tough and unswerving. She was staring right at Geordie and him back at her.

He smiled with one side of his face, as Sheen had noted he was apt to do. The response he wanted.

'Which is why Moore stitched you up, cos you wouldn't play the game?'

'Yes,' she confirmed.

'The video, the one you said was from a hotel near Londonderry, is there a copy?' he asked.

Aoife had said the hotel was near Derry, Geordie's use of the city's full title a reflection of their divergent backgrounds. Geordie was from Protestant east Belfast,

Aoife from the Catholic west. One word meant a world of difference – only in Northern Ireland. Still, differences could co-exist, as their unlikely partnership was proving.

'Moore said there was just one copy. That was destroyed,' she replied.

'You believe that?'

'So far another hasn't come my way. If someone else had one, they would have tried to use it by now,' she replied.

'Or maybe someone is waiting until you have enough for their blackmail to be worthwhile,' observed Geordie.

Aoife paled visibly. 'Setting up hidden CCTV is not as easy as they make it look in the movies. Unless it's very discreet, people notice. Peelers especially will notice, particularly those who have a taste for extramarital affairs and marching powder.

'It may be nothing, but there's a real creep, a fella called Burgoyne, he works for Securitel, the alarm and surveillance company, down at the waterfront development. I had dealings with him during the investigation. The way he spoke to me, it was like he knew me, like he could see right through my clothes. Or already had,' she added.

Geordie tapped his pen against the little black book. 'Not an awful lot to go on here, if I'm being brutal,' he said. 'I'll start with the drugs. That kind of weight of coke could have come from a police seizure,' he said.

'Meaning an inside job?' asked Sheen.

'Well, somebody put it there, and it wasn't Aoife,' said Geordie.

'Surely Internal Investigations has already seized the CCTV at Ladas Drive station?' suggested Aoife.

'Aye, probably. I would. But remember, Internal will start with you, not start by looking for someone who ruthlessly framed you,' said Geordie. 'Still, I'll cover all angles, rest assured.' That same half-smile etched itself up the left side of his face. 'I love a good mystery, but this is taking things to a different level,' he said.

Geordie heaved himself off the armchair, said he was going to make a start.

Aoife spoke before Sheen had a chance. 'What about Hayley?'

All eyes fixed on Hayley White, who stared back at Aoife, the germ of an objection on her face.

Aoife was having none of it. 'Hayley is on board too, that was what we agreed, Sheen?' she said.

'Hayley's going to pair up with you, Geordie,' Sheen said quietly.

He hadn't covered this with Geordie last night; should have. Fact was he forgot.

Geordie gave him a look that said it all. 'This one's not even a cop,' he said, thumb cocked in Hayley's direction.

'Hayley's my friend. And she's an intuitive; she can help. If I'm not permitted to go after the person that did this to me, then Hayley will be there,' explained Aoife.

Geordie, however, looked more confused. 'Sheen, please tell me you're not bringing a psychic along, mate,' he said.

'I'm not a psychic,' said Hayley quietly. Geordie started to say something, face like he'd sucked a lime. 'But I'm not an idiot,' continued Hayley. Geordie stopped. 'I've no interest in getting in your way, but Aoife wants my help and I'm prepared to offer it,' she said. 'I don't know much about police investigations, but I know this one isn't exactly what you'd call conventional so far. It's not fair of you to make a big deal of me not being a cop.'

Geordie didn't reply, his red-veined face had darkened. He shot a look at Sheen, who shrugged. Hayley had a point. Geordie stomped over to the door, pulled it open.

'Keep in touch,' said Sheen.

'Aye,' he growled, exited.

Hayley followed, but at her own pace.

'Good luck,' said Aoife.

Hayley gave her a small smile and returned the farewell. Sheen had a feeling Hayley White wouldn't need it. His attention turned to the scant details of the historic murder on the display boards, and then the thin case files on the breakfast bar.

The same couldn't be said for him.

CHAPTER TWENTY-ONE

Aoife had taken Geordie's place on the pile of laundry after he and Hayley had left. Sheen unpacked one of two manila folders, spread the pages and enlarged photographs along the length of the breakfast bar. It was Father Phil Rafferty's murder file. Sheen glanced up from his work, invited her over. The case was, of course, the whole point of her being there. She raised herself off the chair, moving more slowly than she needed to, and joined Sheen.

'From the scene, I'd say we are looking for a man, younger rather than old. I don't read signs of a struggle, but from the blood spatter patterns and the positioning of the remains it looks like he was literally carried from one side of the room to the other. And Father Phil Rafferty wasn't a small guy,' mused Sheen, his eyes on the images.

Aoife forced her own gaze down. 'Makes sense,' she replied, but only to stave off the stunned silence she knew would set in if she did not say something quickly.

Before her were spread the images of Father Phil's defiled body, and the sacristy. The thick film of congealing blood, so dark it was almost black, spread across the surface of the dresser, touching the open Bible. The abomination of Father Phil's posed remains: his head perched like a medieval spoil of war on top of the wooden chair where he had been lodged. The cruel cuts that had been etched into his skin, alien and evil, and, somehow most terrible of all, his genitals on show, a humiliation to crown this destruction of a good person. She blinked away a film of tears, swallowed the knot in her throat. She was on a job. She was good at this. She was going to catch the animal who did this.

'Looks like his head was severed here,' she said, her finger resting on the vile image of the congealed pool of blood on the dresser surface.

Sheen followed her direction, hummed agreement. 'Meaning Father Phil was held up and over the surface,' said Sheen, but then he paused, glanced at Aoife, reading her reaction to his playing out of events.

She met his eyes, gave him nothing, even though that knot was back in her throat again.

Sheen continued. 'He was decapitated, and then his body was moved, positioned in the chair,' he surmised.

'Where the rest of the defilement of his corpse was carried out,' she finished for him. Her voice was, somehow, cool and steady. 'Assuming he was held in place while the beheading took place,' she said, but the sentence was cut short, the knot suddenly high in her palate.

188

Sheen was there for her. He rested a hand on her lower arm, and, mercifully, removed it again equally stealthily. Kindness can summon tears more swiftly than cruelty sometimes.

'This took some serious strength. Maybe even more than one person, now I see it again,' Aoife concluded. She squinted at the image. 'And as you said, no obvious signs of a struggle,' she said. Even a Catholic priest could be forgiven for fighting for his life. Especially when the death that was about to be visited on him was as ghastly as this.

'Which brings us to this,' said Sheen. He sifted through the spread of documents, handed her a sheaf.

She scanned the headlines, echoed by Sheen as she read. 'Initial toxicology report states Father Phil had a near-lethal level of diamorphine in his bloodstream. It probably would have killed him. Though, in the end, I don't think that's the cause of death.' She glanced up from the report. 'He was drugged?'

'Unless he was a closet user,' countered Sheen.

'Course not.'

'Explains the incapacitation, no evidence of a struggle,' offered Sheen.

True, but, equally, a hammer blow to the skull would have done much the same job. And hammers were easy to come by, diamorphine wasn't. Assuming Father Phil was injected with the drug, the murderer or murderers would have had to get close enough to administer. So why go to the trouble? Aoife raised the question.

189

'No idea,' conceded Sheen. 'But it's significant,' he said.

He spread out the papers from the second file, that of Rhonda Sterrit, the teenage girl murdered and dumped at the front gate of her own home the same day Father Phil had been slain.

'Rhonda Sterrit's autopsy is later today. I can be there, for some of it anyway,' said Sheen. 'I'll look for links to Father Phil,' he said. 'Oh, and no prints found, at either scene. But they did detect small deposits of a dark fibre, at both, different from Father Phil's or Rhonda Sterrit's clothes. I've asked for a comparison to see if they match, still waiting. And red candlewax,' said Sheen.

Aoife looked up at this. Sheen asked her if it meant something.

'Not sure,' she replied. Her brain felt woolly, underused. Or, perhaps, it was the dregs of the quarter-tablet of OxyContin she'd taken last night when sleep wouldn't come.

Aoife scanned the crime scene photos. The victim's right hand was missing, in its place a prong of white arm bone, trimmed like a butchered rib of beef. Aoife found the photo of Father Phil's severed head, and then pushed it away, her eyes darting from one grotesque image to the other.

'Cuts very clean. Those on Father Phil and the girl,' she commented with a slight shudder. 'The drugs, the precision surgery, maybe we are looking for a deranged doctor?'

'That's what they said about Jack the Ripper, you know,' said Sheen.

'CCTV?'

'Not much. The Sterrits' home is served by a live stream from the intercom at the front gate, but no recording. The father, Gordon Sterrit, was alerted to his daughter's body after someone buzzed the intercom,' said Sheen.

'Don't tell me – no fingerprints found?'

Sheen shook his head. 'And Sterrit didn't see anyone when he went to the door. Beyond that it's not great. Newforge Lane is off the beaten track. Adjacent homes are well set off the road, but a few neighbours do have doorstep cameras. Nothing reported in the file, but we can ask,' he suggested.

'Says here Gordon Sterrit claims to have dropped his daughter off at the entrance of the Methodist Church on the Lisburn Road at 7 p.m.,' read Aoife. 'Statements were taken from the staff, her friends, adjacent restaurant owners, all tell the same story.'

'She never turned up.'

Aoife frowned as she flicked back and forth though the thin file. 'There's no record here of the area being sealed and forensically examined,' she said.

'I know. By the time the call went up that the kid was missing, her body had already been dumped in Newforge Lane. Which naturally enough was treated as the principal scene of crime,' said Sheen.

'Bloody sloppy though.'

'Bloody cuts and understaffing,' said Sheen.

Aoife said she wanted to check the front of the church for herself.

'Newforge Lane becomes Balmoral Avenue before it reaches the Lisburn Road and from there into the city. But go east, it's the Lagan Towpath, and the meadows,' said Aoife.

Sheen was familiar, had enjoyed a few good walks along the path, and ate a great bacon bagel in the converted cottage that now did business as a thriving little cafe. It was a beautiful part of Belfast.

'Multiple entry and exit points, and unlit,' said Sheen.

'And no security cameras,' concluded Aoife. 'We're late off the blocks here, Sheen. This already feels cold.'

'There's something else. Look.' He passed her his phone. She frowned, confused. 'These are the remains of the child's body we dug up in Monaghan at the end of last summer,' he explained.

'Jimmy McKenna, the one John Fryer murdered, back in the day?'

'No. The other body, the one we weren't out to find. It was taken to the mortuary in Monaghan General, over the border. They put the remains in cold storage,' he said.

'My God.' was her only response. The image Sheen showed her didn't look human, let alone the corpse of a child.

'The peat and bog water preserved the body by effectively tanning the flesh. It's why it's that colour.' Brown is what he meant, and Sheen was correct; it looked like a preserved and misshapen leather saddle. 'Hands and head removed,' he explained, though she could see that now.

'You think there's a connection, don't you?' she asked.

In response, he pointed to the photograph of the child's back.

'Impossible,' she said, and picked up one of the grisly close-up shots taken of Father Phil's body seated in the chair. It showed his chest, where the symbol had been carved into his flesh.

'Same pattern,' confirmed Sheen. 'It's the symbol of Saturn, an occult sign, linked to rebirth or something. If it's not connected, then it's the biggest coincidence I've ever come across on the job,' he said. 'But that's not all.' Sheen had more. A quick online search for Solomon's seal had confirmed that the herb found lodged inside the body of his bog boy had meaning too, both biblical and pagan. Some said King Solomon himself placed his seal upon it, but it was also associated with the planet Saturn.

'Black magic?' she asked.

'I'm not sure yet, but get this,' he said. Sheen gave her a potted summary of what he knew about the covert British Army plot to sow fear and superstition along the border in the 1970s, roughly the same time the child's body had been dumped in the Monaghan bog. He also filled her in on what he'd discovered about Trevor McHenry, with Fahey's help. Sheen had spoken to Fahey first thing that morning. Asked him to dig around and find anything he could about the Sterrit family, same for Father Phil Rafferty.

'Let me get this right. We think this might be some long-dormant, loony former soldier who got a taste for the occult and has taken up serial murder?'

'We don't know for sure that our killer or killers have been dormant,' clarified Sheen.

Aoife ran one hand through her hair. 'This thing feels boundary-less already, too much,' she said.

Sheen had looked into the case of the boy O'Rawe, the child whose burned and dismembered body was found on the shores of the Lagan in 1976. His gut told him there had to be a connection, but O'Rawe's murder had never been solved and the lead detective was now dead. After a trawl through family members, Sheen had found that both his parents had passed and his siblings had emigrated. He could understand why. Not a total dead end, but trying to breathe life into a second cold case to resuscitate another felt like a hiding to nowhere. Especially while someone was killing people here and now.

'The historic route has yielded what it will for now. Unless McHenry reveals names of his troop, I can't see an easy way to approach it from that end. So it's Fuck, Fuck, Wank, Shit, Cunt, and back to basics,' he said.

Aoife shook her head, couldn't resist a small smile. 'Family, Forensics, Witnesses, Scene, CCTV,' she replied. The essential first steps to taking management of a murder enquiry, some of which they'd already just explored.

'Impressed,' said Sheen, nodding, and he did appear to be. 'The Clonard crime scene is still preserved. We go there first. Let's see if something's been missed. The Sterrits are back in their house and I want to interview them myself.' He paused for a second. 'Priests don't have wives and kids. Who's his next in command?' asked Sheen.

'Father Macken,' said Aoife.

'Then we want a word.'

The photograph of Rhonda Sterrit's body caught Aoife's eye and she picked it up.

'Look at this,' she said, sharing the photograph.

Sheen scrutinised the image. 'What am I seeing?'

'Look at her left hand,' she replied.

'Appears that rigor has started to set in, given the position of the fingers,' he noted. 'It's like she was holding something,' he said finally.

'Exactly,' said Aoife. She'd been reluctant to make the inference for him, better that he saw it first for himself, more objective.

'That's something we can ask the parents when we meet them. Come on, let's go. Are you hungry, by the way? There's a deli beside St Anne's Cathedral, does a smashing Italian sub,' he said, already half out the door. Oddly enough, she was, despite the details of what they had just shared. She'd forgotten just how famishing detective work was.

Sheen paused partway down the first flight, turned and looked back up.

'I'm glad you called me, Aoife. Good to be working with you again,' he said.

As Aoife descended the stairs in Sheen's wake, her mind again returned to what he'd said about Jack the Ripper and their killer, both so brazen and bloody and hungry for death. She stopped briefly at the bottom step and let Sheen open the front door. The pale light of day did little to fill the gloom of the communal hallway. Those similarities needed to end; the Ripper had never been caught.

CHAPTER TWENTY-TWO

The woman awoke from her dream with a jolt and then waited until the sound of her own scream subsided in her mind. The same horror show that had played so many times before. The only dream she ever had. She blinked and the world came into smudgy focus. First, she saw the contours of her bedroom, but they re-formed. The weak light from her back door revealed the scarred wooden table, a knife and half a raw hamburger, and the bare kitchen beyond. Her mind still played this waking trick, though it had been a long time since she'd taken her thin sleep anywhere but in this chair.

The minutes sifted by in slow silence punctuated by the distant bird calls heralding another day, claiming their rights. That and the unsheathing sword in her gut, cutting and burning inch by inch as her body awakened. This was just the beginning; the pike of agony would grow. Even if she remained still, it would burrow into her all the same and find her core. Unless she resurrected herself from this seat and got to the kitchen cupboard where some temporary salvation awaited, she'd be damned to pain so intense that she'd never be able to move.

Unlike the birds, she had no claim on the new day. Time was not on her side.

'Ehhhh!' She clutched her gut with both bony arms, as though to carry away the pain, but to no avail. She was fully, horribly alert now.

She dug her fingernails into the fabric of the armchair and managed to stand up, gasped and inhaled. She shuffled to the kitchen cupboard. Her clothes, already sour and unwashed, started to soak up yet more sweat as her legs and back grew slick with the exertion. But the movement helped a little, as though she were in some way outpacing the tide of the pain.

She stopped, one hand rested on the laminate kitchen counter, her breaths mixed with sobs. She readied herself then reached up to the top shelf of the cupboard, her hand trembling lightly as the boring pain drilled on, deeper and deeper. Her fingertips touched one of the remaining syringes, pre-loaded with a fat dose of diamorphine. She knocked it off the shelf and noted as it landed on the countertop that the needle was still capped with a plastic protector. Which was good; the morphine would be sweet oblivion, but at a price. If she managed to make it back to her chair, she'd never be able to get off it again. She left it where it fell and then slumped against the counter, fighting to breathe. The morphine had done its job on the priest and on Sterrit's daughter, but they were just the beginning.

There was more work to be done.

She reached up and clawed into the bare cupboard once more, this time slid out the pack that had once contained twenty cigarettes. On it, a single message, all other brand marketing banished: SMOKING CAN HARM YOUR UNBORN CHILD. Another sound came from her, closer this time to a laugh. It echoed briefly. She shook out the remaining hand-rolled smokes of the half-dozen she'd pre-made. She'd laced each with Angel Dust: PCP. The street drug had started life as a veterinary painkiller. And of all its potent charms, it was this that she needed most right now. The purple plastic lighter clinked out of the pack too, followed by the thin phial that contained the remaining drops of the PCP solvent.

She picked up her smoke, or rather 'fry'. The Internet site where she'd found the drugs also provided the street lingo, and a guide on how to roll your own using the PCP solvent. This she required, but the preparation of lethal doses of diamorphine she understood already. Half a lifetime in nursing had its benefits. Still, the World Wide Web had proved to be most enlightening, even for a latecomer. In fact, without it, the dead priest would be planning his pastoral duties, and the young Sterrit girl would be eating her breakfast.

She paused and searched herself for a flicker of regret, but there was none. Even her hatred, so hot in her dreams, was a cold memory.

'Have you any good left in you at all?' she enquired. No response from the empty room, and no answer from her.

Her eyes rested again on the syringe of morphine. She could have made the girl suffer, the priest too. Instead, she'd killed them softly. So, perhaps, a little of her soul remained intact. Or, maybe it was just the enduring power of habit. She'd taken the Nightingale Pledge, a nurse's version of the Hippocratic Oath. All her life, she'd been an angel of mercy, soothed the sick and stopped the pain.

'Agghhh,' she moaned. Another dull explosion of hurt slowly spread from her centre in sickening waves.

She managed to get a flame from the lighter on her second attempt, touched it to the tip of the fry and sucked on the acrid smoke, inhaling hard and deep. She clamped her jaw closed and held the burning smoke in her lungs. First came pain from the pressure, followed almost instantly by a numbness starting in her extremities. It flowed down her fingertips and arms. She exhaled, dragged again, the burn less caustic now, her lungs and chest soothing as the numbness reached her torso. But with it that swooning sense of a world untied from its moorings, cocktail hour gone wrong. She gripped the kitchen top with one hand, then emitted a mirthless giggle as the Angel Dust found her dopamine centre and played a little jingle down her brain's pleasure pathway. Just as suddenly her dry laugh disappeared.

She pushed off the kitchen worktop, took one final, smaller hit, and then carefully killed the burning tip of the fry in the black hole that she'd already scorched into the laminate surface. Too little, the pain would overcome her, but too much . . . ? She'd be in convulsions, coma, and death. So, she'd be careful, but it was worth it. Angel Dust wasn't just a painkiller. When she'd worked as an emergency room nurse in the Bronx, a cop told her how to spot patients they brought her way who'd been using it.

Look for the wet, naked guy wearing two sets of cuffs.

Indeed, she was sweating again, but this time not because of the pain.

Now she felt its power.

Strength drummed through her, like a thick voltage that could be tapped for fury. She was panting with the exertion of holding this energy at bay. Yes, she could snap a set of cuffs, a platoon of men would scatter like pins at her feet. Her eyes flitted left and then right, for there in shadows of the still-murky room was a broiling snake-like movement, the creatures that appeared to feed from her wrath.

If there was good in her once, then there was no good left in her now.

Since the chemotherapy it was like there was nothing left inside her at all, she was just a husk. That young nurse had said it true when he turned the tap on to let the noxious, bright red liquid enter her. It didn't just attack the cancer; it killed everything she had once been.

Ready to let the Devil in, darlin'?

She strode from the kitchen and stopped. Her half-lit reflection looked back from the dirty mirror on the dining-room wall. Here was her frail, black-clothed frame, hollow-chested, and her head bald but for stray wisps of grey hair.

Before God and those assembled here, I solemnly pledge;
To adhere to the code of ethics of the nursing profession.

Above her, extended from her back and shoulders were wings, luscious and sleek as a raven. They quivered with each thump of her heart. From the shadows, the liquid snakes seeped closer, seeking her.

I will not do anything evil or malicious.
I will not knowingly give any harmful drug.

Her black wings flexed and folded, sent a faintly dusty waft of air into her face, the silken fan of a feather rested against her hand. She could run her fingers through her plumage. The untethered room made her sway once more and she looked away. When she returned her eyes to the mirror her wings were gone, for now.

Yes, she'd let the Devil in, so long at her door. While there was life in her, she would raise hell, and kill them all with the strength of a hundred men.

CHAPTER TWENTY-THREE

Geordie stopped the car on the lower Newtownards Road in east Belfast. A double yellow line with two wheels on the pavement.

They were outside a private members' club. Hayley read the sign over the painted-out window: BEANO'S: COLD BEER, POOL TABLES, BIG SCREEN SPORTS.

It was closed and looked as dead as the rest of the widely spaced commercial buildings on this part of the road. Hayley glanced up at the tattered remains of Union Jack flags clinging to lamp posts, a leftover from the 12th of July celebrations.

Not a part of town she knew, or one she would readily elect to visit.

She glanced at Geordie.

'Don't worry, you don't have to come in,' Geordie said. Then an added reassurance. 'I can lock you in the car till I come back. There's no alarm in this old thing, so you won't set it off or anything,' he said.

'No thanks,' she replied.

Geordie raised his eyebrows, reached for the glove compartment at her knees then seemed to think better of it, and moved to leave.

'If we're going to work together, I'll need to know what's going on,' she said.

He closed his door, appraised her. Worse than the mild exasperation he exuded was the infuriating tenderness in his eyes. It was a look she knew too well. It was pity. For the first time since this madness had begun, even including their discovery of Father Phil dead and mutilated, Geordie's look triggered a flash of anger, white and electric in her breast. She gripped the worn fabric of the seat.

Geordie smiled at her. 'You're tagging along, we're not working together,' he corrected.

'Fine,' she replied. 'But when Aoife asks me for an update, I'll explain that to her. And you can explain it to Sheen,' she said.

Geordie sighed, got out, leant into the car. 'Don't go anywhere. If I'm not out in about ten minutes, give Owen Sheen a call,' he said.

'Tell him what?'

'Tell him to come, fast as he can,' he said, no longer smiling.

She looked over at the closed facade of Beano's, dead to the world.

'Looks closed,' she said.

'He's in there, he always is,' he said, and then he closed the door.

From conversation to sudden quiet. Geordie approached Beano's white painted door, stood there for a moment, and rocked his head from side to side, a boxer getting ready for the ring. Then he raised his fist and banged it. Above the door, she now noticed, there was a small white security camera, almost completely camouflaged. The door opened a crack. Words were exchanged and Geordie stepped inside. Across the road there was a clatter of shutters as a cafe opened for business.

A slow minute passed.

The cafe owner set out a small aluminium table and twin chairs, went back inside. She didn't blame him, it was too cold to eat al fresco, must be for die-hard smokers. All was still and quiet from Beano's.

If I'm not out in about ten minutes, give Owen Sheen a call.

She opened her door a little, felt the cold air surge in, listened, but could hear nothing more than the muted sounds of a wintering city; street traffic from the near distance, the despondent rake of a crow, the swish of the wind. Then there was a shout, muffled but male and coming unmistakeably from the direction of Beano's. Her heart rate spiked.

Tell him to come, fast as he can.

'Shit,' she hissed, fumbled in her handbag for her phone, but dropped the lot, all over the mud-caked rubber floor mat. Her hands searched, chanced on something hard which she snatched and too quickly raised her head. She banged the back of her skull on the glove compartment as she sat up.

'Shit!' she said again, stared at the object in her hand. Not a phone, but a black sock, and inside what felt like two hard balls. Hayley grimaced, reached into the large football sock. Little else was clean in this vehicle, why should this be any different? Her fingers found the spheres, smooth and cold to the touch; she pulled them out.

Two red snooker balls, each about two inches in diameter. She slid them back into the sock sleeve, clacked the makeshift weapon into one palm. She could see its use. Hayley looked over at Beano's. All was quiet once more. She felt the weight of the sock in her right hand. She popped open the glove box. Inside was a handgun, black burnished steel in a soft brown holster. She reached in and tentatively slipped it free, its weight as reassuring as the ball sock. Geordie's personal protection weapon, the one he'd reached for, instinctively. But also, the weapon he'd left behind. Meaning he was unprotected.

Hayley watched a man position himself in a chair outside the front of Beano's. He was a big guy and looked mean into the bargain. He filled his lightweight white Puffa jacket to capacity, and this, added to his close-shaved skull, made him look like the Stay Puft Marshmallow Man from *Ghostbusters*. If she paused to think about her next move any longer she would freeze and do nothing. Hayley got out of the car, slammed the door and strode confidently towards Beano's.

The man squinted at her as she approached him. Beano's front door was slightly open, and that was good, solved her first problem. She glanced at his scowling face, pictured the Stay Puft Marshmallow Man and almost started to laugh, her stomach doing flips. She kept it in, barely. Instead she dropped him a wink as she felt the reassuring weight she was packing in her coat pocket. He glared at her.

'Beano's expecting me,' she said before he had a chance to open his mouth. His face creased into a grimace of what looked like real hatred. Which was a bit worrying; he'd not exactly been provoked.

'He's not here,' said Stay Puft, getting up.

Hayley kept coming, her eyes on him. He hesitated.

'Sure, he's always here,' she said, the grit in her voice taking both of them by surprise. She glanced up at the snub-faced CCTV camera, as though to evidence the fact, then nudged open the door and walked on in. From behind her she heard the scrape of the chair on the pavement, Stay Puft on his feet. She moved quickly, eyes blinking to adjust to the murk within.

The entrance alcove opened up into a club room. There was a small bar on the left wall, glass-fronted fridges filled with cans of lager and stout on either side, one draught tap. In the central area was a pool table, another right at the back, the obligatory super-size flatscreen television on the right-side wall, as advertised. All in all, almost exactly how she'd envisioned Beano's to be when they first pulled up outside.

'Oi!' Stay Puft's bellowing voice, but still behind her.

Hayley didn't turn round and she didn't stop. She was headed for the pool table at the back, its overhead yellow light swinging slowly on its cord like an inverted tent, casting crazy shadows. There was Geordie, back and shoulders pushed down on the worn green baize by a small, stocky man in his late fifties, white hair and matching goatee, well-muscled arms barely covered by his tight white T-shirt. Beano, she presumed. Geordie's lip was bruised, a nasty looking blood blister. Beano had the spear of a broken pool cue pointed into the vulnerable meat under Geordie's chin.

'Mackers, what the fuck is this!' Beano enquired as she stood beside the pool table and crossed her arms. Beano had clearly noticed her, but his eyes were still on Geordie, who was taking an avid interest in the broken cue.

'Boss, she, ah, she's a peeler.'

Mackers was now right beside her. She could actually feel his desire to hurt her, like the heat off an Aga oven on a cold day.

Geordie glanced her way at the mention of her new job title. She stayed stoic.

'Bitch, you need a warrant to be here. Private club,' said Beano, the point of the cue still half buried in Geordie's craw.

'Not if the door was open,' said Geordie, no smile on his mug now, just good old-fashioned shit-scared. Beano took his eyes from Geordie, looked at her.

Anger dissipated in a cloud of confusion, followed by revised understanding.

Hayley White had seen it all before. She returned his stare with a terse smile.

'And unlike Geordie no one checked my credentials at the door,' she said, patting the weight in her side pocket. 'So you boys best break it up and say sorry, or Mackers is going to need a new knee cap. Maybe you too, Beano,' she added. For effect, hoping she'd not overplayed it.

Beano let go of Geordie, threw the broken cue to the floor. Clearly not; maybe she was getting the hang of this.

'You didn't say you were on the job,' said Beano to Geordie, who proceeded to manoeuvre himself off the table with a grunt and a grimace.

'Didn't get the chance,' he replied. 'I need to ask you something.'

A moment of silence between the men; the mood shifted and settled.

'Fuck it. Let's have a drink and one for your partner too,' Beano said, 'partner' delivered with a point as sharp as the discarded spear.

'Too early for me,' she responded.

'Mackers, mind the front. And shut the door,' said Beano.

Mackers made his exit, one last glare at her before he did.

Beano jabbed a finger towards the small bar, where he free-poured two whiskies. Geordie took a stool, and then his drink. She joined him. Beano stayed behind the bar. He shovelled ice cubes into a white cloth and slammed it on the bar between them. Geordie nodded, took a knock of Scotch, and then raised the pack to his lip. Beano drained half his booze, swallowing with a hiss. Hayley watched and listened.

'Well?' asked Beano.

'A friend of ours is in a jam,' he said, motioning his head in Hayley's direction.

'That so,' said Beano, expressionless.

'Aye, it is. Someone misplaced a quarter of a kilo of fine powder in her locker. Her work locker,' said Geordie.

Beano's expression changed now, real surprise.

'News to me. Not much I can tell you. Assuming I'd want to tell you anything,' he added.

'If it's come from the street, I need to know the source,' replied Geordie.

Beano swirled the last of his whisky in the glass but set it down untasted.

'I'd appreciate it. For old time's sake,' added Geordie.

'Not sure. If I had to cut a wire, I'd probably say this came from the Wombles,' said Beano.

Hayley listened. Womble was a derisory name used to describe the outlawed UDA, the Ulster Defence Association. One of the two main loyalist paramilitary outfits active during the Troubles and supposedly put out to pasture. It was Cecil Moore's alma mater, the man who had been blackmailing Aoife. They controlled much of the hard drugs in Belfast and beyond; a business they shared uneasily with their loyalist nemesis, the UVF, the Ulster Volunteer Force and the dregs of the IRA, Dissident republicans.

'Why so?' pushed Geordie.

'Hunch,' said Beano. Now he did finish his drink. Geordie matched him, set his glass down, and waited. Beano stayed silent, eyes moving like a chess player planning a series of moves. Hayley contributed nothing but a quiet look, which made it two against one. Beano broke the silence. Despite her misgivings, Hayley was beginning to see the attraction in the police game after all.

'The first boy to get whacked this time round was Henry Orr, middleman from Carrickfergus,' explained Beano.

Hayley knew the name; it had been all over the news a number of weeks before. An ageing former UDA prisoner turned community activist. He'd been the first man to die in the tit-for-tat murders that still continued. Speculation had been rife that Dissident republicans were involved.

'Heard Orr was murdered by Dissidents,' said Geordie.

Beano shrugged. 'Probably. But why start a war?' he asked.

Despite being sworn ideological enemies, the last thing the opposing paramilitary gangs wanted was conflict. It got in the way of their shady business.

'So, you heard there was missing product involved?' asked Geordie.

'Something set the Coca Colas onto him. Them boys are all about the money, freeing Ireland one drug deal at a time,' he simplified.

Coca Cola was the street slang for the Real IRA, one of the main Dissident republican groups. Their sparse support base called them the Real Thing, just like Classic Coke's old branding slogan. Belfast humour, it was always there, and would always be black as a pint of stout.

'So, Orr ripped off the Dissidents. Then the Dissidents whacked Orr. Cue murders galore,' speculated Geordie.

'That's only one way of seeing it,' said Beano.

'What's another way,' Geordie said.

'Someone ripped off the Dissidents. And someone pointed a finger at Orr, maybe even set the old bastard up to take a bullet,' said Beano.

Geordie flicked the rim of his glass with his finger. 'Your man Crazy Horse, Orr's second in charge?' asked Geordie.

Beano did not confirm or deny, but he followed Geordie's lead. 'I heard he's taken himself out of Carrickfergus and is back living with his mother in Rathcoole. Word on the street is he's moved back into town wearing his old boss's boots, kicking up a lot of dust too, building himself a wee kingdom. Now his gaffer's gone. Know what I mean?' said Beano.

Crazy Horse, the only thing Belfast loved more than dark humour was nicknames.

Geordie raised his eyebrows. 'Crazy Horse whacked Orr,' he replied.

'Or got the Dissidents to do the spade work for him, and then cashed in his chips,' said Beano. 'Just another way of seeing it, mind,' he added.

'And what happened to the missing product that was nicked from the Dissidents?'

'Sounds like you know more about that part of the story than I do, mate,' replied Beano.

Geordie eased off the stool, business apparently concluded. Hayley followed. Geordie reached for his wallet, but Beano raised a hand.

'This one's on the house,' said Beano. Hayley noticed that he was not, as far as she could tell, alluding to the empty glasses on the bar.

'Cheers,' said Geordie, his fingers touching his chin.

Beano raised an eyebrow. 'Next time, just a drink, that's us square,' he added.

Geordie nodded and said fair enough.

They walked back through the club and out, past Mackers, who ignored them completely. Geordie pulled the car in a big U-turn and headed back down the Newtownards Road towards the city centre. He spoke first.

'You did well in there. Cheers,' he said.

'Welcome,' she said. 'Quicker than Owen Sheen?'

'By a long way,' he agreed.

'Why did he have a broken pool cue under your chin?' she asked.

'I put his son away, about five years ago for manslaughter. He killed his best mate in a fight at a party. He got ten years,' he said.

'Oh. So, he'll be out soon,' she said.

Georgie scoffed, shook his head. 'Topped himself in Maghaberry. Overdose,' he said, matter of fact.

'Right. So, Beano blames you?'

'Who else can he blame?' replied Geordie.

'Is that man, Beano, a paramilitary?' she asked.

Geordie looked over, his face once again traced with irritation. But then he shook his head, started to answer her.

'Na, ordinary decent criminal, wee lowlife. He was my tout, but off the books, you know? Not a signed-up informer or anything. Cash in hand when he could help me, and I'd turn a blind eye,' he explained.

She waited before speaking again, could hear the drill of the tyres on the asphalt, taste the lingering staleness of the car's interior.

'To what?' she said.

'You really want to know?' replied Geordie. He waited a beat but got no answer from Hayley. 'Scrapbooks; used to be. These days it's probably just stolen property. Might run a few girls,' said Geordie.

'What are scrapbooks? And are you telling me that man's into selling women, people smuggling?'

Geordie sighed heavily. 'I never said he was smuggling people. I said he was running a couple of girls, women.'

'Oh, then that's fine. Sure, he's like Women's Aid really,' she snapped.

Silence again, the tyres burred, the creak of the wheel under Geordie's tightening fists.

'What's scrapbooks?' she repeated.

Geordie growled. 'Porn. Borderline stuff,' he said. 'Great Dane meets sexy blonde. Barely legal reveals all. He had a cut-and-paste business. They'd ship in illegal mags, take out pages from different books, and put them back together in a different order, mixed up. Like a scrapbook. Years ago, before online porn took off and put it all in the shade. It was a loophole. Harder to prosecute if the original publications weren't being sold on,' he said.

'My God. And you turned a blind eye to this? Bestiality? Child pornography?'

'Never that! Not little kids,' barked Geordie, but he did not look at her. 'So some sick fucker got his joys from a dirty book under the counter in Smithfield Market! I got names. Put murderers away. Not everything in life is so black and white, Mother Teresa.'

'Where are we going now?' she asked.

'Rathcoole. I want a word with Crazy Horse. See what he knows about a missing bag of powder that ended up in Aoife's locker,' he said.

Rathcoole was a staunch loyalist housing project on the outskirts of north Belfast. Silence settled.

'I didn't tell Mackers that I was a police officer, by the way,' she added.

Geordie shrugged. He pushed his tongue against his still-swollen lip, looked painful.

'Put my piece back in the glove compartment, seeing as you're not a peeler,' he said.

Hayley reached inside her coat pocket, pulled out the ball sock and let it swing between her and Geordie. He did a quick double take, then a smile creased the left side of his face and he burst out laughing. Hayley allowed herself a small smile in return.

'Break Mackers' knees indeed!' announced Geordie.

She dropped the sock into the footwell with a clack and her nascent smile fell away.

She wished that she had, now she knew what those men did. She looked out the window and the dull expanse of the Belfast sky, grey as dishwater. Hayley White was suddenly unsure she wanted to play this game after all.

CHAPTER TWENTY-FOUR

Sheen's sub was still wrapped in its tissue and rested snug with Aoife's, both untouched on the back seat of his car. Neither had said it out loud but having lunch before visiting the Clonard Monastery crime scene was probably ill-advised. Sheen found a parking space outside the gates of the monastery and they both got out, approached the side entrance that led to the sacristy. It was still taped off, a white forensics tent fixed to the wall, obscuring the door. A uniformed PSNI man was on guard.

Sheen showed his warrant card, introduced himself and Aoife simultaneously and held his breath. If the young man in uniform asked to see Aoife's police credentials this could be tricky. And if he reported back up the chain of command that she was with Sheen and attempting to enter a sealed crime scene then this could get serious, especially when Paddy Laverty got wind of it. The uniform glanced at Sheen's identification, they exchanged a few words about the weather, and both Sheen and Aoife entered the sheltered shell of the white tent unhampered. Sheen made a mental note to follow this up with the sergeant running Grosvenor Road station at some point when this was all over. Really, the crime scene was inviolable. If the chief constable turned up to take a look he wasn't getting in unless he was working the case, no exceptions made. Sheen signed and dated the entry logbook, just his name, as Aoife stepped into a white paper forensic suit and zipped it up. He found a large in the same cardboard box, plus shoes and a mask, and got suited and booted.

Inside it was almost full dark. Sheen stepped on one of the white plastic stepping plates, reached for the switch that would turn on the powerful halogen standing lamps that had been set up.

'Ready?' he asked Aoife.

She gave him a small nod, her eyes large and peering from above the face mask. She didn't look it.

Sheen hit the switch. An instant flood of clean, clinical light illuminated the small room. Black blood, congealed and hard-looking, coated the surface of the sideboard, had dripped to the ground where it had pooled and solidified. The parquet floor was spattered and smeared with the brownish-red gore. Sheen could taste it, iron and awful, despite the mask.

Aoife moved first, carefully entering the crime scene using the stepping plates. She stood in the middle of the room, hands on hips, taking stock. Her gaze was focused and full of scrutiny, that fold of concentration dented between her eyes. Despite the trauma Aoife was fully professional. And despite the horror of the scene, Sheen couldn't pull his eyes from her. She lowered herself down, scanned the smears and bloody scuffs on the floor.

'See something?' asked Sheen.

'Not easy. Looks like one set of footprints to me,' she replied.

This suggested one killer. And also that Father Phil had not walked or struggled when the blood started to pour.

'Here,' she pointed.

Sheen came closer. It looked like the smeared imprint of the upper half of a shoe or boot, no distinct markings. Sheen took out his mobile, snapped a few photos.

Aoife stepped around him, was back at the entrance. 'And here, this one's a bit clearer,' she said.

Sheen followed, repeated the process. 'What size do you reckon that is?' he asked.

'It'll be in the report,' she said absently. 'I'm a five, and it's bigger than mine,' she added. Sheen was ten, and it looked smaller than his. Not particularly helpful, it made their print about average.

'His feet might be average, but his power wasn't,' said Sheen. He had stepped over to where the blood had set on the wide sideboard, the place where Father Phil had probably been decapitated. He took a few photos from directly above, getting as much detail as he could: the pool of blood, the Bible, the floor below. It had all already been meticulously documented by the CSIs, but this was his methodology, and these gruesome snaps would find their way onto his murder wall. Unpleasant but important; thus far in his career, it had never failed him.

Sheen put his phone away, and with a grimace he touched the congealed liquid, cold and viscous on his white-gloved fingertips. Aoife was beside him, watching as Sheen moved his fingers over the wood, stopping when he found what he had been looking for. A score in the surface of the wood, running across from left to right.

'Looks like you were right. There's a groove cut into the wood here. I'd say it was a serrated blade by the feel of it,' he said, removing his fingers. Then he added, 'Sorry, Aoife, it was the only way.'

'Think we're done here,' said Aoife in response. 'But why not ask Hayley to have a go?'

Sheen felt his stomach muscles tighten as he choked down the urge to object. Instead, he nodded and said he'd text Geordie, ask him to swing round as soon as he had a chance.

Aoife navigated the steps back to the entrance and Sheen followed. A thrum from her phone; Aoife paused, extracted it from inside her suit.

'Father Macken. He says he is in the monastery, waiting for us,' she said.

Aoife had called and left a message for the young priest as they drove here. Although the monastery was not being used to celebrate Mass while the sacristy remained a crime scene, the main body of the building had already been cleared for the public to visit and pay respects. He turned off the halogen, returning the room to darkness, and followed Aoife out where they both got changed.

A few minutes later, Sheen and Aoife walked up the central aisle of the monastery, its baroque columns straddling their path, the vaulted roof suspended above their heads, its intricate mosaic work part-obscured in the shadows of the half-lit building. The lingering clove and cinnamon scent of burnt incense, the old smell of varnished wooden pews, and the newer, higher odour of fresh flowers. There had been bouquets and wreaths on the front steps, scribbled messages of loss and prayers on each, and an overflowing dam of them against the closed altar rail, which they now approached. A man in black stood up from the corner of the front pew. He turned around, tall and dark-haired, chocolate-brown eyes and strong jaw.

'Father Macken, thanks for agreeing to speak to us,' Aoife said, approaching and shaking his hand.

He held her palm in his and her gaze too. The young priest's strong face creased.

'It's nice to see you, Aoife.'

Aoife turned, introduced Sheen, who shook his hand, suggested they take a seat.

'That a Brummie accent I hear?' asked Sheen.

'Walsall,' corrected Father Macken. 'Cockney?' he enquired.

'I was born in the City Hospital here in Belfast, bit far to hear the Bow Bells, so definitely not. Grew up in Highbury, though,' he said. He read the genuine surprise in Father Macken's handsome face. 'Long story. Probably not for now,' he added.

'Father, DI Sheen is in charge of investigating Father Phil's murder. We're going to need to ask you a few questions,' Aoife said.

Father Macken nodded, agreement and understanding.

Sheen stepped in. 'How long had you known Father Phil Rafferty?'

'Five years. When I first started at Clonard.'

'Explain to me how this works. Is it like in the police where I see a vacancy in the PSNI advertised, I go for the job, get the position?' he postulated.

A little laugh from Father Macken, short and dry. 'Ah, no, it's more like the army than the police. I'm a Redemptorist.' Sheen shook his head, wanting him to explain. 'We are a missionary order, dedicated to labouring among the neglected and disadvantaged,' he said.

'So, you were sent here and so was Father Phil?' clarified Sheen.

Father Macken nodded. 'Could have been anywhere in the world. And once we join a community, we tend to stay there for life. Poverty, chastity, obedience, accessible sermons,' he explained.

'So, Father Phil had served here, for how long?'

'Nearly fifty years.'

Sheen nodded, ran his eyes over the swollen bank of flowers and wreaths along the altar rail, each one from a person or family that Father Phil had ministered to. He took a breath.

'Father Macken, in that time were there ever any allegations made against Father Phil?' he asked, looking the younger man in the face, gauging his reaction, not just his response.

Aoife spoke. 'Father Phil was a good man, a great man,' she cautioned, her hand on Sheen's arm.

Sheen let her but kept his eyes on Father Macken.

'Nothing. That's the truth. In this day and age things can't be buried and dismissed anyway. Rightly so,' he added softly, his brown eyes meeting Sheen's.

'Look at the flowers, Sheen. He was loved,' Aoife said. She got off the pew and moved to the wreaths, then started towards a small shrine on the right side of the church, where candles could be lit, prayers sent up, he assumed.

Sheen dropped this line, for now, asked Father Macken the standard set of questions: whether Father Phil had seemed distracted, mentioned anyone who was threatening him, whether there'd been anyone unusual hanging around the monastery or their dwelling. No, no, three times no. Sheen enquired about his alibi.

'I was at home. The lady who comes to clean was there that morning, she was able to corroborate that,' he added.

Sheen squinted into the shadows along the far wall to their left, adjacent to the altar rail.

'That door leads into the sacristy?' he enquired.

'It does.'

'You have CCTV in this place?'

Father Macken shifted in his seat, nodded up at the back of the monastery.

'Up there. We stream our Novena Masses worldwide. In fact, you're live online as we speak,' he said.

Sheen studied the angle of the camera; it was focused on the altar. Still, it was a win, maybe a breakthrough.

'Other cameras?' he asked.

'Just the one,' said Father Macken.

Sheen's heart sank, but just a tad. 'You have a backup of this?' he said.

'Think so, but only for a set period, then it re-records over itself,' said Father Macken.

Sheen took out his small black notepad, scribbled his email address, gave it to Father Macken.

'Gonna need that emailed to me, soon as,' he said.

Father Macken said he'd do it.

'Sheen!' It was Aoife. He jumped up and paced over to where she was standing in front of the shrine. Looming above them was a white marble statue of a saint, a cross held to his breast.

'Look at the candles,' she said. Sheen glanced down at the iron rows containing the small aluminium shells. Some were still half full of hard wax, others had burned out, and all were squashed and flattened.

'Red wax,' he said, the significance dawning on him.

'This was my candle,' said Aoife, pointing to an almost intact little red cup of wax. It looked like it had not burned for very long. 'I set it a few moments before Father Phil suggested that Hayley and I go into town,' she recalled.

'These have been flattened,' said Sheen.

He took a plastic bag from his pocket, picked up Aoife's candle and sealed it. They could have it tested, but chances were there'd be no DNA, though they might be able to confirm a match for fibres. He looked across the breadth of the church to the small door that led into the sacristy. If this was their killer, they might have him on camera if he'd walked straight across. Another ripple of exhilaration, but he kept it down. Best not raise hopes too soon.

Aoife was thinking in a different direction. 'He must have been hiding. In the monastery, I mean,' she said, turning to look at Sheen. He could see the anger in her eyes, but also something else, a look he knew all too well, the guilt. 'We probably walked right past him,' she said quietly.

'If that's the case, we'll have him on CCTV,' replied Sheen quickly, but though he'd said it with conviction, he did not feel the words. For a killer who'd managed not to leave a print or a hair, getting caught on camera would be sloppy indeed.

Aoife shook her head, walked off down the side aisle headed for the front door.

Sheen slipped his phone out, messaged Geordie to come if he could. And to bring Hayley White.

Sheen called over thanks to Father Macken, and then looked again at the squashed and lifeless candles, and at the cold stone eyes of the icon standing above him. If Aoife was correct, then she and Hayley White were the last people before the killer to see Father Phil Rafferty alive. He turned and walked back through the monastery, breathing in its age. Father Phil had served here for nearly half a century. Fifty years was a lot of history, much of it horrifically violent. And Father Phil Rafferty, for all the good he'd supposedly done, had made an enemy of someone.

CHAPTER TWENTY-FIVE

'This is Crazy Horse's ma's street,' said Geordie. He was speaking in a half-whisper, which was unnecessary given they were the only people sitting in a parked car with the windows up.

Hayley considered his words for a moment. 'Mad Mare?'

Geordie's eyes were on the road; he clearly wasn't listening.

They were parked on a street in Rathcoole, a giant housing estate on the outskirts of north Belfast. It was built in the 1950s to house those displaced from inner city slum clearances in Belfast, and it was, at one time, the largest housing development of its kind in Western Europe. Most of the homes they had passed were white-rendered, or red-bricked terrace with paved front gardens and, inexplicably, solar panels on rooftops. All was presided over by twin blocks of flats; at least twenty floors apiece, that stood sentinel at the entrance of the estate. Hayley knew this place was almost one hundred per cent Protestant, though in the early days of the Troubles it had been mixed. But soon communities had become utterly polarised, and inhabited separate ghettos on opposite sides of the city, though their homes and streets were government-built carbon copies. Some things would just never make sense to her.

'Right, I'm going to have a word. No need for you—'

'I'll stay here. I know the drill,' she finished for him.

Geordie got out. She watched him saunter along the road, and then he crossed over, out of sight. Hayley checked her phone. No messages. She started to scroll through photographs people had posted on a social media site, feeling her brain grow numb. Hayley closed her eyes, and then pocketed her phone.

A weight thumped against the side of the car; the driver's door opened. Hayley flinched.

'Sorry.'

It was Geordie, back again. He bundled in, started the motor and hastily screeched the car in a tight three-point turn, wheezing lightly. He burned off, eyes moving back and forth from road to mirror. They reached the twin towers and exited the estate.

'Change of plan?' asked Hayley.

Geordie nodded his head, face grim. 'House's being watched,' he replied.

Hayley tried to recall the cast of characters outlined by Beano earlier. 'Dissidents?'

Geordie sneered. 'Those clowns haven't a clue,' he said. 'Worse. Special Branch. Least that's who he used to be with,' he said.

'Who?'

'The guy who's parked across the street from our man's mother's abode. Fella by the name of Thompson. *Bad* egg,' he explained. Geordie was flustered, but Hayley also sensed something else. The guy was shaken.

'What's this mean? For Aoife?' she asked.

A shrug from Geordie, who still checked his rear view like he had developed a tic.

'For Crazy Horse it means he's golden; he won't be the next scum bag who gets whacked in this turf war,' said Geordie. 'Not while that boy Thompson has his back.'

'Crazy Horse's an informer?'

'Looks that way.'

Based on what Hayley had pieced together from the surreal exchange with Beano, Crazy Horse had ripped off the drugs that were found in Aoife's locker from republican Dissidents and had set his boss up to take a bullet for it.

'So, you think Special Branch know what Crazy Horse has done?' asked Hayley.

Geordie nodded, and then a message alert sounded from his phone which he found in his pocket. He read it while driving. 'That's Sheen. He wants us both down at Clonard, the crime scene,' explained Geordie. They'd put some distance between themselves and Rathcoole. As they cruised along the Shore Road, the docks and Titanic Quarter approached on their left. He scrubbed off some speed and returned to the topic of Crazy Horse.

'The Branch must know that Crazy Horse stole the powder. What either of them might know about it ending up in Aoife's locker, no idea. But there's no way we can start asking Crazy Horse those kind of questions' – Geordie cocked his thumb over his left shoulder as though the man was seated behind them – 'with Thompson watching him. We need to find another way,' he said.

'What do you know about this guy Thompson?' she asked.

'Shady bastard and trigger-happy too. Took a lot of scalps and quite a few of them personally,' he said. Hayley assumed he meant he'd killed people. 'Shoot first and shoot to kill,' confirmed Geordie.

'Did he see you?'

Geordie shook his head emphatically. 'Definitely not.'

'Can I ask you a question?'

Geordie glanced her way, half a frown, but nodded.

'How come Internal Investigations looked into you?'

Aoife had told Hayley that Geordie had been drummed out, lost a portion of his pension because of it. He'd made his disdain for Internal Investigations clear back at Sheen's apartment.

'On the face of it they had me for boozing on the job,' he said.

Hayley thought about the large breakfast whisky he'd shared with Beano, didn't ask if it was true.

230

'But that was an excuse. Boozing was standard, especially with my generation of peeler. It was really because I'd put Special Branch's nose out of joint,' he said.

'This guy Thompson?'

'Amongst others. They were running touts, guys who were literally getting away with blue murder. I wouldn't stand for it,' he said.

Hayley thought about Geordie's permissive attitude to Beano's disgusting cut-and-paste business, his acceptance of his prostitution of women. And yet, the same man had clearly fallen hard on the sword of his own principles.

'So, they complained?'

Geordie laughed. 'They were pissed off, if that's what you mean. All very polite and nicey-nicey to start off with. As soon as I told them they could go and fuck themselves, things changed. Got to a point where I'd be doing my garden and dodgy boys would creep past in a car, scoping out my home.'

'You mean they gave your address to terrorists?'

Geordie said he suspected it. 'And if some Provo had ventilated me in my front garden, I'd have had a hero's funeral, my name on the plaque in Ladas Drive and someone would have got a full pension. Boys like Thompson would never have been fingered for it,' he said.

'So, what happened?'

'In the end the internal investigation was launched by my own DCI, and he was a good guy. Did it to protect me, get me offside because he knew I'd never back down,' said Geordie.

Hayley took a moment to drink this in. She could see why Geordie wanted to steer clear of Special Branch and Crazy Horse, if he was a protected informer. He'd learnt the hard way how dangerous it could be to get in their way, but Geordie had stuck to his principles. His ideals were a bit bent out of shape, but she could see why Owen Sheen had asked him to be part of his team.

'So, mind if I ask you a question?' said Geordie.

Now it was Hayley's turn to shrug.

'What's the deal here? All this,' said Geordie, waving in her general direction.

'You mean why am I dressed like a woman?'

'Aye.'

'Because I am a woman, Geordie.'

'Since when?'

'Since always. Ever remember being at school, when you're a little kid, and thinking I don't belong in this uniform, I'm not interested in the toys they give me, I'm not a boy like the rest of these children, I am a girl, I want to have a baby some day?'

'No.'

'I do. From the very start, from as early as I can remember,' she said.

Geordie didn't reply, but she braced herself for a quip, a dismissal, or nothing at all.

'That must have been tough for you,' he said.

'Yes, Geordie, it was. And it still is,' she replied.

They'd descended into the underpass of the Westlink; Geordie indicated for the Falls Road exit. Clonard

Monastery was not far away. Hayley's stomach dipped.

'Your family OK with it?'

Hayley had spent half a lifetime hiding herself behind the male persona she'd been socialised to accept. Only since returning from England did she begin to be herself.

'Parents are dead; they never knew. I have a sister and a brother. Her I see, but he wants nothing to do with me.'

'That's a pity. You have a day job?'

'Supply teacher.'

'Fuck me, you have some balls, I'll give you that!' exclaimed Geordie. He glanced at her, his expression the purest form of a man with his foot in his mouth.

Hayley could only laugh. After a moment's hesitation he joined her.

'You have family, Geordie?'

'The ex-wife's in Spain. I don't get an invite. My son's a copper in Glasgow, see him sometimes. Daughter works for a bank in Hong Kong. She did well,' he said.

'Siblings?'

Geordie fell quiet. 'I have a brother somewhere, no idea where. Things were up and down when I was a child. Spent time in and out of care homes. Like Tara Boys' Home,' he said grimly.

'Heard of it. That must have been difficult,' said Hayley quietly.

'Don't talk to me. If I never wear another pair of ugly brogues my whole life it'll be too soon,' he said, laughing gruffly, but Hayley didn't detect any honest cheer. Geordie fell silent for a few seconds, and then said, 'And that wasn't the worst of it. But it was the making of me,' he said.

Geordie pulled into Clonard Monastery. Aoife was on the steps waiting, raised a hand. Seconds later Sheen emerged. Geordie parked, turned to her.

'World's a hard place. You have to find your own way,' he said, and extended his hand.

Hayley thought of Beano's prostitutes and Geordie's stand against those who let killers walk. She gave Geordie's hand a firm shake, feeling certain that some kind of deal had just been made.

CHAPTER TWENTY-SIX

Oswald Smith was standing, very appropriately, with his back to the wall in a basement corridor of Palace Barracks, Holywood, about five miles north-east of Belfast. This was the official HQ of MI5 in Northern Ireland. He could smell the underground car park that opened at the end of the passage to his right, engine oil and rubber. Glass doors led inside to his left, but they were hidden from view, like him, behind a sharp corner. His office was upstairs, but this was where Oswald needed to be. He knew this nook was a CCTV blind spot, a place where he could stand and think and not be watched. He rested his head against the grey concrete of the wall, cold and harsh against his prematurely bald crown. His zinc eyes did not flinch; he let his skin taste the texture, and his thoughts run the sequences that needed to be considered.

Last July, Cecil Moore, the one-time UDA godfather and full-time drug lord, had told Oswald, an MI5 handler, to jump, and Oswald could do nothing but ask how high. Moore's measurements had amounted to the death of an informer in PSNI custody that had been passed off as suicide (not as difficult as one might imagine), and the depositing of a quantity of Class A drugs in the work locker of DC Aoife McCusker (much more complex, but something Oswald had managed to orchestrate with virtually no turnaround time). Since then, Oswald had watched and waited for any sign that what he had done in July might return to haunt him.

Until now, nothing. Cecil Moore was dead. With him gone, the hold he'd had over Oswald had appeared to have been neutralised. Oswald had been naive: thought himself the spider when he'd first arrived in Northern Ireland; agile, devious, still. But all the while that he was enlisting Moore and his cronies as informers and assets, Moore had been taking the measure of Oswald, determining his weaknesses and weaving a web too sticky and intricate for any prey to escape. And that was what he had swiftly become. He had, in fact, been groomed, to give it its proper title. This time he permitted a thin smile, fleeting and bitter. But now he was the spider and beholden to Moore no longer.

But there were loose threads. Thus his vigilance, because once snared, twice shy.

Threads: like the fact that when Oswald went searching for information on the phone of a very dead Cecil Moore in the PSNI's evidence lock-up, he'd found that the SIM card was missing, and nothing of interest on the device.

Threads: the fact that the crime report had stated that the same phone was discovered on the person of an injured and unconscious Aoife McCusker, the very woman Moore had tasked him to damage with the drugs, just another delicate insect that had wandered into Moore's snare. Or perhaps she was not so delicate? After all, Moore was dead, McCusker was still alive. Had McCusker managed to secrete the SIM from the phone? Had she watched what Moore had stored on it? Did she still have it? Oswald had visited her in her sparse hospital room, searched it high and low and found nothing. Same went for her bloodied and scorched clothing in the evidence lock-up. No SIM, no videos, as though it had simply vanished.

Threads: someone else had recorded that footage for Moore. It was a professional job, the sort of quality he'd seen at play from the security service, in fact. If someone else recorded it, then someone else had watched it, and someone else knew of its existence.

Threads: like the fact that DI Owen Sheen from the Metropolitan Police was still in Northern Ireland despite the false start of the Serious Historical Offences Team. A man who had been seen at the same crime scene last July from which Cecil Moore's SIM went missing and the man who had visited Aoife McCusker's hospital bed as she recuperated. And now, Oswald had recently confirmed, Sheen had been ushered through the back door to join Paddy Laverty in Serious Crimes and was ghost-piloting a murder investigation with none other than Geordie Brown, a one-man wrecking ball brought out of alcoholism to protect and serve.

Until now, these threads were just that; loose ends, and unfinished business to be tied up one by one when the time was right.

Thompson's phone call had changed everything. A tripwire had been triggered.

Thompson had spotted Geordie Brown sniffing round the door of his latest asset, the so-called Crazy Horse, a rising star in the UDA. Could mean absolutely nothing, but Geordie Brown connected to Sheen, who connected to McCusker. And it was Crazy Horse who had provided Oswald with the drugs placed in McCusker's locker. It had all worked out splendidly, until now. But if Geordie Brown got to Crazy Horse, and Crazy Horse talked, then thread upon thread, it all led back to Oswald.

He tapped the access code into the glass face of his phone and opened a message to Thompson. Two emoji icons, no words; Thompson would know exactly what he meant. The first was an open, unblinking eye. Next, a pair of footprints. Watch them, follow them. He wanted eyes on Geordie Brown. Which also meant leaving Crazy Horse unwatched, and unguarded. Next, he swapped phones; this time used a burner he would destroy. This message was for a Dissident republican who lived in the ghetto of Ardoyne in north Belfast. He typed in the address of Crazy Horse's mother in Rathcoole followed by the thumb down emoji and the line of 'Z's indicating sleep. But this was a sleep from which Crazy Horse would never awaken.

He pressed send, closed his screen, and took a big breath of the flat underground air. That would be enough, for now. There were other options, but eliminating Crazy Horse should act as a fire break. Thompson would keep him informed and could be relied on to keep his mouth shut. He was one of those who had 'moved down the road' as the saying went. A former member of the old RUC Special Branch discreetly enlisted in the service of MI5 after the creation of the PSNI. Men like Thompson would never make the grade if they walked into Whitehall and tried to pass recruitment; the psychometrics alone would have him flagged as dangerous. But this was not the mainland, and as was the way of it, in Belfast things were done differently.

Oswald pushed his back off the wall, turned left towards the entrance of the barracks, his face a mask of confident calm. He would watch Geordie Brown with interest, and if he put his drinker's nose where it didn't belong, it would be a big thumbs down and lights out for the old thief-taker.

He'd sleep with the dead, and not just him, the woman who was apparently tagging along with him too.

CHAPTER TWENTY-SEVEN

Sheen and Geordie had distracted the uniformed officer who was guarding the Clonard crime scene. When his back was turned, Aoife ushered Hayley through the tented entrance, and swiftly got her suited and booted. Neither of them signed the visitor log.

Aoife stood back on the first of the plastic stepping plates and let Hayley step gingerly into the shadowy sacristy.

'I can switch on the halogens if it helps.'

Hayley didn't respond at first, but then shook her head, slowly, and raised a hand, her back now to Aoife. Aoife stayed quiet. After a few seconds Hayley spoke, but her voice was distant, dreamy.

'No, it's OK. What I'm trying to see isn't under the spotlights.'

Aoife waited. Hayley stood still. It was impossible to tell from her vantage point whether Hayley's eyes were open or closed. A shiver ran up and down Aoife's arms, studding her flesh hard enough to rasp against the paper suit. The darkness in here seemed pervasive; her eyes had barely adjusted to the gloom. In these shadows, the evil of the act seemed to find a dark companionship. Aoife wanted to speak, and truth be told she wanted to run away from this horrible desecration. Hayley remained still and silent. Aoife watched as she waved an arm gently through the air in front of her, as though to dispel a smoke that only she could see. Then she spoke. Still facing away, her tone that same dreamy drawl that suggested her words were as much for herself as Aoife.

'The person that did this had a great strength. Not natural. It was . . .' She trailed off and lapsed into a short silence. Aoife was about to speak when a long minute had ticked by, but then came Hayley's voice again, making her flinch. 'A *hollow* strength, there's emptiness in the core,' she finished.

Hayley moved from her vantage point in the middle of the room for the first time, made her way over to the high-backed wooden chair where Aoife had discovered Father Phil's humiliated body.

Aoife's heart had skipped up a notch. The strength was something Sheen and she had surmised, but they'd had the full facts at their disposal and the crime scene photos. Hayley hadn't.

Hayley was close to the chair now and lowered a gloved hand to the wood, and then turned to Aoife for the first time, her wide eyes darting a question: *Can I touch this?* Aoife nodded twice and watched as Hayley rested her hand over the wood for a minute or more, her head cocked to the right, as though listening for something. She flexed her fingers and then slowly pressed her palm against the carved wood, where Father Phil's severed head had been lodged.

It would be cold, sticky-wet to the touch.

'Ah,' a gasp from Hayley, who now took her hand away. In the half-light Aoife could see the palm of her white glove was dark.

'What is it?' asked Aoife, unable to stop herself.

Hayley turned and her eyes were wide, wet glass in the gloom of the room.

'It's cold. Like there's nothing left. Just the cold and dark,' she replied.

Aoife understood she wasn't talking about the texture of the wooden chair. Aoife was about to interject when Hayley spoke again, her voice quavering ever so slightly. What she said next wasn't exactly revelatory; the carnage that had been wreaked on Father Phil spoke volumes for the anger, the hatred that must have inspired the act. Still, Hayley's words stayed in the air of the sealed, blood-thick sacristy.

'Nothing but vengeance, just hollow, awful vengeance. And this isn't over. Can we get out of here, please?'

Aoife led them out and they changed. Aoife nodded to Sheen. He eyed their exit over the shoulder of the uniformed officer, who was still listening raptly to Geordie, doing a fair job as a stand-up comedian. She gulped the fresh air, thankful for the sane world beyond the thick stone walls that had held them like a tomb.

CHAPTER TWENTY-EIGHT

As Sheen buzzed the intercom at the gate of the Sterrits' home on Newforge Lane in the expensive south side of Belfast, Aoife scanned the sloping lip of drive that led on to the road. This was where Rhonda's body had been. There was no sign of any blood, or of anything at all to suggest that such a gruesome thing had happened so recently. Over the decades, so much blood had spattered the streets of Belfast, all now washed away, and forgotten by many. But there would always be those, the ones who had been left behind to count the cost, for which the stain and the pain would never really go.

What Hayley had to say about the Clonard crime scene was intriguing but largely useless, though he didn't say this to Aoife, who sang her praises all the way here. Geordie's news about the drugs that had turned up in Aoife's locker was more helpful, though worrying. He'd suggested they had originated from the Dissidents in north Belfast, most likely via someone in the UDA in Rathcoole. Someone Geordie was certain was being protected by Special Branch. He had not admitted it, but Sheen could tell that this discovery had rattled Geordie, who said he was going to work on another angle. When he'd mentioned Dissident republicans, Sheen had again thought of that ghost Oswald, and the UDA took things way too close to Paddy Laverty's remit at present to leave Sheen comfortable. He'd told Geordie to his keep ear to the ground and keep him informed.

Sheen pressed the buzzer again. Hocus-pocus was good at selling books and films, but when it came to real police work, nothing trumped knocking, or buzzing, on doors.

A woman's voice crackled through the small speaker. Sheen identified himself and held up his warrant card to the small, black eye of the intercom's surveillance camera. The chunky metal gate started to retract along a runner. A woman, probably in her late forties, waited at the open front door. She was without make-up, a caramel-brown dressing robe draped thickly over her shoulders, covering her like a blanket. Her face had the strong structure of a natural beauty, but Aoife suspected that she had aged years in the last days, and her eyes were weary.

Sheen proffered his warrant card once again, but it was given barely a glance.

'Mrs Sterrit?'

She nodded, closed-mouthed. 'Call me Rachel. Thought the other detective was in charge of Rhonda's case? The young man,' she said in reply.

'Not any more,' said Sheen, and she nodded again, this time with a little more conviction than before. She offered Sheen her hand and he shook it.

'Aoife McCusker,' said Aoife, following Sheen's lead.

They were still on the doorstep. Rachel Sterrit pulled the dressing gown closer to her body. Her eyes settled on the gate.

'Rachel, we are going to have to come in, if that's OK? We need to have a word with you and your husband,' Sheen said.

She blinked, opened the door, and invited them both in.

Gordon Sterrit was at the big kitchen table. He was older than his wife, by at least twenty years. His pinstriped suit trousers were crumpled, and there was a couple of days' white growth on his cheeks. A half-empty bottle of blended Scotch whisky stood by his elbow. He stared at them with red-veined eyes as his wife ushered them in and made introductions. Rachel Sterrit wandered away, and moments later Aoife heard the soft plink of piano keys from the adjacent lounge.

'We are sorry for your loss, Mr Sterrit,' said Sheen.

Sterrit scoffed, unscrewed the metal cap of the Scotch and splashed a big serving into a crystal tumbler.

'Are you? You don't look too sssorry,' he slurred. He took a large mouthful of whisky and downed it, teeth clasped, a man taking his medicine, strong but necessary. 'Sorry, sorry, sorry. Big deal,' he continued.

The man was plastered. To Aoife, it looked like he

was just refilling from the night, and maybe days before, not starting afresh this afternoon.

'I'm in charge of investigating Rhonda's murder,' said Sheen, his voice firm. He pulled out a heavy wooden chair with a scrape and sat next to Gordon Sterrit. Sheen took out his black notepad, and then put his hand on the bottle of Scotch, made space between them.

Gordon Sterrit lunged for the bottle, tugged it away from Sheen and started to refill.

'I'll answer your questions. Sure, already answered your questions,' he said.

Sheen started to speak, walked Sterrit through the details of how he had uncovered his daughter's body. His answers were slow and slurring, and emotionless. In the few minutes that Aoife stood there, she heard nothing new and little detail from Gordon Sterrit that was not already documented in the case file she'd scanned as they drove here from Clonard. Then again, this man was a barrister, top of his game. Well used to selecting his words with precision and care, maybe if he was shit-faced or sober.

Sheen glanced over at her. She nodded, understanding. Aoife backed slowly from the room and approached Rachel Sterrit, who was still discordantly playing single notes on the piano. For the first time, Aoife now pondered whether Gordon Sterrit wasn't the only one who was self-medicating the grief and shock of their daughter's death. She gently placed a hand on Rachel Sterrit's arm. The music stopped, the last key ringing a lonely D in the big room.

'What age were you when Rhonda was born?' asked Aoife.

Rachel turned to her, the question, as Aoife had hoped, managing to prick the bubble she was in.

'I was thirty-seven' she said without hesitation, the response followed by the briefest of smiles, which melted away as instantly as a snowflake on an iron griddle. Rachel's eyes filled up. Another smile traced its way over her mouth, this one bitter and rueful. 'I thought I might never have a child,' she said.

Aoife nodded, feeling the woman's pain but reluctant to stop now that she was talking. Unlike her husband, she was, at least, making sense.

'Your husband, he's a lot older than you?'

'Twenty-one years,' she confirmed. 'I met Gordon at the Central Masonic Lodge in Belfast. I was married before, you see; our paths crossed on a wives' evening. My first husband was a police officer, RUC,' she said. No smile this time, another bad memory.

'Was he killed, on duty?' chanced Aoife.

Now Rachel Sterrit did smile, one that fell far short of reaching her eyes, and emitted a rasping laugh. 'No such luck. He was carrying on with a young thing from his job. Took himself, his low sperm count and her skinny arse off to New Zealand,' said Rachel. 'Looking back, the Lodge pretty much arranged my marriage to Gordon. He'd managed to remain single. But they pride themselves on looking after their own. I don't have any regrets. Didn't, I should say,' she added.

Aoife did the mental maths. Gordon Sterrit married Rachel when he was in his fifties, earliest. Meaning he'd spent a lifetime as a bachelor up until that point.

'Rachel, in that time, did Gordon or you make any enemies, anyone who you think might hold a grudge?'

A second's hesitation, just a flicker, and then it was gone.

'Gordon's a lawyer. He makes enemies every day he goes to work. It's his job,' she said.

Aoife said she understood but pushed for specifics. For the first time, Aoife detected a touch of steel in Rachel Sterrit's response.

'I answered these questions already, for the other detective. No. I can't understand why someone hates us so much,' she said. Her voice cracked now, and tears came, fast and flowing.

Aoife handed her a tissue. 'Mr Sterrit's taking this hard too,' she offered.

'Gordon never touched a drop of drink all the time I've known him. It was something that mattered to me after your man I was hitched to,' she explained, wiping her nose.

'Has he said anything, anything at all that might be important?' pushed Aoife.

Rachel sniffed and raised her brows. She exhaled, held Aoife with the same defeated look she'd seen at the front door.

'He sat at that table all night. He was ranting and raving before he fell asleep. Shouting about the sins of the fathers,' she said, then paused, looked up and started to quote. '"Prepare a place of slaughter because of the iniquity of their fathers." It's from the book of Isaiah. Looked it up on Google before I fell asleep,' she said.

Aoife made a mental note.

Rachel moved, started to walk back towards the kitchen. Aoife followed, saw Sheen raise himself from the table and give her a brief nod as he replaced his notepad in his jacket. Said it all: speaking to Gordon Sterrit had been a waste of time. Rachel Sterrit had not given much, but as was so often the case it had been worth speaking to the woman in person, sometimes as much for what wasn't said. Gordon Sterrit was stony-eyed, his face set, staring at the wooden tabletop.

'Mr Sterrit, Rachel, thank you for your time. As we make progress you'll be the first to know,' Sheen said, walking out of the kitchen, headed for the grand front door.

Aoife remained. 'Mr Sterrit, one last thing,' she said. He looked up laboriously. 'Did Rhonda have anything in her hand, when you found her outside at the front gate?'

Sheen was back by her side, and watched for Sterrit's reaction, just as she did. Gordon Sterrit's eyes widened, his lips fish-mouthed, and then his features went into lawyer lockdown. Too late, his drunken tell had escaped and made his denials hollow and flimsy.

'No, no. She wasn't holding anything,' he said. His words, for the first time since they had arrived, were clearly enunciated and sounded well thought through.

Her question had sobered him, albeit temporarily. Sterrit reached for the bottle and started to pour once more, a larger knock than his last.

'Thank you, sir, and you, Rachel,' said Aoife, making her way out the front door. It was closed immediately.

Sheen was by her side as they waited for the gate to slide open.

'He's lying,' he said.

'Through his teeth,' agreed Aoife.

Sheen's phone rang. 'Fahey,' answered Sheen, and then paused, took out his notebook and scribbled. 'Cheers mate, yeah, send me a message too,' he said and ended the call.

Aoife recognised his name: Sheen's journalist contact. 'Got something?' she asked.

'Looks like Gordon Sterrit fell out with a former colleague, man called Williamson Golding. Sterrit was his mentor. Apparently he makes his living prosecuting police malpractice,' said Sheen. He opened a new message on his phone, Fahey presumably. Sheen scanned the message. 'At one point they were tight; same Masonic Lodge, part of the Black Preceptory. Whatever that is,' he continued.

'Sort of a posh Orange Order,' clarified Aoife.

'And most interestingly, Golding was a former special forces soldier, SAS.' Sheen said that McHenry told him one of his troop was still in Belfast, and that he'd be easy to find.

'One of the guys involved in the border black ops?' she asked.

Sheen said it looked likely.

'Want to go back and grill Sterrit about this?'

'Waste of time. But I want a word with the mysterious Williamson Golding,' he replied.

CHAPTER TWENTY-NINE

Simon Nixon parked in his pastor's space outside his whitewashed stone Baptist Church on the outskirts of Moira, well into the open countryside south-west of Belfast city. He switched off the headlights and popped his belt. Before he had a chance to change his mind he opened the driver's door and hefted first one leg, and then the other out of the footwell.

He uttered a stifled little gasp, beads of sweat on his high forehead. His knees: they screamed in complaint. Tendons of rusted wire coated in acid. Simon gulped in the cool dusk air, tasting the ever-present warmth of fresh manure. He was forty-two years old, but for his knees and clattering 2002 Mercedes estate alike, it wasn't about the date of production, it was about miles on the clock. Rugby throughout preparatory and boarding schools, same at Queen's University where he'd added mountain hiking and a couple of charity marathon runs for good measure. By the time he was in his mid twenties, Simon was popping pills every time the weather changed from dry to damp. When he was working as a pastor in Uganda in his thirties, he'd needed to roll out of the small camp bed he'd slept in each night and work his legs like the Tin Man from *The Wizard of Oz*, but once oiled, he'd be good to go. But that was then, and this was now, and Simon was rusted solid.

He'd been on his feet and moving most of the day, and that was good. But on the journey back he'd got lodged behind a tractor pulling a full load of black-plastic-wrapped silage. Simon supposed he could have overtaken, but he didn't trust the old coffin he was driving in to spit out the necessary power when he put his foot down. And, if truth be told, he didn't trust his knees to punch the clutch and accelerator as instructed to overtake safely. When at last the tractor had turned off into an unmarked laneway ten or so miles from his home, he was given a lesson in how to overtake aggressively from twenty or more blaring, anger-contorted drivers.

He'd also learnt that at least one, perhaps a tourist or someone of Italian descent, understood the sign for the cuckold.

Simon dug his heels into the thick blanket of loose stone and moaned as he straightened his legs. The toothache-like throb eased exquisitely, and he uttered an involuntary little laugh. But then his headache spoke up, filled the void his knee pain had left. The doctor had told him no more anti-inflammatory pills. His stomach couldn't take it, and yet his eyes moved to the closed glove compartment where a pristine foil-backed sheet of the fat 400 mg pills lay like the Promised Land. He'd started to drink turmeric and black pepper tea, filthy stuff but incrementally it had done some good. But when one needed instant salvation, pass the pinks. He closed his eyes, breathed in the free and good country air. Christ Jesus on his cross bore the sins of mankind. *God give me the strength to carry this gift and see the good in all things.* Simon raised himself up on the wing of his prayer and found, as always with a prayer (and when he'd straightened his long legs), the pain wasn't so awful after all. But his head was still hammering. A nice cup of tea and a slice of toast would come to the rescue.

He glanced up the hill, saw his yellow porch light, though from up there one could not see him, or the little church. Denise was home and very soon he would be too, in his recliner, and scribbling whatever poem or homily on life that came to him for his blog and Twitter feed. But first he needed his pad and fountain pen, which he'd left absently on the lectern in the church. He slammed his car door closed, scrunched tentatively across the gravel, found his legs amenable. He paused, squinted into the murk to the far corner of the grounds, which served as a car park when his parish congregated. There, masked in the deep shadows of the overhanging oak, a car. It was small and painted dark and almost as beat-up as his. It hadn't been there this morning when he left. In the past, he'd had some trouble. Couples had used the car park at night. Simon peered at the car, attentive for any sign of life (or any movement, perhaps the vehicle rocking on its springs, for example), but all was silent and still this night.

A double hoot from an owl blinked in and out of existence, made him jump. He followed the sound with his eyes, and then traced a slow, scanning look along the perimeter of the grounds, seeing only soft shadow, the greens and purples and blacks of day's end. His eyes returned to the parked car. An absurd thought entered his mind: *It's watching me.*

Ridiculous, and yet Simon stood his ground, as one did when a wild dog strayed close to the campfire in Uganda, its eyes gleaming like burning glass, when the animal in a man stared back. It was empty, abandoned. Perhaps it had broken down and had been parked in what was deemed a safe place? That was the reasonable explanation. Come now, let us reason together, says the Lord.

Simon raised a hand to his forehead, once more demanding his attention, and turned from the car. He'd report it to the police first thing in the morning if it had not moved on. He plucked the long iron key from his parka coat pocket; it was still warm to the touch. It found easy purchase and turned smoothly in the big timber door. Familiar scents of old wood, polish and paper greeted him as he entered. His was a church of the Bible and pulpit, no incense, no mystic candles, no blessed water. For Simon, there was only the Holy Book and the Gospels, like his father before him. Though unlike his daddy, Simon preferred to minister in the sticks, away from Belfast and the glare of public attention. And for Simon, unlike his father, politics and religion were separate things. He loved both God and Ulster, but they never met or merged from his pulpit.

But then again, judge not lest ye be judged. Daddy lived through dark days, a time when the people of Ulster were wandering in a wilderness and when the rifles of the IRA were being used to spill Protestant blood. Thank God it was all over; now may the Lord of peace himself give you peace at all times, in every way.

Simon traced his steps to the pulpit with a practised ease, navigating the darkness as though in light. He pawed the hollow cavity under the pulpit, found what he needed, careful not to let his fountain pen slide off; it would be harder to find it if it rolled off along the—

A sound, coming from the open doorway; a shuffle, or sifting, of feet on stone, causing Simon to spin, shoulders half-hunched.

'Who's there?' he commanded.

His rich voice filled the cave-like interior of the stone church, as it had done on so many Sunday services. But he'd never pronounced the Word with this edge of alarm and urgency.

This was his church. It was a house of God.

'I warn you that this church is protected by CCTV. Your movements are being monitored by Securitel as we speak,' he said. Not true. The only watchful eyes on this old psalm hall were those of the Lord.

Simon's eyes settled on a dark well of shadow to the left of the door, where there were tall stacks of wooden chairs. The distance from there to the open doorway was about half the gap that he needed to cover to get back to the exit. He edged tentatively up the main aisle of the church, could hear his own breathing, enormous in the silence. And yes, he could feel a watchful pair of eyes on him, as surely as he'd felt the Spirit of the Lord course through him when he'd preached, hands on his pulpit. There was another presence in this room with him. It was in the shadows and that was where it belonged.

It was not the Lord his God.

'Everyone who does evil hates the light and will not come into the light for fear that their deeds will be exposed!' he roared.

Simon inched closer to the door. His heart was booming, hands slick.

A scratch and rustle, from the open mouth of the front entrance. Simon gasped, dropped his writing pad. He waited; face frozen, eyes wide, rooted to the smooth stone under foot. Another flurry of wind, and this time he saw the scratching gyre of dry leaves as it pirouetted in the doorway, and settled once more, dropped by the breeze. Simon Nixon exhaled a chortle of pure relief, trailing off into a self-chastising scoff. His reflections tonight would be something about the nature of evil and fear. But he'd also take a dose of painkillers and soon after, go to bed. Simon bent and scooped up his pad; his knees crunched and he groaned, at once full of worldly concerns once more.

'I wish my great pain could be weighed,' he muttered. Job, 6:2–4 Perhaps he could include something about pain in the emerging reflection?

An explosion of noise instantly filled the silent chamber, the ear-rending smash of wood on wood, coming from behind him. Simon's pad hit the deck once more as he spun to meet the cataclysm of sound. His frantic eyes scanned the darkness, and, better adjusted now, he could make out the toppled steeple of wooden chairs scattered across the pews and reaching to the foot of the lectern at the head of the church. On instinct, he flashed his head back in the direction they'd come from, where the remaining stacks of chairs still stood.

Simon surveyed the wreckage once more, heart bellowing for him to move and run and not stop until he was out the door and up the hill and home. But the pastor of the church stood his ground, shirt clinging to his sweaty torso. A speedy tally confirmed what he already knew. There were a dozen pine chairs in each stack, tall as him. Desmond, their handyman, had parked them in place using a flat-based steel trolley and even then Desmond had grunted and perspired when it came to edging the stacks in place using his body weight. And Desmond was young and farmhand-strong.

Someone (or something) had toppled the substantial stack like he would have been able to scatter matches across a kitchen table.

Simon's decision-making brain turned the sign on the door to CLOSED at that particular revelation, but it at least had the presence of mind to tell his right thumb to flick the lid off his fountain pen and to hold it like the sword he now wished he had. Then his amygdala lit up and his body flushed with enough noradrenaline to make him run like a pacesetter in the Belfast Marathon, knee pain be damned. He made it to the doorway, not taking his eyes from the vacant corner where the chairs stood sentinel. Movement from the open door snapped his attention, but too late.

A figure all in black rushed to meet him, filling the frame as he struggled in slow motion to reach the exit first. It had been crouching down in the shadows on the threshold, like a condensed ball of darkness, waiting for him. Simon uttered a dry, stifled shriek as it raised its arms. Black wings of cloth blotted out the muted light of the almost complete dusk beyond.

He had time to think: *It's a demon.*

And then it rushed at him, emitting an awful, high-toned screech. He tasted the stale foulness of its odour, realised he'd stopped dead, and before he had a chance to sprint off again, it slammed into him, feverish and ghastly and sharp-boned. Simon, already off balance, was shoved and sent sprawling towards the pews and scattered chairs, had a second to pray this was a dream. But the thing kept coming, its claws clamped on him, accelerating him with a running shove that sent him careering out of control. He flipped over the unforgiving back-beam of a pew head first, barely avoided smashing his skull, and cartwheeled into the next row. His left knee, always the better of the two, connected with the mahogany armrest and Simon had just a nanosecond to register the high cracking sound of his kneecap splitting before his eyes filled with white light, and the twin blasts of pain from shoulder and knee filled his universe. The light dissipated to a faint purple glow from the still-open church doorway. He was on his side, in the central aisle. Both hands cupped his broken kneecap, the lead instrument in a symphony of pain.

The dark thing that had sent him tumbling approached. Its black veil billowed from its form like burnt rubber, and Simon watched, able only to gasp for air. Closer now he saw its spindle-thin legs, moving in an awful fast-forward precision, like a spider surging towards its quarry. It leant into him; he felt its heat, tasted its foul and stale air. Prying fingers found his wallet. Seconds later it fell to the floor with a heavy splat next to his head.

'Nixon.' His name, whispered and awful. This was the sound of judgement.

Simon groaned, could see the texture of the limestone paving by his face, and the heat of the thing close above him once more. A faraway stab spoke up from his buttock, and then the almost instantaneous flood of warm relief pulsated from his core, blossoming out. Hot, acrid breath on his face, but he didn't mind, nothing mattered.

'No more pain,' it said, and that was true.

He was lifted once more, but this time like a babe in arms. Though he sensed his knee swinging limply against the joint and could hear the scratch of bone on bone from his ruptured collar, there was no more pain. He strained to call to mind a verse, a fitting word from the Holy Book, but as he was carried out of his church, Simon closed his eyes and the numbing darkness swallowed him, like a whale.

CHAPTER THIRTY

Belfast, Northern Ireland
Friday 21st December

The law offices of Williamson Golding were located near the redeveloped Belfast dockside in what looked to Sheen to be a converted granary store. Glass-fronted and transparent, he could see through the clear walls all the way to the other side, and the open breadth of the river beyond. It was just shy of 9. a.m., and the place was in full swing. He moved his eyes from first floor to third; saw men and women dressed for business at open laptops, others sat together at long tables, or walking and talking, clutching folders secured with the proverbial red tape.

He didn't fancy it. The natural human proclivity is to nosey on our neighbours and being stared at all day would be off-putting. What if you absently picked your ear, or worse? Also, and more importantly for a law firm like this, the open-plan layout posed an obvious security risk. The glass was no doubt well reinforced, not easy to penetrate via a listening device unless a window was open, and Sheen could see none, but there were lots of people out there adept at lip-reading, and plenty of private dicks, press and corporate espionage agencies more than willing to pay good money for their underhand services. Anyone could stand here and video the office surreptitiously. These days there was nothing more normal than a person, phone in hand, apparently in their own world.

'Bit exposed, wouldn't you say?' asked Aoife from beside him. She nodded up at the corporate bods settled round a table on the second floor, a geezer with a grey beard in front of them, like he was about to present.

Sheen glanced at her, nodded with a small smile of approval. Her instincts were, as usual, spot on. The makings of a true detective were nature, not nurture, he was certain of it. When Sheen looked up again, the glass box of the conference room had been blacked out, its transparent walls now opaque as the washed-clean blackboards of every new school year he remembered as a kid. Not so naive it would seem, and not so transparent.

'Maybe not so sharing and caring after all,' he said, and started for the double entrance doors, glass of course, which silently parted well before they were even close. Sheen showed his warrant card to the young brunette woman on reception and asked for Williamson Golding, with no real hope of either finding him in the building or being directed to his office if he was there. The woman adopted a pained expression and tapped on a keyboard. She told him the next available slot with

Mr Golding would be next Tuesday at 7.45 a.m.

'This is a murder enquiry. And it's not his legal services we're interested in,' said Aoife. 'We can take him out of here, drive him up to Antrim station and he can answer our questions in an interview room when it suits us,' she went on.

The brunette, Abigail, he now noted from the badge on her lapel, looked truly devastated at such an eventuality. But of course, they would do no such thing, and Aoife McCusker, she without a warrant card or legal right to investigate said murder case, would do well to keep her trap shut. Williamson Golding was a former soldier, then copper turned lawyer, who now made his living prosecuting police malpractice and generally being a white knight for every scumbag who'd found himself on the receiving end of a PSNI taser. Detective work might be an instinct, but caution and reticence were learnt skills.

Sheen edged in front of Aoife, who was leaning on the counter staring at Abigail.

'But I'm sure that won't be necessary, Abigail. Why don't you call his extension, ask his PA if he can spare us five minutes? I'm sure a man like Mr Golding will be more than happy to help if he can,' assured Sheen.

Abigail reached for the phone. Before she could punch the extension as instructed, the lift behind Sheen and Aoife at the other end of the entrance foyer pinged. Sheen saw her eyes widen and her expression shift between abject terror and awe. It could only be Golding.

Sheen turned, saw him front and centre of the small entourage of black-cloaked and wigged barristers who now billowed their way. Fahey had sent him a picture. Sheen had time to think about the dark fibres found at Father Phil's murder scene, and the likely match they'd also recovered from young Rhonda Sterrit's remains. Golding's group was about to breeze right past them. Abigail had frozen. Sheen took a big step into their path, blocked their way. The layers of urgent-sounding conversation from the barristers stopped abruptly, as did they. All eyes were now on Sheen.

'Hello, Mr Golding. DI Sheen, PSNI, Serious Crimes. We're hoping you'll find a few minutes to answer a couple of questions,' he said.

Nothing from the group, Golding was still, a glacial stare fixed on Sheen. He was almost a foot smaller than the two young men and one woman who accompanied him. But no mistaking his presence, Sheen nearly obeyed the command those dagger eyes silently broadcast: *Get out of my way.* Almost, but persistence was another virtue of police work, this trait most certainly learnt through hard experience. Sheen stood his ground and offered his hand. Golding did not respond.

'We're investigating the murders of Father Phil Rafferty and Rhonda Sterrit. You were old mates with Rhonda's father, Gordon Sterrit, back in the day, right? I understand you had a falling-out some time back.'

'I'm expected in court, DI Sheen. If this is urgent, you can call my office for an appointment.' Scottish accent, as expected, but worn smooth at the edges. But the hard rock of working-class Glasgow wasn't far from the surface. And it was visible too; the finger of a fat white scar touched his eyebrow and disappeared beneath the false tight curls of his wig.

'Nothing urgent, Mr Golding, only the murder of a child and priest,' countered Sheen.

He stood his ground. From behind Golding, words spoken from the tallest of his crew, the guy who looked like a young BFG from the children's story; dish ears, hound-dog eyes and lanky bones.

'He said we're due in court. Now I suggest you stand aside, sir, or—'

'Or you're gonna call the police, are you?' asked Sheen.

'Or I'll have you hung up for contempt of court, young man,' interjected Golding.

Sheen remained impassive. That said, Golding could do it; he needed to be careful how far he pushed this.

'No need to go down that road,' he said, slowly sliding out of the way.

Sheen let the entourage get to the sliding doors and then called Golding by his surname, no prefix this time. He stopped, slowly turned, and his juniors parted. Sheen saw a flare in his eyes now, the cold appraisal of the seasoned barrister was gone. This was the hard stare of a young SAS trooper with blood on his hands in the dead of night. The eyes of a killer, perhaps not a murderer, but most definitely a killer, Sheen was certain of that. He'd looked into similar eyes across countless

266

tables in sweat-filled interview rooms. This was the real Williamson Golding, the man he wanted to speak to. And it hadn't taken a world of provocation from Sheen for him to turn and face him. Sheen stuck his hands in his jacket pockets, moved to make up some distance between them.

'Wanted to ask you about British Army black ops along the border in the '70s. And about a dead boy I pulled from a peat bog too,' he added coldly.

Sheen felt that flame flicker in his breast at the mention of the boy's body, and perhaps Golding saw some of the heat in his eyes too. Either way, he'd got Golding's attention, maybe because of the black ops, or the child's body, or both.

'Go on ahead, send the car back for me, I'll be a few minutes, no more,' he said to his group, a soft smile on his face.

The three juniors made their way to a Bentley that had pulled up outside. Golding's smile disappeared as the limo's doors closed and it purred away. He beckoned Sheen with a twitch of his head to follow him out of the building. Golding walked, Sheen and Aoife followed.

'Killing livestock and creating mock black masses part of the SAS handbook when you served, was it?' Sheen said.

'Never served in Ulster, DI Sheen.'

'Did some of your boys go too far, maybe got a taste for it? What's a headless donkey compared to a headless child? Who cares about a single Paddy kid against the success of a mission like that? Worth it, was it?'

'Oh, aye, I heard about that. In the paper, right? Very Hammer Horror. But nothing to do with me.' He laughed. 'I was in the army, well-known fact, but as I said, not here. Ask the Ministry of Defence. I was stationed in Germany most of the time. Caught a bad dose of the clap one winter, but that's about as undercover as my career ever got,' he said.

Sheen knew the MOD never confirmed anything about Special Forces personnel while still alive, sometimes not even after death. And Golding would know it too.

'Not what Trevor McHenry's been saying. Captain McHenry as he was then,' said Sheen.

Not exactly true, but Golding's eyes widened momentarily at the mention of McHenry. No doubt at all that Golding was the person McHenry had alluded to when Sheen spoke to him outside Andy's Booze Hut on the Glencairn estate. Golding absorbed the hit, and then deftly sidestepped.

'I heard about you, Sheen. About both of you,' Golding said quietly. His eyes narrowed on Aoife, before returning his attention to Sheen.

Meaning what? Their well-publicised adventure from the previous summer? Sheen's long-dead brother, public knowledge for those who choose to go looking? Or, perhaps, he meant Aoife McCusker's suspension and her loss of custody of her daughter Ava? In which case,

Sheen was on thin ice indeed, a simple request to look at Aoife's credentials could scupper everything.

'I wonder what those over-privileged kids you're working with have heard about you?' asked Sheen. 'Oh, I'm sure they know the official line. Working-class boy soldier, a decade in the dirt with the RUC, before you self-educated and turned to the law. And so nobly went after the very coppers you'd served with. Inspiring. I'm sure they lap it up.'

'To be working class, there needs to be work. When I was a boy my mother sent me to school with a blade for protection instead of a packed lunch,' he replied.

Sheen had cut him, not in the way he'd hoped, but still, he'd managed to get past his armour once more. He glanced involuntarily at the scar on Golding's forehead. Further down the street the Bentley swung into view, coming to pick up Golding. A change of direction was needed to keep him talking now.

'How do you know Gordon Sterrit, Mr Golding?'

'He was my mentor. Gave me my first posting at his chambers, as I'm sure you already know. It's not a secret,' he said.

'But you two were more than just professional colleagues though? You were members of the same Masonic Lodge and in the Black Preceptory together. Brothers. Isn't that how you like to refer to one another?'

Golding remained tight-lipped. The Bentley was about halfway down the street now; their window with Golding was closing.

'And let's not forget the Ulster Israelites too, so many little clubs. Fun times, but then you severed all ties. Why'd you guys fall out, Mr Golding?'

The scales had fallen over Golding's eyes once more, though not before Sheen registered the surprise he'd betrayed when he mentioned the Ulster Israelites. Fahey was brilliant; he'd found something Golding thought was safely dead and buried there. Fahey had told him that the Embassy of Israel in London said they knew nothing about the group and thus far Sheen had no more to go on. But over the summer Sheen had seen the Israeli flag flying in Protestant districts, the Palestinian banner in nationalist areas. Northern Ireland may mean little to those in the Middle East, but the opposite clearly was not the case. The question was, why did Williamson Golding want to keep this part of his past hidden?

'I've nothing to add, DI Sheen. If you want to bring me in as a person of interest and question me under caution, you know you can. But we both know you won't,' he said, glancing over at Aoife.

The Bentley pulled to a stop by the kerb.

'Why do you think someone wanted to kill Gordon Sterrit's daughter, Mr Golding? She was just a child. Not much older actually than that child I dug out of the Monaghan bog,' he went on. He was firing more or less blindly now. Potshot questions loaded with the still-mysterious details of this case. His time was all but up here. He'd got lucky already; perhaps he'd get lucky again?

'There are a lot of evil people in this world. Some men make enemies of them, and some people are just unlucky. Like your lost boy in the bog maybe. I've not spoken to Gordon Sterrit for years. And I do mean years, DI Sheen. You'd be better asking him yourself,' replied Golding, one hand on the Bentley's now-open rear door.

'Were you one of those enemies?' asked Sheen.

Golding gave him an impatient shake of his head. They both knew Golding's alibi could be checked, and Sheen had no doubt it would be sound. A man like him would have the sense to distance himself from a crime or make a clean job of it.

'I knew Gordon in another life, DI Sheen.' He inhaled deeply from the fresh wind coming up off the Lagan. 'There was a time in this wee country that some people were out to build a new Jerusalem. I got to a point where I had no stomach for it any more, know what I mean?' he said, and slid into the car.

Sheen put his hand on the top of the door, held it open.

'No, I can't bloody well say that I do. But I think you fell out with men you once called brothers. Trevor McHenry was in charge of your troop, right? And yet he refused your offer of counsel, got sent down for a hard stretch rather than take your help.'

Direct hit, a thick vein bulged in Golding's neck. His hand shot out, gripped the inner door handle. 'That was his mistake. But for the record he knew me no better than you do,' he spat.

Sheen released his own hand before Golding's forceful pull on the door could trap it. The Bentley instantly took off, faster than before.

'What do you make of that?' asked Aoife.

Sheen dug his fists into his jacket pockets, rocked on his heels and put his chin into his chest. Golding and Sterrit had been balls deep together in every esoteric society most people knew about in Northern Ireland and at least one that no one had really heard of. Sterrit had been more than a mate; he'd helped raise Golding from non-officer soldier to trainee barrister. Sheen wouldn't be surprised if Sterrit had bankrolled Golding's education too. And yet Golding seemed untouched by the news of Rhonda Sterrit's death. How any of this linked to past or present crimes was no clearer than it had been before. But Golding's dismissal of McHenry had sounded less of a denial of their relationship as a refutation of McHenry's judgement of him. His head was beginning to ache, hardly a surprise.

'That Williamson Golding is a changeling who doesn't keep friends,' said Sheen. 'Plus he's a man with scars, so much so he feels the need to right wrongs for a living.'

His mind turned to Rhonda Sterrit's impending autopsy. But then his stomach growled.

'I'll probably regret it, but right now I need a fresh buttered Belfast bap with ham and mustard,' said Sheen.

Aoife said she knew just the place.

'Thought you might,' replied Sheen. They started to walk to where he'd parked the Sig, and as they did another transparent room in the building above them flicked to impervious blackness, shielding the goings-on inside Williamson Golding Ltd from the prying eyes of the passing world.

CHAPTER THIRTY-ONE

Forensic autopsies are official business. They are meticulously documented, and that includes a record of those present. So Aoife McCusker agreed to step back and take stock of the likely points of abduction of Rhonda Sterrit near the church on the Lisburn Road. Sheen waited in the Northern Ireland Regional Forensic Mortuary deep in the bowels of the Royal Victoria Hospital off the Falls Road in West Belfast. Despite its location in the Catholic, nationalist heartland of the city, it was collectively and affectionately, known as the Royal, by both communities. He listened to the sharp squeak of turning wheels as the steel gurney, on which Rhonda Sterrit's body rested, approached. He'd already exchanged introductions with Maurice Gibney, one of two assistant pathologists from the Northern Ireland State Pathologist's Department, who now pushed the gurney into the spotless, white-tiled room. Gibney had explained that he'd completed some preliminaries:

documenting the clothes Rhonda had been wearing and weighing the body. Two porters entered and lifted the body, still clothed in a plastic white sheet, from the gurney to the autopsy table. The table was stainless steel, slightly bevelled on each side, and Rhonda's body now rested on a thick, black rubber hump which caused her chest and abdomen to stand proud from the level of the table.

Sheen noted there were two drainage channels that fed to a dark hole in the tiled floor. He took a deep breath. Aoife had done well to avoid this. The air was an amalgam of formaldehyde, disinfectant alcohol and the pervasive dampness that seemed to fill every cavity of the mortuary.

'Thrash metal fan in your day?' asked Sheen.

Gibney was wearing a Slayer T-shirt, the inverted pentagram in a circle that was part of the thrash metal band's logo partly visible behind the rubber apron that covered his chest. Gibney snapped on a pair of long black latex gloves. Sheen enjoyed music, considered his tastes eclectic, but drew the line at bands that attacked the senses and were a punishment to listen to.

His eyes lingered on the sharp corner of the occult symbol on Gibney's shirt, printed in blood-red on the black fabric. Slayer sang about the Devil and eternal damnation, if he recalled. Sheen's eyes moved to the contours of Rhonda Sterrit still concealed beneath the white sheet. Police investigations, like any other aspect of life, could throw up uncanny echoes of themselves.

It meant nothing of course, but at another level, maybe deep in his Irish roots, Sheen could feel the chime of related things now he was hunting the killer. And the sound was discordant and unsettling.

'Still am,' he replied, his eyes smiling and then made his black-gloved fingers into the heavy-metal horn sign.

Sheen allowed himself a small scoff. Gibney was at least his age, and the harsh white overheads reflected off his hairless dome in a spot of light. He didn't look like a headbanger. Dress code aside, he did look like a professor of dentistry and biomedical sciences, which in fact he was. No accounting for musical taste. A flap and swish from the rubber doors behind Sheen, and then he was joined by a woman, maybe in her mid-forties, though it was difficult to tell. Like Sheen she was dressed in a gown and mask. They shook hands.

'Jennifer O'Donoghue. I'm here from the BHSCT,' she explained.

Sheen introduced himself, and then looked to Gibney, who read his confusion. Forensic autopsies were usually attended by the pathologist, a senior representative of the police or, as was the case with Sheen today, the SIO in a murder enquiry.

'Jen's representing the Belfast Health and Social Care Trust. She's a paediatric pathologist. For child deaths, Jen gets brought in,' explained Gibney, fixing a head-mounted microphone and attaching it to a recording device secreted on his belt.

'Oh, I see,' answered Sheen.

Child protection, though Gordon Sterrit and his wife had no other children. A shiver of unease at this thought; perhaps it was not the Sterrit's children who were now at risk.

Gibney nodded. 'Ready?'

Sheen and Jennifer O'Donoghue said they were.

He slowly drew back the white sheet. First Rhonda's head was revealed, then a thick swathe of brown hair with the kink of natural curl, dark at the roots but edging to auburn under the strong overhead lights. Sheen stared at her face. The skin was waxy, her eyes partially shrunken in her sockets, the orbits tinged with a darker blue, a match for the sapphire tint of her lips, now closed and sealed for ever. Here was a young girl with an old-fashioned name who'd never live to fulfil it in womanhood.

Sheen concentrated on Gibney's low-toned narrative detailing the age, gender and circumstances of Rhonda's presentation to autopsy. Gibney tugged the sheet and it gave a silken hiss, as he exposed the rest of her body. Sheen followed the reveal, saw her partially budded breasts, the small patch of her pubis, the milky smoothness of her thighs. He instinctively dropped his eyes, aware of Jennifer O'Donoghue standing close by. The naked body of a teenage girl was something he had no business with. But the copper in him knew differently. Sheen forced his eyes away from the cracked tile at the wheels of the steel gurney and back to the table, his gaze coldly dispassionate and watchful.

He took a step towards her body, absorbed all the details before him: the spattering of freckles on the nose, the chipped aquamarine toenail varnish, the elliptical dark brown birth mark on the soft muscle of her left shoulder and, of course, the butchered stump at the end of her right arm. Her flesh here was trimmed neatly to expose the white fork of her protruding radius and ulna forearm bones. The corpse was other-worldly in its stillness, and, now that he'd surmounted his learnt proprieties, unmistakeable in its lifelessness. Sheen had seen so many bodies, and the inherent deadness was always the same, absolute as a thud of clay on a coffin lid. This was a shell, and one that each of us was destined to leave behind.

He had little interest in wakes or graves, but catching murderers and avenging the innocent were the things that made him tick. And a corpse could hold the key to the killing. Here was the last witness to a murder, and one who would reveal her answers, but only if he asked the right questions.

Gibney was measuring Rhonda's height from heel to head. He added this to the outline diagram of a body in a flipchart, and then extended the tape from the top of her shoulder down her right arm to the clean cut that marked the place where her hand had been removed. The location and dimensions of the amputation point were noted precisely, and then he set to work archiving the nature and size of the bone protrusion. Forensic autopsies took time. Gibney would inspect and record every bodily blemish and bruise (confusingly they called them 'lacerations' on the record for reasons Sheen had never got to the bottom of). The report would take longer, weeks at least.

Sheen raised a hand. Gibney stopped what he was doing, answered Sheen's silent interruption with a twitch of his eyebrows.

'Do we know whether this,' said Sheen, gesturing to the stump and protruding bones, 'happened while she was still alive?'

Gibney shrugged. He was going to give him a non-committal answer. Sheen's experience of pathologists, even those who welcomed police involvement, was that their preferred seating arrangement was to be right on the fence.

'I'd say no,' he responded. 'Either that or she was totally unconscious when the procedure took place.'

Straight answer, one-sided too. Sheen noted the use of the term 'procedure'. Gibney could as well have used its sister term, 'operation'. The meaning would have been the same and Sheen could see the sense in both. The wound at the end of Rhonda's arm didn't look like the ghastly result of a torture inflicted. It was surgical, deliberate. Which begged the question: what purpose did this disfigurement serve?

'Because it's so clean?' enquired Sheen, using the best term that came to hand, but Gibney took his meaning, nodded.

'Yeah, no obvious signs of struggle or haste. This took some time. A degree of skill too. Rhonda must have been still while the person worked,' he said.

Sheen exhaled a breath, felt a little weight lift. Whatever terror this child had gone through being abducted, at least she didn't suffer through the awful mutilation.

'But probably alive,' Gibney added.

Sheen asked for his thinking.

'The body arrived all but drained of blood,' he said.

Sheen flicked through the mental images of Rhonda's crime scene photos. There'd been a little blood on the entrance ramp outside her home where she'd been dumped, but nowhere near the quantity one would expect if her hand had been hacked off in that location.

'So, this was done elsewhere – I mean, from where she was discovered,' Sheen said.

'And while her heart was still beating,' added Gibney, 'though she was probably unconscious at the time.'

'Maurice, did you conduct the autopsy on Father Phil Rafferty this week?'

'The Clonard priest? Not me,' he said with a shake of his head.

'Initial toxicology suggests he may have had a near fatal dose of diamorphine,' said Sheen.

'Blimey, that was a quick turnaround. And you want to know if this body shows similar signs?'

'Is there any way to tell? I mean, right now?' asked Sheen.

Gibney's eyes told of a wry smile under his mask. 'We'd need to wait for a full toxicology analysis. To be certain, that is. If she were alive, I'd be on the lookout for markedly slow breathing, constricted pinpoint pupils, lethargy to the point of being in a comatose state,' he said.

Sheen's turn to give Gibney a look; the one thing that was certain in this sterile room was those under examination were long dead.

'Patience, DI Sheen.' Gibney beckoned Sheen closer and pointed at the fingers of Rhonda's left hand. 'See this?' he asked.

Sheen nodded. Her fingertips were deep purple, darker, but not far off the shade of her lips. Sheen had assumed it was a version of the nail varnish that Rhonda had used to paint her toes.

'That unusual?' asked Sheen.

'Not in cases of heroin overdose that I've come across from time to time,' replied Gibney.

A little flutter of birds took flight in Sheen's chest. The toxicology would confirm it, but this was Gibney's way of approving his suspicions, without going on the record and stating it as a scientific fact. Same as Father Phil, meaning they were after the same murderer. This, not the chopping and amputations, was the real leitmotif; this was their killer's signature. Sheen knew it as surely as he'd known Gordon Sterrit was lying. And not because the drugging was obvious; rather it was because the use of the drug was discreet. Whatever sick fulfilment this gave to the murderer, it was a private satisfaction, not paraded like the posed bodies.

'Can you see a mark where she's been injected?'

'No, you can see that for yourself,' he said, moving a black palm across the girl's body.

Sheen moved his face closer to the corpse, inspected her arms and neck from both sides of the table. Gibney was right: there was nothing.

'Can we turn her over?' asked Sheen.

Gibney nodded, took charge of Rhonda's hips, while Sheen levered from beneath her shoulders, taking care not to let the body roll down the side of the rubber hump on the table. Jennifer O'Donoghue, silent throughout so far, took a small step back. The men heaved Rhonda Sterrit up on her side. Her hair fell on her face.

'There you are,' said Gibney.

Sheen glanced down the exposed underside of her body near to where Gibney stood. There was a dark purple bruise on her left buttock, radiating out from a dot in its centre. Gibney hunkered down, both hands still keeping the body in position with Sheen's help. 'This could very well be a puncture point,' he surmised.

Sheen helped him position the body on its back again. There was no doubt. Sheen had seen puncture points on other corpses, and this was one.

'We good?' asked Gibney.

Sheen nodded and thanked him.

Gibney reached for a small-handled scalpel from the tray on wheels at the head of the table and started to speak once more in the same low monotone that had denoted his narrative for the record. As he did so he made a long, perfectly steady incision from Rhonda

Sterrit's pubic region to just below her chest bone, and then completed the two arms of the Y shape, by cutting from each shoulder joint in turn, ensuring each incision joined the stem of the first long cut. As was accepted practice for post-mortems on women, Gibney carefully curved each arm of the Y to undercut the discreet swell of Rhonda's breasts. To Sheen it somehow made the awful intensity of the experience better. Gibney had given Rhonda the respect of a woman she would never now grow to become.

The flesh parted under the blade without resistance, skin splitting instantly to reveal the thin stratum of body fat, yellow as old papyrus. By the time Gibney's scalpel had completed its work, and his probing, pulling hands took over, Sheen could see the pale tone and texture of the abdominal muscles, the darker meat of the vital organs, and the off-whiteness of the lungs which Gibney separated, inspected, and made note of on his flipchart diagrams. There was, of course, no blood. Sheen tried not to dwell on the comparison with spatchcocked raw chicken that his mind was sending up, but to no avail. Nevertheless, he remained stoic without too much effort, but knew that the cloying, cloudy visceral smell that had filled the air would stay in his nose and linger in his imagination all day. People at their first autopsy expected the copper reek of fresh blood, but this was different, mushroom and dank. Earthy in fact, like the bogland he'd spent so much time searching this autumn.

By the time Gibney had set down his rib-cutters and reached for the bone saw, Sheen decided he'd seen enough. Jennifer O'Donoghue was nowhere in sight, having taken a hastily announced and very extended toilet break somewhere between the liver and the diaphragm.

'Off so soon?' asked Gibney, eyes full of mischief.

'Afraid so. Can we get a wiggle on those tox reports?'

'Do my best, send them your way,' Gibney replied.

Sheen thanked him and left to get changed, stopping to wash his hands thoroughly before splashing some cold water on his face. His phone, appropriately dead to the world in the basement of the forensic mortuary, vibrated and chirped to life from his jacket as he walked to the car. He settled into the bucket of the driver's seat.

The first was an email. The bone spectrum analysis from the toenail sample taken from the Monaghan bog body had been returned. Sheen read it a few times, finally extracted the headline. The boy had been a city kid, not a farm child. And yet the little boy Declan O'Rawe from Terrytole was a rural child found dead in urban Belfast. If anything, this news made things less clear, rather than more. More alerts from his phone distracted his attention.

Three missed calls from Dermot Fahey, his journalist. Plus two messages, one text and one picture. He read the text.

WHAT THE FUCK?! CALL ME NOW!

Instead, Sheen scrolled up to the image.

'Jesus Christ,' he said.

It was a severed right hand, in a cardboard box. The fingers protruded over its edge, and Sheen identified it instantly as Rhonda Sterrit's. The fingernails were stained blue, deepening to dark purple at the cuticles. Another image arrived from Fahey. This showed a folded sheet of paper in the box. Sheen managed to make out the words TOP SECRET before two more messages arrived. The first was from Fahey, which simply said *This too* . . . but the other was from Aoife, telling him she'd found something important. She didn't know the half of it. He hesitated, considering whether to call Fahey or Aoife first, but only for a heartbeat. He hit Aoife's number. She picked up after one ring.

'Sheen—' she started, but he cut her off.

'I'm coming to get you. You're not going to believe what just turned up.'

CHAPTER THIRTY-TWO

There was a steady flow of early afternoon traffic on the Lisburn Road, but the pavement outside the Methodist Church was empty apart from Aoife McCusker.

She stood at the thick granite steps of the building that led on to the street, and stared up at its brooding face, all the darker in the weak light of the low sun. Rhonda Sterrit had been dropped off a little further down the street on the same side, according to Gordon Sterrit's statement. Made sense: their home on Newforge Lane was about two miles west of here. The natural stopping point was about ten metres from where Aoife now stood, where a double yellow strip led to the corner. It would have been traffic-free. Sterrit said he had driven off, didn't check that she had made it into the building. It was an oversight, but Aoife didn't blame him. Any other day, the kid would have made it safely to her choir recital and bused it home with her pal.

But Rhonda Sterrit had never even made it into this church. The triangulation analysis of her mobile phone signal confirmed she'd been in the vicinity at the time. Then the signal went dead. Disappeared, just like the thirteen-year-old who had owned it. Rhonda's phone was still unaccounted for, but the child had been gone barely long enough to arouse concern that she was missing. Still, this whole area should have been shut down, the streets combed for forensics as soon as Sterrit had confirmed this was where his daughter had been last seen.

A gust of wind eddied up the road, coming from the north and full of ice. Aoife gritted her teeth, pulled her inadequate coat close to her body. Another blast of Baltic air, and this time her thoughts turned to Ava. Had someone had the presence of mind to remind her to wear a coat today? Water formed in her eyes and not just from the searing wind. She squeezed them closed, demanded of herself that she stop. She would not do this, not on the job, not here and now. Yet when she blinked away the tears, another thought, so much worse than the first.

What if she had started to develop?

Ava was approaching her tenth birthday, and she was a big girl for her age. So many of them were. Children grew up faster these days, the girls especially. *What if she needed a training bra and no one had noticed? What if she'd started her period? What if these things had been noticed, but not by someone who had her best interests at heart?*

At that she turned from the door of the church and headed for her car. Ava would be at school, and soon she'd be getting out. She'd be able to catch a glimpse; a look was all she needed for now. Then she'd be able to rest and give the case more attention. Aoife stopped dead and dropped her car keys back into her bag from where she'd hurriedly hooked them. If Ava spotted her, her baby girl would come running and that would be that. She'd get into the car and Aoife would drive away and she wouldn't stop. But when they caught up with her (and of course they would), they'd take Ava away again and then it would be for good.

Aoife turned around and retraced her steps. Her eyes were dry, face set. Ava wasn't with her, but at least she was alive. She was alive, and soon enough she would have her home. Right now, there was another little girl who needed her. This one would never be coming home, and the maniac who'd killed her, and most probably Father Phil too, was still out there and was going to kill again.

The traffic had dried up as it is apt to do at times. Aoife studied the twenty feet of pavement between the place where Rhonda had left her father's car and the entrance to the church.

People don't disappear into thin air.

And even if the road was in the lull of a quiet moment just like this one, Sterrit had dropped Rhonda off at 7 p.m. It would have been dark, yes, but it wasn't the dead of night. Plus, the front of the church had been open, and this section of the pavement would have been well illuminated. She raised her eyes and noted it was also overlooked by a street lamp. They blinked to life no later than 4.30 p.m. during winter. This place would have been practically floodlit. And Rhonda wasn't a toddler. Aoife knew just how vocal girls could be when they let it rip. And yet, potential witnesses claimed to have seen nothing, heard nothing. All of which meant that either Rhonda knew her abductor and left the scene willingly or was secreted away with great force, great stealth, or perhaps both.

She imagined a black van decelerating, men tumbling out, grabbing Rhonda and bundling her into the vehicle and speeding off. Aoife's eyes darted from the door of the church to the side of the road. No, not the way it happened. Staff at the church reported no screeching of tyres, nothing out of place at all, same went for the restaurant owner directly opposite. It was possible that Rhonda was lured away by someone she trusted, but unlikely. The family had few close relatives, none of whom lived in Belfast, and fewer close friends, all of whom checked out. Which suggested this was a crime of stealth, rather than strength, though whoever had murdered Father Phil had displayed both.

Aoife moved her eyes along the swan necks of the lamp posts that shrunk in regular intervals down the road. She was about to turn away, and then she saw it, maybe a quarter of a mile or so away. A black CCTV mast, its twin cameras directed up and down the road.

One camera was pointed in her direction, although not perfectly aligned. The case notes didn't say anything about a CCTV check. Perhaps it had been requested, but more likely they'd not got around to it by the time the case was transferred. CCTV was ubiquitous in Belfast city centre, but not as all-seeing as some would perhaps believe. Many of the new masts erected in the last five or so years were positioned at trouble spots. Others, like this one, served the purpose of traffic monitoring. The PSNI had access to all feeds but they were managed by Securitel, the large telecommunications company based on the redeveloped Titanic Quarter. Roving CCTV vehicles acted as a supplement to support the still-patchy citywide coverage. Still, this was a possible break, and one that so far had gone untapped.

Aoife gauged the approximate reach of the street lamp above her head and took several long steps backwards, one eye on the pavement so she didn't blunder into anyone. In the gloom of a Belfast winter's evening this area would be in relative darkness, a blind spot for the CCTV mast for sure.

'This is where the bastard got you,' she said.

The killer had chosen his vantage well. But it only worked if Rhonda didn't walk straight into the church.

'Why'd you leave the light, Rhonda?' she said quietly.

The kid was young and well-heeled, but no child these days will accept the offer to pet a puppy or obey a command to get into a car.

'What turned your head, girl?'

Aoife dropped to her haunches, one hand on the cold pavement, looking but not yet seeing. If the CSIs had been called in when they should have been something might have been found. To start to look now was lunacy and ultimately pointless. Anything she found would be inadmissible, it would never enter the evidence chain, but still Aoife persevered, slowly edging across the pavement, headed for the kerb. She felt eyes on her and looked up, saw an elderly woman with a walking cane and pull-along shopping trolley standing behind her. She'd had the run of the road while standing and thinking but as soon as she started to behave like a mad person, there was an audience.

She smiled. 'Lost my earring,' she said.

'You got a matching pair on you,' observed the woman, and then muttered an appraisal of what Aoife had in fact lost.

Aoife returned to her scrutiny of the pavement. 'Fuck off, then,' she whispered pleasantly.

She made it to the kerb and had started to push herself up, and then she stopped. There, in the dead leaves in the heart of a storm drain, something glinted dimly. She slipped on a pair of latex gloves from her pocket and, making pincers of her fingers, slipped her hand into the open slot of the drain as far as it would go. The first time she felt only the rasp of dead vegetation. She withdrew her hand, flexed her fingers and tried again. This time her fingertips touched something cold, metallic. She gave one more stretch and pushed her hand deeper, praying it wouldn't get stuck. Her fingertips pinched closed over hard metal and she slowly dislodged her hand, wincing as the steel of the drain tried to trap her knuckles.

She raised herself off the hard ground and studied her quarry. It was a small silver crucifix, attached to the remains of a fine link chain that she knew would have led to four spaced beads, one for the Our Father, and three denoting introductory Hail Mary prayers. This was once part of a set of rosary beads. She glanced back at the grey Methodist Church. It hadn't come from in there. But had it been enough to make Rhonda Sterrit walk from the light into the darkness, believing she was safe, when in fact she was not? The image of gutted red candles at the Altar of St Gerard flashed in her mind. Their killer had been present in Clonard, had blended in during a Catholic Mass. And now, evidence that the same person had managed to lure Rhonda Sterrit to her death, maybe using a similar ruse.

And what better disguise for a man to hide behind when inside a monastery or outside a church than being dressed as a priest or a preacher? The fibres found at both crime scenes had been black. Just like the clothes Father Macken had been wearing earlier when Sheen had interviewed him in Clonard.

She dropped her find into a small plastic bag and pulled out her phone, eager to tell Sheen. If they could get lucky with the CCTV they'd have a face to match the description. No sooner had she sent her message than her phone vibrated; Sheen calling her back. At least he was eager, she'd give him that. And, despite the brief dalliance with facial hair, he was sexier than ever if truth be told. She answered the call, ready to tell all.

'Sheen—' she started, but he butted in. She listened, first with interest, and then, as Sheen continued, with mounting horror.

CHAPTER THIRTY-THREE

Gordon Sterrit poured another dram and watched as the empty glass stayed empty.

He turned the bottle of Scotch upside down. Five beads of whisky slowly dropped. He looked at the meagre yield bleakly before letting go of the bottle. It fell on its side with a hard clatter before rolling to the edge of the kitchen table where it stopped, balanced on the edge like the Kyaiktiyo Pagoda. He sucked the last of the Scotch from his crystal tumbler and looked over at the half-open cupboard under the sink. That's where this bottle had been squirrelled away, a coat of kitchen grease on its shoulder, and old enough to taste a bit dusty.

There wasn't another drop of drink in the whole house.

Hardly a shock; until a few days past, he'd been teetotal. Sterrit emitted a laugh with no warmth, started to raise himself up and thought better of it. Legs were like rubber. He should have gone out and bought another while he still could. But he'd chanced upon the now-empty bottle under the sink and set to work.

He was way too far gone now; the thought of such an undertaking was on par with setting off on an Antarctic expedition. Instead he held the glass, thinking about nothing in particular but feeling the unwelcome intrusion of sobriety, small spears of detail, what had led him to hunt under the sink and submerge in alcohol once more.

Rachel had pleaded with him to stop drinking and talk to her. Her voice had been grating. She'd been right in his face. Had he shoved her? Did she slip? Either way, Sterrit retrieved an image of her staring up at him accusingly from the kitchen floor. Harsh words, maybe from him, probably. It was time to say sorry, best to get in with that first. Sterrit jolted from his reverie, pushed the chair from the table with a brain-scourging scrape.

'Rachel!'

His slurred call went unheeded. He relaxed back into his seat as he remembered. She'd left and taken a bag with her. She had chucked something at him from the hallway. He drowsily looked along the length of the kitchen, until his bleary gaze settled on the glint of gold against the skirting board at the far wall.

That was her wedding ring.

Sterrit closed his eyes, growled and then began to whimper. He stopped abruptly; eyes open. Rachel walking out wasn't what had sent him in search of more booze. He'd already broken the seal on the bottle by the time she'd started to aggravate him with her talk.

That London cop – Sheen was his name – had been here. He'd asked him things, something that his lawyer's mind had flagged at the time and now, as the thunderous, ball-bearing rattle of the imminent hangover filled his brain, he could hear again.

Ever heard about a British Army campaign along the Monaghan border to raise a black magic panic?

Sterrit had read the newspaper article some time ago with interest but little concern. It hadn't said much. So perhaps Sheen had read it too. But why did he mention it to Gordon Sterrit, whose only daughter had been murdered and dumped with a hand amputated at his front door? So far as anyone knew, he was a man with no connection whatsoever to the British Army. Another question, this one had come from the woman.

Did Rhonda have anything in her hand, when you found her outside at the front gate?

He'd destroyed the document, and only he and McKeague now knew that it had been placed on Rhonda's body. And yet they'd asked questions, somehow Sheen *knew*. And it was only a matter of time before a man like Sheen would return; and he'd keep asking questions, especially if there were more bodies, and more documents. Whether Sterrit answered him or not, Sheen would make the connections; coppers like him always did. As surely as death itself, Sheen would visit him again. First he'd come with questions, but then, with answers.

Rhonda's amputated lower arm, the bone clean and trimmed of flesh protruding from the ghastly stump.

McHenry's border campaign, one part of an old game of foul play, the tip of all their old secrets.

Another newspaper headline came to mind, this one from months before, just a little story, buried away in the depths of his Sunday paper.

CHANCE DISCOVERY OF A SECOND BOG BODY

And hadn't Detective Sheen been there too? Yes, yes, he had, crusading into the depths of the past to discover that which had long ago been Disappeared.

And as the fridge freezer droned beside him, Sterrit finally made the connection. He could see the answer in his unblinking, bloodshot eyes as he stared far past the kitchen, through the walls of his home. He could see it clearly for the first time.

Rhonda's murder wasn't about the secret document. Another laugh from Sterrit, this one serrated with the cutting edge of self-ridicule. What a bastard liar he'd been; at some level he'd known all along. Known from the second he dialled McKeague's number and summoned him, not just from his sunny retirement, but from the past. Probably, McKeague knew too. If not now, then he would soon.

This wasn't political. This was personal.

Sterrit closed his eyes and brought the empty tumbler to his face and as he inhaled the ghost of the whisky the years fell away like so many dead autumn leaves.

He'd been dozing, too much Scotch. That was how he'd console himself later, when it all was over. Or rather, how he'd manage to absolve himself. His head was buzzing with a swarm of angry hornets, attacking his inner forehead. He pinched the bridge of his nose, tasted the peaty fumes of the drink in his sinus, and sour, acidic bile in his throat. The drink was something he needed to keep a handle on. Or, perhaps it had already got beyond that point. The maxim he liked to recount while out with admiring junior partners in the firm was starting to sound more like an epitaph than a clever retort in good company.

'First you have a drink, and then the drink has a drink. And then the drink has you.'

For the young Gordon Sterrit, not yet a QC but tipped for the top, this night would be the last time he let a drink pass his lips for many years to come. His abstinence would prevail until a week before Christmas in the second decade of the twenty-first century, when this night would again eventually catch up with him as the past almost always does.

It was early morning, but still no trace of light behind the closed curtains of the dining room in which he'd slept, fully clothed and alone in his armchair. He stood up and stretched and yawned, thought about starting to tidy up but instead led by a call of nature, headed for the hallway and the stairs. The downstairs of his home smelt of stale tobacco smoke and spilt booze. It would take him a week to air it. Plus, the phantom whiff of mingled aftershaves, not quite masking the sour prickle of man-sweat, thick and hormonal.

Gordon had little interest in sex, which marked him as odd, perhaps. He'd come to understand that, possibly, he may be inclined towards both shellfish and mussels, but unlike yesterday evening's guests had no interest in little boys. But ye without sin should cast the first stone. Plus, the old man had insisted. Said these gatherings were necessary, an unparalleled way for his contacts in the service to harvest information and assets, as he liked to put it. Certainly, Gordon had quietly noted the cross-section of society that these little get-togethers tended to attract, all strictly by invitation only and all hand-picked by the old man. They ranged from politicians to paramilitary hardmen. The kind of people the spooks in grey suits could make good use of once tongues hung as loose as trousers, and later, when they had them dangling on the end of a hook. It meant, of course, that some of the men who'd crossed his threshold and sampled the goods must have been in the security services.

Gordon grimaced as he surveyed the state of his latrine. The boys, the old man assured him, were well fed and well paid. They would be peddling themselves on the streets, freezing and in danger if not for the warmth and comforts of Gordon's residence. At the close of the evening, each was couriered to their home, in a car, no less. Plus, he was always quick to remind, this was their choice. Children they may still be, but in appearance only. Nobody forced them through the door.

Gordon started down the stairs, descended two steps and halted.

A sound, it came from the small attic room directly above his head. He paused, listening, heard it again.

Click, whirl and hiss.

Gordon frowned. He turned and traced his way back up the steps and stood on the landing. From the room to his right the drone of sonorous snores, thick enough to feel as much as hear. He nudged the door. The old man was on his back, white vest stretched across his vast fatty torso and over his parts. This was expected. The old man was responsible for seeing the guests out and the getting rid of the boys. He had a room and bed for the trouble. But for the others there was an understanding; no sleepovers allowed. And yet, the unmistakeable shuffle of movement from above, and then the same noise that had drawn him seconds before.

Click, whirl and hiss.

He climbed the steep gradient of the attic stairs, stood at the closed door and briefly considered knocking, before twisting the handle and opening it. The door, which had no bolt, swung open unhindered.

And horror lay waiting.

McKeague stood there, wearing his white underpants, a pair of socks and nothing else. In his hands he held a Polaroid instant camera. He observed Sterrit with eyes as blank as wet slate and offered him an insolent twitch of jaw by way of greeting.

Sterrit was about to challenge him, but then his eyes were drawn to the easy chair in the middle of the small attic room. There, peeking over the cushioned side he saw two feet, small and white, the balls of the heels calloused and yellowed with toughened skin. Sterrit's stomach dropped; he was suddenly nauseous and dry in the mouth.

His eyes moved to a line of frayed blue packing rope that had been slung over the rafter that crossed the top of the room. It ended somewhere behind the chair. Sterrit uttered a sickly moan. The loose end of the rope rested on the back of the chair where McKeague now stood and it was twisted, as though recently bunched or wrapped round a fist. Sterrit's eyes returned to McKeague, whose gaze was waiting. McKeague nodded his head towards the attic stairs behind Sterrit.

'You'd best wake the old boy up. Got ourselves a fucking problem here,' he said.

Finally, Sterrit found his tongue but it was thick and lame. 'What? Wha?' he managed, before closing his mouth and taking a couple of reluctant steps into the attic.

McKeague had located his trousers. He stepped into them, speaking to Sterrit as he did, matter of fact.

'This one was a right wee goer. But, ah, things got a bit outta hand. Pity,' he said, but he didn't sound regretful. In fact, there was trace of a smirk on his face as he raised the Polaroid and took a photograph of what lay behind the chair, at the end of the rope.

Click, whirl and hiss.

Moments later, the boxy camera spat out a square of celluloid, still slick and milky white. McKeague took it between thumb and forefinger and waved it in the air.

Sterrit took another step closer to the chair, walking on a dead man's legs. He glanced at the small table where a reading lamp had been knocked on its side. There was a stack of Polaroids, flesh tones and close-ups, fanned out. Sterrit looked away, and for the first time saw what lay over the arm of the chair.

A boy's body, too still to be asleep, face down and buckled over the chair.

Sterrit gasped.

The skin was white as cod, and Sterrit knew the cadaver was lifeless before he reached over and touched its shoulder. He withdrew his hand with an intake of breath and took in the details of the body. The child's back and legs were a palate of bruises and welts. Sterrit heard a slap and clasp as McKeague threaded his belt to his trousers and fastened the buckle. Sterrit closed his eyes, but not before he identified the bruised indentations on the buttocks of the dead boy for what they could only be: teeth marks.

Click, whirl and hiss.

Sterrit rounded on McKeague, the scream in his gullet now transformed into a snarl.

'Why the hell are you taking photographs?!' Not, Sterrit would time and again reflect, the most pressing question at hand, but somehow, it was the right one in that moment.

McKeague set the camera down and pulled on his shirt, eyes never leaving Sterrit's face. No trace of shame, and no answer to Sterrit's question. There was nothing there at all.

'Go and wake that old, fat bastard up. This needs to be got rid of, outside of Belfast.'

Sterrit didn't move. Neither did McKeague. This was his home, not a place where he took orders, and not from a man like this. But very soon it could become his mess alone to clean up, and stand accused of. Sterrit broke and walked away. He steadied himself against the attic door frame as the stairs seemed to stretch below him like warm toffee.

McKeague's voice followed him as he slowly descended.

'Put the kettle on will you, Counsellor? I'm gasping for a brew.'

Gordon Sterrit sniffed and wiped a clammy hand over his face. He'd been crying; hadn't realised. His head pounded with a *ka-boom, ka-boom, ka-boom*, sending sickening waves of hangover headache with each wallop from his overworked heart. Only a drink or a sheet of pills would touch it. The empty bottle rested on the precipice of the wooden table. Drunk or sober, this thing wasn't going to go away; he could see that now. In fact, it was going to come back for him. *Sheen* was going to come back for him. He'd lost Rhonda and now Rachel too.

He slammed his big palm on the table. The bottle bounced and fell. It broke with a thick crack on the floor below. Sterrit shoved his chair away from the table with a scrape, stood up and started to walk, one hand on the table like a man at sea. The peaty, fireplace fumes of the broken whisky bottle filled the room.

He leant into the table, picked up the broken head of the bottle by the nose, stood and steadied himself. He sniffed the fumes, tasted the peat, the smoke, the bog.

He never wanted to taste or smell it ever again.

But he never, ever wanted to be sober again.

So, Gordon Sterrit decided he'd have a bath, a good hot bath. He pushed himself off the table, found his old legs co-operative and slowly shuffled through the kitchen, headed for the stairs and his bathroom beyond.

He took it slow, and steady, careful not to drop the jagged splinter of broken bottle which he gripped resolutely in one hand.

CHAPTER THIRTY-FOUR

Dermot Fahey's home was not what Sheen had been expecting. Based on Fahey's eco-conscious bicycle and shabby attire Sheen anticipated he'd live in an upcycled one-room apartment where plastic was banned. In fact, the Victorian three-storey town house on Claremont Street, a stone's throw from Botanic Avenue, was an epitome of tasteful, sandblasted restoration. He rapped the big brass knocker three times, and spotted Fahey's bike chained against a concrete embedded stand in the small front garden. Fahey opened up. He looked shell-shocked. He ushered Sheen and Aoife inside and hastily closed the door after them. The interior didn't disappoint: stripped pine floors, a white runner up the centre of the wooden staircase, framed works of abstract art and an antique-looking mirror along the hallway wall.

'Nice place, Dermot,' commented Sheen.

'Wife's father's loaded,' he answered by way of explanation, and then beckoned them both through a small archway that led into a spacious open-plan kitchen-diner and garden room. He pointed to a distressed wooden table in the dining area. The cardboard box stood on a couple of plastic bags in its centre.

Sheen pulled on a pair of latex gloves from a supply in his jacket pocket.

'That needs to be out of here before my kids come home from school,' Fahey said.

'Where did it come from?' asked Aoife.

Fahey said he found it on his doorstep that morning, hand delivered, not posted.

'Anyone else touched this?' asked Sheen.

Fahey shook his head.

'Where's the document?'

Fahey nodded to the box once more. 'I just dropped it back inside,' he said, wiping his hand down the front of his sweater as he spoke.

Sheen approached, Aoife by his side. He looked into the box. The hand was on its side, ghastly and erratic. No doubt at all it was Rhonda's missing appendage. The fingers, including the blue-tinged nails were a match for what he'd just seen in the forensic autopsy. He gingerly lifted it out, grimacing a little at the dead heaviness, the solidity of it. He rotated it, saw no markings, or carvings, nothing to note, apart from the raw wound that marked the point of separation from Rhonda's body. Whoever had done this had murdered an innocent young girl. At the height of Troubles, this kind of thing was all too commonplace. As both sides battled over the big question of who owned the country and who should run it, murderers and sadists had enjoyed an unparalleled licence to indulge in their worst fantasies. All in the name of patriotism, of course. Not for the first time Sheen wondered whether a place that had released such a force could ever really put it back in the bottle again. He set it back in the box and reached for the folded paper.

'There are two documents here,' he said.

Fahey spoke from several feet away. 'I only noticed the other one after I'd texted you.'

Sheen separated the two pieces of paper, handed one to Aoife, who had also donned a pair of gloves. She glanced from one to the other and commented on what Sheen had also noticed.

'This one looks original. Older, I mean. But that one is a photocopy,' she said, meaning the one in Sheen's hand.

Correct, but a cursory glance suggested they were both from the same source. He gave the facsimile his attention. Across the top of the page in large capitalised letters he read:

TOP SECRET EYES ONLY

Sheen quickly glanced to the header of Aoife's document; saw hers was identical, but the letters were printed in red ink. Presumably the original version of the document in his hand had looked the same. He returned to his find, eyes scanning the page and mouthing the words. Fahey now stood by Sheen's right shoulder.

MEMORANDUM OF THE CIRCLE OF NAVAN
TO: ARCHANGEL
SUBJECT: OPERATION MANNA (OM)
DATE: THURSDAY 20TH OCTOBER 1988
PRESENT: BROTHER JEROBOAM, BROTHER AARON, BROTHER MOSES, BROTHER GIDEON, BROTHER SAMSON, BROTHER DAVID

'The Circle of Navan? Mean anything to you?'

Fahey was wide-eyed, drinking in the words on the page before them, and didn't respond.

Sheen read on.

Brother Moses reports that initial overtures to the State of Israel through contact in the MOSSAD proved fruitless. Request for shipment needed was 'too hot' for them, could sour relations with the USA. Suggested contacts in South Africa led to meetings with BOSS representative [REDACTED] and fixer from the United States introduced to Brother Moses as [REDACTED].

In exchange for an agreed sum of £300,000 sterling, the following shipment has been procured and has successfully docked at Larne harbour:

200 Russian-made Kalashnikov AK-47 automatic rifles

90 American Browning 9mm pistols

500 fragmentation grenades
30,000 bullets
12 Russian-made RPG-7 rocket launchers

Brother Aaron will ensure seamless distribution to trusted parties, with the assistance of Brother Samson. Shipment will be also be used to bolster Ulster Opposition. OM complete success.

'If this is legit then I think we've just found the Holy Grail,' said Fahey. Some colour had returned to his cheeks, and Sheen saw the glint of excitement in his eyes. He reached to take the paper from Sheen, but Sheen drew it away from him.

'Gloves,' said Sheen.

Fahey nodded his comprehension.

'So?' asked Sheen.

Fahey let out a small gasp that widened into a chuckle.

'There's always been talk. Between journalists, usually around tables stacked with empty pint glasses. Pure conspiracy theory,' he said, wetting his lips with his tongue, his eyes still on the paper in Sheen's hand. 'Or so we thought.'

'About this Circle of Navan?' Sheen read the name again, careful not to get it wrong. He pronounced 'Navan' as one would say 'naval'.

'Navan,' corrected Fahey, the first two letters pronounced as in 'nanny goat'.

'Navan, then. You know it?'

'Not in so many words. But of a group, top boys operating above the law in Northern Ireland, oh yeah,' he said, nodding.

'You mean a paramilitary organisation?' asked Sheen.

Fahey shook his head emphatically. 'Nothing so blunt. We're not talking about corner boys wearing surplus army gear and carrying pickaxe handles. They were ten a penny here back in the day. This was different. Once or twice I heard it called The Cabal. They were close to the establishment, connected and protected, but highly secretive; the things they were involved in were never claimed. Until right now I'd never seen one ounce of evidence to suggest such a group ever existed,' said Fahey.

'You're telling me that this was official? Gunrunning sanctioned by Whitehall?' asked Sheen, nodding at the document.

'Not a bit of it. It was zealots run by renegades. Story goes that there's always been a sect within the British Security Services, far right, and ultra-conservative,' explained Fahey.

Sheen understood. He'd heard whispers himself while in the Met. Spooks in grey suits that'd crossed the line from political servants to political puppetmasters. Smear campaigns and off-the-books investigations into left wing politicians they fancied as a red threat. There was even a rumour that they'd plotted to overthrow the British PM Harold Wilson in the 1970s.

'The last line of defence against atheist communism, right?' asked Sheen.

'Something like that. Don't forget that the IRA was fighting their long war for a *socialist* united Ireland. Other Irish republican splinter groups were even redder, outright Trots,' agreed Fahey.

'And this lot?' asked Sheen, pointing to the reference to Ulster Opposition, bottom of the page.

'Other side of the fence entirely. Sort of loyalist militia that was set up after the 1985 Anglo-Irish Agreement,' he said.

'Oh yeah, when the Protestants of Ulster believed Thatcher was selling them down the river to Dublin. People actually believed they would have a United Ireland forced on them against their wishes, correct?'

Sheen could still remember the news footage from the time, the massive banner over Belfast city hall: ULSTER SAYS NO!

'Some did,' said Fahey.

'Evidently,' said Sheen. He set the paper down and pressed his fingertips to his forehead. So much detail, the dense wiring of history behind everything he touched in this investigation. He understood what Fahey was helping to elucidate but how it linked to the Belfast murders, or his bog body, was as clear as mud.

'Sheen, take a look,' It was Aoife, the document in her hand, her eyes glittering.

Sheen snatched it, scanned the text. Header was the same, as was the list of those present (or their code names anyway). His eyes darted back to what he'd just skimmed over.

311

SUBJECT: OPERATION SATURN (OS)
DATE: FRIDAY 15TH JUNE 1975

'Bloody hell,' said Sheen.
'Quite so,' she replied.
Sheen read the body of the memorandum.

Brother Gideon and Brother David report that
Operation Saturn has been accepted as covert
tactic proposal by superiors and unrolled with
modest success. Local media have picked up
on the discovery of animal remains and staged
occult paraphernalia as hoped. Brothers confirm
considerable reduction of civilian encounters in
areas of sensitivity on both sides of the Irish border.

This has enabled Ulster Troop SAS to step up
technical reconnaissance and led to the successful
targeting of two confirmed players and recovery
of a quantity of arms. Local support wanes for
terrorists linked to 'evil', kills and capture have
dented their morale and manpower.

Suggest we widen OS to include longer stretch of
border into Counties Fermanagh and Londonderry.

'Gotcha,' said Sheen, pointing to OPERATION
SATURN printed on the page. He'd been right, all
along. The murders were tied to the covert troops out

of Aughnacloy army base in County Tyrone. Whether it was a rogue soldier who'd been murdering since the 1970s or a copycat killer new to the scene in Belfast, Sheen wasn't sure. But he knew it was the right path, and they were getting closer.

'Guess we know who Brother Gideon is anyway,' said Aoife. She'd been in perfect sync with Sheen's thoughts.

'McHenry,' he replied. He returned his attention to the other document and then his eyes rested on Rhonda Sterrit's right hand. 'I think the original version of this was left with Rhonda Sterrit's body,' said Sheen.

'The thing she'd been holding,' replied Aoife.

'Precisely,' said Sheen.

Aoife looked at the photocopied document. 'Meaning Sterrit is likely one of these code names, same as McHenry?' she asked.

'Let's go back and have a word, shall we? But first I want to speak to Captain McHenry and ask him about Operation Saturn.' And while he was there, he'd hear what McHenry thought he knew about his brother's killing. And by God, McHenry would talk this time. He'd taunted Sheen by saying John Fryer wasn't responsible for Kevin's murder. Probably just a sick jibe, but what if it wasn't? And who better placed than McHenry, master of secrets, to have an inside line on the darkest mystery Sheen had never fully solved?

His phone vibrated and sounded from his jacket. He recognised the tone; it was the Serious Crimes duty desk over at Ladas Drive. Sheen picked up, listened.

'Thanks. Text me the address. I'll need to GPS it, never been there,' he said, ending the call.

'Another body. Dumped in a public toilet near the village of Moira. Hand removed,' he said.

'Shit,' hissed Aoife.

He shared her frustration. They were close to cracking this thing wide open, but quick as they were, their murderer was fleeter on his feet. He set the documents on the table and took a photo of each before returning them to the box as he'd found them.

He turned to Fahey. 'Dermot, you need to call this in, 999. They'll send uniforms over to take a statement and when I get the call, I'll ask Geordie to be here to represent the enquiry. Best that we weren't here. It'll raise questions from Paddy Laverty as to why you called me and not the blues. It's going to take a while. Your kids might need to be somewhere else for a few hours. Sorry.'

'OK, understood,' he replied.

'Good man. And soon as you can, set to work on making more sense of those documents. I'll email you photos. The originals will be taken,' he said.

Nothing he could do about that, but he'd ask Geordie to go slow on entering them into the evidence log. The direction those documents seemed to be taking things could put the frighteners up Paddy Laverty about political fallout as he liked to call it, or worse: they could have the whole case hijacked and taken over by Special Branch.

'I want to know more. Why's it called the Circle of Navan? What you can find about the code names. They sound biblical. If there's a link with that Ulster Israelites group that Sterrit and Golding used to belong to, I need to know.'

'Not a lot, then,' replied Fahey.

'After I find out what's waiting for us up in Moira, I'm going back to speak to Captain McHenry again. What you can't tell us, I have a feeling that he can. And this time he will bloody well talk.'

CHAPTER THIRTY-FIVE

Geordie had always loved a drink but had never been a man for the smokes. Only at Christmas, or maybe at a wedding, and then only ever a cigar. He asked Hayley if she wanted something to eat or drink, as he pulled to a stop, wheels well onto the pavement and parked on a double red line on Royal Avenue in Belfast city centre.

'No, thank you,' replied Hayley.

Geordie got out and she called after him, asked for a Diet Coke. She went to offer him money, but he waved her away and marched across the road headed for the small newsagent and tobacconist. He'd brought Hayley with him when he visited the main office of Securitel in the Titanic Quarter. Sheen had called and reminded him about checking for CCTV; also said Aoife McCusker thought there was a chance the killer had been caught on the footage from a traffic mast on the Lisburn Road. He'd also asked him to get whatever mobile unit footage he could for the area where the Sterrit girl was abducted.

Geordie said that Aoife was the teacher's pet, but he knew what he was doing.

He'd bought a thumbnail USB from Argos before they'd gone to Securitel. According to the wee hippy at the counter it could hold Belfast Central Library, which was good enough for his needs. They'd managed to get an audience with the slimy Mr Danny Burgoyne, whom Aoife had mentioned at Sheen's apartment. Geordie got a nonce vibe from him straight off the bat. Also, he'd definitely rattled him. When Geordie mentioned whether he recognised him from a hotel up in Londonderry he'd broken a sweat and started talking like a washing machine. Lots of words, nothing of value.

So, he was probably the technician as Aoife had suspected, the man the late Cecil Moore had used to record the incriminating footage of her at that hotel. But though Geordie had got a copy of all the CCTV recordings from the streets of Belfast they needed, he'd have a harder time finding any footage that ball of lard wanted to keep secret, with or without a search warrant. And, of course, he was conspicuously without one.

These days filth like him didn't hide their porn under the floorboards. It was encrypted offshore, password protected and virtually impossible to access without heavyweight tech or co-operation from the scumbag. And unless Owen Sheen would permit Geordie a few hours in a basement room with Danny Burgoyne, they had to assume he'd politely decline to help. Dead end. If he still had footage of Aoife McCusker making the beast with two backs with her coked-up former boyfriend, there was little he could do about it for now. And besides, there was nothing to suggest that cretin knew anything more about how the drugs got into her locker. And that was his number one priority.

So, if high tech had failed, Geordie would have to rely on old technology, in his experience many times more effective. He paid for Hayley's drink, some chocolate bars and a fat King Edward cigar and a lighter.

'We got a ticket,' said Hayley as he got back in the car.

Geordie spied the plastic-wrapped present on his windscreen, reached out and ripped it free. He tossed it into the back seat where the rest of them lay balled.

'Meet your sisters,' he said, and pulled out, headed east.

Hayley thanked him for her drink and asked him where they were going.

'Ladas Drive station,' he said, glanced her way.

'Don't tell me, I wait outside this time,' she replied.

Geordie gave her a smile. He was getting used to Hayley; she was good craic. And she knew how to handle herself too; Beano had shit his britches despite his hard man act.

'Yeah, but don't worry, you won't be the only one who has to wait out in the cold,' he said.

Twenty minutes later Geordie walked into Ladas Drive by the side entrance, headed straight for the operation room Sheen had set up, but only to show his face. This was the pretend one, not the real thing: that was back at Sheen's cramped apartment. He needn't have bothered.

Serious Crimes was virtually empty. The only person there was the young detective whom Sheen had replaced on the Belfast murders case. He was seated at one desk in the far corner, tapping a keyboard. He looked up and Geordie bid him good day. Manners cost you nothing. He headed for the bogs, entered the ladies', and did a quick check. The stalls were empty.

Geordie unwrapped his King Edward, deposited the cellophane in one of the little white bins that opened when you waved your hand over them. He found the booth that was directly under the smoke detector, stood on the closed toilet and lit his cigar, relishing the first few draws, blue smoke billowing. He took another three or four and then raised his face to the ceiling and exhaled a stream of smoke up, right into the sensor.

A second later, total mayhem erupted.

The noise was deafening in the confined space. He jumped off the toilet, lifted the lid and dropped his smoke into the pan and flushed. He quickly exited, walked a few steps and pushed the door of the gents' open. He didn't need to go, but nevertheless stood at the ready at one of the urinals. The door opened.

'Fire alarm! We have to get out!' shouted a young guy, three-piece suit. As if Geordie hadn't noticed.

Geordie zipped up and washed his hands; the guy was still waiting.

'I know where to go,' Geordie shouted back over the din.

The young eejit nodded and away he went. It was true; he did know. He'd done enough fire drills in this building to be able to assemble in the back car park with his eyes closed. He also knew the front entrance was off limits. He exited the gents', took a sharp left, marched straight for the front desk, and found it empty as he'd hoped. If the sergeant on duty had locked his computer this little drama would be for nothing, but when Geordie touched the mouse it blinked to life.

'Good man,' thanked Geordie, and reached into his pocket and took out the little USB. He plugged it into the side of the computer as he swiftly navigated what he needed. Front desk had access to the CCTV live feed from which Geordie now observed the organised chaos of a roll call and line-up in the car park. From here he could also access archives, though how far back he wasn't sure.

He searched quickly through the months, found June and earlier empty. Presumably backed up somewhere else or deleted. He opened July. Still intact. Lucky; there must be a six-month cut off. He selected the week either side of the 12th of July, highlighted the files and copied them into his USB, waiting as the timer counted the seconds down until the operation was complete. He looked at the rest of July. There might be something there, but his storage device was full and no way was he was going to email. The sirens that had continued incessantly abruptly stopped. The void filled with a new ringing in his ears.

'Shit,' he whispered. He was running out of time. He removed his USB, found the live feed and disabled it. Next, he highlighted the recordings made for today and deleted them. After wiping the mouse and keyboard with his sleeve Geordie walked to the closed front entrance and kicked it open. The alarm triggered again, immediately filling the building he now left behind him. The front of the station was obligingly empty of personnel, and he let himself out the front gate.

'Cheers for waiting,' he said to Hayley. He'd parked a few streets away and they could both see fire engines now cross the street's entrance, headed in the direction of Ladas Drive.

'It's what I do best.'

'I don't know about that,' he replied. A message from Sheen. Geordie read it, uttered a laugh. 'Owen Sheen says that I'm about to get a call in to take over at our man Fahey's house in Claremont Street,' said Geordie.

'Problem?' asked Hayley.

Geordie said no, but Sheen wanted him to go slow on entering the evidence at the scene. 'And you think you're psychic?' Geordie laughed again.

'I'm not actually,' replied Hayley. She was staring at him, took Geordie a second to process that she was waiting for him to explain. He pulled away, headed back into town, suddenly sober.

'He said some strange documents turned up on Fahey's doorstep. And that child's hand too.'

CHAPTER THIRTY-SIX

McKeague watched and waited, the passing seconds punctuated by the incessant tapping of his right foot on the pavement. In his hand was a cold coffee in a cardboard cup. Half the contents were gone, spilt over its edge.

He had started his vigil at the corner of Chichester Street and Oxford Street, a sound vantage point for the side exit of Belfast's Laganside Courts. Williamson Golding had been easy to track down to this place. He'd called his office, claimed to represent one of their rivals and said he needed an urgent meeting with Golding. They'd tried to discourage him, said it couldn't happen at short notice. Then they'd offered Golding's email address, and after a bit more persistence, had told him he was in court, and that he would be in session most of the day. The office number, the name he'd hidden behind: so easy to find on the Internet. Golding's home address, however, was not so easy; he'd covered his tracks pretty well. McKeague hadn't even bothered to ask for it at his office, the alarm bells would ring. But Golding's abode was what McKeague needed. Best place for a private chat. And, importantly, he wanted Golding to understand that he had got to him.

He checked his watch; he'd only been waiting for half an hour, but to his racing brain it seemed an eternal purgatory of delay. The steadily moving traffic that passed by was slow as sludge to his streaming mind. He'd walked down the road and drifted in and out of St George's Market to keep camouflaged; a stationary figure stood out. A man who looked agitated could stand out too. He steadied his tapping foot. His heart knocked for release in his ribs and McKeague absorbed the thrum by clenching his jaw. Back in the day he'd cracked and ground his back molars down while speeding his way through countless Belfast nights. The warm smells of street food wafting his way from the market were no more appetising to him than his untasted coffee. His stomach was a tight, hard ball, small like his pin-prick pupils that whizzed from the road to the court doors, to the surrounding buildings, searching for watchful eyes that may have taken note of him or cameras pointed his way.

Nobody, it seemed, had taken an interest in this old man.

Movement coming from the side door of the court drew all of his frantic attention. Seconds later two people emerged, cloaks and wigs, big grins. First out was a tall woman, young and thoroughbred. A man followed; smaller, meaner.

It was Golding.

And so much fucking older! But it was definitely him; the same kestrel eyes, set in the cliff edge of his gaunt cheek bones. A big Bentley pulled up, Golding and the lanky bird got in. McKeague pondered briefly if he was banging her. Probably yes, Golding always fancied himself as a ladies' man, for ever the player. Sterrit had said he'd never settled down. McKeague watched from the kerb as the car pulled away and followed the one-way system south before indicating right into May Street. It slowed and passed the corner where McKeague stood. He glanced away as the car entered the street and then sped off. The motor had tinted windows; no way to tell if he'd been recognised. He kept eyes on it, waited until he saw its right indicator flash once more. It was turning into the parallel Victoria Street, and from there would be headed north. Beyond lay the latticework of newer motorway links that McKeague had taken note of using a map; they could get on the M3 and head east through the Titanic Quarter, or due north and join the M2. Either way Golding could soon be out of Belfast or disappear into any number of districts to the east or north. He had to keep him in sight. Not for the first time since returning to his native soil, McKeague needed to be fast.

He turned and sprinted to where he'd double-parked his rental, tore off the parking fine stuck to the windshield, got in and screeched off. He took a hard right into Victoria Street without giving way or slowing down. No sign of the Bentley. He ripped the gears down a notch, made the Fiat squeal in complaint, but felt the car bite the road and add the speed he needed. No sooner had he gained than he had to decelerate hard, red lights in his grill from a line of traffic that had stopped to obey a red light at the Albert Clock memorial. McKeague screamed blue murder inside the closed capsule of his little car, and when the light turned green he broke free from the lane of traffic and hurtled on, eyes wild, searching, but not seeing the powerful limousine.

'You fucking bastard,' he spat, and then, from the corner of his eye, he caught sight of Golding's Bentley. It had swung right onto Waring Street, away from McKeague, who was bearing straight ahead towards Dunmar Link. He braked again and pulled his right hand down hard on the wheel. The car screeched and then rocked on its springs. He barely avoided a side-on collision with a minibus, frozen faces of horror and disbelief framed in its condensation-fogged windows. A cacophony of horns and squealing tyres, and then McKeague stuck his foot down and the little car lurched off. The Bentley was out of sight again but at least he was on the right road. He tried to steady his breathing and wiped his slick palms in turn down his front. He'd slowed down, just a little; the traffic was light, and he'd made good headway. Up ahead he saw the Bentley, five cars on. McKeague followed it as it crossed the River

Lagan, assumed that Golding must have settled in east Belfast. McKeague held his position. Then the Bentley indicated and the big car took a slip road, McKeague in discreet pursuit. He was wrong about the east. They swung back on themselves, and again crossed the river, this time using the Lagan Bridge. McKeague followed as they entered the M3, which very soon after joined the M2. He was headed north after all. His driver had gone round the houses to take him there. Maybe he was being paid by the mile?

Or maybe Golding was conscious of being tailed?

The Bentley had smoothly accelerated to just under the speed limit, and McKeague matched it, but kept his distance. After a while McKeague began to wonder if Golding was taking him out of Belfast entirely, and then, he saw the Bentley's brake lights flare and it indicated left. McKeague watched it leave the motorway and join the Shore Road, still headed north. He slowed way down, let a few cars nip ahead and then took the exit at the last second. If the big car was taking Golding to dinner at the bint's place, then this could be a long game. Either way, Golding's driver was either an idiot or quite the opposite. There was no reason for taking the route he had to reach this part of town. Golding had definitely instructed him to vary the itinerary for security reasons. The habits of an old soldier never really died. McKeague drew back further. Here the traffic was lighter; his tail would be more conspicuous.

When the Bentley turned into the affluent Fortwilliam district near the Antrim Road, McKeague started to smile. This was it; this was exactly the sort of place that Golding would need to live. It befitted his standing as a barrister, ticked all the boxes, but especially the ones that he kept hidden: childhood poverty, malnutrition and violence. He drew right back now, a full street behind the Bentley; he had him, no need to panic. McKeague slowly edged the car around the corner of a residential street, Lansdowne Road. It was wide and tree-lined, with Edwardian detached homes, most with manicured hedges and off-street parking. The Bentley had stopped halfway along. Seconds later, Golding and the woman got out and entered a wide-gated property. He watched the Bentley pull away and then waited. He gave himself a full, excruciating three minutes before getting out of the tin can.

Golding's house was a pile, not just a home, set well back from the road at the end of a snaking white gravel path. There was a triple garage and probably a pool out the back. To his surprise, the farmer's-style front gate was open and unsecured, so McKeague strode up the drive, crunching the gravel under foot as he went. He pressed the doorbell with a knuckle, heard a loud bell chime from within. Seconds later it was opened by the woman, the collar of her white blouse unbuttoned, and blonde hair unfurled to her neck.

'All right, love? Is your daddy there?' enquired McKeague.

Mild surprise, and then her features closed round the fact she'd just been toyed with. But no fear, here was a young thing that had grown up in a time and place where a stranger asking for your da at the front door had never been a cause for panic. But as with so much in this life, it's never too late to learn.

'I'm sorry, can I help you?' she asked. She didn't sound like she was in a helpful mood.

McKeague rasped out a small laugh. A call came from inside asking who it was. McKeague unclenched his jaw.

'Brother David, 'mon out and have a yarn, me old mucker,' sang out McKeague.

The woman's face edged towards concern. She started to push the door closed, but McKeague could hear the rap of heels on hard wood coming their way. Golding appeared, light blue shirt undone, sleeves up. His eyes focused on McKeague, who looked back, unsmiling. A passing moment of confusion, and then recognition, and then a stone-cold stare. Tough boy, young Golding. If he was scared he wasn't showing it.

'It's OK, Emma. Let me deal with this,' he said softly. Emma opened her mouth to speak, big brown eyes saying she didn't want him to. Golding patted her gently on the arm. 'Go on, pet,' he assured.

Emma eyed McKeague warily, and he shot her a wink.

Golding stepped out and pulled the door closed. He was on a raised step, McKeague on the cusp of the gravel drive. They were almost eye to eye because of it, but McKeague still had the advantage. Neither man spoke for a long moment. McKeague broke it; he was in a hurry after all.

'Hope you're as good at keeping your gob shut when it comes to past events, mate,' he said.

'Why are you here, and calling me that name? Have you lost your mind or something?' retorted Golding.

'Touché, Golding. But you see I got a call from Gordon Sterrit of all people. His wee girl was cut up like a side of mutton, dumped on his doorstep. Friends in need and all that bollocks,' said McKeague.

Golding snorted in retort. 'So I heard,' he replied.

'But did you hear that she had a piece of paper in her hand with your name all over it? Well, in a manner of speaking, Brother David.'

Golding's eyes widened at this. But McKeague read less surprise than fast calculation. Perhaps Golding was his man, the source of the leak? If that was the case, then he was also the killer, or knew who was. McKeague's gut told him no; the home, the crusading career, the distance he'd put between himself and the past. It didn't compute. But then, life often didn't.

'What did it say?' asked Golding at last.

'Luckily for both of us it focused on Operation Manna, so Brother Moses was left holding the baby. This time.' said McKeague, scrutinising Golding intently. If he betrayed himself, even a little bit, McKeague would know it. He'd stared enough condemned men in the eye to recognise the flicker of guilt or despair at being discovered. Golding's eyes remained flinty and impassive.

'Sounds like you should have questioned Sterrit in that case,' said Golding.

'Oh, I did. And maybe I will again,' he replied.

Golding stared at him, eyes alive and cunning.

'Sterrit was clean. Why would he leak it? Why would he call me?' McKeague leant over Golding. 'I'm not a man you want as your nemesis,' he said.

'Forgive me if I don't go yapping to my mammy,' retorted Golding.

'The way Sterrit and I saw it, it had to have been someone in the know, someone with a beef against him. Maybe even someone with a beef against all of us, because where there's one naughty document, there will be more. Maybe someone like you,' said McKeague.

'Not guilty,' snapped Golding.

'Oh, but you see, you are. We all are. And guilt can do terrible things to people. Well, so they tell me anyway,' added McKeague.

'I'm nothing like you,' growled Golding, the cold control dissipating from his eyes for the first time.

'Oh, you made your feelings clear, cut your ties, followed the honourable path,' said McKeague, affecting a mock bow. 'And now you battle corruption no less, demand the truth be told, right?'

Golding said nothing.

'Won't be long before a few home truths come out about you unless I nip this in the bud. About both of us,' he said darkly. 'And if we're clean and Sterrit's clean, it leaves one man still alive who could have done this. Where's McHenry?'

'Fuck am I supposed to know? Changed his name, disappeared. He could be anywhere,' replied Golding.

Which was true, but McKeague knew what awaited men after a long stint inside, and more often than not it wasn't a savings account with the means to fly to the other side of the world.

'Anyway,' continued Golding, 'hasn't he suffered enough? The guy did his time, and in his day he was the best. You hear me, McKeague, he was the best,' said Golding, one finger raised and pointed now in McKeague's face.

'I just want a word. Face-to-face, like this. Because I wonder, Golding, is your captain so loyal to you? Last time I heard he wanted nothing to do with you, accepted a hard stretch rather than take your help. If we don't find the leak and put a plug in it, all of this,' he said, gesturing to the house and gardens, 'could come crashing down.'

'McHenry got me wrong,' said Golding.

'Aye, probably he did. Your tastes are not like mine,' he said, nodding towards the big front door behind which Emma waited. 'But if he's our man, then he's going to do you wrong. So, tell me where he is, while I'm asking you, and young Emma, nicely,' said McKeague.

Golding flashed him a look. 'I'm not scared of you, pal.'

McKeague said nothing.

Golding shook his head, eyes moving left to right.

'He's in Glencairn, living under the name of Craigavon,' he said, and gave McKeague a street address. Not two miles as the crow flies. And a shithole, exactly where a fallen old felon would be expected to end up.

'Small world,' observed McKeague. 'What's he do?'

'Drinks,' replied Golding.

McKeague turned and started to scrunch across the vast gravel river of the drive. His mouth was dry as dust, and he felt the weight of his limbs like they'd been dipped in concrete. He was coming down fast, and eventually he'd crash, not even another ounce of speed would keep him awake when that happened. But not yet, for now another few grams would send his rocket skyward again.

Golding shouted his name; he stopped.

'Two peelers came to me. Owen Sheen. London boy. And Aoife McCusker, home-grown. Asking questions about Sterrit's kid,' he said.

'And you said?'

'Nothing.'

'I'll give you that, Golding, you know how to keep your mouth shut,' replied McKeague.

Golding reddened. 'He also said he found a child's body in the bog, down Monaghan way. Dates from the old days,' said Golding. He took a few steps towards McKeague. 'What the fuck did you do, you sick bastard?'

McKeague ignored him, turned again and headed for the gate, half a world away. So now he had two nosey peelers to deal with here too? The more the merrier. But first it was time to go and find dear old Captain McHenry or whatever he was calling himself these days. Golding said he'd suffered enough. McKeague rested a hand on the gate post. He was panting, mouth dry, back and chest wet with the sweats.

'We'll fucking see about that,' he said, and headed to his car.

CHAPTER THIRTY-SEVEN

The GPS got Sheen and Aoife close, but the disused public convenience where Pastor Simon Nixon's body had been found wasn't easy to locate. Exactly the point, Sheen surmised as he retraced his way back along the largely empty Belfast Road just south of Moira in County Down, outside Belfast. Five minutes later, after slowly scanning either side of the route, Sheen spotted the blue lights of a stationary police vehicle parked just off-road up ahead. He also spotted Paddy Laverty talking to a uniform on guard at the police tape, the wind sweeping his greying hair this way and that. Sheen pulled into a lay-by.

'Best if you wait here,' said Sheen.

Aoife sighed but nodded, she'd spotted him too.

He handed her the car keys. 'In case I'm delayed. Or you're asked to move on,' he explained.

He got out and started to make up the hundred metres or so distance to the crime scene, buffeted by the wind, but gulping the clean country air as though it could feed him insight. While he'd been in the Forensic Mortuary at the Royal getting a handle on the killer's signature use of diamorphine, another innocent person had already been murdered and dumped. He needed to be sharper and smarter on this, especially with Laverty snooping round.

Sheen reached the tape, showed his card and signed in. Laverty was a few feet away, gave him a quizzical look.

'D'you walk here?'

'Parked a bit away,' he replied.

Laverty tossed him a forensic suit and mask, beckoned for him to follow him deeper into the crime scene.

'What brings you here?' enquired Sheen, keeping it casual.

'Was in the area, heard that it had been called in. Thought I'd swing by. I am the SIO after all,' he replied.

Sheen grunted his assent; asked who had found the body.

'Some old boy who'd pulled over for a pish,' replied Laverty.

Sheen surveyed the bleak stone structure of the disused toilet block, overgrown with weeds and tall grass. The doors were bricked up. Not exactly a convenient convenience but perhaps old habits die hard, especially for old men?

'Where's Geordie?' asked Laverty.

Sheen had stepped into the white paper suit, and they were following a taped off pathway towards the block. To their left and right similarly attired CSIs were on their hands and knees doing their painstaking work. One was taking a liquid clay mould: a footprint, Sheen assumed. But it was the body that interested Sheen, and he could see the edge of a small tented enclosure peeking from the left side of the old building. Halogen lamps on steel stands were plugged into a generator and already bathed the area in clean light, as the gloom of the afternoon succumbed to dusk. Sheen and Laverty approached the heart of the scene via designated plastic stepping plates.

'Told him to take a run down to Securitel, get the CCTV from Lisburn Road and any mobile units in the area at the time Rhonda Sterrit went missing,' he said. 'Was going to call it in for you to officially action.'

'Well, consider it done. And you can get me up to speed in a minute now that we're face-to-face,' replied Laverty.

Sheen nodded.

'Was that CCTV not already requested?' he asked.

Sheen shook his head.

'Fuck's sake, that gobshite Stevens should be on traffic. But he can't drive for love nor money either,' said Laverty. Sheen assumed he meant the young officer who'd been handling the case before he took over; the one he'd spotted looking perplexed and frantic outside Clonard when Father Phil's body had been discovered.

'We're on it now,' offered Sheen.

'Least there's one man I can rely on,' replied Laverty.

No, one bloody good woman, Aoife McCusker, in fact, Sheen silently corrected him. *The same woman you did a Pontius Pilate on and were happy to see nailed up with every other bent scum copper whose luck has finally run dry.*

'Can't get the staff,' murmured Sheen. A platitude, but in this case, it was almost fitting.

'Ah, sure you know Stevens is the chief constable's nephew?'

Sheen admitted this was news.

Laverty nodded, eyes to the heavens.

They entered the small tent. Super clean white light illuminated a man's body prostrate on the ground, feet to the wall, face down. Two things took his attention; his trousers and underwear were hawked down round his ankles, and his right hand was missing at the wrist. A small glance at the neatly filleted lower arm bones that pronged from the muscle of the limb told Sheen this was the work of the same killer. But not just the precision of the cut; it was the missing appendage, the staged humiliation of the body, it all fitted.

A man dressed like Sheen and Laverty was hunkered down next to the corpse, examining the discolouration of the skin that was visible on the legs. He looked up. Wire-rimmed penny glasses, clever and alert eyes.

'This is Art MacMurrow, police surgeon,' said Laverty.

'DI Owen Sheen. Nice to meet you.'

Art's eyes widened. 'I know the name. An honour to meet the man,' he said. Sheen could feel Laverty bristle at Art's reply. 'I'd like to shake your hand, but,' he said, and by way of explanation opened the buttocks of the body and inserted an oversized thermometer into its anus.

'What can you tell us?' said Laverty, getting back to business and taking the reins. He was the SIO after all.

Art flicked the thermometer gently. 'Judging by livor mortis I'd say the body has been here between five and ten hours,' he said, moving his finger along the line of purple discolouration that marked the lower portion of the legs and buttocks.

'Lividity like this sets in pretty quickly after death. But if you look here,' said Art, motioning them over to his side, 'this effect tells us how long he's been here,' he said, and pressed two fingers into the muscle of the lower thigh. Sheen watched as the light purple tone disappeared to white at the pressure of his touch.

'Anything longer than ten hours and that would stay purple,' he explained. 'But I have to say, I think this man lost a lot of blood before he was placed here,' said Art.

'Meaning he might have been killed and butchered before he was dumped here this morning?' asked Laverty.

'It's possible. No more than a day,' suggested Art.

Made sense; it was obvious from the vicinity that his hand had not been removed in situ, and Rhonda Sterrit's body had displayed the same characteristics. Sheen explained his thinking, then hunkered down beside Art, carefully took Simon Nixon's remaining hand in his own and examined the nails. As expected, they were tinged with blue.

'Can we see his face?' he asked.

Art looked to Laverty for guidance, who confirmed the police photographer had finished with the body. Art lifted Nixon's face from the damp ground. Sheen noted that his eyes were still open, but tried not to be drawn by this. He focused on the dead man's lips. Sure enough, blue-purple tinged, just like his nails, and just like Rhonda Sterrit.

'You think he was drugged, don't you?' asked Art.

Clever man indeed. Sheen explained his findings from Rhonda's autopsy. Art stood back from the body, eyes down, searching. Already he was seeking an answer to the question Sheen had yet to ask.

'There,' he said, pointing at a tiny prick point on Simon Nixon's rear. Nothing as pronounced as the bruise Sheen had seen on Rhonda Sterrit, but there nonetheless. 'You'd have to wait for autopsy and tox reports, but I'd say that's a candidate for a point of injection,' said Art.

Sheen told him about the mark on Rhonda Sterrit, an angry bruise, not like this.

'Everyone's different. Could be she was tense and resistant when injected, this man maybe more tranquil,' he suggested.

Or he'd already been incapacitated, thought Sheen. Simon Nixon was a big man. He noted the swelling round Simon Nixon's left knee and pointed to it. Art confirmed his kneecap had been smashed, and his collar bone was broken too. Whoever had done this had done a number on a pretty big man. Sheen stepped back, took in his surroundings once more.

Getting him here on foot would be quite a job, assuming he was dead when he'd been dumped here. Next, Sheen carefully eyed the surrounding patch of earth, not really expecting to find anything new. The place had been photographed and the body checked already. If there was a document left it would have been found by now. He took out his phone and recorded a few images, as was his way, and then he and Laverty left the shelter of the small tent and stood in the gusting air once more.

'How'd we ID him?' asked Sheen.

'Driver's licence, back pocket. No wallet, no phone. Uniform are at his house, about five miles away, interviewing his wife. He was travelling for work yesterday, due home, never showed. His wee church is located beside his house. She called it in late in the evening,' explained Laverty.

'Why leave the licence unless they wanted him to be identified when discovered?'

'They?' enquired Laverty.

Sheen gave Laverty a run-down on his thinking and what they'd found so far. Namely that this was either one very powerful person, or a tight team, and that there were links, as he'd initially hypothesised, to the body in the bog that his team had uncovered the previous summer. He didn't mention the Circle of Navan, the fact Rhonda Sterrit's hand had turned up on Fahey's doorstep or his suspicions about Williamson Golding's past history with Trevor McHenry. Fahey's emergency services call would have been relayed to him by now, but his phone was on silent in his pocket; the record would show he was here when the news reached him officially. There'd be a drag, and it would serve to keep Laverty half a step out of sync. Until he got the measure of what they were dealing with it was exactly where he needed him to be. One sniff of political corruption and this would be air-lifted from him, and with it his chance to solve the mystery of the body from the bog and to get things sorted for Aoife.

'So, what you're saying is we could have a serial killer who's been on the road since the '70s?'

'Or more likely a copycat, maybe even an apprentice learning his trade?' suggested Sheen, his words sounding barely plausible to his own ears. Then again, the reality of what he seemed to be uncovering here was hardly the stuff of a flatpack murder investigation.

Laverty didn't seem too perturbed by Sheen's idea, but he rounded on him.

'You promised me results, a collar. What you're giving me is a body count, with parts missing,' he said.

Comradeship between reliable men was short-lived.

'I'm hoping for a break on the CCTV. Plus, I'm digging into Father Phil Rafferty's background, and the footage from inside the monastery. There's something that links him to Rhonda Sterrit, and now to this man Nixon,' he offered.

Though at present, he was none the wiser as to what that might be. A run over to Glencairn to shake some answers out of Trevor McHenry ought to change that.

'Good luck with solving a case on CCTV,' said Laverty. 'You do know who this fella's father was, right?' he said, nodding at the small tent where Simon Nixon's body lay.

Sheen admitted he didn't.

'Look him up. Pastor Kyle Nixon, real fire and brimstone preacher from way back. He started his own fringe political party in the 1970s, then that Ulster Opposition thing in the '80s,' said Laverty.

Sheen's heart responded with an involuntary thud at the mention of Ulster Opposition, also in the document that referred to Operation Manna, guns from South Africa and the arming of fringe loyalist groups.

'Oh yeah, I remember that. Dad's Army for Ulster Protestants set up after the Anglo-Irish Agreement in the '80s,' he said.

Laverty gave him an appreciative side glance. 'Well informed for a London boy,' he praised. 'They weren't even that. Middle class twats wearing berets and attending rallies. Toothless,' said Laverty.

Sheen wasn't so sure Laverty was correct about that.

'You think all that stuff could be linked to this,' he chanced.

Laverty scoffed and replied instantly. 'Doubt it. You can't get more personal than murdering someone. You'll not find the answer in a history book. Which is a rare thing in this place,' he said.

Sheen's brain was whirling. Laverty had a point but, in this case, he was very wrong. There was also nothing more personal than *unfinished history*; he knew it all too well. But if he and Aoife were correct and McHenry was Brother Gideon of the Circle of Navan, then Simon Nixon's father could have been involved too. Laverty's mention of Ulster Opposition was too much of a coincidence to be anything but significant.

'This guy Kyle Nixon. Know where I might find him?' asked Sheen.

'Up above or down below, depending on your estimation of him. Long dead,' clarified Laverty. 'Sure, his son was near middle-aged,' he went on.

Sheen's spirits sagged at this news, and then, a fat pulse of excitement ran through him.

His *son*.

Sheen looked over at the small tent that covered Simon Nixon's remains. Butchered and dumped to be found, just like young Rhonda.

Sterrit's *daughter*.

'Simon Nixon, he take after his father?' enquired Sheen, trying hard to keep his tone nonchalant.

'What, like into politics and the like? Na, low profile, and a really good guy, I've been told,' answered Laverty.

The good man, the innocent child, both sacrificed. The importance of Rhonda as Sterrit's daughter, it had been something he'd glanced over, but it was core to this. Both victims were the children of men who'd had skeletons in the closet. A quote he'd read, attributed to the Irish republican hunger striker Bobby Sands: *Our revenge will be the laughter of our children.*

343

But what if some people thought the opposite was true?

A CSI approached, lifted her mask, spoke to Laverty. 'They've been trying to reach you, asked that you check your phone, sir,' she said.

Laverty fumbled past the zipper of his white suit, extracted his phone.

'Bollocks. A UDA man's just been gunned down in Rathcoole. Crazy bloody Horse, he called himself,' he said, already moving off, back in the direction of the road. 'Keep me informed, Sheen,' he shouted without turning. Laverty's words made Sheen think about Geordie's mention of Rathcoole the day before, but no sooner had Laverty turned to go than Art MacMurrow walked his way from the direction of the toilet block.

'C'mere. You'll want to see this,' he said.

Sheen followed him, not into the tent, but around the other side. There was a hole in a bricked-up door. A CSI emerged, a brown evidence bag in hand. Sheen knew what it would be before he carefully removed the document within.

As with the others, this too had the same header, in the original red lettering. It was addressed for Archangel and had the same list of Brothers present. He scanned down the page. And there it was.

Brother Aaron reports the successful launch of Ulster Opposition as a third force against the Anglo-Irish Agreement. Popular support has been strong, and media coverage widespread. The hope is to make this 'our Ulster Workers' Strike' and bring the country to a standstill when necessary.

Brother Samson motioned for arms and munitions, seconded by Brother Jeroboam and Brother Moses has agreed to approach friends in Israel.

Brother Samson has suggested funds could be released from [REDACTED] bank in [REDACTED] and we request blind eye from the security forces in the acquisition of a lump sum, dates and times will be communicated.

Sheen couldn't make sense of all of this. But two things were clear. This document predated that sent to Fahey with Rhonda's missing hand, the one that communicated the successful acquisition of arms from South Africa. And secondly, the main story here was Ulster Opposition, launched by none other than Brother Aaron, clearly Nixon's deceased father. He took several photos of the document, mailed the update to Fahey and then bagged it and gave it back to the CSI. He wanted to hear what Fahey had found, start to properly unpick the Circle of Navan, and work out why someone was targeting their offspring and had murdered Father Phil Rafferty too. So many questions, and the case was finally moving. But he needed to be fast, otherwise it would bury him. One thing he did know; this was larger than Operation Saturn, and more personal than some nutjob former soldier who'd gone off the reservation.

Sheen ran up the path, stripped his protective suit from his body and jogged down the road, eyes searching for his parked car. Trevor McHenry was a man who could answer at least some of these questions, but Sheen couldn't shake the feeling that the Devil himself was breathing down his neck.

CHAPTER THIRTY-EIGHT

'Where'd you go?' asked Sheen.

Aoife had pulled his car up across the road from where he'd left her, and now got out of the driver's seat and back into the passenger side.

'Nixon's place,' she replied.

'Laverty said uniform were sent to his home,' said Sheen.

Aoife nodded, as Sheen did a quick check and U-turned the car before sticking his foot down and moving through the gears, Belfast bound.

'Yeah, they were. Saw them at his house, so I took a look over the little church,' she explained.

Sheen recalled Laverty mentioning that Nixon's Baptist Church was close to his home. Smart move from Aoife, but not if their colleagues had caught her snooping round a possible crime scene.

She read the concern on his face. 'They didn't see me. Place had a big car park, easy to conceal yourself from the house, and the road,' she explained.

Sheen shot her a glance, and she nodded back, their thinking in line. It sounded ideal for a murderer to watch and wait.

'I'll make a call, remind the plods to cover the church grounds too,' he said.

'There's more. The door to the church was open, and inside the place was a mess. Big stack of wooden chairs scattered up the aisle, one of the pews overturned,' she explained.

Sheen thought it through, the beat of his mind matching the spaced-out road lamps that sucked by as he sped along.

'Was the door to the church damaged?'

'No, I checked. Unlocked,' she confirmed.

'So, they lay in wait, waited till Nixon went inside, and took him from there,' he suggested.

Aoife pulled out her phone, touched the screen and held a photo up for him to see.

'Looks that way. This was on the floor,' she said.

It was a man's wallet, brown leather, face down and unfolded. Sheen explained that Nixon's licence was found on his body, and then gave her a potted summary of what else he'd found at the toilet block, including the realisation that both Simon Nixon and Rhonda Sterrit were the children of men who'd apparently been involved in dark dealings with the Circle of Navan.

'So, somebody's targeting the children of these people?' asked Aoife.

'Looks that way, doesn't it?'

'But Father Phil was an old man. No way he was a child of one of these people,' she said, meaning the Circle of Navan.

Sheen tapped the steering wheel, his brain revving but not in gear. Aoife was correct of course. Father Phil Rafferty was important, the first person killed and that had to be significant.

'And speaking as his friend, I can tell you for a fact, Sheen, that he had nothing to do with them,' she continued.

Sheen was less sure about that, but she was correct about Father Phil Rafferty being too old to match his hypothesis.

'Plus, why plant the documents? Why go to the bother of making it ritualistic, but then use the morphine to make it painless?' Sheen asked.

'Where did these documents come from? And why now?' she asked.

Sheen slowed as he entered the narrow streets of Glencairn, trying to remember the way to McHenry's home.

'I'm not sure about the why, Aoife,' he replied. 'But McHenry was Military Intelligence. I'd say the captain is our source. And even though it seems he's named in at least one of those documents, so far he's not been victimised. A safe place to start asking questions about the secret files,' he said, sneaking into a parking spot across from McHenry's house.

'Sheen, those documents were addressed to someone,' she said.

'Archangel,' agreed Sheen. 'No clue,' he added.

'That's not my point. If they were sent memos, then how could McHenry have still possessed them in original form, assuming it was our killer who made that photocopy?'

'I'd say it was an insurance policy that he took out, a copy of the originals made at the time of sending,' said Sheen.

Aoife nodded. 'Looks like he's finally decided to cash it in.'

No lights burned in McHenry's home and there was no answer when Sheen knocked on the front door or living-room window. Even the neighbour with the crooked nose didn't come out. Sheen sighed, started towards Andy's Booze Hut. But from the top of the road he could see its illuminated glass front, and the place was empty, no sign of McHenry.

Try the offy. That's where he's usually to be found.

Or drinking down the allotment.

A boy, maybe thirteen, approached, clacking over the flagstones on a steel scooter.

Sheen raised a hand and he stopped.

'You know where the allotments are, kid?'

The boy pointed across the dark patch of ground adjacent to the line of shops, told them to follow the path. Sheen and Aoife cut across the kids' play area, which also had a range of outside gym equipment.

'Look,' said Aoife, walking a little deeper into the shadows. Tall cans of continental lager were spread across the soft rubber foam surface. Two blue plastic bags rustled in the light breeze, snagged on the underside of a roundabout. She tugged one free. A swing squeaked on its rusted hinge. 'This has been cut open,' she said.

A scream, garbled and ghastly, pierced the still air.

'Go!' said Sheen, already running across the thin path that traversed the playing fields.

Another wail. It didn't sound human, so high-pitched and incessant, barely punctuated by what must be the gasps of the person emitting the sound.

Sheen removed his Glock. He picked up his pace, sprinting now.

The screaming stopped abruptly.

Sheen skidded to a halt, panting hard, his eyes searching.

Aoife arrived at his side, equally puffed.

'There,' she said, pointing to a wooden door in a fenced-off section of the sloping ground. It stood slightly open. Sheen saw a rusted latch and lock hanging by a single screw to the frame, and splintered wood.

Aoife charged on, too fast for Sheen's grabbing hand. He went after her. She was unarmed. Sheen went through the door first, weapon raised. He tracked the Glock in an arc in front of them, and then swung round, checked the blind spot behind the door, up and down the line of the fence, but saw nothing. The ground fell away steeply, portioned off in neat sections, some rich with growing greens, others fallow and bare. Sheen moved down the small central path that led from the entrance, saw a potting shed at the crux of the hill, water butt and standing tap next to it.

He led the way, gun ready, eyes alert. They reached the door. The sliding bolt had been pried off and was on the ground at Sheen's feet, small Yale lock and all. He nodded to Aoife who met his eyes, one hand on the edge of the door. Sheen was ready to enter, gun in hand. He wished to God he'd remembered to bring his torch from the car. He mouthed a count of one to three. Aoife wrenched the door open on three, and Sheen bore inside.

'Armed police. Don't move!' he yelled.

The place was small, two quick checks in front and behind the door told him he was alone. Then he peered deeper into the gloom and saw that the shed turned on an L shape up ahead to the right. He silently explained to Aoife, now next to him. She nodded and he moved, stealthily, in a half crouch. He'd given fair warning and wouldn't do it twice. Sheen reached the blind corner. Before he could hesitate, he ducked and rounded, gun tracking the orbit ahead, his eyes wide.

'Oh, sweet Jesus,' he gasped, absorbing the horror before him. He lowered the gun.

Aoife had pressed her body against his side, and she cried out.

Trevor McHenry had been suspended by the wrists using a line of rope tied round fat hooks on either wall. The rest of the rope was coiled near his partially suspended feet. He was wearing only his socks and underpants, and even in the murk Sheen could see he'd suffered a terrible death. His torso and legs were a canvas of a thousand cuts, shallow slices that had lacerated the skin but probably not severed a main artery. The torturer must have inflicted maximum agony that could be horribly prolonged. Sheen saw a strip of duct tape on the ground. It had probably been used to gag the poor bastard. Until his final moments when Sheen had heard him wail. McHenry's head was slumped on his chest, but from the dark apron of blood that had spread from under his chin, Sheen knew his throat had been cut. He put an arm round Aoife's shoulder. She'd buried her face in his chest. The old soldier had probably begged to be killed.

He'd heard him wail.

Sheen nudged Aoife off him, snapping out of the shock at last. He touched the man's forehead. It was still warm.

'Shit,' he hissed, raised his gun and headed for the entrance.

They'd been close, almost on top of the killer before he'd decided to end it for McHenry or got what he wanted out of him. From outside, faint but not too distant, Sheen heard the dull clink of a clay pot being broken or kicked over. He bounded through the shed and out the door, saw nothing. Then, at the top of the slope, movement; it was the wooden door closing. Sheen took the hill in long strides, barged the door with his right shoulder and was instantly knocked backwards, almost off his feet. He pushed it with both hands, felt it yield, but barely. Two stout kicks told Sheen it wasn't going to budge: he'd put enough doors in over the years to know when he was wasting his time. He cursed through gritted teeth. It opened outwards and the fucker had jammed it good.

Sheen took a step or two back and scanned the fence. It was six feet tall and rested on twin-stacked concrete gravel boards, which made it over eight feet. He holstered his weapon, took a run up and half jumped, half walked up the lower part of the fence, got his right hand over the top to hoist up and over. He cried out in pain and shock, fell off, ended on his arse on the earth, clutching his right hand to his body.

'Fucking hell,' he yelled, more in anger, but his hand was bleeding and hurting too.

'What happened?' asked Aoife, joining him.

'What the fuck is it about Belfast and barbed wire?' he said.

Sheen got up, found a ball of tissue in his pocket and pressed it into his hand. Hurt like a bastard. He took out his gun, raised it to the door. He'd blow the hinges off and squeeze out.

Whispered voices from outside the door.

'Armed police. Open this door,' he commanded.

To his surprise the talking stopped, and, after a lot of scratching and thumping, the door opened. It was the kid, with another, the one who'd given him directions.

Sheen saw on the ground the pickaxe that had been used to secure the door.

'Mister, it wasn't me, I swear to ye,' the kid said, one hand raised. In his other was an open can of lager, same as Sheen and Aoife had found in the playground.

Sheen ignored him, ran back the way he'd come, knowing already that he was too late. He stopped at the edge of the playground, scanned the well-lit streets of Glencairn, saw nothing. He tracked back, was about to call 999 and then instead hit Geordie's number. He answered on the first ring.

'Sheen. Bout ye. Listen, I got my hands on the CCTV, from Ladas Drive nick. Don't be asking me how—' but Sheen broke him off, explained what had happened.

'Holy fuck,' said Geordie. 'Will I meet you back at your gaff, then?' he asked.

Sheen stopped walking, his mind on the killer he'd just let slip past him.

'No, come here, and quick.'

A short time later Hayley stood next to Sheen with McHenry's cooling body grotesquely spread-eagled before them. Bringing her here was a risk, in every way. One more person entering a crime scene, contaminating the evidence; he ought to know better. But she'd been accurate when she said that Father Phil's killer must have been super strong. He'd give her a chance. He had blown his earlier, after all.

Sheen used the torch on his phone to illuminate the body.

'Listen, I can't give you much time. And you can't touch anything,' he added.

Hayley didn't respond immediately, just stood there looking at McHenry. She turned her eyes to Sheen, full of glass and shock. He shouldn't have done this, it wasn't fair, and it sure as hell wasn't good police work.

'Then I'm not sure what you want me to say.'

Sheen didn't respond.

Hayley turned again to McHenry. She moved closer, raised a hand to the taut line of the rope that held one of his wrists. She nodded to it and, after a little hesitation, Sheen nodded back to her. There would be no prints left on it anyway, and they'd be massively unlucky if the part Hayley touched happened to have the only DNA left by their murderer. She slowly closed one hand round the rope and stood, eyes closed, concentrating. Sheen waited, ten, twenty, thirty seconds. Nothing. One of McHenry's eyes now rested on Sheen, demanded his attention. It was empty as the abyss.

Sheen looked away, was about to speak, call it a night, when Hayley's free arm shot out and she grabbed him above the elbow, hard enough to hurt. Her whole body was thrumming, as though the conduit of a hefty electrical current. The rope that she still clasped in her other hand had picked up the vibration and so too had McHenry's body. It was quivering, horrendously animated, alive and writhing in agony once more before Sheen's eyes. He involuntarily tried to take a step back – he couldn't help himself – but Hayley's fingers had bolted to his arm and she held him fast, her spasm now making him shake too.

From what seemed like a long way away, Aoife's voice, strident.

'Hayley! Hayley, are you OK? Sheen, stop this!'

McHenry's body was still dancing, his head shaking from side to side. *No, no, I will not stop, I will not stop.* There was nothing Sheen could do. Words from Hayley, repeated again and again in a hoarse, rising whisper as she exhaled and inhaled, still shuddering, her eyes closed but oddly at peace, as though in repose. And yet, her cheeks were wet with tears.

'Kill me, kill me, kill me, kill me,' she chanted, her plea rising in volume, making Sheen wince, until the words slurred into incoherence and she emitted a terrible, high-pitched wail, relentless and hardly human.

Sheen tried to pull away but was again moored in place by a greater power. The wail, it was a copy of the awful sound he'd heard from McHenry, not just like it, but identical. He'd never be able to forget it.

Just as Sheen thought he was about to lose his calm entirely, Hayley let go of the rope. And then, she let go of his arm. He readied himself to catch her should she collapse, but she stood firm, arms by her sides, head lowered. McHenry's body finally stopped shaking. Hayley wiped her face on her sleeve.

'I want to get out of here now,' she said quietly.

Sheen showed her the way, wanting to ask her what she'd found, but holding back on questions and praying he hadn't fouled up the scene entirely for this waste of time. A part of him, which until very recently had been a dyed-in-the-wool sceptic, was now pretty sure that McHenry had not only begged for his life, the poor bastard had also begged to be killed near the end.

They made their way out of the allotments and Sheen called 999 when they reached the playground. He needed to get Aoife and Hayley offside pronto, told Geordie to bring them to his apartment. Fahey would probably be there, assuming his wife was back from work to look after the kids. Sheen said he would join them as soon as he could.

'It was a different killer. Whoever murdered Father Phil didn't kill this man,' said Hayley.

Sheen quickly ran the numbers: no secret documents at the scene, no missing limbs and no sign of a morphine injection. At least one of the above was obvious to see, but the other details were case-specific, so far shared between him and Aoife.

'Go on,' he said.

Hayley slowly shook her head, as though straining to select the right words.

'The person that did this enjoyed it, didn't want it to be over. It's almost like,' she paused, 'like it's a hobby?' she said, but was clearly not content with the word.

'A sport?' said Sheen softly.

Either Hayley knew more about serial offenders than the average person, or it was more proof that she was genuine.

She nodded her agreement. 'When I touched that rope, I saw Captain McHenry's face. Just before he died, it was a mask of agony and despair. It was very strong, like the killer had taken a picture, taken it away with him,' she said.

'Like a trophy, you mean?' asked Sheen.

'Exactly like that. And it's not his first.'

CHAPTER THIRTY-NINE

McKeague pulled in a few houses away from the address in Fruithill Park in West Belfast that Trevor McHenry had finally given him. This was where he'd find the woman McHenry had foolishly decided to pass the documents to, the woman who fancied herself some kind of avenging angel.

His gut instinct, those tinkling bells he'd heard way deep down, that the answer was in his book of souls, was right. McHenry had held out for longer than he'd expected. Almost became hard work for him, but not quite. His new knife was a razor; he'd have to mail it home to Spain after this was finished. He popped the boot and found his Polaroid. McHenry's moment of death had been a missed opportunity. There wouldn't be another. Like the blade, the photographs, if he got any, would be forwarded to a post box in Málaga he used for such purposes.

He forced himself to unlock his jaw, felt it throb. His head was light; legs were like jelly. Weakness had replaced power as the speed waned once more in his system, and he would soon be running on empty. But first, he'd unfuck this situation or, as Sterrit preferred, provide necessary containment. And with a bit of luck, he'd enjoy a frolic to remember, and capture. He mouthed another two wraps, which left just one in his stash, and strapped his camera round his chest.

McKeague approached the house. It was a large semi-detached, but run-down and looked vacant. He walked up and rang the doorbell, knocked the door three times too for good measure. Follow the path of least resistance, always. The speed started to kick in his blood, a bass beat tripping in his ears.

No reply. The place exuded emptiness. He stepped back, scanned the empty eyes of the windows, turned his attention to the wide wooden doors of the double-fronted garage. They were secure, brass padlock and thick silver chain. The small side entrance was also locked, new padlock threaded through the draw bolt. He pressed the wooden trellis that crowned the door and felt it give. He punched it three times and it fell inwards. There was no barbed wire or broken glass, and it was not very high now that the trellis was gone, eye level with McKeague. He glanced both ways, but the street was sedate, and flipped the camera round to rest on his back. He took a small run up, leapt up and over, torso first, wriggled his upper body through the gap, swung his legs over and dropped to the yard below. He stopped, still and listening, but there was no life here.

He tried the back door. Locked. McKeague took an empty clay flowerpot from the back step and used its base to punch a hole in the glass. He paused, alert for movement from the adjacent home that overlooked him, but all was quiet. He cleared the glass shards, reached in and turned the key, still in the lock. He entered, crunching on glass, senses alive, one fist now moulded into the handle of his blade. The stink hit him as a drone filled his ears. McKeague grimaced; the place was rotten, smelt like a tramp's crotch. He walked from the kitchen into an adjacent diner. The sound was louder here, a somnolent hum. A mound of flies, heaving from a lump of what looked like rotted meat. In one corner was a mop bucket, more flies ballooned from its rim. McKeague waved the fat flies from his face as they rose and then settled again on their quarry. The kitchen was bare. He moved. Went from room to room, eyes searching for files, books where documents could be secreted, a computer; there was nothing. The bitch's house looked like she was already dead. He checked upstairs. A few old magazines were on a bedside table. Like the rest of the floor, it was thick with dust.

He came back down, exited the back door and took in fresh air. The door to the garage was secured with another small padlock, this one old-looking. He popped it with the steel shaft of a mop that he found in the back garden. The wooden door creaked on its hinges. Inside the garage was cool and dank, oil and old cut grass in his nose. And something else, heavier, rusted and organic. It was a smell he knew well. And that same lazy buzzing sound filled the room.

It was blood.

He found a hanging light string, pulled it and squinted as the interior was flooded in a yellow glare from the overhead strip. The workbench along the far wall was carpeted in fat black flies; they rippled and droned, revealing the red gore beneath on which they feasted. McKeague ignored it, walked to the shelf above the bench where what he wanted had caught his eye.

He slid out the sheaf of papers. The header told him he had what he came for.

CIRCLE OF NAVAN

Unlike the copy Sterrit had shown him on his phone which was in colour, the header printed in red, these were black and white photocopies. He scanned the list of once-familiar names, and then read each file quickly, his own blood beginning to boil with each page.

McHenry had been busy. And there were more questions, those he didn't get around to asking him. Like, who was this Archangel, the person he'd been reporting to?

'Not relevant,' he chastised himself.

And right now, that was true. Whoever McHenry had been feeding reports to over the years managed to sit on these secrets for long enough and were probably unaware he'd been making duplicates for his own purposes. The woman who owned this dump was his problem, the source of the leak. He'd heard on the radio that Nixon's son had been killed. Probably meant another document had also escaped. No matter. He flicked through the ream, found the one that concerned him most. All it would take was one bit of evidence that proved he was Samson. McHenry swore there was nothing, but this time last week there'd been no documents about the Circle of Navan, and here we fucking all are.

He stuffed the copies into his jacket and went back through the house, exited the front door. His prey was out there, but he knew where he'd run her to ground. He started the car and checked his fuel. Just like him the wee rental was running low, but there was enough in the tank to take him to where he needed to go. It was time for the endgame to finally unfuck this mess.

And time for a long overdue run down the country. He'd not been there for years.

CHAPTER FORTY

It was evening time before Sheen finally got back to his apartment, and still no sign of Dermot Fahey. After leaving Trevor McHenry's murder scene he'd gone back to speak to Williamson Golding, this time catching him at his home address. Sheen had got precisely nowhere. Golding was as inscrutable and closed as he'd been earlier in the day. He didn't even flinch when Sheen told him about Trevor McHenry and how he had died. He was more concerned about getting ready for some charity dinner that he was a benefactor of. Sheen had noticed the silver-flocked invitation on the little table by his front door. Shared Futures Foundation, some sort of cross-community youth federation, building tomorrow today, apparently. But Golding was no philanthropist; he was a seriously cold fish. That said, he'd displayed something close to real trepidation when he'd first opened his front door to Sheen's unannounced visit. And it wasn't nerves at being questioned by a copper, something Sheen had seen so many times. It was almost as though he'd been expecting someone else.

Hayley and Aoife were tidying up the remains of a Chinese takeaway. Geordie was busy on Sheen's laptop, still working through the CCTV footage. Sheen asked him if he'd had any more luck with surveillance footage from mobile units at the time Rhonda Sterrit was abducted and later dumped outside her home at Newforge Lane.

Geordie didn't look up. 'Zero,' he said. 'And the Lisburn Road camera gave very little. A small dark car left the scene at the time we think Rhonda was lifted. Impossible to make out any more details unless we call NASA or something,' explained Geordie. 'Oh, and that CCTV that Father Macken mailed you from Clonard was good footage, but all it showed was the altar and the Mass. Sorry.'

More or less what Sheen had expected; very rarely were cases cracked on the back of useful CCTV. Their request for footage from Sterrit's neighbours was equally barren. This suggested that their killer had physically carried Rhonda Sterrit's body to her home, presumably on foot under cover of darkness through the adjacent Lagan Meadows.

Sheen sighed and ran a hand over his rasping face. He'd wanted to speak to Gordon Sterrit again too, preferably when he was sober, but when he called his home it was answered by a police officer. Rachel, Sterrit's wife, had returned to the family home and found him dead in a bath of blood, a piece of broken bottle next to him. It was the document; he must have worked out they were onto him, and now he'd taken his secrets about the Circle of Navan, and probably much more, with him. Given the details of the case, Sheen had no sympathy for him, but felt bad for Rachel. Her daughter and husband dead in a matter of days, her whole life ripped asunder, and for what?

Aoife offered to reheat him some chow mein, but he declined. What he really wanted was a smoke, more badly than he would have ever thought possible. He'd resisted the urge so far, so he settled for a big mug of tea, allowed himself a few digestives. He thanked Aoife, who handed him the steaming drink, and the world was almost instantly a better place a few sips in. When he looked up, all eyes in the small apartment were on him. His team wanted answers, as did he, but he'd come up short. A buzz announced Dermot Fahey's arrival from the street below and Sheen gave him access using his intercom by the door. Moments later he entered the apartment. Brief introductions made, Fahey declined a cup of tea and set out on the breakfast bar papers he'd brought and then started to align them on the pin board.

'I've been digging,' he said, his back briefly to Sheen and the team. When he turned, his eyes had unvarnished excitement, all the colour back in his cheeks. Sheen was glad to see it. Poor guy had looked seasick when that box containing Rhonda Sterrit's hand had arrived on his doorstep. But now he seemed to have something new.

'I was correct about the Circle of Navan,' he said. Fahey went on to elaborate. The name of the group indeed alluded to an ancient ceremonial monument in modern day Armagh, Northern Ireland. The circular mound was reputed to have been the site of an even more ancient temple, and later the seat of power for the Ulaid, a Gaelic kingdom in north-eastern Ireland which flourished in the Middle Ages.

Hayley asked the obvious question. 'How come a group like this, pro-British, pro-status quo for Northern Ireland staying in the United Kingdom, used an ancient *Irish* name like that?'

'This is where it gets interesting for us,' he answered, but his eyes twinkled at Sheen when he spoke. He turned his back to them and started to write the names of those listed in the Circle of Navan documents on one of the white boards as he spoke. 'This place is also associated with an identity that was pre-Celtic, pre-Irish in any modern sense. There's a kind of creation myth that suggests the original settlers of the land, known as Tuatha Dé Danann, literally the people of Danu, set up camp here. It's where history and mythology merge,' he said.

Sheen raised a hand. 'Fascinating but I'm lost. What's with the names?' he asked. At least two he recognised, Moses and Samson, both biblical.

Fahey had a small smile on his lips. He pointed to the names.

'You see, one interpretation of this is that Tuatha Dé was a lost tribe of ancient Israel, the tribe of Dan to be precise.'

'You're shitting me,' said Sheen, making the connection. Fahey slowly shook his head.

'Same as the Ulster Israelites,' said Sheen. It was the group that Williamson Golding and Gordon Sterrit had both been members of.

'That's right,' said Fahey. He moved to the board and pointed at the document that had been found in the same box as Rhonda Sterrit's hand. Sheen recalled that this was what had arrived as a photocopy.

'We agreed that this one was probably originally left with Rhonda Sterrit's body, right? And that Sterrit or someone else had destroyed it?'

Sheen nodded his agreement.

Fahey wrote Brother Moses next to Sterrit's name. 'Moses is sometimes remembered as the Giver of the Law. And what did Sterrit do?'

'Lawyer,' replied Sheen.

Next Fahey pointed to the copy of the other document, the one that detailed Operation Saturn. 'As we surmised earlier, this one must refer to McHenry. Saturn is a bit of a smoking gun, but the name Brother Gideon, it fits too. Gideon led military campaigns to defeat Israel's enemies. He developed the strategy of guerrilla warfare, the Israelites' chosen method of fighting for many centuries,' said Fahey.

Sheen approached the board, pointed to the third document, the one discovered close to Simon Nixon's remains. 'Brother Aaron must be Nixon. Nixon Senior, I mean, the father of the murdered Pastor?'

'The first high priest of the Israelites. Nixon obviously had no issues regarding his own self-worth,' suggested Fahey.

Same went for them all, thought Sheen, the melodramatic bastards. But they weren't playing. The stuff detailed in those documents was heavy duty; arms smuggling, illegal cross-border military action, militia-building. Sheen thought of what Fahey had said about Navan being in Armagh. Not far at all from the Monaghan bog where he'd discovered the boy's dismembered corpse, the thing that had set him searching in the first place. Geographically close, but, if the documents were legit, the murder of a little boy made even less sense if pinned on this group. They'd fancied themselves as players on a bigger stage, with a warped sense of being defenders of the realm. And yet the bodies that had turned up this week said there was a connection: the documents, the missing limbs, the symbolism. It had literally been carved out for him to see but Sheen couldn't. He resisted the urge to reach for his smokes, and instead asked Fahey to tell him more.

'Not sure how much more I've got, to be honest. This one,' he said, pointing to the final document outlining Operation Saturn, 'it mentions a Brother David working with, we can only assume, McHenry,' he said.

Sheen nodded, saw where he was taking him.

'David was believed to have been a boy warrior who defeated an enemy much more ferocious than himself,' Fahey explained.

'Golding?' said Sheen. He'd been part of McHenry's troop, despite his denials, and he was at least five years younger than McHenry and Sterrit. Definitely would have been younger than Nixon's father, who was now dead. Sheen pointed to Brother Jerobam's name.

Fahey shrugged. 'No idea. Jeroboam was the first king of the northern Kingdom of Israel. I thought royal family, but then that's ridiculous, even for this set-up.'

The final name Sheen recognised: Samson.

'Isn't he the one who lost his strength after they cut his hair?'

'Aye, well done you. He was also exceptionally strong, impossible to beat and a bit of a freelancer, you know? Never attached to one army for very long,' said Fahey.

Sheen's thoughts turned to the way that McHenry had been strung up like a rag doll, and the ease with which his torturer and killer had evaded him at the allotment.

After Fahey had finished talking, Sheen explained what he'd deduced from Simon Nixon's death: that their killer was targeting the children of those listed as members of the Circle of Navan. He also offered him a potted summary of McHenry's fate and what he had concluded from it: he'd been murdered by someone other than the killer they were hunting.

'You mean we have another killer on the road here, not just the maniac who murdered the priest and the girl?' asked Fahey.

'Looks that way,' replied Sheen.

'Convince me,' said Fahey.

Sheen had chewed it over in his mind again and again since finding McHenry's body. He was far from convinced himself, but he trusted his instinct, and, against his better judgement, he had started to trust Hayley White.

'Hayley was certain McHenry was murdered by a different killer and I'm inclined to agree. MO was totally different,' said Sheen. 'We liked McHenry for the documents, but no way was he the killer. The guy was barely capable of lifting a beer can, and my first meeting with him took place at the same time Father Phil Rafferty was butchered.'

'But if he was the source of the documents . . .'

'Then he was in league with our murderer,' finished Sheen. 'And given the death that he endured, I'd say he gave whoever tortured him a name this evening.'

'So, we have some nutjob hunting the original nutjob, and no clue who either of them are?'

Sheen didn't reply, but Fahey was correct. His eyes moved over the names on the white board, two of which remained a mystery: Jeroboam and Samson. Somebody had savagely tortured McHenry to death; the same someone had to have an interest in stopping old secrets from seeing the light of day.

'If Golding is Brother David then go and pay him a visit. Tell him the killer's picking off the kids of his old pals,' suggested Fahey.

'Mate, I did. Told me he didn't have any kids. Closed the door on me,' said Sheen.

He could bring Golding in and question him properly,

but he had nothing to pin him down with. Golding would walk, and it would be a waste of time. Two more names: Samson and Jeroboam. And now two killers at work, and again that feeling that he was too slow with time running low.

A text alert from his phone; it was from the Serious Crimes incident desk. He read it and shared it with Aoife.

'Pastor Nixon's missing hand?' she asked.

Sheen nodded – who else's? It had been dumped on the doorstep of the BBC studios in Belfast city.

'No more documents,' commented Aoife.

Sheen growled. 'This is a dead end. Sterrit and McHenry are dead, Golding can't be forced to talk, and we now have somebody in play who's tortured enough information from McHenry to be at least a step ahead of us,' he complained.

Fahey's phone rang and he took the call in the kitchen.

Sheen turned to Geordie and asked him if he'd anything to report. He looked up from Sheen's laptop and beckoned him over. Aoife and Hayley joined him.

'Been looking at the Ladas Drive footage. As expected, there's a whole section that corresponds to when we think the drugs were put in her locker completely erased. See?' he asked.

Geordie fast-forwarded through the minutes until he reached the early afternoon in question and then he slowed down. Aoife McCusker could be seen entering the station and a short time later, on the split screen, then entering the female locker room. She was carrying a backpack.

The feed then ended with snow on the screen. Geordie forwarded the film and it abruptly came back to life. The time reading showed that thirty minutes had been lost.

'Bastard,' whispered Aoife.

'Tried my best,' retorted Geordie.

Aoife gently punched him on the fat of his shoulder.

'Joking aside, I wasn't going to let that put me off. These are the main cameras. There's also a feed from those pointed outward, monitoring adjacent streets and blind corners round the station,' he explained.

'And?' asked Aoife.

'And look what I found,' he said. Geordie enlarged the screen after forwarding to a point about halfway through the recording. Sheen noted that the clock now read bang on the section that had been erased from the main camera's footage. This feed showed a portion of a sidestreet that led to a small entrance door near to the corner of Ladas Drive station. The road was only partly visible, much of it blanketed in afternoon shadow. A car approached, moving fast. Seconds later the same vehicle swerved to a stop in the shadows. Sheen squinted, but it was impossible to make out the motor, let alone the number plate. With patience and time, they'd place it from when it sped in, but it would be tricky.

Geordie forwarded the feed, then slowed. Another car approached, this one moving as fast as the first, and after presumably turning, it parked beside the waiting vehicle. The driver's door opened, and a man got out. Geordie pressed pause as the man turned in the direction of the camera. Not a great shot, but it was enough. He could see the glare of reflected light from his receded hairline, noted the dark suit, as forgettable and bland as the man's features and zinc eyes.

He was a grey man, the perfect spook.

'Oswald Smith, as I live and breathe,' said Sheen. The same guy who claimed to work for the Northern Ireland Office, lurking in the background as events unfolded last July. The same man who'd turned up to warn Sheen and Aoife off the Dissident republicans, men he was no doubt running as informers.

'You know him?' asked Geordie.

Sheen said he did and asked him to play the recording. Oswald had a brand name plastic bag in one hand. He walked to the passenger side of the waiting car where he exited the frame. Seconds passed. He re-emerged, this time without the bag, got into his car, reversed abruptly and exited the frame.

'Get ready,' said Geordie, sounded grim.

'You fucking bastard,' hissed Aoife.

A man had entered the frame. He looked to Sheen, even from the grainy footage, to be coping with the ravages of a bad hangover. Or was still part way through a several-day bender. Shirt untucked, hair on end. And in one hand he clutched the same plastic bag Oswald had brought from his car. No prizes for guessing what it contained: about a quarter of a kilo of uncut coke, soon to be found in Aoife McCusker's locker.

'Charlie Donaldson,' said Aoife.

Sheen did a double take. *This* wretch was Charlie Donaldson, the man with whom Aoife had so unwisely embarked on an affair? The bloke who'd exposed her to so much risk and entrapped her for Cecil Moore? Aoife had said yesterday that this guy was weak, and she was damn right about that. But she'd also suggested he was a victim in all of this. And on that point she was sorely mistaken.

Aoife was on her feet, had marched to the door, grabbed her coat and was halfway out.

'Aoife, stop,' shouted Sheen.

She spun round and he could see the rage in her blue eyes.

'I'll murder that traitorous bastard,' she hissed.

Geordie set the laptop down and marched over to her. He took her by the arm and hauled her into the apartment, shutting the door.

'In good time,' he said.

Aoife made to dash past him, but he stood in the frame, plugged it. End of conversation. She turned to Sheen once more, the anger in her face melting into frustrated hurt.

'I understand, but Geordie's right.' It was all he could say. It seemed to be enough.

She sat on the stool by the breakfast bar, head on hand.

Hayley approached her and put an arm round her. 'We have him now,' she said quietly.

Not quite. What they'd discovered wasn't exactly proof, but it was good enough to have the bastard brought in and sweated. By the looks of him he might crack wide open too. If he talked, the next stop would be that snake Oswald, someone Sheen would take a personal satisfaction in dragging into the light like a sleeping vampire. If Donaldson kept quiet, then like everything else in this case so far, it would be close but no cigar. The sight of Oswald and the thought of Dissident republicans made Sheen think about the drugs. Which, in turn, made him think about the UDA member that Geordie said was being protected by Special Branch.

'Geordie, what was the name of that UDA man from Rathcoole?'

'Crazy Horse.' The same name that Laverty had mentioned earlier.

'What?' Geordie must have registered the change in his expression.

'Laverty told me that Crazy Horse was shot dead this afternoon.'

Geordie took a moment to absorb this. 'Thompson, the guy who was guarding him, must have been told to step down. No way anyone could have got to Crazy Horse with him there,' he said.

'From what we have just watched on that footage, Oswald is behind this. Which means it was likely him who had Crazy Horse taken out today.'

'So, Thompson must work for that spook Oswald now, not Special Branch,' said Geordie.

'If he had Crazy Horse murdered we have to assume that Oswald knows we are onto him. We need to be quick,' said Sheen.

'We also need to be very careful,' added Geordie.

Fahey emerged from the small kitchen. 'You're not gonna believe who just called me. Dylan Martin's widow,' he revealed.

Sheen took a second to place the name. 'The journalist you worked with? The one who ended up dead in Morocco?' said Sheen.

Martin had been the bloke who'd named McHenry as being involved in what they now knew to be Operation Saturn. Right before he was framed for manslaughter.

'Yeah, she says she'll talk to me. Woman fucking hated me. I can't believe it. Asked me to meet her tomorrow, but I won her over, said I can come over now,' said Fahey.

'Nice one,' said Sheen.

'Hope so. She said she has something to tell me, wouldn't do it on the phone. Says Dylan Martin wasn't investigating the Satanic panic thing when he was murdered after all. McHenry was talking to him about something else,' he said.

Sheen told him to keep him informed and Fahey promised to, before darting out, taking the stairs two at a time.

Sheen walked over to his boards, ran his hand through his hair and tried to see the case again, but through new eyes.

Aoife spoke from behind him. 'Sterrit, Nixon, Golding. Your theory works for them; clearly connected to the Circle of Navan. But Father Phil? Still doesn't make any sense why he was murdered,' she reminded him.

Aoife was correct. Fahey had discreetly fed back to him that his research into Father Phil Rafferty came back clean. No history of child abuse, no known enemies. He'd worked tirelessly for the Clonard community, even played a part mediating between paramilitaries and the British government in the very early stages of the peace process.

'These biblical names, the fact the killer's targeting the children of these men, I can't seem to make the connection,' she said.

Sheen turned around; an image seared into his mind. He snatched the case file where he'd put the few additional photographs he had not added to the boards, took Aoife's head gently in both hands and kissed her on the forehead.

'Sheen!' she said.

'I'm bloody glad I didn't just say that,' said Geordie.

Sheen scattered the contents of the file on the bar, found the picture he wanted. It was a detailed shot from Father Phil's murder scene, a photo he'd taken of the top of the sideboard where, if they were correct, the killer had hacked off the priest's head.

'Look,' he said, holding the photo up to show Aoife.

She squinted and a crease formed between her eyes. 'The Bible,' she said.

Sheen set the photo down and pointed at the open book.

'It was open. You think that was coincidental?' Sheen opened his phone and searched for the reference, which was just about visible, though the text was not.

'Judges 19,' read Aoife.

Sheen started to read from the search results on his phone. 'Tells the story of a Levite's wife or concubine, who was raped and murdered in his absence. When the Levite finds out he cuts the woman's remains into twelve pieces and sends her body throughout the land, showing up the evil that had been committed,' he said.

'The hands, that's why he's sending them to the press,' said Aoife.

'Exactly, and that's why he's killing their kids. The politics is incidental. This is personal,' said Sheen.

The crease in Aoife's brow deepened. 'You're saying that whoever's doing this had their child taken from them? That body you found in the bog is over forty years old; it would make our killer maybe as old as eighty, it's not possible,' said Aoife.

'Maybe not a parent, but they're family, I'll bet my life on it,' he said, but Sheen's jubilation had started to deflate.

Geordie had come over and was looking at the scattered photos. He picked one up.

'What's that?'

It was the photo of the portion of the shoe that had been left with the boy's preserved body in Monaghan General. Sheen gave Geordie the run-down and read the block capitals once more, the letters he'd assumed may have formed part of a name.

ORAN

'It's a name all right but not a kid's name. O'Halloran,' said Geordie.

Sheen's heart spiked. 'Geordie, what are you telling me?'

'It was the name of a shoe shop in Belfast, well known. They supplied all the shoes for the boys' home I did a bit of time in. Tara Boys' Home, it was called,' he said quietly.

Hayley was staring at Geordie, her mouth open.

Sheen thought of the shoe, the body of the boy, a boy who had gone missing but had never been missed. Who was more vulnerable and expendable than a child in care in the '70s? Sheen ran over to where he'd hung up his jacket, dug in the pocket and pulled out the bag containing the shoe.

'Geordie, look. Is this the same shoe, like the one you used to wear?'

Geordie took the remains of the shoe from the paper bag and turned the rubber sole over in his hands. After a few seconds he spoke.

'Yeah, that's an O'Halloran brogue,' he said, a twinge of sadness in his voice.

Sheen had no idea that Geordie had been in care, but then again, why would he? Sheen asked him where the shop was.

'Lisburn Road. Used to be. Gone now.'

'And the home?'

'Same place, but off the main drag. They converted it into luxury flats,' he said.

Sheen got Geordie to write the address in his

notepad. Sheen's hand was shaking when he took it and read it. It was just streets away from where Rhonda Sterrit had been abducted. This was it, the break they needed, and as expected the answer had been staring them in the face.

'Geordie, you're a diamond,' said Sheen.

'Don't even think about it,' warned Geordie.

Sheen pulled on his jacket. 'Aoife, I need you with me,' he said, and headed for the door.

'What about us?' asked Geordie.

'Go and nab that bastard Donaldson. Bring him in,' said Sheen.

'Wait, let me see it.' It was Hayley. She asked for the remains of the old shoe and Geordie passed it to her. Hayley reached and took it in one hand, but let out a cry, dropped it and took a step back. She'd gone an unhealthy shade of white. Sheen watched her, transfixed. If she was acting, she'd done a good job. Aoife went to her and put an arm round her friend's big shoulders. Hayley ignored her. Her eyes turned to Sheen.

'You see something?' he asked.

Hayley nodded, eyes wet.

'You don't want to know,' she said. 'But I can tell you that whoever it was killed Trevor McHenry also murdered the wee boy who wore that shoe.'

CHAPTER FORTY-ONE

Aoife and Sheen stood at the front gates of what had been the Tara Boys' Home on a leafy residential street off the Lisburn Road. They were about a quarter of a mile from the Methodist Church where Rhonda Sterrit had been taken. The former boys' home was impressive, but Aoife felt its presence as more cold than welcoming. Situated off the road at the end of a curved garden path, the detached structure had double-breasted bay windows, ground and first floor, topped with twin peaked roofs in dark slate. They looked to Aoife like two witches' hats, and this, plus the black slate roof and dark granite paint that covered the exterior render, added to the overall gothic feel. She'd never want to live here.

'No thanks,' she commented as they approached the under-lit front door.

Sheen grunted his agreement and rapped the pane. A uniformed porter appeared, the sort of attendant Aoife had seen while in New York, but never until now in Belfast. Sheen showed his warrant card; the guy invited them in. He was big-set, with a wide face and full head of white hair.

'Can I help you?' he asked.

She and Sheen had chewed over exactly what they hoped to find here. Geordie had told them the home closed in the '80s and lay vacant for more than a decade before being redeveloped. In short, their chances of finding anything here were slim, but it was all they had.

'This place used to be a boys' home. We're hoping to get some information about those years. Lists of residents, that kind of thing,' said Sheen.

The porter nodded, but his response was not helpful.

'Well before my time, sir. I've worked here for over twelve years, but always while this has been a residential property,' he said.

'Anyone else work here who may remember it as a home?' Aoife tried.

The porter shook his head.

'Is there a basement, some place where old files could have been stacked away?' asked Sheen.

The man's face sparked to life. 'There is a basement, but they converted it into a pool and sauna, but that was only about six years ago,' he said.

'Before that?' she asked.

'Odds and sods. Old furniture and the like. There were filing cabinets too,' he said.

'Dumped?' Aoife asked.

He gave another shake of his head, and a flutter rose in response from Aoife's stomach. They had a chance here.

'Some of the junk was, but the files were just wheeled down the end of the garden and put in the shed. My son-in-law did it,' he said.

Sheen told him they needed access.

A minute later Aoife followed the beam of Sheen's Maglite as he led the way across the expansive lawn. They stopped at the shed. It was large, more of an outhouse. Sheen used the keys the porter had handed over to open the lock, and they both stepped inside. No light, only the torch which Sheen set on the edge of the first of three wide file cabinets as he tugged open the top drawer. The air was stale, though not acrid: dust and disinfectant.

'Empty,' breathed Sheen.

Aoife repositioned the torch, took the second cabinet: the first drawer was full. She walked her fingers through the pages, reams of invoices from a catering company. They were made out to Tara Boys' Home at least. She closed it, started on the second.

'Anything?' asked Sheen.

Her reply was drowned out by another hollow-sounding crash as Sheen slammed a drawer closed, his curse in its wake. Aoife worked her way through two more drawers, more invoices and paper-clipped bundles of receipts.

Sheen continued to rampage. He'd done one full cabinet and now had turned to number three. One drawer in and he kicked it, proceeded to pull the clearly empty drawers from their cradles and tossed them to one side.

'Not helpful, Sheen,' she chided, fingers working meticulously through the last drawer in what was evidently an accounts file. Nothing related to a register of children in care as they'd dared to hope, but lots on the supply of industrial-sized packs of toilet paper and bleach. She blew a stray strand from her face, slammed the final drawer shut. There were no other cabinets.

Sheen was pacing, a debris of drawers around him. This was always going to be a punt. Then, an idea, the most obvious one that she'd somehow missed.

'Sheen. We didn't do an Internet search. Can you believe that?' she said, pulling out her phone.

It was true; in the rush to arrive here neither of them had bothered to try what had become any researcher's first port of call. She glanced at her phone, no bars. Sheen had his own phone out, clearly the same result. He swore colourfully. Then he booted the empty cabinet which rocked and clattered on its side. For someone who hadn't been smoking in his apartment, he was certainly behaving like a man who'd been denied his fix. She snatched the torch.

'You're a child,' she hissed, moved to pass him.

The beam of the torch danced across the innards of the toppled cabinet.

Aoife stopped.

She turned and focused the light on what she'd just spotted. There was a folded document stuck to the inside wall of the cabinet, where one of the drawers had been. She reached down and pulled it off, dry with age. Sheen hunkered down beside her. Aoife opened it, careful not to tear the paper. Her eyes widened. She blinked and reread the first lines again, to make sure what she thought she'd seen was actually there. It was a page of minutes from a meeting of the board of trustees of Tara Boys' Home, dated 1978. There, listed amongst several names she did not recognise were two she did.

'Gordon Sterrit,' whispered Sheen.

'And Kyle Nixon,' said Aoife.

Aoife and Sheen moved as one, out the shed door and up the garden path. Her phone had three bars by the time she reached the front garden of the now luxury flats. Immediately she searched for Tara Boys' Home, scanned the results. Sheen was on his phone too.

'Missed call from Fahey,' he said, phone to ear.

Aoife sifted through the results, one ear on Sheen's hurried conversation. He interrupted Fahey and explained where they were and what they'd discovered. From what she'd snatched, it sounded like Dylan Martin's wife had directed Fahey to this exact location; the dead journalist had been investigating the boys' home when he'd been murdered.

'So far, we have Gordon Sterrit and Kyle Nixon on the board of trustees. Looks as though the Circle of Navan wasn't the only club they shared,' he said. Sheen told him he needed help with the other names they'd found. He had his notebook out. The first two names appeared not to elicit a strong response from Fahey. Sheen read out the third.

'Harrison Glover,' he said, paused, listened to Fahey's answer, this time scribbling. He asked for an address and after a brief pause set to work writing down Fahey's response.

'Monaghan? Jesus Christ, that's less than three miles from where the kid's body was buried in the bog,' said Sheen. 'He's our man.'

'He got children?' asked Sheen. More note-taking. Sheen then read the last name they'd discovered.

'Leonard McKeague,' he said. Sheen repeated the name, as though Fahey had fallen silent. Sheen's expression changed from excitement to trepidation; he jotted down a few more words. He thanked Fahey and slapped his notebook closed.

Aoife turned her attention back to her own search. Seconds later she found what she needed.

'Sheen, look!' she said, and held her phone up. It was a public Facebook page for former residents of Tara Boys' Home. It had been there all along; they could have accessed this at any time but, of course, they had no way of knowing Tara was significant. Aoife moved through the small number of postings.

'There,' said Sheen.

Aoife saw it too. She scanned the text, dated from the previous year. The title of the post was 'Still Living In Hope'.

Your help needed. My brother disappeared from Tara Boys' Home when he was thirteen years old in February 1976. His name is Peter Beatty. He was last seen at a 'party' near the Lisburn Road at that time. I can't remember the address. Don't know the names of those present. They told me he ran away, but I don't believe it. If you can help me, please get in touch. Discretion guaranteed. Still living in hope.

The message was signed off by someone called Dolores Beatty, with an email address.

Sheen immediately got back on his phone; seconds later was speaking with Fahey.

'Dermot, I need you to run the name Peter Beatty against your search for kids reported missing. Belfast-based, yeah? Cheers. Let me know,' he said and hung up.

'What'd Fahey say?' she asked.

Sheen was walking and Aoife followed.

'I'll tell you on the way,' he replied.

'Where are we going?'

'Back to where this all began. Monaghan. And we'd best pray we're not too late.'

CHAPTER FORTY-TWO

Geordie could have formally requested Charlie Donaldson's home address from the police database, but to have done so would have required a reason and flagged his enquiry as part of a live investigation. Which his clandestine piecing together of Aoife McCusker's downfall was not, for the time being anyway. He knew that Donaldson used to live up in Greencastle, north of Belfast city, though heard he'd moved. Geordie had phoned Community Relations, found out that Charlie Donaldson had called in sick Monday morning and not made it into work since. He'd blagged it, asked the guy if Charlie was still on a named street in the Greencastle area. Told him he had a couple of tickets to a Glentoran match, vaguely remembered talking to Donaldson about the Irish League ages ago. Rules were rules, but football was football.

'No, sure he's divorced from your woman, and she got that house,' he explained. He adopted a more conspiratorial tone, 'Charlie was ding-donging McCusker, the hottie that worked here last year,' he said.

Geordie played along, said he hoped it'd been worth it. The desk jockey said he thought not, and then gave Geordie what he needed, Donaldson's address.

As he pulled his car up a few doors away from the shared entrance to the block of flats in Dunmurry village on the outskirts of West Belfast, Geordie double-checked that they had not been followed. Once satisfied, he took stock. The area itself was nice enough: middle class and residential. But this little pocket of council houses and two-storey apartments arranged in cul-de-sacs was anything but. Neither the window frames overloaded with flashing festive lights nor the life-sized Santa who appeared to be clinging on for dear life to a top windowsill, raised the overall tone. There was one window in the block they now stood before that was a Scrooge of blank indifference. Geordie pointed to a pile of dog turd on the overgrown grass verge, by way of warning for Hayley who bypassed it, and stood by his side.

'So, this is where you end up when you're caught with your pants down,' commented Hayley.

'Bit more to this than being stung by a woman scorned,' suggested Geordie, his eyes scanning the communal bins and noting the one that was almost overflowing with empty cider cans, and bottles of cheap spirits. The lids of the others were closed. He kicked one; sounded empty, probably meant the collection day had been Monday, maybe even Tuesday morning. Someone was hitting it like a hired donkey, probably the same someone who'd not shown up for work so far this week. Geordie knew all about it; the drink had almost got the better of him after he'd taken early retirement. But even at his worst, it was nothing like this.

They approached the shared entrance; Geordie pressed the buzzer for Donaldson's flat. Through the reinforced glass he could see another, smaller sausage of dog shit, inside the entrance hallway. Hayley was right, Donaldson had sunk low, but it wasn't just his hygiene he needed to mind, living in a hole like this. He'd set up camp a baton-round away from the itchy, strongly nationalist estates of Twinbrook and Poleglass, the sorts of places where Dissident scum floated to the surface and had their way.

People talked, and before long it would be common knowledge that Charlie was a peeler. Very soon that information would reach the wrong people, if it hadn't done so already. Geordie glanced up at the surrounding windows, and then back along the road on which he'd parked, filled with a sudden, probably irrational sense of being watched. There was no sign of eyes on them, but still. He looked to Hayley.

'You sense anything?' She said no, but Geordie walked back to the gate and peered into the deepening late afternoon gloom. The small street was still and empty of people. Parked cars all the way down on both sides, one of them his. An eddy of wind gusted and carried a polystyrene takeaway tray into the middle of the road and waltzed it his way. Geordie turned to Hayley. He'd never be caught living here as a peeler or one who'd retired, and not just because it was a dive. Donaldson was on a self-destruct mission in more ways than one, it would appear.

Geordie leant long on the buzzer once more and waited. No response, so he opted for a different approach and ran his hand up and down all the buttons several times. After a few seconds he heard the entrance unlock with a low buzz. They went in, found Donaldson's flat. It was, as he expected, the one with the dark, undecorated window he'd spotted from the street. Geordie banged the door with the ball of his fist. No answer, so he hit it again, harder this time. One of the neighbours opened their door a crack and closed it without reply when Geordie asked if they knew where Charlie was. People here could probably smell peeler like he could smell that fresh dog shit downstairs.

'Charlie!'

A few seconds passed and then he heard the shuffling sound of approaching steps from inside. A muffled voice spoke from behind the door, asking who's there.

'It's Geordie Brown. My granny's thirty-seven. Yours is sixty-one,' he said.

Geordie had flirted with the Freemasons early in his career, found it useful in securing the odd foot in the door along the way but it had never delivered a promotion or fabled advancement. He'd tired of it long ago, probably his face had never fitted in the first place, or the drink on his breath. Brother Masons identified one another in Belfast police circles by casually asking how old is your granny? Thirty-seven was the number of the lodge Geordie had once belonged to, and he knew that his one-time fellow Mason, Charlie Donaldson, had attended lodge sixty-one.

It did the trick. Geordie could hear the door being unlocked, and then Charlie's face appeared in the crack. He'd kept the small security chain fastened.

'Long time no see, mate,' greeted Geordie.

Donaldson looked fucked: skin like tallow and eyes bloodshot and sunken. Even with the door open just a bit Geordie could smell the stale air from within: sour drink and unwashed skin. But it wasn't just the demon drink for this guy. If Charlie wasn't bang on his own namesake, then Geordie was set to be elected the next pope.

'Heard you retired,' Charlie croaked.

Geordie shrugged.

Charlie glanced at Hayley.

'Back in the saddle. This is Hayley,' said Geordie, but left it at that. Donaldson didn't look too interested anyway.

'Geordie, what can I do for you? I have a bug, need to get back to bed,' he said. Fuck it, the ruse about match tickets wouldn't take him where he wanted to go, which was through this door with as little nonsense as possible.

'Thing is, Charlie, I'm back working the SHOT,' he said. He saw a glimmer of recognition from Donaldson at his mention of the Serious Historical Offences Team, and of unease. 'And one part of recent history I'm interested in is who stitched up our mutual friend Aoife McCusker,' he said.

Charlie Donaldson started to stutter, something about not being able to help, and made to push the door closed. Geordie stuck his foot in the crack just in time and barged his not inconsiderable heft against the wood. The Masons had helped him get a foot in a door one last time. The security chain snapped and Donaldson was knocked backwards. Not quite off his feet, but enough to give Geordie access. The guy was lucky the door hadn't hit him in the face but that could be arranged.

'Cheers for inviting us in,' Geordie continued. He glanced around the hallway and kitchen. Place looked like a squat, or, maybe more accurately, a drug den. 'This place is a tip head,' said Geordie.

Hayley joined him in the doorway and immediately put a hand to her face. Geordie knew only too well that it was possible to do a version of the job while on the piss. But how Charlie Donaldson had not been taken into an office and given his marching orders was a small miracle.

'I-I – get out, how dare you?' he responded.

'Get your shoes on; you're coming for a drive. Want to ask you a few questions about your mate Oswald, and what he gave you to put into Aoife McCusker's locker,' said Geordie.

Charlie Donaldson moved with a burst of speed that caught Geordie entirely by surprise. The bastard was already past him before he'd finished his sentence, headed for the open front door, shoes or no shoes.

Hayley was waiting. Donaldson was shoved backwards and re-entered the flat at almost the same speed he'd tried to leave it. This time he landed square on his arse.

Geordie fished out a set of cuffs, old style, not the newer ones with the rigid plastic centre. He held them up.

'With or without your slippers, or these bangles, you're going to the ball, me old mucker,' he said.

Charlie asked him if he was arresting him.

Geordie lifted his eyes to the ceiling. 'Would it make it better if I did?' he asked. And when things got official it would be Donaldson's drug-addled word against his that he'd come along willingly. Plus, Hayley would be an hallucination brought on by excessive cocaine use. Geordie had arrested a bloke once who swore the Moley was after him.

Charlie's shoulders dropped, he pulled on a pair of trainers and started to get to his feet. Geordie's phone rang and he answered it, eyes still on Donaldson. It was Sheen. Geordie listened for a few seconds.

'We're on our way. Yeah, I'll remember,' he said and then spoke back the name of the address in County Monaghan Sheen had just given him and killed the call.

Donaldson was trying to edge away from them, back into the flat. He strode after him, grabbed him by the scruff and propelled him back up the hall and out the open front door.

'Come on the fuck,' he said and pulled Donaldson's door closed behind them. He manhandled him down the stairs, Hayley keeping up.

'Where are we going?' she asked.

'To finally get to the bottom of all this, by the sounds of it,' replied Geordie.

CHAPTER FORTY-THREE

Oswald didn't have time to go down to his spot in the basement garage. No matter. At this time of day, his part of Palace Barracks was much quieter. Thompson had called him, sounding urgent. His voice was in Oswald's ear as he pushed open the door to the gents' and walked in, phone in hand.

'Wait,' said Oswald, and Thompson immediately stopped talking. Oswald did a scan of the booths, found them and the three urinals empty. He entered the last booth, closed the door and spoke in a whisper.

'Speak,' he said. Thompson did, Oswald listened. Thompson had been slipped, lost Geordie Brown near the Titanic Quarter and didn't pick him up again until he turned up at Owen Sheen's Laganside apartment much later. Thompson told him there had been a fire alarm and general evacuation of Ladas Drive PSNI station in the meantime, a place that Oswald had told him to monitor.

'Was he there?' But, of course, Thompson said he didn't know. How could he? He'd taken his eyes off the old sniffer dog and now there was no knowing what scent he might have picked up. Oswald studied the graffiti-free texture of the dark red paint on the back of the toilet door. If Brown was at Ladas Drive, then what of it? He was sub-contracted on a murder enquiry; it made perfect sense for him to be there.

But first he visited Crazy Horse, *where the drugs came from*, Oswald's mind contested, *and now he's snooping around Ladas, the place where those drugs had been deposited.*

Oswald took a long breath of the aerosol-fragranced air. He needed to remain rational; he'd taken care of the CCTV, on the off-chance that the dullards in Internal Investigations ever got round to scrutinising Aoife McCusker's movements. And yet he was sweating, thinking, and Thompson was still speaking. He blinked away the reverie, gave Thompson's voice his full attention. Thompson said something, a name. Oswald nearly dropped his phone.

'Repeat,' he said, mouth dry.

Thompson did. 'Charlie Donaldson,' he said.

Geordie Brown and the woman Oswald did not know had just taken Donaldson from his flat in Dunmurry. Oswald closed his eyes. He should have neutralised Donaldson when he'd ceased to serve a purpose. Namely, as soon as the drugs had been discovered in McCusker's locker.

But you didn't, he thought, *you left him dangling, like a fat fly waiting to serve up maggots of information to anyone persistent enough to follow the threads. Who is the spider now, Oswald, and who is the prey?*

Prudence is indeed an old maid courted by incapacity.

'Fall back,' said Oswald, cutting off Thompson mid-sentence.

Thompson asked him if he was sure about that.

'Don't question me,' snarled Oswald, his voice brittle in the tiled interior of the gents'. Thompson shut up. Oswald steadied his breathing, said nothing. 'Where are they now?'

Thompson relayed the information he needed. Oswald nodded, calmer now. He knew the road, the direction of travel. He also knew who now needed to step in. He repeated his command for Thompson to pull away from surveillance and ended the call.

Oswald found his burner phone; his fingers moved swiftly, like he was spinning thread. He sent the details of Geordie Brown's car, and direction of travel with a message to a number that he knew was another burner phone. This one was always on and would be read by a man in Lagmore on the Poleglass housing estate in West Belfast. For a Dissident, Oswald had always found him most compliant. He did not wait for a response. That would come later, in the evening news.

He dismantled the phone, popped the SIM card and twisted it, and then flushed it down the toilet. He'd discard the pieces of the burner separately. His mind turned momentarily to those threads which still hung loose: Cecil Moore's missing SIM which had not, as yet, turned up, the fact that Owen Sheen and McCusker were in the vicinity when it went missing and the elusive filmmaker who had provided his services for Moore and who must have seen his video too.

'In good time,' said Oswald softly. Yes, all in good time. Because with certain threads snipped, time would once more be on his side. He exited the booth, walked across the still-empty gents' and washed his hands, as though he'd emptied his bowels. His zinc eyes stared back at him unblinking as the water scalded his hands. The three words of the text message he'd sent to his man in Lagmore made him smile through the steam from the sink.

Three little pigs.

PART FOUR

LET THE DEVIL IN

CHAPTER FORTY-FOUR

Sheen stuck the Sig into fifth gear and punched the accelerator, felt the engine kick him back into his seat and heard it growl. His headlights speared the road ahead as he weaved the car between lanes of slower traffic. He tried Geordie's phone for the second time since setting off, but once again it went straight to voicemail. Aoife had tried to call Hayley – same result. Probably driving through that reception black spot she'd noted a while back. At least it meant they were probably on Aoife and Sheen's tail.

They were well beyond the M1, bound for Monaghan, but this time for the estate once owned by Harrison Glover. Glover was dead, but Fahey had told him that his youngest son, Fingall, still lived on the estate. And Fingall Glover was disabled and vulnerable; he required twenty-four-hour care. This meant he was surely in grave danger from a killer targeting the offspring of the Circle of Navan. Fahey had also told him Glover had been one of the last of the old Anglo-Irish aristocracy. He had a distinguished service record from the Second World War, but Fahey said he was aware of him principally because of his supposed secret service links. That and his far-right politics: he'd been an outspoken critic of the IRA and successive British governments' failure to neutralise them. Even though his stately home was in the Republic of Ireland, Glover was British in the mould of an old colonial, had resided between there and London, and had sat in the House of Lords. Apart from when he made regular trips to Belfast to fulfil his duties as Chair of the Board of Trustees at Tara Boys' Home.

'So, we think Glover was Brother Jeroboam, from the Circle of Navan documents?' asked Aoife, from the passenger seat.

'That's exactly what we think,' replied Sheen. 'I'm guessing he chose that name too, the man who would be king,' said Sheen. His hands gripped the wheel. The sick bastard hadn't been satisfied with plotting gun shipments and terrorising farmers along the border. He, and at least three others, Kyle Nixon, Gordon Sterrit and Leonard McKeague, had also enjoyed the run of Tara Boys' Home after lights-out. And if their body from the bog had indeed once been a resident there, then they were responsible for things that made even the Circle of Navan seem wholesome. Once more, Sheen noted, in war-torn Belfast terrible crimes had slipped by more or less unnoticed and had, so far, gone unpunished.

'What did Fahey say about this McKeague?' asked Aoife.

'He recognised him immediately. Said he's a homicidal bastard, lots of blood on his hands from back in the day. Some kind of freelance operator, never aligned to one paramilitary faction, but did dirty work for almost all of them at one time or another,' explained Sheen.

'What are we talking?'

'Interrogations. Torturing confessions from supposed informers. Fahey said his old mentor, Dylan Martin, believed McKeague was also responsible for a number of abduction, torture and kill murders in the 1970s,' said Sheen.

Aoife shivered. 'Romper room killings,' she said.

Sheen agreed. He'd heard of the name, a sick allusion to a children's television show which dated from the time. Innocent men would be dragged from the streets, beaten and tortured horrifically by large groups of people in illegal drinking dens, and then finally shot dead and dumped for the other side to discover.

'I think this McKeague is our missing link. Brother Samson, the hard man who took on the enemy. Fahey said he'd disappeared when the Troubles ended, assumed he was dead. Plus, no children that he was aware of,' said Sheen.

Aoife expressed her disgust, perhaps at McKeague's crimes, or Sterrit, Nixon and Glover's association with him, or maybe both. Aoife fell silent for a long moment before again speaking.

'Sheen, could McKeague be our killer, the one who murdered Trevor McHenry, I mean?' she asked.

A grisly image of McHenry's body strung up and sliced to pieces. This McKeague had been a known sadist and proficient at extracting confessions from hard men and innocent people alike.

'Christ, of course. Sterrit!' he said.

If McKeague and he had once been close enough to share the kind of secrets they concealed, then it stood to reason they might remain in contact. Sheen flicked through his recent call list using the dash display, found Paddy Laverty's name and pushed it. He motioned for Aoife to remain quiet.

'Sheen.' Laverty's voice spoke through the speakers sounding stressed, commotion from the background. 'You heard?'

'No, what's going on?'

'Someone tried to abduct a child from outside a charity event at the Odyssey,' he said.

Sheen's eyes widened. That was the venue of Williamson Golding's event, the Shared Futures thing. It was a cross-community youth federation. In a manner of speaking, these were his children. Sheen felt the blood drain from his head; his stomach flipped. He'd known about this but not seen it coming.

'Paddy, is the kid all right?'

'Aye. Kid's fine, scared shitless though. Your man Golding, the barrister, his bird got in the way and took a needle to the arm. She's been taken to the Royal, doesn't look good for her,' said Laverty.

'The man who tried to take the kid, did they get him?'

'Who said it was a man? Some wee woman did it. Dressed in black she was, like a nun, headscarf and all. She put a security guard through a plate-glass door before she got away, can you believe that?'

'Details?'

'She was white and old. Her car was dark blue and old. Witnesses,' said Laverty.

Sheen could hear the disdain in his voice. Sheen's mind raced, Aoife stared at him, the same recognition formed in her eyes. The small, dark-coloured car matched the grainy images from the CCTV mast on the Lisburn Road and the dark fibres that were found on Father Phil and Rhonda Sterrit. Aoife had suggested a killer dressed as a priest and she wasn't far off the mark. Doubtless there'd be a match with this woman. Plus, the gargantuan strength also ticked a box. But how she possessed it remained a mystery. Another piece fell into place for Sheen, the question of who she was. The Facebook posting Aoife found called Peter Beatty their brother. This creature must be Peter's sister. And Sheen knew all about seeking justice for a dead sibling. He'd been right to head for Glover's old home in Monaghan. If this woman knew about Harrison Glover's disabled son, Fingall, this is where she'd go next. But if Aoife was right, they were not alone in the hunt for her this night.

'Paddy, I need you to run me a name. Leonard McKeague. Maybe seventy years old. I need to know if he's entered the country recently, get a passport check from main entry points,' said Sheen. Laverty was silent on the other end. Sheen's mind turned to the little boy he'd read about in Clones Library, Declan O'Rawe. He had gone missing in Monaghan, but turned up dead in Belfast, his body burned and bearing signs of torture. 'While you're at it can you dig up McKeague's previous abodes, see if he had a Belfast address?'

'I know that name, Sheen. Want to tell me what's going on here?' Laverty sounded dubious.

Sheen slowed down as he passed a sign for Aughnacloy. Telling Laverty he was soon to cross the Irish border into the Republic where he had no jurisdiction was probably not a great idea.

'I think he's responsible for the killing that happened today in Glencairn. Guy called Paul Craigavon,' said Sheen, using McHenry's new name.

'That man McKeague was a demon. It wouldn't surprise me, though I haven't heard mention of him for donkey's,' he said. He told Sheen he'd look into it, thankfully didn't ask him where he was. He probably presumed he was on his way to the Odyssey.

'Cheers, Paddy. By the way, how far behind the curve am I?'

'About an hour,' said Laverty, ended the call.

About ten miles further south Fahey called.

'What you got, Dermot?'

'Peter Beatty, listed as missing, presumed to have run away in February 1976. Resided at Tara Boys' Home, Lisburn Road,' said Fahey. It was a direct match for the Facebook posting found by Aoife.

'Dermot, you're a star,' said Sheen. It also confirmed what the bone spectrum analysis made on the toenail clipping had suggested: Peter Beatty had been a city kid.

'I know. Be careful, mate,' he said.

Sheen said they would, ended the call and turned to Aoife. No longer would he call the corpse a bog body, or a boy's body, now he had a name.

'Peter Beatty,' said Sheen. They'd found him. And if his hunch was right, he was going to find the bastard who murdered him too.

Seconds later another call came: Paddy Laverty.

'Your man arrived in Belfast on the first flight from Málaga Wednesday morning,' confirmed Laverty. 'Got his mugshot from passport control. I'll send it out to all units; see if we can't pick him up.'

'Address?'

'Used to live on York Street,' said Laverty.

Sheen knew where it was, and the revelation stunned him into a momentary silence. York Street was a stone's throw from Sailortown, the little district where he'd spent the first years of his childhood. That same chiming he'd felt earlier in the investigation, once again at play. McKeague had probably walked the very streets where he and his brother had played football and hide-and-seek. As little boys they could easily have crossed paths with him, and the thought of it gave him a chill. But Sailortown wasn't the only place that was close to where McKeague had lived.

York Street was very near to the spot on the River Lagan where Declan O'Rawe's body had been dumped.

Somebody had gone to great lengths to take him away from where he'd been abducted in Monaghan. But in murder, as with most things, the landscape matters. It makes its impression on us all, as surely as we imprint upon it. And though a killer might want to disguise his deeds, the land will tell its own tale. Through his connection with Glover, McKeague was familiar with the bogs of Monaghan, and when it came to Belfast, it was the alleys and side streets along the Lagan that he knew best. McKeague had murdered Declan O'Rawe, just as he had murdered Peter Beatty.

'See you soon, Paddy,' said Sheen, and ended the call. He explained his thinking to Aoife.

'You know, Hayley told us this already. She said the man who murdered McHenry also killed Peter Beatty,' said Aoife.

'Yes, she did,' agreed Sheen. And if Sheen was correct, McKeague, a seasoned murderer, and Peter Beatty's demented sister were both headed for Harrison Glover's estate, and Geordie was thus far out of reach. He had one more call to make. He reached for the dash and found her name. She answered, but only after six rings.

'Sheen, I'm on duty,' said Pixie McQuillan.

'Good. I'm going to need your help.'

CHAPTER FORTY-FIVE

Geordie gnawed on the peanut-filled chocolate bar he'd bought earlier in the day. Hayley said she didn't fancy one and he didn't offer a share to Charlie Donaldson, who sat in the back seat. Geordie had slapped a pair of handcuffs on him just because. Donaldson asked again for Geordie to remove them, promised that he wouldn't try anything.

'I know you won't, Charlie. But I just want you to get used to wearing them. That's going to be your style for a long time to come, mate.'

Geordie eased off the accelerator. The M1 was far behind them, and he took the speed down to just over seventy as they went through the small townships that led to the Monaghan border. The speed limit was thirty but needs must. Sheen sounded like he needed backup. Donaldson started to talk. Again.

Since leaving Belfast that was all he'd done. Mainly he'd been blaming this guy Oswald for the whole thing, said that he gave him the bag to put in Aoife's locker, said he had no idea what was in it, said he thought it was official business as Oswald was obviously a spook. Basically, he was saying anything that might get his arse off the oven plate. If he said as much on the record then there'd at least be a case for Aoife McCusker, meaning Geordie (and Hayley) had come up with the goods. Geordie also looked forward to getting a search done of Donaldson's flat. The guy was clearly a user, and if they could find traces of the same batch of coke that had been found in Aoife's locker in Donaldson's place, then all his accusations against Oswald would do him no good.

He'd obviously been paid something for putting that bag in Aoife's locker. And Geordie could take a guess what it was.

He eyed Donaldson contemptuously in his rear-view and noted he had the sweats. Good. Geordie was about to return his eyes to the unlit road ahead when his eye caught another vehicle, four cars behind them, matching his speed. His old copper's instinct told him this was something, but he couldn't place it. He drove, eyes on the road for a stretch, and then returned to the rear-view. It was a Land Rover Evoque, brown. And now it was two cars behind them.

'Geordie, you got reception on your phone?' Hayley asked him from the passenger side. He touched his mobile on the dash, found it had no bars.

'Me neither,' said Hayley.

'We're in the boogies down here. You'll get reception

again when you get over the border. Not too far now,' said Geordie.

Headlights blared in his rear-view and side mirror; Geordie squinted. The snarl of a powerful engine and seconds later the brown Range Rover overtook on his right, lurching back into lane and accelerating off just before a large lorry zoomed past where it had recklessly overtaken seconds before. Geordie was doing almost eighty; he must have peaked at over one hundred.

Hayley gripped the dash. 'Jesus, idiot.'

'Someone's in a hurry,' commented Geordie.

The brown Range Rover went over the crest of the next hill and disappeared from sight.

'Country drivers, they're bonkers' said Hayley.

Geordie nodded his agreement, checked his rear-view where a single car now had their tail. This was an Audi, powerful sport's version. This car, however, seemed happy to coast behind them at a distance, despite its superior power. There was something wrong here; he could feel it in his gut. He'd been too busy feeding his face and listening to Donaldson to realise it, but now he did. Geordie's eyes flashed to the road ahead. That Range Rover. He'd seen it before. On the long carriageway that went from Donaldson's home in Dunmurry, back to the motorway.

That's where the Evoque had started following them.

It had come from Poleglass; well-known as a hotbed for headcase Dissidents. Geordie reached for the glove compartment as they approached the top of the hill, their way ahead not visible as yet.

'Hayley, get your head down,' he said and popped the glove compartment for his gun.

But Geordie was too late.

The Audi roared to life and made the distance up between them as they went over the top of the hill. Geordie had time to catch a look in his rear-view of a man with a balaclava leaning out the passenger window with a handgun in his hand. Then he started shooting. Hayley screamed, and the back windscreen shattered.

Geordie stuck his foot down, started to weave between lanes. The Audi kept up, short bursts of gunfire showering them, dull thuds registering hits in the body of Geordie's car. Geordie's wing mirror exploded. He cursed and weaved out of the way of an oncoming line of traffic. The Audi was right on his tail. Several more bursts. Geordie heard the high-pitched whistle of a bullet just millimetres from his left ear, and then the front windscreen went white, a single puncture wound in the middle. Geordie punched the perforated glass, it loosened, he could see a bit of the road ahead, but he was driving more or less blind now. In his rear-view the Audi was gone. Geordie had a second to register the brown Range Rover that was parked in a lay-by on the side of the road, and the masked man who waited on one knee at its front wheel. He had a rifle, looked to be an Armalite, the semi-automatic of choice for the IRA throughout the hottest decades of the Troubles.

'Oh fuck,' shouted Geordie. No sooner had the expletive left his lips than he felt the dull impact of bullets hitting the back of the car. A fraction of a second later came the sharp rattle of more rounds, these missing their target. Geordie stuck his foot down and swerved the car right and then left. He twisted the wheel sharply back to his right, a reflex reaction, and as he did he heard one or both back tyres explode. The car fishtailed into the oncoming lane. Geordie hit the brakes and tried to regain control, but it was too late. The front of the car descended into a culvert that ran parallel to the road and the impact bucked the rear of the car skyward. In slow motion Geordie felt the car rise and start to turn. He looked to Hayley as the world beyond her window rotated and spun. She was wearing her seat belt. He closed his eyes as the car hit the ground. And then the world went a deeper black.

CHAPTER FORTY-SIX

McKeague killed his headlights as he turned into the walled grounds of the old man's estate over the border. The big, iron gates were wide open, and he slowed as he guided the car along the wide, pressed-earth path. He allowed his eyes to adjust to the dark.

Past and present merged. He'd been in the passenger seat, the old man had driven, Counsellor Sterrit in the back, where he clutched a bottle of Scotch like his salvation depended on it. It had been dark, just like this. The February dawn had not yet retrieved the land from the clutches of the night. In the boot, wrapped up in a blanket, was what they'd come here to get rid of.

McKeague blinked into the blue shadows and saw the outline of the big house, its silhouette unchanged. The bulkhead cellar doors were still there; that was where they'd carried their load. The other two had been sick more than once while he set to work with his big butterfly knife, but he'd made them stay, and made them watch. That way if he went down, they all went down. McKeague knew that loose lips were rarely a problem when a man knew he'd be tied to the sinking ship.

He'd sent the old man for an axe when his knife had been found wanting, but he'd returned with a spade. McKeague gave it to Sterrit and watched as he cut off the hands to get rid of prints. That had been easy, but the head was too much for him. Sterrit had turned away, his bottle raised to the low ceiling and he'd taken over. The old man had buried the head and hands in the cellar, promised to throw them into the furnace when it was next lit. McKeague didn't know whether he had or not and didn't much care. Those were his bones. It was Sterrit's idea to make use of one of the big empty wine casks. It had been a tight squeeze, but they'd managed it. And then there followed a long walk, clothed in the morning mist.

McKeague parked the car under the wide arms of a big Lebanese cedar. From the house it would be totally concealed, but as he treaded softly across the fallen needles, he saw that its wide windows were blank and lifeless. No blinking festive decorations, nothing. He stopped short of where the security lamp over the front door would likely pick up his movement. There was a big sign listing shotgun safety protocol, and adjacent to where he stood there was a wooden trough, enclosed on two sides. That's where the guns would be loaded and unloaded. It looked like the old man's estate had been turned into some kind of hunting range. But Sterrit had said Glover's youngest still lived here, the handicapped one.

He skirted round the perimeter of the big building and found what he wanted tucked away down a cobbled path. The old stable yard was gated and the decrepit building he recalled now had a roof of clean, new slate. The small window next to the half-door was framed with glowing LED lights and a wide ramp breached the step. The sort of ramp used for wheelchair access. This was the place. McKeague gently unlatched the gate. He paused.

A bust of gunfire, deadened a little by distance, but not that far off. Followed by several more. Then silence.

McKeague waited. Nothing. Whatever it was it seemed to be a one-off. But it was a bad sign. He studied the small stable building for signs of movement but saw none. The gunfire had clearly not disturbed those within. He slipped through the gate, reached into his pocket for his blade and folded his fingers round the grip. He stopped. His legs were so heavy.

McKeague blinked. He was standing in the middle of the cobblestone yard, swaying gently, eyes fixed on the glowing lights that framed the window. His mouth was dry, heart slow and then fast, no rhythm. He needed to be quick here, but suddenly, he was slow, and tired, and his mind had slipped out of gear.

He was crashing.

He searched his pocket for another wrap of speed but then remembered he'd swallowed the last of them.

'Shit,' he hissed, wiped a film of grease from his forehead. He ground his teeth, actually heard the squeak and then the crack. From behind him, back towards the entrance of the estate, he heard the low hum of an approaching vehicle. He flashed his head round in its direction, ear cocked, but as soon as he did the sound stopped. Someone else had arrived. He recalled Golding's warning, and then thought of the gunfire he had heard.

Two peelers came to me . . . Asking questions.

McKeague moved, headed for the ramp and banged the half-door five times, loud enough to wake the dead. When time was low, the direct approach was best. Lights turned on from within, the sound of a voice, female and Eastern European from behind the half-door. She was probably a live-in nurse.

'Yes. Who is it there?'

'There's a fire!' shouted McKeague.

Immediately he heard the door unbolted and keys turning. McKeague made his hand into a fist round the handle of his blade. The door opened a little. The owner of the voice was a big lump of a girl who filled the frame. She wore a light blue dressing gown which she clutched in one hand to her double chin. McKeague rammed his shoulder against the door and it opened enough to let him grab a handful of the towelling robe. He slammed his blade into the blubber of her throat, and then rammed it straight up. She recoiled, eyes black mirrors of shocked amazement, gurgling as hot blood coursed from the puncture point down her exposed breasts that rolled out as her hand transferred to McKeague's wrist.

She was strong. She started to pull McKeague's hand free from her throat, teeth bared and red, her eyes full of fury now. McKeague gasped; she'd damn near pushed him off the step. He released her dressing gown, used his free hand to steady himself on the door frame. This was not going to happen. He allowed her to push his stabbing fist away another inch, and then leant into the blade, swiped sideways through the fat and tissue, seeking her carotids. And then the blood gushed.

McKeague bundled her back through the door, dropped the knife, its work complete. Both her hands had gone to her neck now, trying to stem the inevitable, and McKeague could feel her weight slump on him as her legs started to buckle and give. Not what he needed right now. He gasped, turned her and pulled open a door. It was a cloakroom, just what he'd hoped. He shoved her in, and she dropped like a controlled demolition, feet twitching. He picked up his blade and closed the cloakroom door. There was blood on the floor, but not as much as he'd feared. The dressing gown had soaked up most of it. He walked to the small sink under the window with the Christmas lights, cleaned his knife and rinsed his hands. He was panting, fucking knackered. He leant against the white porcelain, savouring the cool. That hadn't gone exactly to plan. He eyed the stable yard; all was quiet, for now.

McKeague closed over the entrance door and set about searching. A minute later he found what he'd hoped he would in a narrow steel cabinet next to the back door. It took him another minute to locate the cartridges in the drawer of the kitchen table. He poured himself a cold drink of water and felt his pulse quieten. That was just a hitch; he was back on track now. And at least he didn't feel like he'd turned up to what might be a gunfight carrying a knife.

He opened the door to the stable yard just a little and then quickly padded through the rooms until he found the old man's son, asleep and helpless. McKeague chose the spot where he would watch and wait. Moments later, he heard the sound of the stable yard gate unlatching. He didn't have to wait for very long.

CHAPTER FORTY-SEVEN

Sheen parked up outside the high walls of what had been Harrison Glover's stately home right about when Geordie was enjoying his chocolate bar. The road was deserted, and when Aoife followed Sheen through the wide entrance, they found the grounds silent and empty too. They walked up the broad dirt path. Her eyes were alert for movement, her ears tuned for sound, but there was only the whisper of leaves stirred by the light breeze and the sound of their breathing. Sheen turned to her, pointed at a sign at the head of the path which now opened up to the spread of the big house fifty metres ahead. It was a list of rules for those using shotguns.

'When I came down here on Monday I heard gun shots,' he whispered.

Aoife nodded that she understood. This place and its grounds were not far from where Sheen's team had discovered Peter Beatty's body in a cask. Aoife scanned their immediate surroundings. She could just about make out a massive Lebanese cedar tree about one hundred metres away to their left stretching its arms over a rolling lawn. To their right was a small wooden hut with a half-roof and open front. Discarded shotgun cartridges littered a trough filled with sand at its base. The house itself looked dark and dead; it struck Aoife as a municipal building rather than a home. Sheen pointed to the bulkhead doors, padlocked, and commented that the place looked secure and deserted. Aoife saw a small path that led round the side of the house. She beckoned Sheen and he followed her lead.

A muffled patter of gunfire briefly filled the air in a succession of clipped bursts and then was gone.

They both flinched; she saw Sheen reach for his protection weapon. It had sounded pretty close.

'Shots?' asked Sheen.

Aoife nodded. 'Sounded like an Armalite,' she replied. Aoife had heard rounds like that before, while patrolling in an armoured Land Rover round north Belfast. A gunman had opened fire from behind a wall near a local fish and chip shop. He had narrowly missed their vehicle, but more importantly had somehow not injured or killed the numerous people queuing up for food.

'What the hell's going on here?' asked Sheen.

Before she had a chance to reply, the sound of an approaching engine filled the night, driven hard and headed their way.

'Get down!' She pulled Sheen by the arm of his jacket and they both made themselves small against the side wall of the house, partially shielded by the skeletal spread of a wintering hydrangea.

'Look,' said Sheen.

A busted-up old Ford Fiesta rounded the corner and skidded to a stop close to where the sign she'd read was fixed. It was hard to tell in the murk, but it looked dark blue. The driver's door opened abruptly, and a figure stepped out, dressed in a black shawl and headscarf. She could pass for a nun, as Paddy Laverty had suggested. Her movements were jilted and angular, like a nightmare come to life. She reached into her garments, took out something and seconds later Aoife heard the tell-tale scratch of a flint lighter, followed by flame and then smoke. The smell hit Aoife a moment later; bitter, caustic and chemical. She resisted the urge to cough, clasped a hand over her mouth and nose. Sheen's face told a similar story.

'What is it?' she gasped.

'It's Angel Dust, PCP,' explained Sheen.

She might have an edge when it came to firearms and explosives, but Sheen knew his drugs. Aoife had heard of it when training. As well as inducing serious psychosis, the street drug had anaesthetising properties, so much so that it was known to take three or four officers to subdue an average-sized person on the drug. Not because they'd developed an unnatural strength, but because they were virtually immune to pain, at least temporarily.

The woman, Dolores Beatty, shuddered and then expelled the noxious fumes, as she spread her arms like wings. The smoke billowed round her, and Aoife watched as she inhaled once more and then flicked the glowing stub towards the front of the house. It triggered a security light which bathed her in white. The face that scanned the facade of what had been Harrison Glover's home was sheet-white and slick with perspiration. She was thin enough to pass for a living skeleton, and her eyes burned with a madness that made Aoife want to up and run. She lowered her head, kept still. The security light timed out, hopefully before this woman had a chance to lay eyes on her and Sheen. She blinked into the darkness, tried to adjust, and when she raised her face, she half expected to see the woman's livid mask next to her, close enough to taste the foul fumes of the PCP on her breath.

The area in front of the house was empty.

'She went round the left of the house,' said Sheen.

Made sense, if she was here for Glover's disabled son there must be another dwelling, because he clearly wasn't living in this building. Aoife moved to follow the woman's route, but Sheen said no, started round the house on their path, to the right of the building. If they were lucky it would lead to the same place; they might be able to flank her.

427

CHAPTER FORTY-EIGHT

McKeague could smell her before he'd seen her.

Unwashed clothes, stale piss and something else, bitter, like burning wires. Feet approached from the stable entrance, moving in slow shuffles and then scurrying, stop and start. For the first time since extracting what he needed from McHenry, he felt a small tremor of trepidation. Nothing he could put his finger on, and of course he wasn't scared. McKeague didn't do fear like other men. But there was something about the way the approaching feet moved, and that smell which he could taste in the air now as its owner crept closer to his place of concealment behind the door in this handicap's bedroom. It was as though this woman was dead already.

He ground his teeth mercilessly, blinked sweat from his eyes and tightened his grip round the barrel of the loaded two-bore he held. Fuck, he needed another wrap or two to straighten himself out. This was just comedown jitters; he'd forgotten how the paranoia could slip in and have you. What had started off as sport when Sterrit had called for his help, now felt like a job that needed to be done and done quickly. He'd left his Polaroid in the car, thoughts of furnishing his book of souls far from his mind. From the hallway outside the bedroom a voice spoke.

'Little boy Glover, little boy Glover,' she sang, but it was awful. It made you want to turn away, *run* and cover your ears.

'Ahh, Glover,' she whispered. McKeague stood perfectly still. A hand rap-a-tat-tatted the bedroom door, right next to his face. She'd worked out he was here. McKeague didn't breathe.

The figure stepped over the threshold, small and cloaked in black, but did not turn his way. The smell was rancid – he struggled not to gag – and he could feel the heat coming from her, like she was aflame. The woman hovered over the bed in which the frail form of Glover's son was propped on pillows, an oxygen feed attached to his nose.

McKeague deftly stepped from his concealed corner and raised the barrel of the gun, feeling calmer now and back in charge. Her back was turned to him and he watched as she withdrew a big blade (nice choice) which she held in her right hand. In her left she now had a syringe. She approached the sleeping man, the syringe raised.

'You've been a naughty girl, haven't ye?'

The creature slowly turned her head to look at him, the unsheathed needle poised at the neck of Glover's son. The look in her eyes was not what McKeague had been expecting, and he didn't like it.

'Haaaaaa,' she snarled. It was an angry sound, more animal than human. But her eyes were wide and full. She looked like she was pleased, but in the way a cat is pleased to see a mouse.

Time to end this; he'd had enough fucking dramatics for one day. McKeague lifted the shotgun to his shoulder. These things had some kick, and this bitch was about to get both barrels. She swiped her knife through the air between them but to no effect. Too much distance, and her other hand still held the point of the syringe to the neck of Glover's son.

'Ha yourself, you mad cunt. I win. Time for lights out.' His finger compressed the twin triggers.

CHAPTER FORTY-NINE

Sheen had been right about their path, but wrong about being able to flank the woman.

It led to the back of the big house and from there he and Aoife had been able to scale a fence and drop into the garden of what looked like it had once been a stable.

'This looks inhabited,' she said.

Sheen agreed. There were household refuse bins along the side of the building and a satellite dish on the roof. He tried the back door.

'Locked,' he said.

Aoife pointed to the little path that ran along the side of the building and he led the way.

Sheen nodded to the entrance gate. It was unlatched and ajar. He took out his gun, no longer as alien and wrong in his grip as it had been the previous summer, and slowly inched towards the front door, which was at the head of a gentle ramp. It was also part open. Sheen rested a palm against it and gently pushed it wider, gun trained on the darkness beyond.

Nothing. All quiet. He moved in, but paused when he felt it was sticky under foot. He sniffed and his nose wrinkled at the coppery smell.

'There's blood here,' whispered Aoife from behind him.

He didn't look down; now he moved quickly. As a police officer his first role was the preservation of life; above all others this was his core priority. He swiftly scanned the small kitchen area to his right, deemed it secure, and then walked from room to room following the main corridor through the bungalow, praying he wasn't already too late. From the last bedroom to his left came voices. Sheen moved nimbly but didn't hesitate. He heard what sounded like a hiss or a snarl, followed by muffled words.

'. . . lights out.'

Sheen stepped into the frame of the open door, gun raised.

'Armed police! Drop your weapons!'

On the bed was a frail-looking adult male, propped up on pillows, a breathing apparatus attached to his nose. He was maybe older than Sheen, though it was hard to tell for sure. He must be Fingall Glover, Harrison Glover's son. Sheen guessed motor neurone disease, his emaciated limbs and angled head reminded Sheen of the late Professor Stephen Hawking, an impression compounded by the alert, terrified eyes that locked on Sheen's and screamed for help. The poor guy was inert

432

and trapped, but clearly fully aware of all that now unfolded about him.

Standing over him was their woman in black, who looked utterly deranged and seethingly angry. She had a thick syringe that was full of oily-looking liquid pointed to Glover's son's neck and a serrated hunting-style knife in the other hand. She didn't look his way; she was all eyes for the man who stood at the foot of the bed. Big, maybe six foot five inches tall, he had a double-barrelled shotgun levelled at the woman, but now turned his attention to Sheen, though the gun did not stray. This must be McKeague, the bastard that had killed Peter Beatty and Declan O'Rawe, and God knows how many others. He seemed to know who Sheen was too.

'All right, Sheen, 'mon in and join the party,' said McKeague.

'I said drop the gun, McKeague. Last warning,' said Sheen.

His use of McKeague's name had an impact. McKeague's eyes darted from Sheen to Aoife, and then to the woman who still watched him, teeth bared, knife raised.

'Yeah, we know all about you. You're not going back to Málaga anytime soon, mate,' said Sheen.

McKeague barked a laugh, asked him who he thought was going to stand in his way?

Aoife spoke from just behind him. 'Sheen, if she injects him, that man will die,' she said.

Sheen glanced at the woman, Peter Beatty's sister.

He'd taken his attention from her, but Aoife was correct. If she emptied that syringe into him then it was game over for Fingall Glover. But if Sheen took action and shot McKeague before he could kill her with that two-bore then there'd be nothing to prevent her from murdering the innocent man at her mercy in the bed.

Sheen's hands were slick round the pistol, and it was suddenly heavier than before, weighted with the magnitude of his choice. Either way, he was going to fail as a copper; a life would be lost.

McKeague's eyes twinkled with cunning, as though he could read Sheen's ethical quandary.

'What are you waiting for?' he shouted at the woman. 'Finish that spastic off and come and get me, you stinking hag,' he said.

The woman didn't move, but now she nodded, and when Sheen looked in her eyes, he saw a world of rage and pain and delusion.

'McKeague,' she hissed. 'I know your name.'

McKeague's expression hardened, but she'd rattled him, no doubt.

'That's right, and I killed your brother, that little fucking rent boy. He died with a rope round his neck, nice and slowly. Still have a photo if you want to see it,' he said. At that she screeched.

Sheen grimaced as the abrasive sound filled the room. It was like a bottle bank being emptied and shattering.

'Sheen!' shouted Aoife.

The woman jammed the needle into Fingall Glover's neck; she was pressing it home.

Sheen swung his gun her way, the world a slow-motion chase. This was it, to save a life he had to shoot. Sheen squeezed off two rounds, no slip up or misfires, his injured right hand obeying his instructions to hold steady and pull the trigger. The Glock exploded twice as commanded and no sooner had the sound filled the room than the woman jolted as the bullets hit her feeble chest and she was punched back and into the corner, arms over her head. The syringe was still inserted into Glover's son's neck, but its cargo not yet fully delivered. Sheen moved to pull it free.

'No!' Aoife screamed.

He felt her barge him from behind and send him tumbling towards the bed. But not fast enough. He saw McKeague swing the long arm of the shotgun towards them and watched it erupt.

An explosion of sound and shot blasted his way as he hit the floor. He roared, felt his right arm perforate, the smell of singed leather from his jacket melding with a burnt-pork odour of seared flesh. He turned on the floor, frantically looking for Aoife McCusker, who had surely just saved his life. Movement from beyond the door where she slumped against the wall, looked uninjured, and started to get up.

'Aoife, stay down,' he shouted.

Another blast from the shotgun; Sheen closed his eyes, waited for the pain or the end, but not this time. He looked up in time to see McKeague use the butt of the rifle to dislodge the double-glazed pane in the back window he'd just shot at, and then hurl himself through. Sheen gasped, fell back down on his side. The carpet was wet with blood and his arm was on fire, literally. He patted out the flames, groaning in pain as he pawed his wound, but pain was good, pain meant he was alive and would keep him awake.

Aoife approached.

'The syringe,' gasped Sheen.

'Got it,' she answered.

Sheen watched as she discarded the needle and checked the man in the bed for vital signs. His eyes were bleary; they were losing him. If he died, then what Sheen had done was for nothing.

'Weak pulse,' she confirmed. Aoife moved round the bed and approached the crumpled form of Peter Beatty's sister. Seconds later she told Sheen what he already knew.

'She's dead. And look, this was inside her clothing,' she said. Aoife held up what she had found. It was another document.

Sheen tried to get up but could not. He cried out as he collapsed to the floor again and Aoife returned to him, set the document on the bed. She removed a pillow cover and ripped it in half. After a few seconds appraising his wound, she pulled off his jacket. Sheen gritted his teeth.

'You were lucky, looks like he only got your lower arm.' She tied the improvised tourniquet round Sheen's bicep, super tight.

Another groan escaped from Sheen; getting shot really hurt. He didn't feel lucky. The blood that had been bubbling from his wound at a fair old rate subsided.

Aoife knelt beside him. In the far distance the sound of sirens, seemed to be getting closer.

'I'm fine, go after him,' he urged.

'I'm staying here,' she said.

Sheen pulled her close to him with his good hand.

'Leave me. Don't let that bastard get away.' She was close to him, nose to nose. Sheen thought about the gunfire they'd heard, glanced at the carnage of the room. He told her to take his Glock.

Aoife stayed close, didn't move. 'I'm not legal,' she answered.

Sheen had a little laugh, despite the pulsing pain from his arm, told her that over the Irish border neither was he.

Aoife nodded. She reached for the gun and then leant over him.

'I know that you kissed me, Owen Sheen. When I was in my hospital bed,' she said.

'Did I?' he answered.

'Aye, you did, when I was at my most vulnerable,' she said.

Sheen said nothing but held her gaze.

'What goes around,' she said, and then leant in and kissed him hard, her lips soft and parting.

Sheen felt the merest flick of her tongue over his teeth and then she pulled away and bolted off, leaving the ghost of her caress for Sheen to taste. He gritted his teeth, raised himself up on one elbow and slumped against the bed where Fingall Glover was still conscious, but barely. Sheen shouted for him to wake up, gave him a good shove and the poor bugger jolted. His dreamy eyes rested on Sheen's.

'Good man, good man. Stay with me now,' encouraged Sheen. His eyes focused on the document that Aoife had left on the bedspread. He snatched it and began to read. 'I'll be damned,' he said, and folded it into his shirt. Fahey was going to have a story to tell. There was a dead woman in the corner, a dying man in the bed next to him, and he'd been bloody well shot. And unless he'd imagined it, Aoife McCusker had just kissed him. He hadn't seen this coming at the start of the week.

The sound of the sirens had abated, and the room was suddenly very still and quiet. The taste of Aoife's lips had disappeared. Sheen broke the silence with another groan and inwardly prayed to a God he had no faith in to keep Aoife McCusker safe.

CHAPTER FIFTY

Hayley was walking. Her legs felt like planks, making her stagger. Cold air; her hair was wet, sticky. Her ears were ringing, ten times worse than after leaving any rave or club she'd ever been to.

She reached out a hand, felt the cold, rough texture of the big wall to her left. She stopped, leant against it. The wall stretched to infinity, into the mist.

She let out a little moan, scared and suddenly unsure how she was here. She rested her back against the wall now, looked the other way, the way she must have come.

Wall, road, mist. The trees formed a tunnel of foliage, or it looked like they did.

A weight in her right hand, she was holding on tight to something.

In staccato flashes, things were revealed.

Suddenly awake from a black well, the smell of blood and the world a landscape of shattered windshield, glinting. *Very Christmassy*, she'd thought, her vision had started to blear, her eyes closed, and then she'd jolted awake. Geordie was slumped in his seat, upside down. Like her. There was blood coming from his ears, dribbling from a big slash in his forehead. He was very pale.

There was cold air, gushing in from behind her. She'd strained to look back, moaned at the pain in her neck, in her head. The back window of the car was gone. And there was blood, so much blood. Charlie Donaldson was held in place by his seat belt, suspended upside down, just like she was. Unlike Hayley, Donaldson's handcuffed wrists hung limply above his head. And unlike her, one large portion of his face was missing. One of the many bullets that had been fired at them had entered the back of his skull and exited through his cheek. And one was all it took. Charlie was gone.

Movement from the void beyond the back window. Men approached, upside down and wearing masks. Her eyes had locked again on the gory crater in Donaldson's face, but it looked like it wasn't real. She'd turned away from it, fumbled with her seat belt, punched the release and fell into a ball, fell onto the roof. The world was all wrong.

The contents of Geordie's glove compartment had emptied, and she was on top of it, the mess that had been on the floor too. She'd kept one eye on the approaching men, no longer upside down, her hands searching. Then she felt it, Geordie's gun. She'd never fired a gun. But she'd seen *Die Hard*. She tore it free from its leather holster and felt its dimpled grip on her palms, the only thing that was real.

She'd pointed it at the darkened figures in the black masks and closed her eyes and pressed the trigger, again and again, felt its savage kickback tear at her neck and reverberate through her head. She'd stopped when the gun went silent and her finger elicited a dry click. When she'd opened her eyes, the men were gone. Runaway gone or dead gone, she'd no idea. Hayley dropped the gun, tried to free Geordie, but his seat belt was jammed.

Then she'd searched for something to cut the belt, but there was nothing.

Her hand had found something else; she'd grabbed it.

Then her eyes had started to sting, wetness—

Hayley lifted her hand to her head, winced when she touched her forehead. It came back wet and black with blood. She'd been walking again. The wall was still to her left but now she could see an opening, an entrance. She staggered through the wide mouth of the exposed gateway, and in the distance, maybe coming from another galaxy, the sound of sirens mingled with the ringing in her head, or perhaps she was imagining it. She stopped abruptly.

Geordie.

He was trapped. She had to go back. Hayley turned, ready to retrace her steps, and then the sound of gunshots, several cracks and then a bigger boom, made her peer into the shadows and take stock of her surroundings. This was the place: the country house Geordie had said they were headed for.

Geordie said that Sheen and Aoife had needed their help.

She hesitated, and then another muffled shot sounded out, and Hayley moved, still a little shaky on her feet but head clearer now. Whatever Geordie's woes, he wasn't getting shot at. She looked down and studied the weight in her right fist for the first time. It was the sock, weighed low with the two snooker balls. She clacked it against her free palm and started in the direction of the gunshots, praying she wasn't too late, and for God to protect her.

CHAPTER FIFTY-ONE

Aoife scanned the small cobbled courtyard at the front of the converted stables, Sheen's gun in both hands.

No sign of McKeague.

She hesitated and then skirted the cottage, back the way she and Sheen had entered, and reached the rear where McKeague had emerged from the blown-out window. She searched the shadows, was about to head back and out the front of the building again when she spotted one fence panel sagging. She moved closer; it had been kicked out. The grass on the other side was trodden into a fresh path, leading along the side of the big house.

Aoife paused for a beat and then squeezed through the makeshift opening that McKeague had forced. She moved the gun in a wide semicircle, searching for movement, seeing only the ripple of the grass as a cold wind picked up. She moved, following the footprints and then stopped. They disappeared round the side of the big house, a blind corner. From quite far off a car engine started up, the city sound breaking open the countryside quiet.

McKeague must have driven here. And now he was about to drive away.

'Fuck,' hissed Aoife, and ran for the corner. She skidded to a stop and got flat on the ground, face in the earth. She edged her head round the corner, eyes almost level with the ground, a small target and below the obvious line of sight. She saw no one but heard the car once more, this time revving as though to warm a reluctant engine. She located the source of the sound: a hundred or more metres beyond the wide entrance area at the front of the house, coming from beneath the shelter of the giant Lebanese cedar.

Aoife rounded the corner and sprinted for McKeague's motor, ignoring the distant pulse of pain that came from the old wound in her gut, her right hand locked around the gun. When she'd made up about half the distance, the car's headlights flashed to life, full beams.

The bastard was going to get away from her.

Her arms pumped hard at her sides, legs slicing through the distance in a way she would never have imagined possible at the start of this terrible week. Aoife squinted into the car's beams, getting ready to veer to one side should the small vehicle lurch to life and try to mow her down as McKeague made his inevitable escape.

The car remained still, its engine still idling.

She slowed as she approached, panting hard, but eyes and now gun trained on the stationary vehicle. The driver's door was wide open; a good vantage point and fair protection for a man with a shotgun. She, on the other hand, was entirely exposed. She stopped, the gun in both hands, legs planted wide and stable, ready to shoot. The headlights weren't right in her face, but the angle was tight. She squinted at their glare.

'McKeague, get out of the car. Now!' She focused on the shadows of the car's interior, the open door, searching for the slightest movement, her finger curled round the trigger and ready. She took another step, blinking rapidly to maintain some clarity against the headlights' glare. She stopped dead. Her stomach dipped like she'd just taken an elevator ride up one hundred floors in a single second.

The car was empty.

Crunch and click. Footsteps and a gun locked.

The hard nostrils of the twin bore nudged the side of her skull just above her right ear.

'Drop it,' ordered McKeague.

Aoife could only oblige.

'What a brave wee thing *you* are.'

'Our backup's here. Can you hear the sirens?' Aoife could. But the Gardaí were taking their time, sounded no closer than they had been a few minutes ago.

'I have time to give you one shell. And maybe time to give that lucky English cunt over yonder the other one.'

'I have a daughter,' said Aoife, her voice cracking but mind separate, strangely calm, a woman operating to defuse a primed bomb on her lap.

McKeague laughed, like a saw cutting into fresh pine. 'Cheers love, but wee girls were never to my taste,' he said.

She felt the barrel of the gun slide up ever so slightly as he chuckled at his own perversion.

It was all she would get. Aoife moved fast.

She swept her right arm up in a defensive arc and dived to the ground as she did so. Close combat defence, just a fractional variation from a gun pointed right at you at such close range could create sufficient distance from its trajectory to give you one vital, probably last, chance. The shotgun erupted a few inches shy of the top of her skull, instantly deafening her, the heat of its bark searing enough to singe her hair, and her nose and mouth filled with sulphuric smoke.

'Bitch!'

McKeague landed a well-aimed kick into her gut which exploded like a jar of knives before deepening to a toothache chord that sounded through her whole body. She tried to crawl away but felt the heel of McKeague's boot pin her viciously in the lower spine. She coughed, cried out and rasped in a breath. She tried to squirm away. McKeague flipped her and loomed above her, bathed in the white light of the car's headlights, gigantic and supreme. He was no longer smiling. He stepped towards her, closer, stuck the gun's nose into her stomach. She could feel the hot steel burn through her top.

'This way you'll die slowly, but no matter what, you'll—'

McKeague's head was smashed to the side, right to left. Aoife watched a black line of blood escape from his mouth, captured like a floating ribbon in the headlights, heard the crunch of bone and a clack from whatever had hit him, and then he collapsed, like a man with rubber bones. Her eyes were back on the gun. She braced herself for the blast, but none came, and as McKeague hit the grass she batted the arm of the shotgun off her stomach and away.

'Aoife, are you OK?'

It was Hayley. Her face was a mask of blood. She was shaking, starting to cry. She dropped what looked like a weighted football sock, tottered forwards but then her legs gave up and she slumped to the ground, next to McKeague, who was twitching and emitting a wet gurgling sound.

Aoife said she was fine, got up on her knees and walked to Hayley that way.

They embraced.

'You saved my life, you saved my life.' It was all she could say.

Then there was the sound of many sirens approaching in unison, closer at last. The screech of tyres and engines followed, and soon flashing blue and white lights bathed them both. Car doors slammed, voices raised and commanding, and then a gentle touch on her shoulder. Aoife raised her chin, still cradling Hayley.

A blonde-haired woman looked down at her, her face etched with concern. Aoife thought, *She looks a bit like me.*

'I'm Sergeant Pixie McQuillan. Are you Aoife?'

Aoife nodded, identified herself and Hayley, and told Pixie where she could find Sheen and Glover's son. Pixie looked at McKeague and shouted for medical assistance. She glanced at the shotgun and then to Aoife.

'Who's he?' she asked.

McKeague's eyes were partly open but whatever he saw was very far away. One arm was still twitching but the rest of him was quite still. The right side of his head was dented in, the concave impression pooled with dark blood.

'He's history,' said Aoife.

CHAPTER FIFTY-TWO

Belfast, Northern Ireland
Monday 24th December

'Go on ahead, one more knock,' said Geordie, holding up the paper cup.

Sheen hoped the nurse wouldn't stick her head into the room again. But even if she did, it was Christmas Eve after all. He poured Geordie a generous measure of Black Bush, and one for himself. He glanced at the others, but Aoife and Hayley declined, and Fahey shook his head, pointing at his cup of green tea.

'Your health, mate,' he said.

'Up yer bum, Sheen,' replied Geordie and downed his dark amber whiskey in one gulp, despite the restrictions imposed by the neck brace. He smacked his lips, said he usually preferred Scotch, and then moved his eyes pleadingly to Sheen.

'No more,' said Hayley, 'You're still on medication.'

Geordie had come out worst: severe concussion, dislocated shoulder and broken ribs. He had remained unconscious for almost a day. They'd kept him in over the

449

weekend for good measure. When all was said and done, he, and all of them, had been more than lucky. Hayley had suffered minor concussion, Aoife was bruised, and Sheen's arm would eventually sport some unpleasant new pock-scars, but the wounds had, thankfully, so far resisted infection. Itched like hell though, and he was in a sling, so no driving for a while. Fingall Glover had also survived, although it had been touch and go.

From somewhere down the corridor was the sound of 'O Holy Night' being sung by nurses with lanterns, who stepped slowly past the small ward rooms and perhaps through the whole of the Royal. The Belfast sky was darkening as the day gave up its struggle, though it was still early afternoon. Wisps of grey and black cloud trailed past on the fleet westerly breeze.

McKeague had been less fortunate. He was in a vegetative state in Monaghan General Hospital, but moves were afoot to have him extradited to Northern Ireland in connection with Trevor McHenry's death, though the authorities in the Republic wanted him for the murder of Fingall Glover's nurse. Her name was Agrapina Dalca, from Romania. Her friends knew her as Agra. But that was only the beginning: McKeague's apartment on the Costa del Sol had been searched on the back of his capture and evidence discovered that suggested he'd been a serial murderer for three decades or more. Interpol was involved; the investigation would require co-operation with local forces and searches in Morocco, Tunisia, France and Spain. But so far justice was academic; he was in a coma and showed no signs of emerging any time soon.

Sheen glanced at Hayley White, whom he'd begrudged from the very beginning, and who had saved Aoife's life, and most probably Geordie's skin too, by shooting at the Dissident death squad like she was Wyatt Earp. She'd been spot on with what she'd sensed from the crime scenes whether he liked it or not. It was fitting that the only justice served to McKeague in all of this had been at the business end of her powerful right hook.

Sheen looked to Geordie, who was talking to him. Sheen had been drifting; whiskey in the afternoon, not good.

'So, you're saying that this guy McHenry knew about the goings on at Tara?' asked Geordie.

He meant Tara Boys' Home, where some members of the Circle of Navan had a circle of their own in operation, a paedophile ring. It was also the one Geordie had spent some time in as a child. Sheen looked at Geordie for a short moment, again pondered how much of those days Geordie still kept silent about. In the short pause, it was Fahey who answered.

'That's what it looks like. McHenry was ready to expose the lot of them to Dylan Martin in the early '90s when he found out there was child abuse going on. And then the axe fell,' said Fahey.

'Martin was murdered; McHenry framed and silenced,' said Sheen.

'Why not just talk from his prison cell? He'd already taken a punishment,' said Aoife.

'Yeah, I was wondering that myself, so I did a little digging,' replied Fahey.

'As you do,' said Sheen.

'McHenry had a son, also in the military for a time. He died last year, while jet-skiing off the coast of Malta. He was hit by a speedboat, freak accident. Foul play not expected,' explained Fahey.

A hush settled in the small room.

Geordie spoke first. 'They'd threatened his son. Told him that if he didn't sit quietly and do his bird the son would end up like Dylan Martin,' he said.

'That would be my take, yeah,' said Fahey.

'And with his son dead he had nothing to lose. Sad,' said Aoife. 'But why not just go to the press? Why allow Dolores Beatty to go on such a murderous rampage?'

'In a way that was my fault,' said Sheen. 'McHenry spotted the news about the body we discovered, the one that turned out to be Peter Beatty. He said it himself, told me he knew what we'd found,' he explained. 'It got me thinking, how could he have been so certain that some of the Circle of Navan had been involved? The only logical explanation was the symbolism that McKeague and the others involved used: it was borrowed from McHenry's Operation Saturn. That way if the body turned up, it would be blamed on the same black magic coven or whatever people believed was at work along the border. But those details were never revealed to the press.'

'He had to have seen the body for himself,' said Aoife.

Sheen smiled ruefully. 'I emailed his photo to Michael

Mulligan, the guy who gave me access to Peter Beatty's body in Monaghan General. He confirmed that McHenry had visited him a couple of months back, asked to see the remains, claimed he was with the state pathologist's office in Dublin, had a kosher-looking ID.'

'Some of his old craft still remained, then,' said Aoife. Sheen agreed.

'McHenry had never really forgotten about Tara, kept his eyes and ears open. The fact that he heard about your discovery in the bog shows how alert he was. When Dolores Beatty posted her request for help . . .' said Aoife.

'McHenry was there to give her the answer. Plus, a list of names of those he believed were involved. With his own son gone all bets were off, so McHenry decided to give her the Circle of Navan documents too, bring the whole house down around him. A stab at those who probably helped shut him up twenty years ago. Even if it meant incriminating himself,' said Sheen.

'Williamson Golding wasn't involved in Tara,' said Fahey.

Which appeared to be the case; he was nowhere mentioned on the documents they'd found in the storage room in the back garden of what had been the boys' home.

'No, but he'd been Sterrit's best mate, until he worked out what was going on, just like McHenry eventually did. Then he cut all ties with Sterrit and the rest, but he knew about Tara and kept his mouth shut. That's why McHenry refused his help,' explained Sheen.

'And put him in the line of fire,' said Fahey, finishing his green tea and pulling a face like it was hard liquor.

Fahey was right, but in Dolores Beatty's warped vengeance it wasn't Golding or any of the Circle who would suffer. She would take their children, just as they had taken her little brother from her. In Golding's case his young partner Emma Gribbin was the innocent who took the needle and very nearly died.

'Will we ever find out who this Archangel was, the one that McHenry was reporting to in the secret documents?' asked Hayley.

'You have more chance than I do,' said Fahey with a grin, and then his expression turned serious once again. 'I don't think we will. I think there are a lot of things we will never know,' he said.

Fahey got off his seat, wished Geordie well and them all a merry Christmas and said he'd best get back and do the work of Santa before it got too late.

'I'm gonna make tracks too,' said Hayley. She gave Aoife a hug and promised to meet her at Dawn Mass at Clonard the next morning.

Sheen was rather hoping to have Christmas breakfast with Aoife, ideally in bed. He wished Hayley a merry Christmas, wanted to say something more but didn't have the words. That was OK. He'd see her again, personally and professionally.

Hayley and Fahey were in the doorway, coats on.

'But you got a good story out of it, right?' asked Sheen.

Fahey's face lit up once more.

'Please excuse my profanity, but as I said to you last week, it's a *fucking* good story. And, unlike poor Dylan, I'll publish.'

'You take care,' said Sheen, and he meant it.

In the last document, found on Dolores Beatty's body and in duplicate in McKeague's car, there'd been details of yet another secret mission, Operation Retribution. The Circle of Navan, it strongly suggested, had been behind the Dublin and Monaghan bombings in 1974, four explosions that had killed thirty-four and injured more nearly three hundred. The two men tasked with this atrocity were none other than Brother Samson and Brother David, McKeague and Williamson Golding. Of course, Fahey couldn't print Golding's name, but he was a clever man and people could read the signposts; and of course, the Internet, as they'd found out the hard way, was damn near impossible to police. Sheen wondered what Golding's young girlfriend, Emma, and his colleagues at the law firm would make of this. Several children were among those killed in the blasts.

McHenry had known about this and let it lie, but had been prepared to risk it all and expose the Circle over Peter Beatty's death. The truth doesn't always make sense. Sheen listened to the sound of Fahey's trainers squeaking down the corridor. The nurses had started to sing 'Good King Wenceslas'. What other hard facts had McHenry taken to his grave? He'd taunted Sheen that he knew the truth about his brother's death, that John

Fryer had not been responsible after all. Sheen buried the thought, the aftertaste of the whiskey now a little overbearing in the dry heat of the hospital room. But it would return to haunt him again.

Other ghosts seemed to be at rest. Since revealing the truth about Peter Beatty and exposing the Circle of Navan, the voices that had stolen his sleep, John Fryer's included, had spoken less often. Maybe that was a scrubbed conscience? Or maybe it was the warmth of Aoife McCusker, who'd been sleeping close to him in the dead hours before dawn these past few nights?

'I'm pleased for Fahey,' said Aoife. 'He was bloody helpful.'

Sheen agreed that he was, but he detected a weight of sadness in her words.

Geordie was dozing, eyes half closed.

So far things had not worked out so well for Aoife. Paddy Laverty had accused Sheen of breaking their deal, which in his didicoi morality probably meant he now had a blood feud against him or something. In fairness, Sheen had kept quiet about the Circle of Navan documents, took his investigation across a national boundary without permission, including the use of firearms and the death of a suspect, and used Laverty's new boss's name to authorise a cross-border bone spectrum analysis on Peter Beatty's remains. Plus, he'd deputised Aoife McCusker unofficially and agreed to have Hayley White tag along as a psychic consultant without informing Laverty as SIO. All of this, added to Fahey's preliminary newspaper write-up, which made it clear lots was about go public with political repercussions, and Sheen could see his point.

But on the other hand, the guy had been gifted a high-profile collar, as promised.

Laverty needed to roll with it, see the upside, but he was behaving like an asshole, which, after all, was what he probably was. He and Sheen would not be sharing another pint in Mac's any time soon, and he'd already told Sheen that Aoife McCusker was never coming back to Serious Crimes while he had breath in his body blah, blah, blah. And, of course, he'd refused to intercede with Internal Investigations on her behalf. But fuck him; they still had the CCTV footage of Oswald even if Charlie Donaldson was now dead and could tell no tales. There was still hope and Sheen said so to Aoife, though it sounded weak as the smile she returned him.

A sharp knock on the door. Geordie jolted awake. Sheen and Aoife turned. And then they both got off their chairs.

'Please sit down.' It was Sir Ronnie Stevens, Chief Constable of the PSNI. There was a man in a suit with his back to the door standing behind him, neck like a six pack of frankfurters. Sir Ronnie was wearing civilian clothes, but his chinos and polo top were ironed to sharp creases, his grey hair was trimmed to perfection and his green eyes were as clean and clear as two chips of washed marble. He smelt of soap. His eyes settled on the bottle of Bush.

'Take a dram, sir?' enquired Geordie.

'Don't mind if I do, George,' he replied.

George, not Geordie. The chief was a man who refused to shorten names, and Geordie knew better than to correct him.

Sheen served him an Irish measure, same again for himself and Geordie. Aoife declined, looking serious. They toasted health and the season, and Sir Ronnie pulled up a chair and sat among them.

'Thought I should check in and see who's been making all these waves,' he commented.

Geordie eyed Sheen and cocked an eyebrow. Sheen kept quiet.

The chief took another sip, nodded his appreciation. In fairness the Bush was superior, smooth. He set his paper cup down.

'Last time you were working so hard, DI Sheen, we had quite a summer,' he said. Sheen stayed quiet; so far there was nothing to say. 'And now this.' The chief didn't elaborate. Probably too many things to mention.

'DI Laverty tasked me to find who murdered Father Phil Rafferty and Rhonda Sterrit, sir. And I did,' said Sheen.

Sir Ronnie glanced at Aoife McCusker. She held his gaze.

'That you did,' he said, but he was still looking at Aoife. He smiled, seemed genuine, and returned his eyes to Sheen. 'Do you sail, DI Sheen?'

'No, sir.'

'It's one of my enthusiasms; there's nothing like it. But you have to be mindful, read the weather, and think ahead. If it's too calm, you go nowhere. But if it's too choppy, if the waves are too big,' he said and looked at Sheen pointedly, 'you'll go down, no matter how experienced you may be.'

'How's your drink, sir?' asked Geordie.

The chief smiled again and downed his whiskey, said it was grand.

'Things have been way too calm since July. It's such a waste of resources having people like you languish as politicians bicker,' he said. And then the chief seemed to change tack.

'I had an interesting meeting with a senior colleague in MI5. He came all the way from Whitehall to speak with me earlier. We both agreed that it's in everyone's best interests in this wee country if the recent misfortunes which have befallen DC McCusker begin and end at the door of our disgraced, and recently deceased former colleague, Charles Donaldson. Did you know that a quantity of cocaine powder was found in his Dunmurry apartment yesterday? Exact match for the batch which had been secreted in DC McCusker's locker at Ladas Drive some months ago,' he said.

Sheen tried hard to cut through the whiskey in his brain and keep up, but Geordie got there first and spoke.

'Sir, that's only the half of it. Here, look at this,' he said and started to rummage in his bedside table, still talking. 'I have a USB here which shows Donaldson getting the drugs from—' and then Geordie stopped speaking. He turned and looked at them. 'What did you do with it?' He was talking to the chief.

'George, things go missing all the time. Especially from hospital rooms. They're not secure,' he said, affable. Geordie's face had darkened. 'Or during fire alarms, then too,' said the chief, grit in his throat. Geordie said nothing. The chief turned to Sheen. 'Things like SIM cards from phones, they can go missing too. Even when they're bagged as evidence at crime scenes, DI Sheen,' he said. Sheen felt his face redden, he glanced at Aoife, but she was staring at the floor. Checkmate from the chief. 'Of course, the good news is that Internal Investigations will no longer be pursuing an active case against you, DC McCusker. Why would they? Charles Donaldson was to blame,' said the chief.

Aoife stood up so fast her chair toppled over. 'You mean the drug case against me is dead?'

'As a doornail, if I may permit myself the seasonal allusion,' said the chief.

Aoife stepped towards him. 'Ava will come back?'

'Even I won't be able to arrange that for Christmas Day. But, yes, your daughter will be returned to you,' he said. 'You have my word.'

Aoife gave a small moan, raised a hand to her mouth, eyes swimming.

'Alas, your job is not so straightforward.' Aoife sat down. 'DCI Daly is of a mind that given the circumstances a fresh start is more fitting. And I am inclined to agree,' said the chief.

'But there's barely a skeleton staff in Serious Crimes as it is, sir. Aoife is an exceptional detective. Paddy

Laverty should be put in his place, sir,' argued Sheen.

'I agree that Aoife is an asset, and I won't see her squandered. I'm sure you will find her most valuable in the Serious Historical Offences Team. As of the new year, you're back in business, all of you.' Sheen was lost.

'I thought the SHOT was mothballed. How is this possible?' The SHOT was partly overseen by civil servants from the Northern Ireland Office. While politicians continued to squabble, no working SHOT.

'You know it really was quite a meeting this morning. It seems that my friend from Whitehall has his fingers on many buttons. Says he's able to have management of SHOT transferred to the PSNI, on the understanding that you answer to me and only me as Chief Constable. Plus, he said there would be a large plank of funds made available to strengthen Serious Crimes. We should be able to refurnish that department with top grade detectives very soon.'

'So, you take charge and keep me on a short leash in other words,' said Sheen, unable and unwilling to keep the insolence from his tone.

Plus, the chief would get a pay-off from Westminster in exchange for keeping that snake Oswald's name in the dark. The chief rested his stony green eyes on him briefly but then smiled.

'Help you steer clear of choppy water, DI Sheen,' he said, standing.

Sheen and Aoife followed his lead.

'Oswald Smith was behind those drugs in Aoife's locker, and a lot more besides if my suspicions are correct.'

'Enough! I don't know that name. And I don't want to ever hear you speak it in my presence, or anywhere else again. Is that understood, DI Sheen?'

So, this was it? He'd burnt his bridges with Serious Crimes, Special Branch and the Intelligence Services had his cards marked, and now he was being put in the stocks by the chief constable himself. He could walk away, go back to the Met and start again, but he'd be damned before he let them get the best of him. He still had work to do in Belfast.

'Perfectly, sir,' replied Sheen.

'I'd like at least a year from you, DI Sheen. Can you commit to that?'

Sheen's eyes wandered to Aoife, her face full of colour, hope in her eyes. Sheen told the chief he could depend on him. The chief wished Geordie a speedy recovery, told him to take care with the firewater.

'Oh, I almost forgot. I want you to meet my nephew,' said the chief, stepping out the door and beckoning a young man to enter. He was swimming in a department-store suit, looked like he'd barely started shaving. Just as he had when Sheen first set eyes on him outside the gates of Clonard Monastery.

Sheen offered his hand. 'Sheen,' he said.

'Jackson Stevens,' he replied.

Sheen turned to the chief, was about to explain that he had a full quota of qualified people to choose from, which was true, but the chief's green eyes stopped him before he had started.

'Jackson's going to join your team. Serious Crimes wasn't a tailored fit for this young man. He's a history graduate, after all, with honours. But he'll learn a lot from you, DI Sheen,' said the chief.

And you'll be kept well informed, no doubt, thought Sheen.

The chief left and Jackson stayed.

Aoife threw herself at Sheen and embraced him, hard enough to hurt. He held her.

'Here, 'mon over and sit down,' Geordie offered. Jackson obeyed. Geordie grumbled as he stretched over and lifted the bottle of Black Bush. He poured himself a measure, refilled the chief's cup and handed it to his nephew.

Jackson stared at the amber fuel. 'No thanks, sir. I don't really drink whiskey,' he said.

Geordie laughed. 'Well, it's about fucking time you started. Cheers. Merry Christmas.'

EPILOGUE

The new year had been a busy time for funerals.

First came that of Father Phil, murdered because of a judgement call he'd made so many years before. On paper he'd done the right thing: Peter Beatty had not been baptised Catholic, and so he could not be permitted to enter a Catholic-maintained boys' home. It had been a compromise that his parents had come to as a mixed-religion couple. Just as Sheen's own parents had been. Because of it, Peter had been made a ward of the state when his father was unable to care for the family. In doing so, the siblings had been separated more widely than they otherwise would have been. Dolores was unable to protect her younger brother in the way she wanted. And in the end, he was preyed upon by the worst kind of predator. It was one wrong decision by Father Phil Rafferty in a lifetime of dedicated good work. But Dolores Beatty never forgave him.

And last week the double funeral of Peter and his

sister, Dolores, took place. Sheen had gone to the cemetery office in Milltown; found that there was a family grave, two spaces still available. Hand-dug graves, he subsequently learnt, can contain up to four coffins, a machine dug grave only three. In the ground already was Peter Beatty's mother, abducted and murdered by the IRA. They'd claimed she was an informer. The fact that she was a Protestant living in the republican heartland of the Divis Flats on the Falls Road and was known to have come to the aid of a British soldier who had been seriously injured, probably helped seal her fate in those troubled days. But like so much from the past, it was likely the truth would never really be known. Peter's father rested above her, dead at fifty according to the cemetery ledger, probably from drink and hard living. That was what had taken Sheen's mother after she'd succumbed to the despair of losing her firstborn son.

The Beattys' funeral was scantly attended, but Sheen was one of the few. Four layers of tragedy and pain, the strata of Irish history laid to rest in the cold, wet clay. He went for a pint in Mac's after, and then crossed the Falls Road to the memorial stonemasons where he'd ordered a simple wooden cross for the Beatty family grave. Peter's name would be etched on a small brass plaque for all to see, and never to be forgotten. While there, he'd also ordered a gravestone.

When Sheen made his enquiries about the Beattys' family grave, he'd also located another plot, that of the Sheen family, formerly from Sailortown.

The January wind from the Black Mountain pinched at his extremities and brought him back to the moment. Owen Sheen stood on the bones of his kin, buried beneath the cold sod under his feet. His shovel lay on the ground; he'd use it to nick and cut, and clear the way. The plot wasn't as badly overgrown as he'd dreamt. And being here felt much better than he had expected.

Aoife's arms burrowed into the shelter of his open jacket, and he drew her close. Her cold nose touched the tip of his. Ava was on the path, a diamond on a chain swung from her neck. She was saying she couldn't see the giant's face, that it wasn't there. She swished her head from side to side, wild, frizzy hair swirling in the wind as she altered her perspective, looking at Cave Hill in the distance. Sheen smiled and shouted over that she needed to open her eyes, he was there, and the giant was sleeping.

'I can see it, I can see it!' She was shouting, laughing.

Sheen pulled Aoife in, her lips met his and he kissed her, cold giving way to sweet heat. As he stood between his history and, just maybe, his destiny, he heard Ava's laughter which was carried far on the new year's breeze.

AUTHOR'S NOTE

Killing in Your Name is a work of fiction. Any resemblance to real persons living or dead is purely coincidental, and any reference to real events is done so through the lens of fictional storytelling. Of course, Belfast is real, as is the surrounding countryside mentioned in parts of the book. However, I have taken the liberty of changing and indeed inventing things, when and where it suited my story.

ACRONYMS AND ABBREVIATIONS

IRA: Irish Republican Army. Sometimes also referred to as PIRA or Provisional Irish Republican Army in reference to a split that occurred in an earlier incarnation of the group. Illegal and the largest Irish republican paramilitary organisation which was active throughout the modern Troubles. Aimed to take Northern Ireland out of the United Kingdom and create a United Irish republic.

The Met: The Metropolitan Police Service. The police service responsible for the Metropolitan Police District of London which consists of all police boroughs apart from the 'square mile' of the City of London.

MI5: Military Intelligence Section 5. Also known as The Security Service, MI5 is the

United Kingdom's domestic intelligence and security agency. Since 2007 MI5 has led security intelligence work related to Northern Ireland (previously PSNI).

PRONI: The Public Record Office of Northern Ireland. The official archive for Northern Ireland, which includes CAIN, the Conflict Archive on the Internet, which is a database containing information about conflict and politics in Northern Ireland from 1968 to the present.

PSNI: Police Service of Northern Ireland. The police force of Northern Ireland from 2001 to date.

RUC: Royal Ulster Constabulary. The police force of Northern Ireland from 1922 until it was replaced by the PSNI in 2001.

Special Branch: RUC Special Branch. Undercover police unit tasked with combating the IRA and other paramilitary groups by recruiting informers and working closely with MI5. Later replaced by C3 Intelligence Branch of PSNI, though still referred to as Special Branch.

UDA: Ulster Defence Association. Illegal loyalist paramilitary organisation dedicated to keeping Northern Ireland a part of the United Kingdom.

UVF: Ulster Volunteer Force. Illegal loyalist paramilitary organisation dedicated to keeping Northern Ireland a part of the United Kingdom. Smaller in terms of membership than the UDA.

ACKNOWLEDGEMENTS

Thank you to my wife, Sacha, and my children, Leila and Jack, who, whether I believed it or not, have always had faith in my ability to write. Guys, you are there when that door closes and I disappear into my own world, but most importantly, you are there for me when I return, win, lose or draw.

If a novel is first written with the door closed, it's much more of a collaborative process as soon as the door opens and the real work of editing and rewriting begins. Thank you to my perceptive first readers (Sacha and Kevin Henry this time) for your insightful feedback and positive encouragement.

Writing a book and getting it published are two different things. Without my agent, Lisa Moylett at CMM Literary Agency, the DI Sheen series would still be a dream. As well as making this happen, both she and Zoe Apostolides provided indispensable editorial feedback at a point when the book needed it most.

Thank you to the amazing team at Allison & Busby for giving DI Sheen a home and for everything you have done. The brilliant editorial input from Lesley Crooks and Kelly Smith asked intelligent questions, trimmed, polished and took nothing for granted. To borrow a phrase from my dad, you both have the eyes of a young thrush and the book is much the better for your scrutiny and unpicking. For Christina Griffiths' great work on the brooding, noir cover designs and for the hard work of Susie Dunlop, Daniel Scott and Kirsten Munday behind the scenes in rights, sales and distribution, I offer heartfelt thanks.

Finally, dear reader, I want to thank you. The incredible response which *Blood Will Be Born* received means that at least some of you are likely to be following DI Sheen's antics for the second time with this book. If so, it's great to have you back. Please keep in touch. If this is your first taste of DI Sheen's dark, parallel version of Belfast and beyond, I hope you've enjoyed it enough to join us and read more.

GARY DONNELLY is a writer and teacher who was born and raised in West Belfast. After attending a state comprehensive school, he read History at Corpus Christi College, Cambridge and has lived and worked in London since the late 1990s. *Killing in Your Name* is the second novel in the DI Owen Sheen series and follows on from Gary's debut, *Blood Will Be Born*.

donnellywriter.com   @DonnellyWriter